BLOOD & DOMINION

A VAMPIRE ROMANTASY

CRIMSON CRESCENT SERIES
BOOK ONE

TALORIA PRYCE

First Edition: February 2026

ISBN 979-8-89283-331-8 (ebook)
ISBN 979-8-89283-336-3 (paperback)

Published by Books to Hook Publishing, LLC.
www.BooksToHook.com

CONTENTS

ONE

CELESTE

The blood hits my system like poison.

I know it immediately. The way my veins turn to ice, the way my vision doubles and splits, the way my body rejects what should be sustenance. I'm on my knees in my apartment before I can stop myself, stomach heaving even though there's nothing left in me but the tainted blood I just drank.

Stupid. So stupid.

I bought the bag from a contact in the underground, the same guy who used to set up my fights when I was human. Rhett. Not his real name, probably, who always smelled like cigarettes and moved cash with the efficiency of someone who'd done it a thousand times. I trusted him because I didn't have a choice. Because the blood bank downtown started asking too many questions about my "medical condition." Because I've been a vampire for eight months and I still don't know what the hell I'm doing.

The bag sits on my kitchen counter, half-empty, mocking me. No label. No information about the donor, their health status, or what they might have been taking. Just blood that's probably been sitting in someone's trunk for weeks, contaminated with God knows what. Pharmaceuticals. Street drugs. The cocktail of chemicals humans pump into themselves without thinking twice, because they don't have to worry about someone else drinking their blood supply.

My hands shake as I grip the edge of the counter and pull myself up. The room spins like I've been drinking, which is ironic since alcohol doesn't affect me anymore. Through my window, the city lights blur into watercolor streaks; Atlanta at night, sprawling and indifferent to the fact that I'm dying in a shitty apartment in East Atlanta Village.

The kitchen floor is cold linoleum under my bare feet. I focus on that. The physical sensation. The realness of it. My martial arts instructor used to say that when you're hurt, when you're overwhelmed, you anchor yourself in your body. Find something real to hold onto.

Focus, Celeste. Think.

I stumble to the bathroom using the wall for support, and catch my reflection. At least I still have one. That myth turned out to be false. Though right now, I almost wish I couldn't see what I've become. My reflection in the mirror stops me cold. Even in the dim light from the single bulb, I can see the dark lines spreading under my skin like ink in water. My veins map themselves across my arms, my neck, my face, visible and wrong and getting darker by the second. The pattern is almost beautiful in a horrifying way, like black lightning frozen beneath my skin.

My eyes, usually a warm brown, the one feature I inherited from my mother, look glassy and dilated. My pupils are blown so wide there's barely any iris left. Just endless black.

This isn't hunger. This is poisoning.

I've been hungry before. Eight months of figuring out how to feed yourself when you don't have a maker to show you the ropes teaches you what real hunger feels like. It's a gnawing emptiness, a craving that builds until your fangs ache and every heartbeat you hear sounds like a dinner bell.

This is different. This is my body at war with itself, trying to process something it can't handle. Like my human body that one time I got food poisoning from gas station sushi. Except now I'm supposed to have supernatural healing, and it's not doing a damn thing.

A wave of nausea hits, and I barely make it to the toilet before I'm retching up black, viscous blood. It shouldn't be black. Blood should be red, even old blood, even vampire blood. The wrongness of it makes my skin crawl. I can smell the chemical tang of whatever's contaminating it, sharp and artificial.

When the heaving finally stops, I slump against the bathroom wall, breathing hard even though I don't technically need to breathe anymore. Old habits die hard. Twenty-seven years of being human don't just disappear because some vindictive vampire decided to make you immortal against your will.

You can't die like this. Not in your bathroom. Not eight months after fighting your way out of that underground ring.

The thought of my old life sends a spike of rage through the haze of pain. I was supposed to retire. One more fight. A big one, the kind that would set me up for months, and I'd have been done. Free. I could have helped my sister Simone. She's been struggling since Mom died from an overdose five years ago. I've been sending money when I can for her therapy, her rent. She thinks I moved to Miami for work. Doesn't know I was fighting in underground rings or that I'm dead now. Just... gone from her life.

Instead, some vampire with a bruised ego turned me out of spite and disappeared into the night, leaving me to figure out immortality on my own.

Her face flashes through my memory. Beautiful in that

uncanny way some vampires are, with sharp features and eyes like a predator. She'd challenged me to a private match. Big payout, she said. Just the two of us, no audience, winner takes all.

I should have known something was wrong. Should have listened to my instincts screaming that this woman moved wrong, smiled wrong, looked at me like I was prey instead of competition.

But I needed the money. And I was cocky. Three years of underground fighting, dozens of matches, and I'd never lost. Not once. I was fast, technically skilled, and I had that thing fighters need: the ability to turn off the part of your brain that worries about getting hurt and just *fight*.

I beat her. Decisively. She didn't land a single solid hit.

And when it was over, when I was catching my breath and reaching for the envelope of cash, she'd smiled with too many teeth and said, "No one humiliates me."

Then she was on me faster than I could process, fangs in my throat, drinking deep while I struggled and failed to throw her off. The world went gray at the edges. I thought I was dying.

I was. And then I wasn't.

I woke up three days later in an abandoned warehouse with an unbearable thirst and no one to explain what the hell had happened to me. Just a note scrawled on the back of a receipt: *Welcome to eternity, sweetheart.*

I push myself up from the bathroom floor, legs shaking. My phone is in the other room, sitting on the kitchen counter next to the contaminated blood bag. For a moment, I consider calling someone. But who? My sister thinks I moved to Miami for a "job opportunity." My old fighting contacts wouldn't believe me if I told them I was a vampire. And I don't have any vampire friends because I've spent eight months trying to survive, not socialize.

I need help. Need someone who knows about contaminated blood, about what happens when vampires drink from humans who've pumped themselves full of prescription drugs, birth control, antibiotics, and whatever else is poisoning the food supply these days.

Over the last week, I've been asking around, carefully, because apparently saying the wrong thing to the wrong vampire can get you killed. The vampire community has rules I don't fully understand yet. Territories. Hierarchies. Ancient grudges that play out over centuries.

But the same name keeps coming up, whispered like a prayer or a curse, depending on who's talking.

Maximus.

The gatekeeper. The one who controls access to clean blood in Atlanta. The vampire so old and powerful that everyone either worships him or fears him, sometimes both. No one seems to know exactly how old he is. Five hundred years. Six hundred. Some guy at a bar for supernaturals claimed he fought in the Crusades, but that seemed like bullshit.

What isn't bullshit: he's the only one with a reliable supply of uncontaminated blood. And he's notoriously selective about who he helps.

I've been trying to find him for three days.

It started at the Wax and Wane.

I stumbled onto the bar by accident three months ago, following a vampire who'd just fed on a human in Little Five Points. I'd hoped to corner him, ask questions about surviving this life. Instead, he led me to a door behind a laundromat that opened into something impossible.

The Wax and Wane Bar is neutral territory, run by a pack of wolf shifters who enforce one rule above all others: no violence inside. Break that rule, and you answer to the pack. I've seen what the bouncers look like when they shift. Nobody breaks the rule twice.

It's where I learned that vampires aren't the only monsters hiding in plain sight.

The first night I walked in, I nearly turned around and left. A woman at the bar had eyes that glowed amber, her nails extending into claws as she reached for her drink. Two men in the corner booth had pointed ears and spoke a language that made my teeth ache. Something that looked human but moved wrong, too fluid, too graceful, watched me from the shadows with a smile that had too many teeth.

Shifters. Witches. Fae. Things I didn't have names for. All of them real. All of them drinking together like it was the most normal thing in the world.

I spent weeks just watching. Learning. Trying to understand the world I'd been dragged into.

Now, dying from contamination, the Wax and Wane is the only place I know to ask for help.

Three days of nursing drinks I can barely keep down while asking careful questions. Three days of talking to contacts from my fighting days who've since turned out to be supernatural themselves, shifters who'd been betting on my matches, witches who'd been hiding in plain sight. Three days of dead ends and cryptic warnings.

"Don't waste your time," a vampire named Daphne told me, her fangs flashing as she spoke. "Maximus doesn't help nobodies. You need connections. History. Something he wants."

"Even if you find him," one of the wolf shifter bouncers said, arms crossed over his massive chest, "he'll probably kill you just for knowing his name. He's not big on his reputation spreading."

"I heard he once let a vampire starve to death outside his compound just to make a point," a witch added, stirring her drink without even touching her straw. "Begging doesn't work. Offering money doesn't work. He decides who's worthy, and most people aren't."

Encouraging.

I manage to pull on jeans and a jacket, moving on autopilot. Every movement feels like I'm underwater, slow and distant. My reflection in the hallway mirror shows someone who looks half-dead, which is ironic considering I'm already technically deceased. The black veins have spread to my face now, creeping up my jaw like cracks in porcelain.

How long do I have?

Hours, maybe. My vampire healing should be working overtime, burning through the contamination. Instead, it's like my body doesn't know what to do with blood this toxic. Like it's given up.

I grab my keys, another old habit, since I don't actually drive anymore. Vampire speed is faster, and I don't trust myself behind the wheel when I can hear every heartbeat within a hundred feet. But old routines die hard, and the weight of keys in my pocket makes me feel more human. More normal.

Then I'm out the door and into the night, letting the cold air hit my face like a slap.

The streets of East Atlanta Village are busy even at 11 p.m. on a Thursday. Humans everywhere, laughing and drinking and living their fragile little lives. Couples walking arm in arm. Groups of friends bar-hopping. A guy on a skateboard weaving through pedestrians with the confidence of someone who's never had to worry about predators.

I can hear their heartbeats, smell the blood pumping through their veins. My fangs ache with hunger despite the poisoning, because my body is stupid and doesn't understand that feeding right now would probably kill me faster. I shove the hunger down, focusing on putting one foot in front of the other.

Not desperate enough to feed from a random human on the street. Not yet, anyway.

I make my way toward Little Five Points, cutting through side streets to avoid the thickest crowds. The businesses here are the kind Atlanta is known for: vintage shops, tattoo parlors, and head shops with tie-dye in the windows. The Vortex looms ahead with its giant skull facade, a landmark that used to make me smile. Now it just reminds me that I'm heading toward a meeting that probably won't happen with someone who probably won't help me anyway.

The meet-up spot is an alley behind The Vortex, hidden from the main drag by a fence and a dumpster. I slip into the shadows and wait, counting my breaths even though I don't need them. The black veins continue to spread under my skin, a reminder that time is running out.

Derek, the vampire who promised he could get me a meeting with someone in Maximus's circle, is supposed to show at 11:30. It's 11:25 now.

I lean against the brick wall and try not to think about the fact that I'm trusting a stranger who wanted five hundred dollars just for a conversation. Money I didn't have but scraped together anyway by pawning my grandmother's necklace. The only thing of value I owned, and I handed it over to a vampire I barely knew on the promise of help. But I can't wear it if I'm dead.

The minutes tick by. 11:30 comes and goes.

No one shows.

I wait thirty minutes. Then an hour.

No one is coming.

Of course not.

The poisoning is getting worse. I can feel it now, a creeping numbness that starts in my extremities and works its way toward my core. My fingers tingle. My toes have gone completely numb.

When I try to flex my hands, the response is delayed, like the signals from my brain are traveling through molasses.

I slide down the wall until I'm sitting on the cold concrete, knees pulled to my chest. The alley smells like garbage and stale beer and piss, and somewhere in the distance I can hear music thumping from one of the bars. Life is going on without me. The world is spinning while I'm stuck in this alley, waiting for help that isn't coming.

How cosmically unfair is it that I survived three years of underground fighting, broken bones, concussions, opponents who wanted to actually kill me, only to die because I drank the wrong blood bag?

My vision starts to gray at the edges, darkness creeping in like a vignette.

No. Get up. Move.

But I can't. My legs won't cooperate. The numbness has reached my chest now, making it hard to think, hard to focus on anything except the spreading cold. It reminds me of hypothermia, which I learned about in a first aid class years ago. The way your body shuts down from the outside in, conserving heat for your vital organs until even that isn't enough.

Except I'm not cold. I'm a vampire. Temperature doesn't affect me the way it used to.

This is something else. This is my body giving up.

Is this it, then?

This is how Celeste Moreau goes out. Not in a blaze of glory in the ring. Not protecting someone or fighting for something that matters. Just... alone in an alley, poisoned by her own desperation and stupidity.

I close my eyes and try to remember what my mother's face looked like. It's getting harder.

"You've been asking about me."

The voice cuts through the fog like a blade, deep, measured, and utterly without warmth.

My eyes snap open.

A man stands at the mouth of the alley, backlit by the streetlights so I can't see his face clearly. He's tall, over six feet, dressed in dark clothes that probably cost more than my entire apartment. Black coat, dark shirt, everything tailored perfectly. Even from here, even through the haze of poisoning, I can feel the power rolling off him in waves.

Not the desperate, feral energy of the few young vampires I've met in the bars. Not the cocky aggression of the fighters I used to face. This is something else entirely. Something ancient and controlled and absolutely lethal. Like standing near a barely contained explosion.

He steps closer, and the light catches his face.

Sharp features that could have been carved from marble. Pale skin that hasn't seen sunlight in centuries. Dark hair swept back from his forehead, long enough to brush his collar. Eyes that look black in the shadows but probably aren't, probably some shade of dark brown that just reads as black in low light.

There's something aristocratic about him, like he stepped out of a Renaissance painting. Old money. Old world. Old power.

And he's looking at me like I'm an insect he's deciding whether to crush.

"How tedious," he says, his gaze sweeping over me with clinical detachment.

I try to speak, but my throat feels lined with glass. The words come out as a rasp: "You're... him."

"Maximus," he confirms, like it's the most boring fact in the world. "And you are Celeste Moreau. Former underground fighter. Turned eight months ago. No maker. No clan. Making quite a lot of noise asking for me."

He crouches in front of me, not close enough to touch but close enough that I can see his expression clearly. Bored. Vaguely annoyed. Like I'm an inconvenience rather than a dying woman.

Up close, his eyes aren't black, they're a very dark gray, like storm clouds. Ancient eyes that have seen too much. He's strikingly handsome.

"You're contaminated," he observes, tilting his head slightly. "Microplastics, by the look of it. Probably fentanyl as well, judging by the vein patterns. Did you drink from a bag or directly from a human?"

"Bag," I rasp. My tongue feels thick. "Underground contact."

"Of course." His tone suggests this is exactly what he expected. "You know what happens to vampires who drink contaminated blood repeatedly?"

I shake my head. I've heard rumors, but nothing concrete.

"The contamination accumulates," he says, like he's giving a lecture. "Your body tries to filter it, but modern pharmaceuticals are designed to be persistent. They linger. Build up. Eventually, your healing factor can't keep pace. You either die: true death, not the temporary kind, or you go feral. Lose your mind, attack anything that moves, become the monster from human nightmares. Both options are unpleasant."

"Great," I manage. "Good... to know."

Something that might be amusement flickers across his face, gone so fast I might have imagined it.

"You have perhaps three hours before the damage becomes irreversible," he continues. "After that, even my resources couldn't help you. You'd be better off walking into the sun." He tilts his head and leans closer. "Looking at your vein pattern, you actually look past the point of saving."

He stands, brushing invisible dust from his coat with movements so precise they look choreographed. Like he's already written me off. Like he's about to walk away and let me die in this alley.

The rage that's been simmering under my fear suddenly ignites.

"So you're the gatekeeper," I say, each word an effort. My voice sounds stronger, fueled by anger. "The great Maximus. Everyone's... so terrified of you."

He pauses mid-movement, hand still on his coat.

"You don't... look that scary," I continue, even though my vision is tunneling. "Just well-dressed. Like a... a CEO vampire. Very... corporate."

Now I definitely see amusement. It softens his features for half a second, makes him look almost human, before the cold mask slams back into place.

"Most people beg," he says quietly. "You insult me instead. Interesting."

Something flickers in those storm-gray eyes. Not amusement. Something older. Hungrier.

"Begging... doesn't seem to work."

"True." He regards me for a long moment, head tilted again like I'm a puzzle he's trying to solve. "They grovel. Offer me things I don't need. Promise loyalty they can't deliver. Bore me with their desperation."

"And I'm... not boring?"

"Not yet."

The silence stretches between us. I can feel myself fading, the gray edges of my vision creeping further in. The numbness has reached my core now, spreading through my chest like frost. I can feel my consciousness starting to fragment, thoughts scattering like marbles on a floor.

This is it. My last chance. Either he helps, or I die here.

I should beg. Should offer him something, anything. But I've got nothing. No money, no connections, no skills that would interest an ancient vampire who's seen everything.

All I have is the truth.

"I didn't ask for this," I say, and my voice cracks. "Didn't want to be turned. Had a life. Had a future. And some vampire with a grudge took it all away because I... beat her in a fight."

His expression doesn't change.

"I'm not asking you to save me out of kindness," I continue. "I know you don't do that. But I'm a fighter. I'm useful. I can work. I can..." I trail off as another wave of numbness washes over me. "I don't want to die in an alley eight months after becoming immortal. That's just... pathetic."

He's silent for so long, I think he's going to leave.

Then he extends his hand.

"Come with me," he says.

I stare at his hand. At him. At the impossible, inexplicable offer.

"Really?" I whisper.

His eyes meet mine, and for just a moment, I see something beneath the cold exterior. Something lonely. Something that's been alone for a very long time.

"Yes," he says, and his voice drops lower, softer, "I haven't been interested in anything for a very long time."

I make myself move. Make myself reach. My fingers find his and hold on.

His grip is cool and impossibly strong as he pulls me to my feet like I weigh nothing. The world tilts dangerously, but he steadies me with a hand on my elbow. The touch is impersonal but firm.

"Can you walk?" he asks.

I try to take a step, and my legs buckle. He catches me effortlessly.

"That's... a no," I manage.

"Then hold on."

Before I can ask what he means, the world shifts. He sweeps me up into his arms like I weigh nothing, one arm under my knees, the other supporting my back.

"Wait..." I start, but then we're moving.

Vampire speed.

The city becomes streaks of light and color, buildings blurring past in ribbons of neon and shadow. The cold November air whips past us but doesn't touch me; he's moving too fast, creating some kind of pocket of stillness around us. I can't see details, can't process anything except the sensation of movement and the solid strength of the arms holding me.

I should be terrified. My instincts should be screaming that I'm in the grip of a predator, being carried to some unknown location with no way to fight back or escape. For all I know, he's taking me somewhere to kill me quietly, away from witnesses.

Instead, I hold on to his coat and think: *At least I'm not dying in an alley.*

The journey lasts seconds or hours; I can't tell anymore. Time has become elastic, unreliable. The poisoning has spread so far that I can barely hold a coherent thought. All I can do is focus on the feeling of being carried, of moving through space at impossible speeds.

When we finally stop, when solid ground reasserts itself beneath us, and the world snaps back into focus, we're somewhere else entirely.

We're in a foyer. No, calling it a foyer is like calling the ocean a puddle. The space is massive, with ceilings that soar at least twenty feet high. Marble floors in black and white create a pattern that draws the eye toward a grand staircase. The walls are painted a soft cream color, decorated with art that even I can tell is original and probably worth more than most people make in a lifetime.

I take in as much as I can from his arms, my head lolling against his shoulder. Everything is pristine. Perfect. Not a speck of dust, not a thing out of place. The kind of cleanliness that speaks of either obsessive attention to detail or serious money for staff. Probably both.

And it's silent. Not just quiet, silent. The kind of silence that only comes with serious soundproofing and serious security. I can't hear the city at all, can't hear traffic or voices or anything that would indicate we're still in Atlanta.

"Where are we?" I ask, my voice barely a whisper.

"My home," Maximus says, already moving toward one of the doors. "My sanctuary. The place that very few vampires ever see."

He says it without pride or threat, just a statement of fact.

Even through the haze of contamination, I notice details. Security cameras in the corners, subtle but visible if you know to look. Doors leading off in multiple directions, all closed. Windows, but with heavy curtains that would block out any sunlight. Everything is designed for function as much as beauty.

He carries me through a door into a room that's clearly a medical facility, or the vampire equivalent. Pristine white walls, medical equipment I half-recognize, a table in the center that looks like a hospital bed. There's a mini-fridge in the corner with a glass door, and through it I can see rows of blood bags, all neatly labeled.

Clean blood. Uncontaminated. More of it than I've seen in eight months of scrounging.

A man is bent over a counter near the fridge, his back to us, organizing blood bags and making notes on a clipboard. Human, by the heartbeat. Sandy blonde hair, wearing scrubs with a white lab coat.

He turns at the sound of our entrance and freezes. He appears to be in his late forties. His eyes go wide at the sight of Maximus carrying a stranger into the facility, then widen further when he sees the black veins crawling up my arms.

"Sir?" The word comes out startled, but he's already moving, setting down the clipboard and reaching for equipment. Whatever shock he felt disappears behind professionalism. "Contamination?"

"Severe. Microplastics and opioids. At least two hours symptomatic."

Maximus lays me down on the table, his movements careful despite his strength. The surface is cool against my back, but I'm too weak to shiver.

"Stay still," he says to me, then to the human: "Monitor her vitals. I'll handle the blood."

The man attaches sensors to my chest with quick, professional motions. His hands are steady now, the initial surprise locked away. "I'll need samples once she's stabilized."

"Dr. Dalton handles medical needs for my people," Maximus adds, handing me a blood bag. "Do what he tells you."

He moves to the fridge and pulls out a blood bag, checking the label with the same precision he seems to apply to everything. Then he hands it to me.

"Drink," he says. "Slowly. Your system is compromised. Too fast and you'll just vomit it back up."

I take the bag with shaking hands. The blood inside is rich red, not the murky dark color of the contaminated bag. I can smell the difference; clean, pure, free of the chemical tang.

I pierce the bag with my fangs and drink.

The relief is immediate and overwhelming. It hits my system like cool water on burned skin, like oxygen after drowning. The black veins under my skin start to recede, slowly but visibly. The numbness in my extremities begins to fade. My thoughts clear, sharpening back into focus.

I didn't realize how bad it had gotten until it started getting better.

"Not too fast," Maximus warns, watching me with those ancient gray eyes.

I force myself to slow down, to take measured sips instead of gulping. It's hard. Every cell in my body is screaming for more, faster, *now*. But I listen to him.

When the bag is empty, I lower it, wiping my mouth with the back of my hand.

"Better?" he asks.

"Yes." My voice is steady now, no longer rasping. "Thank you."

He inclines his head slightly, acknowledging the gratitude without commenting on it.

"You'll need more," he says. "But we'll space it out. Let your system process the contamination properly. You'll stay here tonight. Possibly longer, depending on how quickly you recover."

"Stay here," I repeat. "In your... sanctuary."

"Yes."

"Why?" The question bursts out before I can stop it. "You don't know me. You don't owe me anything. Why help me?"

He's quiet for a moment, studying me with an intensity that makes me want to look away. But I hold his gaze, refusing to be the first to break.

"You didn't beg," he finally says. "You didn't grovel or promise me things you couldn't deliver. You were honest about what you are and what you've lost. And when faced with death, you insulted me instead of pleading."

"That's it?" I ask incredulously. "You saved my life because I have a bad attitude?"

Something flickers across his face; that almost-smile again.

"I saved your life," he says quietly, "because I haven't met anyone interesting in a very long time. And you, Celeste Moreau, are interesting."

Before I can respond to that, before I can even begin to process what it means, he moves toward the door.

"Rest," he says. "I'll return in an hour with another bag. Don't leave this room."

Then he's gone, the door closing behind him with a soft click.

I sit on the medical table in a stranger's home, a stranger who might be the most powerful vampire in the city, and try to understand what just happened.

My life was supposed to end tonight. In an alley, alone and afraid, poisoned by my own desperation.

Instead, I'm here. Alive. Being called *interesting* by an ancient vampire who looks at me like I'm a puzzle he wants to solve.

I look down at my arms. The black veins are still visible but fading, my vampire healing finally kicking in now that it has clean blood to work with.

Dr. Dalton is still there, checking monitors, making notes on a tablet. He glances at me with something that might be professional curiosity.

"Your recovery rate is unusual," he says, more to himself than to me. "Fledglings typically take longer to stabilize from contamination this severe."

"Is that bad?"

"No. Just..." He pauses, frowning at the readout. "Different. I'll need to run some bloodwork once you've had more time to process the clean supply."

He moves toward the door but stops, looking back at me with an expression I can't quite read.

"For what it's worth," he says quietly, "you're in good hands. Maximus doesn't save people unless he means it."

Then he's gone too, leaving me alone with my questions.

TWO

I close the door to the medical facility and stand in the hallway for exactly three seconds before Marcellus appears. He moves silently despite his size, six-foot-four and built like the enforcer he is. Two hundred years old and utterly loyal, which is the only reason I tolerate his occasional questions.

I found him two centuries ago, a fledgling abandoned by his maker and half-feral from hunger. Gave him purpose when he had none. He's been my second-in-command ever since, the only vampire I trust completely.

"You brought someone here," he says. Not a question. He would have been alerted the moment I entered the property with another vampire.

"I did."

"Into the sanctuary."

"Yes."

His jaw tightens. But bringing an unknown vampire into my private residence violates every rule I've established over the last four centuries.

"She's contaminated," I explain, moving past him toward my study. "Microplastics and opioids. Severe poisoning. She'll need monitoring."

Marcellus follows. "And this required bringing her *here*?"

"She was asking about me. Using my name all over the city."

That stops him. For a moment, his hand drifts toward the blade he keeps at his hip, old instincts from his human life as a soldier.

"You should have killed her," he says flatly.

"Perhaps."

"Then why didn't you?"

I enter my study without answering. The room is exactly as I left it three hours ago, desk cleared, books shelved with precision, curtains drawn against windows that will face east when the sun rises. Everything in its place. Everything controlled.

I pour myself a drink from the crystal decanter on the side table. Whiskey, aged fifty years. It does nothing for me physiologically; alcohol stopped affecting me centuries ago, but the ritual is soothing. The burn in my throat is a memory of being human.

"Maximus," Marcellus presses. "Why is she here?"

I take a drink before answering, letting the silence stretch. Thinking about the last three days. About how I found her in the first place.

"Three nights ago," I begin, "I heard whispers at the Wax and Wane Bar. A young vampire asking about me. Using my name carelessly. Demanding introductions."

"And you tracked her."

"Of course I did."

It hadn't been difficult. Celeste Moreau left a trail wide enough for a fledgling to follow. She'd been to the Wax and Wane three nights running, asking questions of anyone who would listen. Vampires, shifters, even a witch or two. She'd offered money she clearly didn't have, approached strangers with the kind of desperation that makes supernaturals nervous. The wolf shifters who run the bar had flagged her to me as a potential problem. Reckless. Desperate. Exactly the kind of behavior that gets vampires killed.

I'd followed her from the bar back to her apartment in East Atlanta Village that first night. Watched from the shadows as she climbed the external stairs to a second-floor unit in a building that had seen better decades. The kind of place where humans live paycheck to paycheck, where no one asks too many questions.

"I observed her for three nights," I continue. "Learned her patterns. Her habits."

"And what did you learn?" Marcellus asks, settling into the chair across from my desk.

I swirl the whiskey in my glass, remembering.

The first night, I'd simply established her location and confirmed she lived alone. Watched the lights go out in her apartment around 3 a.m. Noted the fire escape that provided easy access, and the lack of security beyond a basic door lock. Vulnerable. An easy kill, if that's what I decided.

The second night, I'd watched more carefully.

She'd emerged from her apartment around 10 p.m., dressed for training. I'd followed her to a twenty-four-hour gym three blocks away, one of those budget chains that caters to night shift workers and insomniacs. She'd worked out for two hours with the focused intensity of someone who'd spent years honing their body into a weapon.

I'd observed from the parking lot, standing in shadows where security cameras couldn't catch me. Watched through the windows as she ran through martial arts forms on the mats in a corner. Precise movements. Controlled power. The kind of discipline that comes from thousands of hours of practice.

She'd trained like she was preparing for war.

When she'd finished, she sat on the mat for ten minutes. Just sat there, staring at nothing. The look on her face had been... lost. Like she was trying to remember who she was supposed to be.

I understood that feeling.

"She's a fighter," I tell Marcellus. "Underground circuit, based on her skill level. Trained in multiple disciplines, I observed elements of Muay Thai, Brazilian Jiu-Jitsu, and possibly Krav Maga. She moves like someone who's been in real fights, not just sparring."

"That makes her dangerous."

"That makes her useful."

Tonight had been the most revealing.

I'd positioned myself on the roof of the building across from her apartment, my enhanced vision allowing me to observe through her window with perfect clarity. An invasion of privacy, certainly, but I've long since stopped concerning myself with such niceties. Privacy is a luxury afforded to those who aren't security risks.

She'd been pacing her apartment like a caged animal. I'd watched her pick up her phone a dozen times and then set it down again without calling anyone. The conflict on her face had been evident even from a distance.

She had someone she missed. Someone she couldn't talk to anymore.

The frustration. The anger. The sheer *rage* at her situation.

I'd seen it all written on her face, and something in my chest had tightened.

She hadn't asked for this existence. That much was clear. She wasn't one of those humans who romanticized vampirism, who sought it out thinking immortality would solve their problems.

She'd been turned against her will and abandoned to figure it out alone.

Like I was.

The parallel had struck me then, though I'd tried to dismiss it.

"Her maker abandoned her," I say to Marcellus now. "Turned her and disappeared. No guidance. No instruction. She's been a vampire for eight months, and she's surviving on instinct and whatever she can piece together from observation."

"Many vampires have survived worse."

"And many have died. She was drinking contaminated blood. Would have continued until it killed her if I hadn't intervened."

Marcellus studies me with those too-knowing eyes. "You still haven't answered my question. Why did you intervene?"

I finish my whiskey in one swallow and set the glass down with more force than necessary.

"Because she interested me," I say finally.

The silence that follows is profound.

"She... interested you," Marcellus repeats slowly, like he's testing words in a foreign language.

"Yes."

"In the two centuries I've served you, I've never seen you interested in anyone. You barely tolerate most vampires. You've killed three in the last year alone for far less than using your name publicly."

"I'm aware of my own patterns, Marcellus."

"Then explain this deviation."

I stand and move to the window, pulling the curtain aside to look out at the dark grounds. "Tonight was the third night. And it was the most concerning.

"She paid a vampire named Derek five hundred dollars. He promised to connect her with someone in my circle. Arrange a meeting. He had no intention of following through. Took her money and planned to leave her waiting in that alley until she either gave up or died.

"She had a blood bag she'd purchased from somewhere. Not from a legitimate source. I watched her drink it. Then halfway through, she stopped. Even from across the street, I could see the moment she realized something was wrong. The way her body went rigid. The way she dropped the bag and stumbled toward the bathroom.

"That's when I knew I needed to act. She'd been poisoned, and based on what I could see, she had hours at most. Derek was never coming. But I was already there."

I turn back to face Marcellus. "I saw myself in her. Who I was in those first years after Luciano. When I was still trying to hold onto who I'd been, before I learned that caring about anyone makes you weak."

Understanding crosses Marcellus's face. "You pity her."

"No." The word comes out sharp. "Pity is condescending. I respect her. She's been dealt an impossible hand, and she's still fighting. Not begging. Not giving up. Fighting."

"And when you found her tonight?"

"She insulted me instead of pleading for her life." I allow myself a thin smile. "Told me I looked like a CEO vampire. Very corporate."

Despite himself, Marcellus smirked. "You saved her life because she has a flip mouth?"

"Essentially."

He shakes his head, but something in his expression softens. "You're more human than you pretend to be."

"Don't," I say sharply.

"Maximus..."

"I said don't." The command cuts through the air like a blade. "I helped her because she has useful skills. She was a fighter. That requires tactical thinking and combat ability. She'll work off her debt, and then she'll leave. This is a transaction, nothing more."

Marcellus doesn't argue, but the skepticism on his face is clear. He's known me too long to believe my own lies.

"What do you need from me?" he asks instead.

"Monitor her vitals remotely. She'll need another bag in forty-five minutes, but I want to observe her recovery rate first. If she destabilizes, alert me immediately."

"Should I run a background check?"

"Already did." I move to my desk and pull up the file I compiled over the last three days. " Celeste Moreau. Twenty-seven when turned. Underground fighter in Atlanta for three years, forty-three fights, forty-three wins. Made enough money to support herself and send funds to a sister in Savannah. Mother died of an overdose five years prior. Father unknown/absent. Turned eight months ago by Valentina Russo. No contact with her maker since."

Marcellus leans over my shoulder to read the screen. "Valentina Russo. I know that name."

"You should. She's part of Konstantin's circle."

That gets his attention. Konstantin, older than me, ambitious, and my primary rival for control of Atlanta's blood supply. We've been playing a careful game of power for the last century, neither strong enough to destroy the other, both too proud to negotiate peace.

"You think the turning was deliberate?" Marcellus asks.

"Unknown. Could be spite, could be strategy. Valentina is known for holding grudges." I pull up another file, surveillance footage from an underground fighting venue. "But look at this."

The video shows Celeste in a makeshift ring, facing off against an opponent twice her size. The fight is brutal, efficient. She moves with the kind of precision that comes from years of training, reading her opponent's tells, exploiting openings. The fight lasts less than three minutes before her opponent is on the ground.

"She's good," Marcellus observes.

"She's exceptional. And according to my sources, she was scheduled for one more fight, a big payout, when she disappeared. That's when she was turned."

"Valentina took that from her."

"Everything. The fight, the money, her human life. All of it." I close the video. "If Konstantin is involved, it complicates things."

"Then throw the girl out. Don't let her become leverage."

He's right, of course. The logical move is to heal Celeste enough to survive and send her away before she becomes entangled in politics she doesn't understand.

But I don't want to.

The realization unsettles me more than I care to admit.

"She stays until she's stable," I say. "After that, we'll assess."

Marcellus knows better than to argue further. "I'll set up monitoring. What about Elena?"

Elena. My human donor coordinator, responsible for vetting and managing the clean blood supply. She'll have questions about an unfamiliar vampire in the facility.

"Go brief her. Let Celeste rest."

"And the girl's diet? Beyond emergency bags?"

"Standard protocol. Clean sources only. I want her fully recovered before we determine what to do with her."

Marcellus nods and turns to leave, but pauses at the door. "You know this will spread. You brought someone into the sanctuary. People will talk."

"Let them."

After he leaves, I sink into the chair behind my desk and close my eyes.

What am I doing?

Six hundred years of careful control, of keeping everyone at arm's length, of building walls so high no one can reach me. And I'm compromising it for a woman I met an hour ago.

But when she looked at me in that alley, when she saw me as just a man instead of a monster or a myth, something shifted. Something I thought had died centuries ago stirred back to life.

I open my eyes and pull up the security feed from the medical room. Celeste is still sitting on the table where I left her, looking around the space with obvious assessment. Cataloging exits, I'd guess. Analyzing potential threats. Fighter's instincts even when recovering from near-death.

Even through the camera, I can see her details clearly. Long dark hair falls past her shoulders. Pale skin that makes the fading black veins more visible. Brown eyes that move with focused intensity as she assesses the room. Athletic build beneath the torn clothes. A fighter's body, lean and purposeful. She's beautiful, I realize with detachment. Not the fragile, decorative beauty that bored me centuries ago, but something sharper. More dangerous.

She shifts slightly, testing her movement, flexing her hands. I can see the black veins have receded significantly from this angle. Her vampire healing is working now that she has clean blood in her system.

Faster than I would have expected, actually. Fledglings usually take longer to recover from contamination this severe.

She's smart. Capable. Dangerous.

Everything I observed over three nights is confirmed in these small movements. She's not just a fighter, she's a survivor. Someone who assesses, adapts, and overcomes.

I close the security feed and try to focus on the stack of reports on my desk. Supply chain updates, donor screening results, and intelligence about Konstantin's movements. The endless work of maintaining control.

But I can't focus.

My mind keeps drifting back to tonight's observation. To the moment I realized she was dying but still holding herself together with whatever discipline she'd learned as a fighter. Still trying to control what she could control, even as everything fell apart. The way she'd walked to that alley, knowing she might die there, but going through the motions anyway, because what else was there to do?

I understood that feeling too well.

How many centuries have I spent going through motions? Maintaining my empire, managing my network, executing strategies I've refined over hundreds of years. All of it efficient. All of it controlled.

All of it empty.

When did I stop living and start merely existing?

I stand abruptly and move to the window, pulling back the curtain. Outside, Atlanta sprawls in the darkness, millions of humans sleeping, living, dying, completely unaware of the predators moving through their city.

I've watched the city transform over the decades. Seen it burn during the Civil War. Seen it rebuild. Seen it become a sprawling modern metropolis while I remained frozen in time, unchanging and untouchable.

Lonely.

The word surfaces before I can suppress it.

Time to go back.

I straighten my coat and check my appearance in the mirror by the door, an old habit from when such things mattered. The reflection shows what it always shows: a man frozen at thirty years old, dark hair and aristocratic features, and eyes that have seen too much.

I look the same as I did when Luciano turned me in 1395.

But I don't feel the same. Not tonight.

Tonight, something has shifted.

I collect another blood bag from the secure refrigerator in my private quarters and make my way back to the medical facility. Each step feels weighted with significance I can't quite name.

When I open the door, Celeste looks up immediately. Her eyes are clearer now, more focused. I confirm that the black veins have receded significantly, though they're still visible under her skin like fading bruises.

"You came back," she says.

"I said I would."

"People don't always do what they say."

"I do," I tell her, and it's true. I may be many things, cold, ruthless, unforgiving, but I keep my word. Always. It's one of the few principles I've maintained from my human life.

I hand her the second bag. "Drink. Same pace as before."

She takes it, but this time she holds my gaze while she drinks. Watching me watch her. Testing boundaries, maybe. Or just trying to understand who I am and what I want from her.

I should look away. Should maintain an appropriate distance between us.

I don't.

Instead, I pull up a chair and sit, the first time I've sat in her presence. The gesture is deliberate. Sitting puts us at the same level and reduces the power differential slightly. It's a concession I rarely make.

"What happens after I'm recovered?" she asks between sips.

"That depends."

"On what?"

"On whether you're as useful as I think you are."

Her eyes narrow slightly. "Useful how?"

"I've been watching you for three days," I say, deciding honesty is the most efficient approach. "Followed you. Observed your patterns. Learned what I needed to know."

She stops drinking. "You've been stalking me."

"Surveillance, not stalking. You were using my name all over the city. That made you a security risk. I needed to assess whether you required elimination."

"And you decided I didn't."

"Obviously, since you're here and not dead in an alley."

She processes this, and I can see her mind working. Not panicking. Not offended. Just... calculating. What does it mean that I tracked her? What does it tell her about my resources, my methods, my intentions?

"What did you learn?" she asks finally.

"That you're a fighter. Underground circuit. Forty-three wins, no losses. That you were scheduled for one more big payout when you were turned. That you have a sister in Savannah you can no longer contact. That you train every night like you're preparing for a war."

Something flashes across her face, pain, quickly suppressed.

"You sent money to your sister," I continue. "Regularly. You lost that ability when you were turned."

"Stop." Her voice is tight.

I do; I've made my point, I know everything I need to know about her. But I've also exposed something raw, and pushing further would be cruel rather than strategic.

"You asked what happens next," I say, changing direction. "Here's the truth: I don't help people out of kindness. I built my network on mutual benefit. You need clean blood and guidance. I need... capable people."

"To do what?"

"Whatever needs doing. My operations are extensive. There are always tasks that require someone with your particular skill set."

She studies me for a long moment. "You want me to work for you."

"I want you to work off your debt. After that, you're free to leave or negotiate a more permanent arrangement."

"And if I say no?"

"Then you leave as soon as you're stable, and you're on your own. No access to my network. No clean blood supply. No protection."

I let that sink in. She's smart enough to understand what I'm offering and what I'm not. This isn't charity. This is a transaction.

"How long?" she asks.

"That depends on how quickly you heal and how useful you prove to be. Weeks. Possibly months."

She finishes the blood bag, sets it aside, and meets my eyes directly. "I have conditions."

That surprises me. Most vampires in her position would simply agree to anything. But she's negotiating.

"Go on," I say.

"I'm not killing humans. I don't care what you need done."

"Agreed. I have no interest in drawing that kind of attention."

"And I'm not turning anyone. Even if you order it."

"Also agreed. Forced turnings are beneath me."

She nods slowly. "Then we have a deal."

I stand and extend my hand. After a moment, she takes it. Her grip is firmer now, the poison receding enough that her strength is returning.

"Welcome to my employ, Celeste Moreau," I say. "Try not to make me regret this."

"Same to you," she replies.

And despite myself, despite six hundred years of emotional control, I almost smile.

THREE

CELESTE

Maximus leaves me in the medical facility with instructions to rest, which is hilarious considering I've been a vampire for eight months and still don't entirely understand what "rest" means anymore.

I don't sleep the way I used to. It's more like... shutting down. Going dormant. My body enters a state somewhere between sleep and death, and I wake up feeling neither refreshed nor tired. Just... existing.

But I'm not ready to shut down yet. Not here, in a stranger's compound, no matter how fancy the medical equipment or how clean the blood supply.

I swing my legs off the table and stand carefully. The room tilts slightly, but nowhere near as bad as before. The second bag of clean blood did its job. I can feel my body repairing itself, vampire healing working the way it's supposed to when it has proper fuel.

The black veins under my skin have faded to faint shadows. If I weren't looking for them, I might miss them entirely. My strength is returning, that supernatural power that still feels foreign even after eight months. Like wearing someone else's body.

I explore the medical facility slowly, cataloging details the way I used to before fights. Know your environment. Identify exits. Understand the terrain.

The room is pristine, with white walls, stainless steel equipment, and everything organized with obsessive precision. There's a sink in the corner, cabinets that probably contain medical supplies, and that refrigerator full of blood bags. Each one is labeled with a date, blood type, and what looks like a donor ID number.

This isn't some makeshift operation. This is a system. Infrastructure. The kind of thing that takes years, maybe decades, to build.

How powerful is Maximus, exactly?

I move to the door and press my ear against it. Vampire hearing picks up sounds from deeper in the building. Footsteps. Voices too low to make out words. The hum of climate control systems.

The door isn't locked.

That surprises me more than it should. He told me not to leave, but he didn't actually restrain me. Either he's confident I won't try to escape, or he's confident he could stop me if I did.

Probably both.

I crack the door open and peer into the hallway. Empty. The floor is the same black and white marble as the foyer, lit by recessed lighting that's probably on automated timers.

Everything about this place screams money, power, and control.

I step into the hallway, closing the door quietly behind me. I'm not trying to escape. Where would I even go? But I need to understand where I am. What I've agreed to.

The hallway extends in both directions. To the left, it leads back toward the foyer I remember from when we arrived. To the right, it continues deeper into the building, with multiple doors branching off.

I go right.

The first door I pass is closed, but there's a small window set into it. I peek through and see what looks like a server room, rows of equipment with blinking lights, climate-controlled, and humming with power. Serious tech. Not what I expected in a vampire's compound.

The second door is open, revealing a library. Floor-to-ceiling bookshelves, a rolling ladder, and leather chairs positioned near a fireplace that's currently dark. The books look old, like, really old. Leather-bound volumes with titles in languages I don't recognize.

How long does it take to collect a library like this? Centuries, probably.

"You were told to rest."

I spin around, my body automatically dropping into a defensive stance before I can stop myself.

The man standing behind me is massive. Six-foot-four at least, built like he could bench press a car. Dark skin, close-cropped hair, and dark brown eyes that assess me with the cold calculation of someone who's decided I'm a potential threat.

He's also a vampire. I can feel it now that I'm paying attention, that sense of recognition, like my body knows it's in the presence of another predator.

"And you are?" I ask, straightening but not relaxing.

"Marcellus. Maximus's second-in-command." His voice is deep, with an accent I can't quite place. Old world. European, maybe. "You should be in the medical facility."

"I was. It got boring."

His expression doesn't change. "Return to the medical facility."

"Or what?"

"Or I will escort you there. Forcibly, if necessary."

I believe him. There's no bluster in his tone, no ego. Just a statement of fact. He's bigger than me, probably stronger, and definitely has more experience.

But I've fought people bigger than me before. Size isn't everything.

"Maximus said I'd be working off my debt," I say, keeping my voice level. "That makes me an employee, not a prisoner. So unless there's a specific reason I need to be locked in that room, I'm going to explore my new workplace."

Marcellus studies me for a long moment. I can almost see him calculating, is subduing me worth the effort?

"Stay out of Maximus's private quarters," he finally says. "Stay out of the donor areas. Stay out of the security center. Everywhere else, you're free to explore until he returns."

"Where is he?"

"That's not your concern."

Fair enough.

Marcellus turns and walks away, his footsteps silent despite his size. I watch him disappear around a corner.

I continue my exploration, more carefully now. The compound is massive, corridors branching off into wings, staircases leading to upper floors. Everything is pristine, organized, controlled. Like Maximus himself.

I find a training room on the ground floor and pause in the doorway. It's equipped better than any gym I've ever used: mats, weights, a boxing bag, and even weapons mounted on the walls. Swords, staffs, knives. All of them look functional, not decorative.

My fingers itch to test them. To move, to fight, to do something physical after lying on that medical table.

But I keep moving instead. There'll be time for training later.

I pass what looks like a dining room, formal, with a table that could seat twenty. Do vampires even use dining rooms? I guess if you're hundreds of years old, you keep up appearances.

Eventually, I find a sitting room with floor-to-ceiling windows overlooking the grounds. I can see gardens, perfectly manicured. Security lighting illuminates paths between hedges and fountains. The whole estate is probably walled, gated, and monitored.

A fortress disguised as a mansion.

I sink into one of the chairs, expensive leather, probably Italian, and stare out at the grounds.

What the hell am I doing here?

A few hours ago, I was dying in an alley. Now I'm sitting in a vampire lord's compound, having agreed to work off a debt I don't fully understand to a man I barely know.

My phone is still in my apartment. My clothes, my few possessions, everything I owned. Even if I could go back, Maximus knows where I live. If he wanted to kill me, he could have done it a dozen times over the last three days.

The fact that he didn't, that he watched me instead, learned about me, decided I was worth saving, that's what unsettles me most.

What does he want from me?

He said I was interesting. That I didn't beg. That I was useful.

But there's something else. Something in the way he looked at me in that alley. Like he recognized something.

"You must be Celeste."

I turn to find a woman standing in the doorway. Human, by the sound of her heartbeat. Mid-thirties, professionally dressed in slacks and a blouse, dark hair pulled back in a neat bun. She's pretty in an understated way, and her expression is cautiously friendly.

"I am," I confirm. "And you are?"

"Elena. I coordinate the donor network for Maximus." She steps into the room, maintaining a respectful distance. "I heard we had a new arrival. Wanted to introduce myself."

"The donor network," I repeat. "You manage the clean blood supply."

"Among other things. Vetting, scheduling, and health monitoring. Making sure our donors are safe and our vampires are fed." She smiles slightly. "It's more complicated than it sounds."

"I bet."

She settles into the chair across from me, crossing her legs. There's no fear in her body language, which is interesting. She works with vampires every day. Either she's incredibly brave or incredibly stupid.

"How are you feeling?" she asks. "Marcellus said you were badly contaminated."

"Better. The clean blood helped."

"You must not have been as bad as he thought to have cleared up so quickly." She pauses, frowning slightly. "Actually, Dr. Dalton mentioned something about your bloodwork. He said the markers were unusual. Not bad, just... different from what he typically sees in fledglings." She shakes her head. "Anyway. I've been doing this for eight years. We've had contaminated vampires brought to the containment wing before. That's medical protocol. But I've never seen Maximus personally bring someone here as a guest. Give them free run of the compound. That never happens."

"He told me that."

"So you understand what it means."

"That he's making an exception. That I should be grateful and not cause trouble."

Elena laughs. "Something like that. But also... he doesn't make exceptions. Ever. So the fact that he made one for you? That's significant."

I don't know what to say to that.

"I'm not trying to make you uncomfortable," Elena continues. "Just... be careful. Maximus is..." She searches for words. "He's fair. Honorable, even by vampire standards. But he's also been alone for a very long time. He doesn't let people close. Doesn't trust easily."

"He watched me for three days before deciding whether to kill me or save me," I say dryly. "Trust isn't exactly his strong suit."

"No, it's not." Elena's expression softens. "But if he's given you a chance, he means it. Just don't make him regret it."

"Second person to tell me that today."

"Because it's true."

Before I can respond, a sound cuts through the building. A scream, raw, agonized, inhuman.

I'm on my feet instantly, every muscle tensed for a fight. "What the hell was that?"

Elena's face has gone pale. "The containment wing."

Another scream, closer this time. Then the sounds of struggle. Something crashing.

"Stay here," Elena says, standing quickly.

"Like hell."

I follow her out of the sitting room and down a corridor I haven't explored yet. The screaming gets louder, more desperate. Other sounds join it, snarling, the crash of furniture breaking, voices shouting commands.

We round a corner and nearly collide with Marcellus. He's moving fast, his expression grim.

"Get back to the medical facility," he orders me. "Now."

"What's happening?"

"One of the contaminated vampires is going feral. We need to contain him before..."

Another crash. A door somewhere ahead bursts open, and a figure stumbles into the hallway.

It's a vampire, male, maybe twenty when he was turned. His eyes are wild, unfocused. Black veins cover every visible inch of his skin, pulsing with poison. He's breathing hard, saliva dripping from exposed fangs.

Feral.

He sees us and lunges.

Marcellus moves to intercept, but I'm faster. My body reacts on instinct, eight months of vampire reflexes combined with years of fighter training. I sidestep the lunge, grab his arm, and use his momentum to throw him into the wall.

He hits hard and goes down, but he's up again in seconds. No pain response. No tactical thinking. Just pure rage and hunger.

He comes at me again, and this time I don't hold back. I'm not trying to kill him, just subdue him. Control the threat.

But he's strong. Stronger than he should be. The feral state has stripped away everything except the predator, and predators are dangerous.

We grapple, slamming into walls, his teeth snapping inches from my throat. I manage to get behind him, arm around his neck in a chokehold, not that vampires need to breathe, but the pressure point still works.

"Little help here!" I grunt.

Marcellus is suddenly there with a syringe. He jabs it into the feral vampire's neck and depresses the plunger.

The effect is almost immediate. The vampire's struggles weaken, then stop. He goes limp in my arms, unconscious.

I lower him to the floor carefully and step back, breathing hard despite not needing oxygen.

"What the hell was that?" I demand.

Marcellus is staring at me with something that might be respect. "Sedative. Should keep him under for a few hours."

"That's not what I meant. What happened to him?"

Elena appears with two other vampires, security, by the look of them. They lift the unconscious feral vampire and carry him back toward wherever he escaped from.

"Contaminated blood," Marcellus says. "He's been deteriorating for days. Tonight, he finally went completely feral."

"And you keep him here?"

"Where else would we keep him?" Marcellus's voice is sharp. "Throw him out to attack humans? Kill him when there might still be a chance to reverse the damage? This is what Maximus does. He tries to save the ones who can be saved."

I look down the hallway where they carried the feral vampire. "Can he be saved?"

"Unknown. We're still researching treatments. But if we don't try, he's definitely lost."

I process this. Maximus maintains a containment wing. Keeps vampires who are going feral from contaminated blood, tries to treat them instead of just putting them down.

That's... not what I expected.

"You did well," Marcellus says grudgingly. "Quick thinking. Good instincts."

"I've fought before."

"So Maximus said." He studies me for a moment. "Perhaps you will be useful after all."

Before I can respond, another voice cuts through the hallway.

"What happened?"

Maximus strides toward us, his expression controlled but his eyes sharp. Taking in the scene, me with torn clothes and fresh bruises already healing, Marcellus with the empty syringe, Elena looking shaken.

"One of the contaminated went feral," Marcellus reports. "Michael. We have him sedated and secured now."

Maximus's gaze shifts to me. "You helped subdue him."

It's not a question.

"Yes."

"I told you to rest."

"I was exploring. He attacked. I reacted."

Something flickers across his face, too quick to identify. Then he turns to Marcellus. "Increase Michael's sedation dosage. I want him monitored every fifteen minutes. If he destabilizes further, notify me immediately."

"Understood."

Maximus looks at Elena. "Make sure the other containment subjects are secure. I don't want any more incidents tonight."

"On it." Elena hurries off.

Then it's just me and Maximus in the hallway, standing too close, both of us assessing the other.

"You should have stayed in the medical facility," he says.

"Probably."

"But you didn't."

"No."

"Why?"

"Because I needed to understand where I am and what I've agreed to. And because I don't take orders well when I don't understand the reasoning behind them."

I expect anger. Irritation, at least. Instead, his expression softens almost imperceptibly.

"Fair enough," he says. "Come with me. If you're well enough to fight feral vampires, you're well enough for a tour."

He starts walking, and after a moment's hesitation, I follow.

FOUR

I lead Celeste through the compound, acutely aware of her presence behind me. She moves quietly, fighter's instincts, but I can hear every footfall, every shift of fabric as she takes in her surroundings.

"This was built in 1887," I say as we walk through a corridor lined with portraits. "Originally belonged to a railroad baron. I acquired it in 1923."

"Acquired," she repeats. "That's a polite way of saying what, exactly?"

"I bought it. Legally. With money I earned through legitimate investments." I glance back at her. "I'm not what you think I am."

"And what do I think you are?"

"A monster who kills and takes whatever he wants."

She's quiet for a moment. "Are you?"

The question is direct. Honest. I appreciate that.

"Sometimes," I admit. "When necessary. But I've learned that building systems is more effective than burning them down. Control comes from infrastructure, not chaos."

We turn into another wing, and I gesture to the doors we pass. "Medical facilities you've already seen. The security center is off-limits. Donor coordination offices. My private quarters are on the third floor, also off-limits."

"And the containment wing?"

"Necessary. The blood crisis is worse than most vampires realize. Contamination isn't just making us sick; it's destroying us. Turning us into mindless predators." I stop at a window that overlooks the grounds. "I keep the ones who might be saved. Research treatments. Try to reverse the damage."

"That's... not what I expected."

"What did you expect?"

She moves to stand beside me, looking out at the gardens. "Someone who hoards power. Uses people. I didn't expect mercy."

"It's not mercy. It's pragmatism. Every vampire who goes feral is one more threat to our secrecy. One more reason for humans to hunt us. I'm not saving them out of kindness, I'm saving them because their survival benefits the larger system."

But even as I say it, I know it's not entirely true. There's something else. Some remnant of who I was before Luciano broke me. The part that still remembers what it means to protect people.

"You're lying," Celeste says quietly.

I turn to look at her. "Excuse me?"

"You're lying to yourself. Maybe you started doing it for pragmatic reasons, but that's not why you continue. I saw your face when Marcellus mentioned Michael. You care what happens to him."

The observation is too perceptive. Too close to truths I don't examine.

"You've known me for three hours," I say coldly. "Don't presume to understand my motivations."

"Fair enough." She doesn't back down, doesn't apologize. Just accepts the boundary I've drawn. "So what's the tour really about? You don't seem like the type to waste time on pleasantries."

Smart. She sees through the pretense.

"I need to assess your capabilities," I say. "You subdued a feral vampire with minimal assistance. But I need to understand your limits before I give you actual assignments."

"You want to test me."

"Yes."

"Fine. When do we start?"

"Now."

I lead her to the training facility, a converted ballroom on the ground floor, equipped with everything necessary for combat training. The space is vast, with high ceilings and reinforced floors designed to withstand vampire strength.

Celeste walks to the center of the room, her eyes taking in the weapons on the walls, the mats, the equipment. She moves like she belongs here. Like she's spent her life in places like this.

"What were you before you were turned?" I ask, even though I already know the answer.

"Underground fighter. Three years."

"Why underground instead of professional?"

"Money was better. Fewer rules. And I liked the freedom of it." She picks up a practice staff from the rack, testing its weight. "Didn't have to deal with promoters or contracts or people telling me how to fight."

"Control."

"What?"

"You valued control. The ability to choose your fights, your terms."

She sets the staff down and meets my eyes. "Yes. And then it was taken from me."

I understand that better than she knows.

"Show me," I say, moving onto the mats. "Demonstrate what you can do."

She doesn't hesitate. Doesn't question. Just attacks.

She's fast, vampire speed combined with trained precision. The first strike comes at my head, and I block it easily. But the second and third come in rapid succession, each one targeting a different vulnerability.

She's not just fast. She's tactical.

I counter, testing her reflexes. She adapts immediately, shifting her stance, reading my movements. We trade blows for thirty seconds, neither of us landing anything significant, both of us assessing the other.

Then I increase the pressure.

I move faster, hitting harder, using my full strength. Most fledglings would fold under this kind of assault. But Celeste holds her ground. She can't match my power; I have six centuries of vampire strength, but she compensates with technique. Redirecting force instead of meeting it head-on. Using my momentum against me.

A move straight from jiu-jitsu.

She sweeps my leg, and I let myself go down, curious to see what she'll do. She follows me to the ground, going for a submission hold, but I reverse it before she can lock it in.

We separate and come to our feet simultaneously.

She's breathing hard, unnecessary, but old habits, and there's a gleam in her eyes. Not fear. Excitement.

She likes this.

"Good," I say. "Your technique is solid. Your instincts are excellent. But you're still thinking like a human fighter."

"What does that mean?"

"You're limiting yourself. You have supernatural strength and speed now. Stop fighting like you're fragile."

I see the understanding dawn on her face.

"Again," I say.

This time, when she attacks, there's less restraint. She uses vampire speed properly, blurring across the mat. Her strikes have more power behind them, less concern about hurting herself.

Better.

We fight for another five minutes, and I find myself... enjoying it. When was the last time I sparred with someone who could keep up? Marcellus, perhaps, but his style is different, pure power and aggression. Celeste fights like water, flowing around obstacles, adapting constantly.

It's been centuries since anyone impressed me in combat.

She fights like poetry written in violence. Like someone taught her body to speak a language most people never learn. I want to watch her fight forever. I want to see what she becomes with proper training.

I want things I haven't allowed myself to want in three hundred years.

The alarm shatters the moment.

A high-pitched wail that cuts through the entire compound, followed by automated announcements: "Security breach. East wing. Multiple hostiles."

I'm moving before the announcement finishes, Celeste right behind me.

"Stay close," I command. "Do exactly as I say."

"What's happening?"

"We're under attack."

We reach the security center in seconds. Marcellus is already there, monitoring multiple screens showing different angles of the compound.

"Eight hostiles," he reports. "Vampires. They breached the east wall using explosives. Moving toward the donor coordination offices."

Not the blood storage. Not my private quarters. The donor offices, where we keep records.

"They're after the network," I say, understanding immediately. "They want to know who our donors are."

"Konstantin," Marcellus says grimly.

Of course. My rival wouldn't attack my supplies directly, too obvious, too crude. But if he could identify our donors, he could compromise them. Turn them. Kill them. Destroy the entire network from the inside.

Strategic. Intelligent. Exactly what I would do.

"Lock down the donor wing," I order. "Move all personnel to the safe room."

Marcellus is already on his comm unit, issuing rapid commands to security teams. "Donor wing sealed. Personnel evacuating to safe room. I'm with you."

"I'm coming too," Celeste says.

"No. You're staying here where..."

"I can fight. You just saw that. You need numbers, and I'm offering."

I want to refuse. Want to lock her somewhere safe. But she's right, I need numbers, and she's capable.

"Fine. But you follow my lead. No heroics."

We move toward the east wing at vampire speed, Marcellus flanking my left, Celeste on my right. I can hear the intruders ahead, breaking doors, moving through rooms with efficient precision.

Professional. Trained. Not random thugs but soldiers.

We round a corner, and there they are, eight vampires in tactical gear, working in coordinated pairs. One of them sees us and shouts a warning.

Then it's chaos.

I take the first two myself, moving faster than they can track. Six hundred years of experience against their comparative youth. I don't intend to kill them. I need them conscious for interrogation.

Marcellus engages three more, his fighting style brutal and direct.

That leaves three for Celeste.

I want to help her. Every instinct screams at me to protect her. But I force myself to trust her capabilities, to focus on my own opponents.

I hear the sounds of her fighting, the impact of strikes, the crash of bodies hitting walls. She's holding her own.

More than holding her own.

I incapacitate my opponents efficiently and turn to check on her. She's taken down two of the three, and she's grappling with the last one. He's bigger than her, stronger, but she gets behind him and does something complicated with his arm that makes him scream.

The joint breaks. He goes down.

She steps back, ready for more threats, scanning the corridor with sharp eyes.

"Clear," Marcellus announces.

The security team arrive moments later, responding to the breach alert. Marcellus gestures to the unconscious attackers. "Secure these eight. Detention wing. I want them conscious and able to answer questions."

I move to the donor coordination offices. The door has been breached but not fully opened. We got here in time. I check the secure servers. No access. The intruders never made it to the actual records.

But it was close.

While the security team handles the prisoners, I turn to

Celeste. She has a split lip that's already healing, bruises forming and fading on her arms.

"You fought well," I say.

"Thanks. They were better trained than I expected."

"Konstantin's people. He doesn't send amateurs."

She processes that. "This is going to happen again, isn't it? More attacks."

"Yes. He's testing our defenses. Looking for weaknesses."

"Then you need more than just you and Marcellus."

She's right, though I don't want to admit it. I have an inner circle. Lieutenants, trusted operators who handle various operations. But my core leadership? That's just Marcellus and me. The inner circle follows our decisions and executes our strategies. What I need is another vampire at the highest level. Someone who can make critical decisions, see the full picture, and be trusted with everything.

Vampires like the one standing in front of me, blood on her clothes and determination in her eyes.

"Come with me," I say.

I lead her and Marcellus to my study, where I pour three glasses of whiskey.

"What you saw tonight is going to become routine," I say, handing Celeste and Marcellus a glass. "Konstantin wants my network. He'll keep attacking until he either succeeds or I convince him it's not worth the cost."

"So convince him," she says.

"I'm trying. But that requires strength. Numbers. People I can trust in positions of power."

She looks at me curiously.

"You want me to be more than just someone working off a debt," she says slowly. "You want me in your inner circle."

"Yes."

Marcellus's expression tightens. "Maximus..."

"She proved herself tonight," I cut him off. "She's capable, tactical, and, most importantly, she has no allegiances to anyone else in this city. No history. No baggage."

"She's a fledgling with eight months of experience," Marcellus argues. "You're talking about giving her access to our most sensitive operations."

"I'm talking about recognizing talent when I see it." I turn to Celeste. "You're wasted as simple muscle. I saw how you fought tonight. You think strategically. You adapt. You read situations and respond intelligently."

"What exactly are you offering?" she asks.

"A position. A real one, not just working off debt. I'll train you properly. Teach you everything you need to know about vampire politics, power structures, and survival. In exchange, you become part of my core team. You help me defend this network and expand it."

"And if I say no?"

"Then you work off your debt as we agreed, and you leave when you're done. But you'll never be more than a fledgling struggling to survive in a city controlled by vampires who see you as competition or a liability."

It's not a threat. Just reality.

She looks at her glass, swirling the whiskey thoughtfully. "If I say yes, I need something in return."

"Name it."

"I have a sister. Simone. She's in Savannah. I've been sending her money, *was* sending her money, to help with therapy, rent, life. She thinks I moved to Miami for work. She can't know what I am, but she still needs help."

"You want me to provide for her."

"As part of my compensation. However, you need to structure

it. Anonymous benefactor, scholarship, trust fund, I don't care. Just... take care of her."

I'm quiet for a moment, studying her. "You're negotiating for someone else before yourself."

"She's all I have left. And she has no idea I'm gone."

"I'll set up a trust. She'll receive monthly deposits from a fictional remote employer, your 'Miami job.' As long as you're in my employ, she'll be taken care of."

The relief is apparent on her face. "Thank you."

"Don't thank me. You'll earn it."

She takes a breath, steadying herself. "And one more thing."

"Go on."

"Help me find the vampire who turned me. I want answers about why she did it."

"Valentina Russo," I say. "That's her name."

She looks up sharply. "You know who she is?"

"Part of my research over the last three days. She's connected to Konstantin, part of his inner circle."

I see her processing this. The vampire who ruined her life works for my enemy.

"Then finding her serves both our interests," she says carefully.

"Perhaps. But hunting her down will bring complications. Konstantin won't take kindly to us targeting one of his people."

"But you'll do it anyway."

I exchange a glance with Marcellus. He knows what I'm about to agree to and doesn't approve. But complications are inevitable anyway.

"Yes," I say. "I'll help you find her. But on my timeline, when it's strategic."

She extends her hand. "Then we have a deal."

I take her hand, and something passes between us. Recognition. Understanding. Her grip is strong. Fighter's hands. Scarred knuckles, no hesitation.

"You know," I say, "most people would be terrified right now. You just negotiated terms with a six-hundred-year-old vampire like you were buying a used car."

"I've faced worse odds in the ring."

"Have you?"

"No." Her eyes glint. "But you don't need to know that."

I fight a smile. "Welcome to the inner circle," I say. "Try not to die."

She smirks. "Same to you."

I wake from dormancy in the guest room Maximus showed me to after our meeting last night.

The bedroom is spacious, with a king-sized bed that's far more comfortable than anything I owned as a human, blackout curtains drawn tight against the windows, and furniture that probably costs more than I made in a year of underground fighting.

I sit up and take in my surroundings properly now that I'm awake.

There's a note on the nightstand, written in precise hand-writing:

Your apartment has been cleared out. Your belongings are in the closet. Training begins at 8 PM. Don't be late. —M

I check the clock on the wall. 7:30 p.m.
Thirty minutes.

I shower quickly in the attached bathroom, marble and chrome, because of course it is, and find my clothes neatly organized in the walk-in closet. My clothes, from my apartment. He wasn't kidding about clearing it out.

Everything is here. My worn jeans, my training gear, even the few personal items I owned. A photo of my sister Simone from three years ago, back when I could still see her. The receipt from my last fight, still stained with blood.

My entire life, packed into three boxes and transported here without my permission.

I should be angry about the invasion of privacy. Instead, I'm relieved I don't have to go back to that empty apartment and face the ghost of my human life.

I dress in training clothes, black leggings, sports bra, tank top, and head out to find the training facility. The compound is more alive. I can hear voices from other parts of the building, footsteps, the hum of activity.

How many people work here?

I find the training room easily, muscle memory from last night, and Maximus is already there. He's changed into different clothes, black pants and a fitted long-sleeve shirt that reveals the fighter's build usually hidden beneath his formal wear. Lean muscle. Clearly, someone who's spent centuries training.

"You're early," he says without looking up from the tablet he's studying.

"You said don't be late."

"I said training begins at eight. It's 7:52."

"Is eight minutes early a problem?"

He finally looks at me, and something in his expression might be amusement. "No. It suggests you take this seriously."

"I take not dying seriously."

"Good. That's the first lesson: everything we do here is about survival. Mine, yours, the vampires who depend on this network. Sentiment is a luxury we can't afford."

He sets down the tablet and moves onto the mats. "Last night you fought well. But you fought like you were in the ring, with rules and referees and the expectation that someone would stop the fight if it went too far."

"And real fights don't work that way."

"No. Real fights end when someone is dead or incapacitated. There's no tapping out. No one to save you if you make a mistake."

He attacks without warning.

I barely block the first strike, and the second one gets through my guard, slamming into my ribs hard enough that I hear something crack. The pain is sharp and immediate, but I force myself to move through it. Vampire healing will fix it.

"Don't freeze," he says, pressing the attack. "Pain is information. Use it."

I adapt, shifting my weight, protecting my injured side while using my good side to counter. He's faster than me, stronger, but I'm learning his patterns. The way he favors his right side slightly. The way he drops his shoulder before a kick.

Maximus sweeps my legs, and I hit the mat hard. For a moment, the ceiling above me isn't the training room. It's older, stone, lit by something too bright and clinical. I smell rain and old buildings and something sharp, medicinal.

Then I blink, and it's gone.

"You hesitated," Maximus says, offering me a hand up.

I take it, unsettled by whatever that was. A dream fragment? A memory? I've never been anywhere that looked like that.

For two hours, he beats the hell out of me.

Every time I think I'm getting the hang of it, he changes the parameters. Adds weapons. Changes the terrain. Forces me to fight in positions that would never happen in a controlled match.

"Underground fighting made you predictable," he says, circling me while I catch my breath. "You learned to fight one-on-one, in a defined space, for a set amount of time. Real vampire combat has none of those constraints."

He gestures to Marcellus, who's been watching from the sidelines. "Again. But this time, two opponents."

Fighting both of them at once is brutal. Every opening I exploit with one leaves me vulnerable to the other. I take hits I can't block, make tactical choices that would work against one fighter but fail against two.

But I'm learning. Adapting. Finding the rhythm of fighting outnumbered.

When Maximus finally calls a halt, I'm covered in bruises that are already fading, and exhilarated in a way I haven't felt since my last real fight.

"Better," Maximus says. "You adapt quickly. But you're still holding back."

"I'm not..."

"You are. You're fighting like you're afraid of hurting us. Of going too far." He steps closer. "We're vampires, Celeste. You can't hurt us permanently. Stop pulling your punches."

He's right. Some part of me is still calibrating force for human opponents. Still afraid of killing someone by accident.

"Tomorrow night, same time," he says. "We'll work on that mental block."

Before I can respond, Elena appears in the doorway. "Sorry to interrupt, but Celeste is supposed to shadow me tonight. Donor coordination training?"

Maximus nods. "Go. Learn how the network operates. Understanding the system is as important as protecting it."

I follow Elena out of the training room, my body aching in that good way that comes from being pushed to your limits.

"Rough session?" Elena asks sympathetically.

"He doesn't seem to believe in easing people in."

"No, he doesn't. But you'll be better for it. Everyone he trains becomes exceptionally dangerous." She leads me down a corridor I haven't explored yet. "Come on. I'll show you the real heart of this operation."

The donor coordination wing is nothing like what I expected. It's professional, almost corporate. Offices with computers, filing systems, and medical equipment for health screenings. There are three other humans working here, all of them focused on their tasks with the efficiency of people who know their jobs matter.

"This is where we manage everything," Elena explains, leading me to her office. "Donor recruitment, health screening, sched-uling, payment processing. We currently have one hundred twenty active donors in rotation, with another fifteen in the vetting process."

"One hundred twenty donors. How many vampires does that support?"

"Thirty, if we're running at full capacity. The inner circle takes priority, of course. The rest goes to vampires in the city who've proven trustworthy and can afford our services."

"Afford?"

"Clean blood isn't free. Most of our donors are compensated generously. It's expensive to maintain them, health insurance, regular medical checkups, premium payments. We pass those costs along."

She pulls up a database on her computer, showing profiles of donors. Names, blood types, medical histories, and feeding schedules.

"How do you recruit them?" I ask, studying the screen.

"Various ways. Some are people who need money and are willing to sell their blood. Some are enthusiasts. Humans who find vampires fascinating and want to be part of that world. We screen them carefully with medical and psychological evaluations. Can't have donors who are unstable or trying to use access to vampires for their own agenda."

I notice something in one of the profiles. "What does 'voluntary-conditional' mean?"

Elena's expression shifts slightly. "That means they agreed to donate, but with certain... requirements."

"What kind of requirements?"

She's quiet for a moment, clearly weighing how much to tell me. "Some donors are people who got into trouble. Financial debts they can't pay, legal issues that make employment impossible, and people who need to disappear for their own safety. Maximus offers them a deal: donate blood regularly, and he makes their problems disappear. They're not forced, technically. But their options are limited."

I feel something cold settle in my stomach. "That's coercion."

"That's survival. These people would be dead or in prison otherwise. Instead, they're alive, healthy, and compensated. Is it morally gray? Yes. But the alternative is vampires hunting randomly, killing people, exposing us all."

She's not wrong. But it still sits uncomfortably.

"How many donors are 'voluntary-conditional'?" I ask.

"About fifteen percent. The rest are genuinely voluntary, people who want the money and understand the risks."

I study the profiles more carefully. Ages ranging from twenty-one to fifty-five. Various backgrounds. Some are listed as "high-risk" with notes about monitoring for contamination.

"What happens if a donor becomes contaminated?" I ask.

"We remove them from the rotation immediately. Pay them a severance and cut all ties. We can't risk anyone drinking contaminated blood; you saw what happens."

Michael. The feral vampire from last night.

"Can contamination be reversed?" I ask.

"We're researching it. Maximus has been funding medical studies for years. So far, limited success. If we catch it early enough, sometimes. But once someone goes fully feral..." She shakes her head. "We haven't found a way back from that."

We spend the next hour going through procedures. How donors are scheduled to avoid over-tapping any single person. How blood is tested before storage. How payments are processed through shell companies to maintain anonymity.

It's sophisticated. Careful. The kind of system that takes decades to build and constant vigilance to maintain.

"Why do you do this?" I ask Elena. "You're human. You could work anywhere. Why manage a blood supply for vampires?"

She considers the question carefully. "I was a phlebotomist and blood bank technician. Worked at the hospital for six years. Eight years ago, my younger brother was killed by a vampire. Drained and left in an alley in Midtown. The police wrote it off as a mugging gone wrong, but I knew better. I had to identify his body. The puncture wounds on his neck weren't from any needle I'd ever seen, and no mugger drains a body of that much blood. I make puncture wounds for a living. I know what they're supposed to look like."

Her voice is steady, but there's old pain beneath it. "I started investigating on my own. Used my access at the hospital to pull records on similar cases. Found a pattern of victims going back years, all with the same type of wounds, all in the same neighborhoods. I started staking out those areas at night. Asked questions I shouldn't have been asking." She pauses. "Turns out, when a human starts poking around vampire hunting grounds, word travels fast. One of Konstantin's people found me before I ever found him. He was going to kill me to keep me quiet.

"Maximus stopped him. Saved my life. Then he made me an offer: he'd been running a blood network for decades, but it was becoming too large for him to manage alone. The contamination crisis was starting to accelerate. He needed someone who under-stood blood banking, medical screening, donor health, someone who could professionalize the operation and scale it properly. Someone who had reason to want this to work."

She pulls up historical records, newspaper clippings about unsolved murders, patterns of disappearances. "I'd spent my entire career managing blood supplies. This was the same work, just... different clientele. And it meant my brother's death could lead to something that prevented other deaths."

"So you have the skills and the motivation," I say quietly.

"Exactly. Maximus doesn't hire people just because he feels sorry for them. He hired me because I'm qualified, and I'm invested in making sure this system works."

"Even with the 'voluntary-conditional' donors?" I ask.

Elena's expression tightens slightly. "Especially with them. Those people have options now that they didn't before. Is it perfect? No. But it's better than Konstantin's people draining them in alleys and leaving their bodies for their families to find. Like they did with my brother."

I understand the logic. Doesn't mean I'm comfortable with all of it.

"Come on," Elena says, standing. "There's someone I want you to meet."

She leads me to a medical room where a woman in her thirties is having blood drawn by one of the medical techs. The woman looks healthy, relaxed even.

"Celeste, this is Monica. She's been one of our donors for three years."

Monica smiles. "New vampire?"

"New to the network," I confirm.

"Elena runs a tight ship. You're in good hands." She doesn't seem afraid at all. "I donate twice a month, make enough to pay my rent and student loans, and the health benefits are better than anything I could get working retail."

"You're okay with vampires drinking your blood?" I ask.

"Honey, I grew up knowing vampires were real. My grandmother was a donor back in the seventies, before things were organized like this. She had scars all over her neck from messy feeding. This?" She gestures to the neat IV setup. "This is civilized. Plus, I get regular health screenings, dental coverage, and I'm building savings. It's a better deal than anything else available to someone like me."

After Monica leaves, I turn to Elena. "Is everyone that comfortable?"

"Most. We screen out people who seem afraid or coerced. Fear affects blood quality, adrenaline, and stress hormones can cause contamination issues." She checks her watch. "You should probably get back. Marcellus wanted to talk to you about security protocols."

I find Marcellus in the security center, a room filled with monitors showing every angle of the compound. He's studying footage from last night's attack, his expression grim.

"You wanted to see me?" I say from the doorway.

He doesn't look away from the screens. "Maximus trusts you. I don't."

"I gathered that."

"You've been a vampire for eight months. You have no connections, no history in this city, and suddenly you're in the inner circle." He finally turns to face me. "That's either incredibly good luck or incredibly good planning."

"You think I'm a plant."

"The timing is suspicious. You start asking about Maximus all over the city. He tracks you down. You nearly die from contaminated blood. Convenient excuse to need his help. He brings you here, and within twenty-four hours, we're attacked."

"You think I signaled them somehow."

"I think you're either an enemy asset or you're dangerously naive. Either way, you're a liability."

I step into the room, keeping my hands visible and non-threatening. "I understand your suspicion. If I were in your position, I'd feel the same. But I'm not working for Konstantin. I don't even know who he is beyond what I've heard in the last day."

"That's what a good plant would say."

"True. So what do I need to do to prove myself?"

Marcellus studies me for a long moment. "Time. Consistency. One mission isn't enough. I need to see that you're loyal when it matters, when there's something to lose."

"Fair enough."

"And if you betray us," he says quietly, "if you're working for Konstantin or anyone else, I will kill you. Slowly. Maximus may be willing to see potential in you, but I've seen too many people betray him over the centuries. I won't let it happen again."

"He saved my life once," he continued, "two centuries ago, when I was a fledgling abandoned by my maker, half-feral from hunger. He gave me purpose when I had nothing. I won't let anyone destroy what he's built, and I won't let anyone hurt him."

There's weight in his words, personal history that explains the fierce protectiveness.

"Understood," I say.

He turns back to the monitors. "The vampires who attacked last night weren't random thugs. They were trained. Professional. And they knew exactly where to hit, the donor coordination offices. That suggests someone gave them intelligence about our layout."

"An inside leak?"

"Possibly. Or extensive surveillance." He pulls up different footage showing the perimeter of the compound. "We sweep for bugs weekly, check for magical scrying, and monitor all communications. But Konstantin has resources. If he wanted to map this place, he could."

I study the attack footage. The way the vampires moved in coordinated pairs. The precision of their breach point. The fact that they targeted records specifically.

"They weren't trying to destroy the network," I say slowly. "They were trying to steal information about it."

"Correct. If Konstantin can identify our donors, he can compromise them. Turn them, threaten them, or simply kill them. Cut off our supply without direct confrontation."

"So what do we do?"

"We accelerate the security upgrade Maximus has been planning. Biometric locks on all sensitive areas. Additional cameras. More security personnel." He looks at me directly. "And we figure out who leaked our layout. Because someone did."

A chill runs down my spine. "You think there's a traitor in the compound."

"I think it's the most logical explanation. And until we identify them, no one is above suspicion." He pauses meaningfully. "Including you."

Before I can respond, an alarm sounds, different from last night's breach alert. This one is lower, more urgent.

Marcellus is on his feet immediately, checking monitors. "Perimeter sensors. Something triggered the north wall detection."

"Another attack?"

"No. The sensors are designed to detect magical signatures.

Someone is trying to scry the compound." He's already moving toward the door. "Stay here. Watch the monitors. If anything changes, alert me immediately."

He's gone before I can argue.

I sink into the chair he vacated and study the monitors. Dozens of camera angles showing empty corridors, secure rooms, and the grounds outside. Everything looks normal.

But normal is deceptive. Twenty-four hours ago, I was dying in an alley. Now I'm in the inner circle of a vampire lord's operation, surrounded by people who half-believe I might be working for the enemy, learning that the clean blood keeping me alive comes from a system built on moral compromises I'm not sure I can accept.

Marcellus thinks there's a traitor in the compound. Elena lost her brother to the chaos Maximus is trying to prevent. And I'm sitting here with access to everything, trusted by someone who shouldn't trust me yet.

I don't know if I made the right choice in accepting Maximus's offer.

But I'm here now. And the only way forward is through.

I watch the monitors and wait for whatever comes next.

CHAPTER
SIX

The scrying attempt lasted twelve minutes before our wards disrupted it.

I stand in the north section of the compound, studying the area where the intrusion occurred. I can't sense magic the way a witch can, but six hundred years of existence teaches you to recognize the aftermath. The way shadows sit wrong in the corner. The faint smell of something burnt and metallic that lingers after a spell.

"Can you trace it?" Marcellus asks from behind me.

"Not without a witch of our own. But it has to be Konstantin's people." I turn away from the wall. "He has three in his employ that I know of, each specializing in different forms of magic. This one seems more like Adrienne's style. Mapping our layout, testing our defenses."

"You're certain?"

"Who else would be scrying our compound the same week they sent a physical assault team?" I shake my head. "He's preparing for something larger. The attack is to test our response time, now magical reconnaissance. He's being thorough."

"Which means we have time."

"Or it means he's already confident enough in his intelligence that he's moving to the final planning stages." I start walking back toward the main building. "Either way, we need to accelerate our preparations."

Marcellus falls into step beside me. "About the girl..."

"Her name is Celeste."

"About *Celeste*," he corrects, his tone suggesting he's humoring me. "I don't trust her."

"You've made that abundantly clear."

"And yet you've given her access to everything. Training, donor coordination, security protocols. In less than 48 hours, she's learned more about our operation than vampires who've worked for us for years."

"She's intelligent. She learns quickly. That's an asset, not a liability."

We enter through the east wing entrance, and I immediately check the security panel. All systems are functioning normally. No breaches, no anomalies.

"She could be feeding information to Konstantin," Marcellus says quietly. "The timing of the attacks..."

"I've considered that." I have. Extensively. The logical part of my mind that's kept me alive for six centuries has analyzed every possibility. "But her reaction during the attack was genuine. You can't fake combat instincts like that. She fought to protect this compound, not sabotage it."

"Unless that's what she wants you to think."

I stop walking and turn to face him. "What do you want me to do, Marcellus? Throw her out based on suspicion? Kill her to eliminate a potential threat? Or do you want me to do what I've done for six hundred years, observe, analyze, and act when I have actual evidence?"

He's quiet for a moment. "I want you to be careful. You're... different with her."

"Different how?"

"You smile when she insults you. You spend extra time training her personally instead of delegating to me. You watch her when you think no one's looking." His expression is concerned rather than accusatory. "In two centuries, I've never seen you care about anyone. Now suddenly you're invested in a fledgling you barely know."

"I'm not invested. I'm utilizing a useful resource."

"You're lying to yourself."

The words hit harder than they should. Because he's right. I am lying to myself.

I've spent the last two days trying to rationalize my interest in Celeste. Telling myself it's strategic. That she's useful. That her skills make her valuable to my operation.

But the truth is simpler and more dangerous: I'm fascinated by her.

The way she moves. The way she thinks. The defiance that should irritate me but instead makes me want to push her further, see how far that spirit extends. The way she looked at me in that alley, not with fear or worship, but with the kind of honest assessment you'd give an equal.

No one has looked at me like an equal in centuries.

"I'll be careful," I tell Marcellus. It's the best I can offer.

He doesn't look convinced, but he nods. "The prisoners from last night's attack are secured in the detention wing. Ready for interrogation when you are."

"Good. I'll handle that personally."

Marcellus leaves to continue his security sweep, and I make my way to my study. It's nearly 3 a.m., that dead zone between night activity and dawn when the compound is quietest.

I begin to review intelligence reports. Planning countermeasures against Konstantin. Analyzing the scrying attempt for additional information.

Konstantin's activities over the last month show a pattern. Increased recruitment. More vampires entering Atlanta from other territories. Shipments of weapons, both conventional and those designed specifically for vampire combat. He's building toward something.

The question is whether he's building an army to take my territory by force, or if he's planning something more subtle.

My phone buzzes. Elena, texting from the donor coordination office:

ELENA

Need to discuss Michael's condition. Not improving.

Michael. The vampire who went feral last night. Celeste helped subdue him. I'd seen her on the security feed. She moved with instincts that saved lives.

I head to the medical wing where Michael is being held in one of the reinforced containment rooms. Elena is there with Dr. Dalton, the human physician I keep on staff for specialized medical needs.

"Show me," I say.

Through the observation window, I can see Michael strapped to a medical bed. The black veins have spread across his entire body now, pulsing with contamination. His eyes are open but unfocused, and he's making sounds, not words, just animalistic noises.

"The sedation is barely keeping him under," Dr. Dalton

explains. "His system is fighting the treatment. The contamination has progressed too far."

"How long does he have?"

"Hours. Maybe a day. After that, even if we keep him sedated, his body will start shutting down. He'll either die or go fully feral the moment we reduce the medication."

I've seen this too many times. Watched vampires deteriorate from contaminated blood, tried every treatment I could research or fund. The success rate is less than ten percent, and even that requires catching the contamination early, like I did with Celeste.

"Keep trying," I say. "If there's any chance..."

"There isn't," Dr. Dalton says gently. "I'm sorry. The kindest thing now would be to let him go peacefully."

Kindness. What a strange concept to apply to ending someone's existence.

But he's right. Michael is suffering. Keeping him alive in this state is cruelty, not mercy.

"I'll do it myself," I say. "Tomorrow night, after we rise. Make him as comfortable as possible until then."

After they leave, I stand at the observation window alone, watching Michael's labored breathing.

This is what Konstantin wants. He wants the blood supply so contaminated that vampires either die or go feral. Wants chaos. Wants the careful system I've built to collapse so he can seize control in the aftermath.

I won't let that happen.

I spend the next two hours in the detention wing, interrogating the prisoners from last night's attack. They're well-trained; Konstantin chose them carefully. But everyone breaks eventually with the right pressure.

By the time I'm done, I have confirmation: Konstantin is planning a major assault within the next two weeks. The attack last night was reconnaissance. He wanted to see our response time, our tactics, our numbers.

And he wanted to know if the rumors about Celeste were true.

Apparently, word has already spread through Atlanta's vampire community that I brought someone into my sanctuary. That I'm training a fledgling personally. That I've added her to my inner circle with unusual speed.

Konstantin thinks she's either a weakness he can exploit or an asset I'm grooming for succession. Either way, he sees her as significant.

Which means she's in danger.

The thought bothers me more than it should.

I return to my study as dawn approaches. The windows are already sealed with blackout systems, but I can feel the sun rising. That instinctive pull toward dormancy that comes with sunrise.

I should rest. But instead, I pull up the security feed.

Celeste is in her room now, sitting on the bed, staring at nothing. She looks exhausted but not defeated. Just... still. Sitting with unusual quietness, staring at nothing.

Something about her posture suggests she's wrestling with something. Weighing decisions. But I can't know what.

I should look away. Close the feed. Let her have privacy in whatever she's processing.

But dawn is approaching, and she's still awake. Still sitting there. A fledgling of her age should be feeling the pull toward dormancy by now.

I find myself leaving my study and walking through the compound toward her room.

I knock softly on her door. "It's Maximus."

A pause. Then: "Come in."

She's still dressed in training clothes, sitting cross-legged on the bed. Her eyes meet mine, questioning.

"You should rest," I say. "Dawn is coming."

"So should you."

I step into the room, leaving the door open, maintaining propriety even as I violate my own rules about keeping distance.

"The donor system," she says after a moment. "Some parts of it bother me."

"Which parts?"

"The 'voluntary-conditional' donors. It feels like coercion."

"It is coercion. But it's controlled coercion with compensation and protection. Before I built this network, those same people would have been drained by random vampires and discarded. At least this way they're alive and benefiting."

"That's what Elena said."

"Elena understands because she lost someone to the old way. The chaos. The random violence." I move to the window, even though I can't see through the blackout curtains. "I'm not asking you to approve of every aspect of what I've built. But I am asking you to understand why it exists."

"To prevent chaos."

"Yes, to prevent chaos," I confirm. "Because chaos serves Konstantin. Order serves survival."

She's quiet for a long moment, staring at nothing. "My mother died of an overdose five years ago," she says quietly. "Fentanyl, though she thought it was something else. Bought pills off someone she trusted. She was dead before the ambulance arrived."

I'm very still. "I'm sorry."

"It's why the contamination crisis matters to me. People trusting the wrong source, thinking they're safe, and dying because of it. Vampires drinking contaminated blood aren't that different from humans taking tainted drugs. Same desperation. Same bad luck." She looks at me directly. "That's why I can accept the moral compromises in your donor system. Because the alternative, random feeding, contaminated blood, vampires going feral, that's the chaos that killed my mother. Just in a different form."

I understand then why she didn't just agree to help; she's invested in preventing this kind of death. It's personal for her in ways I didn't realize.

She's quiet for another moment. "Michael is going to die, isn't he?"

So she understands the severity of what she saw.

"Yes. Tonight. The contamination is too advanced."

"How many others are in the containment wing?"

"Four. In various stages of deterioration. We're trying to save them, but..." I turn back to face her. "This is why the network matters. Why protecting the clean blood supply is worth the moral compromises. Because the alternative is watching people like Michael lose themselves to poisoned blood."

"I understand." And I can see she does. Doesn't mean she's comfortable with it, but she understands.

"You fought well tonight," I say, changing subjects. "You're adapting faster than most vampires do in their first year."

"I had good training before I was turned. Just translating it to vampire abilities."

"It's more than that. You have instincts that can't be taught. Situational awareness. The ability to assess threats and respond appropriately." I pause. "You're wasted as just muscle. I meant what I said about grooming you for the inner circle."

"Marcellus doesn't trust me."

"Marcellus doesn't trust anyone. It's why he's so good at his job."

She almost smiles at that. "Fair enough."

Dawn is pulling at me now, that biological imperative that's impossible to ignore. I need to rest before the day bleeds my strength.

"Get some sleep," I tell her. "Tomorrow night, I want to test your tactical thinking. See how you handle strategic problems, not just physical ones."

"What kind of problems?"

"The kind that are waiting for me the moment I wake at sunset." I move toward the door. "Welcome to the inner circle, Celeste. It's not glamorous. It's not easy. But it matters."

"Maximus."

I pause in the doorway.

"Thank you. For saving me. For trusting me enough to show me all of this."

I should deflect. Should maintain my cold facade. Should remind her that this is transactional.

Instead, I tell her the truth: "You're welcome."

I leave before I can say anything else that compromises the walls I've spent centuries building.

In my private quarters, I lie down as dawn fully breaks. The pull toward dormancy is overwhelming now. But even as I feel consciousness slipping away, my last thought is of her.

Of the way she looked at me just now, with gratitude, yes, but also with that same direct assessment that first intrigued me. Seeing me. Really seeing me.

Not the powerful gatekeeper. Just... Maximus.

A man who's been alone for so long he'd forgotten what it felt like to be seen.

Dangerous, I think, as sleep claims me. This is so dangerous.

But I can't seem to make myself care.

CHAPTER
SEVEN

I wake to complete darkness and the disorienting feeling of not knowing what time it is without looking at a clock.

The blackout curtains in my room are so effective that no light penetrates.

I reach for it on the nightstand. 7:43 p.m.

Just after sunset. My body knew somehow, pulled me out of that death-like sleep right as the sun dropped below the horizon. Vampire biology is doing its thing.

I shower and dress quickly, unsure what tonight will bring. Maximus said he wanted to test my tactical thinking.

Knowing him, it's probably something that will make me question every assumption I have.

I find him in his study, surrounded by maps and documents spread across a massive desk. He's changed into more casual clothes than his usual formal wear, dark jeans, and a Henley that makes him look less like a Renaissance painting and more like an actual person.

"You're punctual," he says without looking up.

"You didn't give me a specific time."

"No, but most fledglings would sleep until 9 or 10 p.m. You woke with the sunset."

"So did you."

"I've been doing this for six centuries. You've been doing it for eight months." He finally looks up, studying me. "Your body is adapting faster than it should. Interesting."

I'm not sure if that's a compliment or just an observation.

He gestures to the maps. "Come here. Tell me what you see."

I move around the desk to stand beside him. The maps show Atlanta and the surrounding areas, marked with different colored pushpins and notations in his precise handwriting.

Red pins cluster in certain areas. Blue pins are more spread out. Green pins form a perimeter around specific neighborhoods.

"Are the red pins vampire territories?" I ask.

"Close. Red pins are locations where contaminated blood sources have been identified. Blue pins are our verified clean donor locations. Green pins are neutral zones, areas where neither I nor Konstantin have established control."

I study the pattern more carefully. The red pins are concentrated in areas I recognize, downtown, certain suburbs, and college neighborhoods.

"The contamination is worse in areas with younger populations," I say slowly. "College students. Young professionals. People more likely to be taking pharmaceuticals or using recreational drugs."

"Correct. Which is why our donor base skews older and more rural. But that creates its own problems."

He pulls up a spreadsheet on a tablet. "We currently serve thirty vampires, including my inner circle. Each vampire needs to feed approximately twice a week. That's sixty feedings weekly, or about 240 per month. Each donor can safely provide blood once every two weeks. "So we need a minimum of one hundred twenty donors just to maintain current operations."

"And you have exactly that?"

"We aim for more when possible. Buffer for emergencies, donor turnover, and geographic distribution. Right now we're running tight. Some vampires can't travel to central locations easily, so we need donors spread across territories." He pulls up another map. "This is where it gets complicated."

This map shows territories marked with names. Konstantin's territory covers a significant portion of the city, east and south. Maximus's territory is northwest and central. There are smaller territories marked with other names I don't recognize.

"Several vampire lords control territories across Atlanta," Maximus explains. "Konstantin and I are the strongest, but we're not the only players. Dmitri, Vivienne, Chen, Okonkwo, and Santos all have their own domains, their own agendas. And there are smaller territories held by minor lords who've allied with one of us or maintain careful neutrality."

"And Konstantin wants your territory."

"He wants the entire city. But he's strategic enough to know a direct assault on my territory would be costly. So instead, he's trying to undermine the blood network. Force vampires who depend on me to either turn to him or starve."

I study the maps, the data, the careful notations. "You're playing a long game."

"The only game worth playing. Quick victories fade. Sustainable systems endure." He looks at me directly. "Which brings me to today's test. I need you to solve a problem."

He clears the desk and pulls up a new map, this one showing a neighborhood I don't recognize.

"Three weeks ago, five vampires in this area started showing signs of contamination. All of them had been feeding from our network, from donors we'd vetted as clean. This shouldn't be possible."

"Someone compromised the donors."

"That's the obvious answer. But when we investigated, the donors checked out. Clean blood, no new medications, no drug use. And yet five vampires got sick."

He hands me a file folder. "This contains everything we know about those five vampires, the donors they were assigned to, and the timeline of contamination. I want you to figure out what happened."

I take the folder and move to the couch, spreading out the documents. Maximus returns to his work, leaving me to puzzle through the information.

The five vampires are all relatively young for vampires, between fifty and one hundred years old. All of them fed from the same rotation of donors over the three-week period. The donors' medical records show nothing unusual.

But something catches my attention. One donor, a man named Jack Mercer, appears in all five vampires' feeding schedules. Not unusual by itself, but the timing is specific. All five vampires fed from blood bags sourced from Mercer's last donation. Same batch. Same contamination.

"Jack Mercer," I say. "He's the common factor."

"We investigated him thoroughly. He's clean."

Something clicks. "What does Mercer do for work?"

"He's a mechanic. Works at an auto shop in Decatur."

"Mechanics are exposed to chemicals constantly. Brake fluid, coolants, solvents, degreasers. Most of it absorbs through the skin over time." I look up at Maximus. "Mercer wasn't taking anything. He was absorbing it at work. My sister dated a mechanic who got hospitalized from chemical exposure. The doctors said the toxins built up in his bloodstream through his skin. Those automotive fluids are dangerous in ways people don't expect."

Maximus is very still. Then he pulls up Mercer's work schedule and cross-references it with the donation dates.

"He worked a double shift the day before his donation," he says slowly. "Overtime repairing a fleet of cars with coolant leaks. Sixteen hours of direct chemical exposure."

"There's your contamination source."

He stares at the data for a long moment. "We've been screening for pharmaceuticals and recreational drugs. Not industrial chemicals."

"You couldn't have known."

"I should have." He sounds genuinely frustrated, the first time I've heard real emotion in his voice that isn't carefully controlled. "Six hundred years and I missed something this obvious."

He looks at me, and something in his expression shifts. "Twenty minutes. You solved in twenty minutes what my people have been investigating for three weeks."

"I had fresh eyes. And personal experience that happened to be relevant."

"Nevertheless." He sets down the tablet and gives me his full attention. "This is why I brought you into the inner circle. You see things differently. Make connections others miss."

The praise feels genuine, which somehow makes it more uncomfortable than if he'd been condescending.

"What happens to Mercer?" I ask.

"We'll rotate him out of donor duty. Pay him severance. He did nothing wrong, but we can't risk further contamination." Maximus stands. "Come with me. I want to show you something."

I follow him through the compound to a wing I haven't explored yet. He unlocks a door with biometric scanning, fingerprint, and retinal scan, and leads me into what looks like a war room.

The space is dominated by a large table with a three-dimensional model of Atlanta built on it. Buildings, streets, and territories are all marked with the same color coding from the maps. But this is interactive; he touches a building, and information displays on nearby screens.

"This is how I manage the network," he says. "Real-time tracking of donors, vampires, feeding schedules, threat assessments. Everything integrated."

I walk around the table, studying the model. It's impressive, the kind of system that requires serious resources and technical expertise.

"How many people know about this room?" I ask.

"Three. Me, Marcellus, and now you."

That stops me. "Why are you showing me this?"

"Because if something happens to me, someone needs to be able to maintain the network." He touches a section of the model, and several buildings light up red. "These are Konstantin's known assets. We monitor them constantly."

"You're preparing for succession."

"I'm preparing for contingencies. I've survived six centuries by planning for every possibility."

He's not wrong, but something about this feels significant. Like he's investing in me in a way that goes beyond just utilizing a useful resource.

Before I can process that, an alarm sounds, different from the attack warnings.

Maximus's expression hardens. "The containment wing."

We move fast, vampire speed, carrying us through corridors to the medical wing. Marcellus is already there, along with Dr. Dalton and two security vampires.

Through the observation window, I can see Michael thrashing against his restraints with inhuman strength. The sedation has failed. He's fully conscious and fully feral.

"How long?" Maximus asks Dr. Dalton.

"Sedation stopped working about ten minutes ago. We tried increasing the dosage, but his system is rejecting it."

Michael's eyes are completely black now, no trace of consciousness remaining. Just hunger and rage.

"Keep him contained," Maximus orders. "Prepare to move him to the execution chamber in five minutes. Full restraints."

"He's suffering," I say quietly.

Maximus looks at me, his expression unreadable. "Yes."

He dismisses everyone except Marcellus and me. The three of us stand at the observation window, watching Michael destroy himself in increments.

"This is what Konstantin wants," Maximus says. "What happens when the blood supply fails completely. Vampires reverting to base instincts. Becoming the monsters humans fear."

"Can't you help him?" I ask, even though I know the answer.

"There's only one way to help him now." Maximus's voice is flat, emotionless. But I see his hand clench slightly at his side. "Marcellus, prepare the chamber."

Marcellus nods and leaves. Maximus continues watching Michael for another moment, then turns to me.

"You don't have to watch this."

"Yes, I do."

He studies my face. "Why?"

"Because this is what I'm fighting to prevent. I need to see what happens when we fail."

Something flickers in his expression, approval, maybe, or just acknowledgment.

"Then come."

He leads me to an adjacent chamber, a smaller room with reinforced walls and a drain in the center of the floor. The purpose is obvious and grim.

Marcellus returns with a long silver blade. "Ready."

Maximus takes the blade and turns to me. "Silver stops our healing. A clean strike to the heart, and it's over instantly. No suffering."

"You've done this before."

"More times than I care to count."

Michael is brought in, restrained by three security vampires and heavy chains. Even with their combined strength, they struggle to control him. He's snarling, thrashing, eyes completely black. There's nothing human left in them. No recognition. No fear. Just rage and hunger.

"Michael Torres," Maximus says formally. "You've served this network with honor for twenty-three years. You deserved better than this end. You will be remembered."

It's a ritual. A way of giving meaning to something senseless.

Maximus moves with precise efficiency. The blade slides between Michael's ribs, finding his heart with practiced accuracy. Michael gasps once, then goes still.

It's over in seconds.

The security vampires carry the body away for whatever disposal method Maximus has established. Marcellus takes the blade and cleans it without comment. And Maximus stands very still, staring at the space where Michael died.

"Go rest," he tells me without looking over. "That's enough for tonight."

But I don't leave. Instead, I ask the question that's been building since I got here: "How many have you killed this way?"

"Thirty-seven. Over the last five years." He finally looks at me.

"The blood crisis is accelerating. It used to be one or two vampires per year. Now it's averaging almost one per month."

"And Konstantin is making it worse."

"Deliberately. The more chaos, the more desperate vampires become. Desperate vampires make poor decisions. Poor decisions create opportunities he can exploit."

"So what do we do?"

"We fight. We protect the network. We find ways to reduce contamination." His voice is tired in a way I haven't heard before. "And we do what needs doing, even when it costs us."

I understand then what Elena meant. Why she believes in what Maximus is building. Because he's not just hoarding power, he's trying to create order in a system that's collapsing. Trying to prevent more deaths like Michael's.

It doesn't make everything okay. Doesn't erase the moral complications. But it makes me understand why people follow him.

"I'm sorry," I say. "For Michael. For having to do that."

"Don't be sorry for me. Be sorry for every vampire who's suffering because our food supply is poisoned. And then help me fix it."

"How?"

"By being what you are. Sharp. Tactical. Unafraid to see things clearly." He meets my eyes. "You solved the Mercer problem in twenty minutes. That kind of thinking is what we need."

"I got lucky."

"You were prepared when luck came." He moves toward the door, then pauses. "Get some rest, Celeste. Tomorrow night, you attend your first inner circle strategy meeting. I want you to see how we actually make decisions."

After he leaves, I stand in the chamber alone for a long moment. The drain in the floor has already been cleaned; there is no evidence of what happened here except the lingering smell of death.

This is my life now. Not just fighting and feeding, but being part of a system that tries to prevent horrors while sometimes perpetuating smaller ones. Not good or evil, just survival with whatever honor can be salvaged.

I think about Michael. About the Mercer problem. About Maximus standing very still while he killed someone he'd known for twenty-three years.

And I think about the fact that Konstantin is out there right now, planning his next move. Building toward something that will force more vampires into Michael's situation.

I'm not naive enough to think I can stop it all. But maybe I can help reduce the body count.

Maybe that's enough.

CHAPTER
EIGHT

I stand at the window of my study, staring out at the grounds. Michael died less than an hour ago. The execution chamber is already cleaned. No blood. No evidence. Just an empty room that will be used again, inevitably, because the contamination crisis isn't slowing down.

Thirty-seven vampires.

That's how many I've killed this way over the last five years. Not in battle. Not in self-defense. Mercy killings, each one a failure of the system I've built to protect our kind.

Michael Torres was the thirty-seventh.

I should feel something. Guilt, perhaps. Regret. But six hundred years has taught me that sentiment is a luxury I can't afford. Michael was suffering. I ended his suffering. That's all there is to it.

Except it's *not* all there is to it, and I know that.

The compound is quiet now, that deep silence that comes in the hours before dawn when most vampires have already gone dormant, and the humans are finishing their shifts.

85

Celeste is still awake. I can feel her presence in the building like a weight I'm constantly aware of. She's in her room, probably processing what she witnessed tonight. The execution. The casual brutality of ending a life to prevent worse suffering.

I wonder if she'll still look at me the same way tomorrow night.

I wonder why I care.

My study is exactly as I left it, desk organized with military precision, reports stacked in order of priority, maps spread across the secondary table. Everything controlled. Everything in its place.

I pour myself a drink. The whiskey burns going down, a sensation I can appreciate even if it doesn't affect me the way it once did. Another memory of being human, back when alcohol could dull the edges of reality.

My phone buzzes. A message from Lord Ashworth, one of the minor vampire lords who controls territory in Dunwoody.

LORD ASHWORTH

Blood crisis affecting my people. Losing donors to contamination faster than I can replace them. We need to coordinate.

I read it twice, analyzing the subtext. Ashworth has managed to stay neutral in the conflict between Konstantin and me for years. The fact that he's reaching out now means he's genuinely desperate.

Ashworth's message is the third I've received this week from smaller lords. They've maintained their independence by staying out of the power struggles between the major players, but the contamination crisis doesn't respect neutrality. Their donors are getting sick just like everyone else's.

Which means the careful balance of power in Atlanta is shifting.

Konstantin knows this. He's counting on it.

I pull up the intelligence reports Marcellus compiled earlier tonight. The pattern is unmistakable. Konstantin's recruitment has jumped forty percent over the last month, mostly young vampires, the kind who are easily swayed by promises of power and belonging. We've intercepted three weapons shipments in the last two weeks alone: silver ammunition, specialized blades designed for vampire combat. He's established four safe houses in what used to be neutral territory, expanding his reach block by block. And the communications are even more concerning. Ethan runs my intelligence network, and his sources have picked up increased contact between Konstantin and vampire lords in neighboring cities.

He's not just planning an assault on my compound. He's building a coalition. Positioning himself as the solution to the crisis, while painting me as the problem, the gatekeeper who hoards resources while others suffer.

It's a smart strategy. I'd do the same in his position.

My phone buzzes again. This time, it's a message from an unknown number, but I recognize Konstantin's style immediately:

UNKNOWN

Heard you had some excitement tonight. Lost a contaminated vampire, gained a fledgling with interesting connections. Tell me, old friend, is she worth what you're about to lose?

I stare at the message for a long moment.

"Old friend." He uses that phrase deliberately, knowing it will irritate me. We were never friends. Allies, perhaps, centuries ago, when we had common enemies. But Konstantin's ambition has always exceeded his patience, and our alliance fractured the moment I refused to support his vision of vampire supremacy.

The fact that he mentions Celeste is troubling. Word has spread faster than I anticipated. Her presence here, her rapid elevation to the inner circle, it's already being analyzed, weaponized, turned into a potential vulnerability.

Konstantin sees her as either a weakness he can exploit or a threat he needs to eliminate.

Both assessments put her in danger.

I don't reply to his message. Engaging would only encourage him. Instead, I forward it to Marcellus with a note:

> Timeline accelerating. Increase security protocols. Begin preparations for siege conditions.

A reply comes within seconds:

MARCELLUS

> Already in progress. Security teams briefed. Perimeter sensors enhanced. Safe room stocked for eight weeks. Do you want Celeste moved to secure quarters?

I start to type "yes," then stop.

Locking her away would keep her safe, but it would also prove Konstantin right, that she's a weakness I'm trying to protect.

I delete the message and type instead:

> No. But assign her a combat partner for all field missions. And accelerate her training schedule. She needs to be ready.

The response is immediate:

MARCELLUS

> Understood. I'll handle it.

I set the phone down and move to the windows. The blackout curtains are already drawn, but I can feel dawn approaching.

I should rest. Tomorrow night will be full of meetings, strategy sessions, and preparations. But my mind won't settle.

Thirty-seven vampires.

The number sits heavy in my chest. Each one a name I knew. Michael Torres had been part of my network for twenty-three years. Before that, he'd been a teacher. High school history. He used to joke that teaching teenagers prepared him for the discipline required of vampire life.

Now he's ash in an urn, waiting to be scattered according to his wishes.

The others come back to me in fragments. Jessica, contaminated six months ago. A former nurse who'd understood the medical risks intellectually but couldn't overcome her addiction to a human boyfriend who used opioids.

They blur together after a while. The contaminated. The feral. The ones I couldn't save.

I used to keep detailed records of each execution. Names, dates, causes of contamination, final words if they were lucid enough to speak. I told myself it was important to document everything, to learn from each failure, to improve the screening process.

But really, I was trying to convince myself that killing them mattered. That ending their suffering was noble rather than practical. That I was still capable of caring about individual lives instead of just managing a population.

I stopped keeping records two years ago when I realized I was lying to myself.

Now I just count.

Thirty-seven.

My phone buzzes a third time. Another message from Konstantin:

UNKNOWN

Two weeks, Maximus. That's how long you have before everything you've built comes crashing down. Choose wisely, join me, or watch your precious network burn.

There it is. The provocation I've been waiting for. He's forcing my hand, trying to make me react emotionally instead of strategically.

The old Maximus, the one who was human, who led soldiers and protected his men with loyalty that bordered on suicidal, would have responded with immediate violence. Would have gathered his forces and struck first, consequences be damned.

The Maximus who was enslaved by Luciano for 150 years learned to wait. To plan. To control every variable before making a move.

But this Maximus, the one who's been alone for 300 years since he killed the woman he loved, keeps getting distracted by variables that shouldn't matter as much as they do.

Like whether she'll look at me differently after tonight.

I pull up the security feed from her room before I can stop myself.

She's still awake, sitting cross-legged on the bed with a notebook I don't remember giving her. Writing something. Her dark hair falls forward, partially obscuring her face. She's changed out of her training clothes into something more comfortable, soft pants and a t-shirt that make her look younger, more vulnerable than the fighter I've been training.

As I watch, she stops writing and stares at nothing. Her expression is troubled. Thinking about Michael's execution, probably. About what she witnessed. About what it means to be part of a system that sometimes requires killing the people it's meant to save.

She's been a vampire for eight months. Still processing the moral complexities of immortality. Still adjusting to a world where right and wrong aren't always clear.

I should turn off the feed. Give her privacy. But I keep watching, fascinated by the small details. The way she absently tucks her hair behind her ear. The way her shoulders tense when she's thinking hard about something. The way she finally closes the notebook and sets it aside with a sigh.

"You're obsessing."

I don't turn around. Marcellus moves silently, but I felt him enter my study. He has a key.

"I'm strategizing," I say.

"You're watching her sleep."

"She's not sleeping. She's writing."

"That's somehow less concerning?" Marcellus moves to stand beside me. He glances at the screen, then back at me. "You need to rest. Dawn's coming."

"Soon."

He's quiet for a moment. Then: "Konstantin's message. You think he'll actually attack in two weeks?"

"No." I finally look away from the feed, meeting Marcellus's eyes. "I think he'll attack sooner. He wants me off-balance, reactive. The two-week timeline is bait. He'll strike within the week, probably in the next few days."

"Which means we need to accelerate everything."

"Yes." I pull up a tactical map on my tablet, showing the compound and surrounding territory. "Double the perimeter guards. I want eyes on every approach. Implement the rotation schedule we discussed; no one works more than four-hour shifts. Tired guards make mistakes."

Marcellus nods, making notes on his own device. "What about

the donors? If he's planning something big, he might target them directly."

"Move the high-value donors to the safe house in Decatur. The rest can shelter here if needed; we have space in the residential wing." I mark several locations on the map. "And I want Celeste trained on defensive positions. She needs to know where to fall back if we're breached."

"You really think she'll fall back?" Marcellus raises an eyebrow. "She's a fighter. She'll go toward the threat, not away from it."

He's right, and I know it. The thought makes my chest tight.

"Then make sure she knows how to survive going toward the threat," I say. "I want you taking lead on her combat training. More time with you, less with me."

Marcellus raises an eyebrow. "We've been training her together. Why the change?"

"She needs to adapt to fighting without me. You have a different style, more aggressive, less controlled. If I'm engaged elsewhere during an attack, she needs to be able to work with you seamlessly."

"That's a tactical reason." His tone suggests he doesn't believe it's the only reason.

He's right. The truth is, I can't watch her fight anymore without cataloging every vulnerability, every opening an opponent could exploit, every way she could get hurt. It's compromising my ability to train her effectively.

Marcellus studies me for a long moment. "You care about her."

"She's a valuable asset."

"You're lying to yourself again."

I turn to face him fully. "And what would you have me say?" The words come out sharper than I intend. "That I've been watching her? That I can't stop cataloging every vulnerability, every way she could get hurt? That I've spent six hundred years building walls and she's dismantling them without even trying?"

Marcellus is quiet. Then: "I'd have you say you're in trouble."

"I know." I close the security feed. "I know."

The words hang in the air between us. Heavy. True.

I've spent six hundred years building walls. Keeping everyone at a distance. Telling myself that attachment is weakness, that caring leads to pain, that love is a luxury I can't afford.

Three hundred years ago, I loved someone. Turned her to save her life. Watched her go feral. Killed her myself when she attacked innocent humans.

I swore I'd never put myself through that again.

And now here I am, watching a woman I barely know write in a notebook at 4 a.m., and I can't look away.

"Get some rest," Marcellus says quietly. "Tomorrow's going to be difficult."

He's right. Then there's Celeste's training, the interrogation of the remaining prisoners from the attack, security preparations, contingency planning...

The list is endless. It always is.

But as Marcellus leaves, I know that's not what's actually keeping me awake.

It's not the strategic concerns. Not the tactical planning. Not even Konstantin's threats.

I tell myself it's because she's new. Untested. A potential vulnerability I need to monitor closely.

The fact that I don't believe my own rationalization should concern me more than it does.

Tomorrow night, I'll accelerate Celeste's training. Have Marcellus push her harder. Prepare her for what's coming. Make sure she's ready to survive what Konstantin is planning.

It's purely tactical. Konstantin has already identified her as significant. That makes her a target whether I want her to be or not.

The fact that I'm more concerned about her survival than any other member of my inner circle is simply because she's the least experienced. The newest variable. The one most likely to make a fatal mistake.

That's all it is.

It has to be.

I lie down as dawn breaks, that familiar pull toward dormancy finally overwhelming. But my last thought before sleep claims me is of her face when she looked at me tonight after Michael's execution.

Not with horror or disgust or fear.

With understanding.

Like she saw exactly who I am. Violent, carrying six centuries of blood on my hands, and chose to see me anyway.

But she didn't see everything.

There are things I haven't shown anyone. Not Marcellus. Not anyone in three hundred years. The darkness Seraphina wove into my blood as a gift I never asked for. What it can do when I let it off the leash. What it costs every time I use it.

Someday she might see that too. I don't know what terrifies me more—that she'll run, or that she won't.

CHAPTER
NINE

CELESTE

I wake with the memory of Michael's death still fresh in my mind.

The blackout curtains keep the room in complete darkness, but my internal clock tells me it's just after sunset. Night five since Maximus found me in that alley. The days blur together when you sleep through them and only exist in darkness.

I sit up slowly, testing my body. The bruises from training with Maximus and Marcellus are gone, healed while I slept. Vampire recovery is still startling sometimes. I could get used to never having lingering injuries, even if I can't get used to everything else.

My phone shows several messages. One from Elena asking if I'm okay after "last night." She must mean the execution.

Another from an unknown number that I assume is Marcellus:

UNKNOWN

Strategy meeting 9 PM. Conference room. Don't be late.

I shower quickly and dress in dark jeans and a fitted black

shirt, professional but practical. I'm not sure what the dress code is for inner circle strategy meetings, but I figure I can't go wrong looking like I'm ready to either negotiate or fight.

When I check my reflection, I barely recognize myself. Five nights ago I was dying. Now I'm preparing for a leadership meeting in a vampire lord's compound, having watched a man be executed and somehow made peace with the moral complexity of it.

My old life feels like it belonged to someone else.

The compound is more active tonight. I can hear voices from other parts of the building, footsteps, the hum of activity that suggests everyone is preparing for something. The atmosphere feels different from previous nights, tighter, more urgent.

I make my way to the conference room, arriving ten minutes early. The door is partially open, and I can hear voices inside.

"...can't sustain these losses. Three more donors contaminated this week alone." A male voice I don't recognize.

"Which is exactly why we need to consolidate resources." That's Marcellus. "Maximus has a proposal..."

"Maximus always has a proposal." A woman's voice, sharp and skeptical. "Usually ones that benefit him more than the rest of us."

I hesitate in the hallway. Should I wait? Announce myself? The message said 9 p.m., and it's only 8:50.

"You can come in, Celeste." Maximus's voice carries through the door. Of course, he knew I was there. "You're part of this meeting."

I push the door open fully and step inside.

The conference room is large and professional, a long table surrounded by chairs, screens mounted on the walls displaying maps and data. Around the table sit six vampires I haven't met before, plus Maximus and Marcellus. Elena is here too, the only human, standing near a display screen with what looks like donor statistics.

All eyes turn to me as I enter.

"This is Celeste Moreau," Maximus says, his tone formal. "She's joined the inner circle. Some of you may have heard about the attack four nights ago. She helped defend the compound and proved herself in combat."

The vampires study me with varying degrees of interest and suspicion. I recognize the type; they're evaluating me, trying to determine if I'm a threat, an asset, or irrelevant.

I've been evaluated before. In the ring, before every fight. This isn't that different.

"The fighter," one of them says. A woman, tall and elegant with pale skin and silver hair pulled back in a severe bun. She looks like she could be anywhere from forty to four hundred. "I heard Konstantin's people didn't make it past you."

"I held my ground against three of them," I say. "But only because Maximus and Marcellus were handling the others. We worked as a team."

Something approving flickers in her expression. "Honesty. Refreshing." She extends a hand. "Nadia. I manage operations in the eastern territories."

I shake her hand, noting her grip is firm but not crushing. Testing me, maybe, but not trying to dominate.

The others introduce themselves as I move around the table.

Julian is stocky and muscular, with a Scottish accent that makes even formal introductions sound warm. Scars visible on his hands and neck suggest he saw combat in his human life. "Security coordination," he says simply. "Multiple sites."

Isabelle looks barely twenty, petite and French, but she moves with the confidence of someone much older. "I handle the finances. Everything from donor payments to equipment procurement." Her accent is subtle, refined.

A thin man with light brown hair and restless energy shakes my hand while somehow still typing on his tablet, a feat of multitasking that seems habitual rather than rude. "Ethan. Intelligence." He says it quickly, eyes flicking between me and his screen. "I run networks throughout Atlanta's supernatural community. Information brokers, bar contacts, a few people inside Konstantin's territory." He's younger than the others, I realize. Not in vampire years, maybe, but in presence. His fingers never stop moving on the tablet, but his eyes are sharp, cataloging details about me even as he works.

Caleb is quiet, watchful, with dark eyes that seem to catalog everything about me in seconds. "I manage the containment facilities. Off-site location." His voice is soft but carries weight.

The last man is older, distinguished, with silver hair and the bearing of someone used to authority. "Dr. Elias Sullivan," he says. "I maintain a cover identity in the human medical community. Blood banks, medical suppliers, and hospital contacts. They think I'm a private physician with wealthy clients who require discretion."

"Now that introductions are complete," Maximus says, moving to the head of the table, "we have significant developments to discuss."

He pulls up a map of Atlanta on one of the wall screens. Several areas are highlighted in red.

"Konstantin has accelerated his timeline. Intelligence suggests he's preparing a major assault within two weeks, possibly sooner. We need to be ready."

"How reliable is this intelligence?" Nadia asks.

"Very. We interrogated the attackers from three nights ago." Maximus brings up additional data. "They were reconnaissance.

Konstantin wanted to test our response time, our defensive capabilities, and to verify rumors about personnel changes. He also sent a message demanding I hand over control of the blood network. An ultimatum I refused."

"Personnel changes? Meaning her," Julian says, nodding toward me. Not hostile, just stating fact.

"According to the prisoners we interrogated," Maximus continues, "word spread quickly through Atlanta's vampire community that I brought someone into the sanctuary. Konstantin sees Celeste as either a weakness he can exploit or a threat he needs to eliminate."

"Which is it?" Isabelle asks, watching me carefully.

I hold her gaze. "I'm here to help defend this network. Whether Konstantin sees that as a threat or tries to use me as leverage, that's his problem to solve, not mine."

Julian grunts approvingly. "Direct. I like that."

"Beyond the immediate threat," Maximus continues, "we have a larger problem. The contamination crisis is worsening. Yesterday we identified and resolved a new contamination source, industrial chemicals absorbed through skin contact. One of our donors works as a mechanic and was unknowingly contaminating his blood with chemicals from car fluids."

Dr. Sullivan nods grimly. "I've expanded our screening protocols to include industrial exposure, but there are hundreds of potential contaminants we weren't testing for. The crisis is evolving faster than our safeguards."

"Which plays into Konstantin's hands," Julian observes. "Desperate vampires make poor decisions."

"Do we know how he's maintaining his supply?" Nadia asks. "His network should be experiencing the same contamination issues we are."

"We don't know," Ethan admits, and frustration cracks through his rapid-fire energy. "Our intelligence on his operations has significant gaps. I've cultivated sources for years, run pattern analysis on his movements." His fingers tap against the tablet, restless. "Nothing. Konstantin's been building this for decades. He's patient in ways that make him hard to track. And he's got magical countermeasures on everything. Scrying attempts, surveillance, even basic reconnaissance gets blocked." He shakes his head. "I've never seen anyone this careful. It's like trying to map a building with no windows."

"Which is why we need a different approach," Maximus says. He looks at me. "Celeste, you fought in underground rings for three years. What do you know about the operations? The venues, the management?"

Everyone's attention shifts to me. I wasn't expecting to contribute this early in the meeting.

"I know the scene pretty well," I say, organizing my thoughts. "Or at least, I knew it as a human. But looking back now, things make more sense." I pause, thinking through the memories with new context. "About two years ago, there was a shift. New management took over several major venues. The operations became more professional, better organized, better funded, bigger payouts. They started recruiting fighters aggressively."

"What kind of recruiting?" Julian asks.

"Offering contracts. Training facilities. It was more organized than the usual underground scene. A lot of fighters moved to those venues." I lean forward. "I stayed independent because something felt off. Too much money, too professional. The people running it moved wrong, looked at fighters wrong. I thought they were connected to organized crime or something."

"You didn't know they were vampires," Maximus says. Not a question.

"I had no idea vampires existed until Valentina turned me. But now? Thinking back on how those managers moved, how they acted at night, never during day events..." I shake my head. "It was vampire-run. I just didn't realize it at the time."

"Konstantin," Marcellus says. "Has to be."

"He's been using the fighting rings for recruitment," Maximus agrees. "Young vampires looking for purpose, humans who are already comfortable with violence. It's strategic."

"How many venues shifted to this new management?" Nadia asks me.

I think back. "At least five that I knew of in Atlanta itself, maybe more in the suburbs. Each one running fights twice a week minimum. They were pulling in the best fighters, the ones with records like mine."

Ethan is typing on his tablet. "If they're recruiting even conservatively from those venues over two years..."

"That's a substantial force," Isabelle finishes. "And we had no intelligence on this."

"Because you weren't looking in the underground fighting world," I say. "Those venues don't advertise to the general public. They're word-of-mouth, cash-only, locations change constantly. You need to be part of that world to even know where the fights are."

"This is valuable intelligence," Maximus says, his eyes on me. "Ethan, I want you to prioritize finding these venues. Map them, identify patterns, see if we can determine where Konstantin's training facilities are located."

"On it," Ethan says, already making notes.

"Impressive." Julian leans back in his chair, studying me with new interest. "Three years in that world and you kept your head down, stayed independent, trusted your instincts when something felt wrong. That's not just survival. That's intelligence."

"Thank you." I'm not sure how to take the compliment. In the ring, praise usually preceded a request for something.

"Most humans wouldn't have noticed anything off about vampire-run operations." He stands and moves around the table toward me, casual, unhurried. "You've got good instincts. We could use more of that around here."

He stops beside my chair, closer than strictly necessary for conversation. His hand lands on my shoulder. Friendly. Familiar. Like we've known each other longer than twenty minutes.

"If you need help getting oriented, learning the city from our perspective, I'd be happy to show you around." His Scottish accent makes the offer sound warm. "I know all the territories. Could be useful for someone new to the operation."

I open my mouth to respond.

A sound cuts through the room. Low. Barely audible.

A growl.

It's coming from the head of the table.

Every conversation stops. Ethan's fingers freeze above his tablet. Nadia goes very still. Julian's hand lifts from my shoulder like he's touched something hot.

I turn to look at Maximus.

He hasn't moved. Still seated, still composed, hands still folded in front of him. But his eyes are fixed on Julian with an intensity that makes something primal in me want to bare my throat in submission. His jaw is tight, a muscle ticking beneath the skin. And that sound, that low, rumbling warning, is still vibrating in his chest. So quiet, I might have imagined it if the entire room wasn't frozen.

What the hell?

Julian takes a full step back from my chair. "Just an offer," he says, and his voice has lost all its warmth. Careful now. Cautious. "Standing invitation. For operational purposes."

Maximus doesn't respond. Doesn't blink. The growl recedes, but the tension doesn't.

The silence stretches. One second. Two. Three.

I don't understand what's happening. Julian was being friendly. Aggressively friendly, maybe, but nothing that warranted... whatever this is. I've seen Maximus face down attackers, execute a man, interrogate prisoners. I've never seen him look at someone like he's considering how many pieces to leave behind.

Over what? A hand on my shoulder?

Finally, Maximus looks away. Back to the maps on the screen, as if nothing happened. "Ethan. The surveillance gaps."

His voice is perfectly controlled. Like the last thirty seconds didn't exist.

Ethan clears his throat twice before he can speak. "Right. Yes. The, um, the eastern quadrant has the most exposure..."

The meeting resumes, but something has fundamentally shifted. I can feel eyes on me now. Quick glances. Reassessments. People putting pieces together that I don't have access to. Nadia catches my gaze across the table. One perfect eyebrow arches. The corner of her mouth twitches.

She looks like she's trying very hard not to smile.

Julian returns to his seat on the opposite side of the table. He doesn't look at me again. Doesn't look at Maximus either. Just stares at his tablet like it contains the secrets of the universe.

I sit very still, something fluttering in my chest, trying to process what just happened.

Maximus growled at someone for touching me.

I sneak a glance at him. He's listening to Ethan's report, face neutral, completely focused on strategy. Like nothing happened. Like he didn't just make a sound that belongs in a nature documentary about apex predators defending their territory.

But his hand, resting on the table, is clenched into a fist.

And when his eyes flick to mine for just a second, there's something in them that makes my breath catch.

Then he looks away, and I'm left with my body humming and absolutely no idea what any of it means.

The meeting continues for another hour, covering defensive preparations, donor security protocols, supply chain redundancies. I listen more than I speak, learning how decisions are made, who defers to whom, where the power dynamics actually lie.

Maximus is clearly in charge, but he lets others contribute. Nadia and Julian seem to have the most influence, their opinions carry weight. Isabelle handles all the financial decisions. Ethan provides intelligence but doesn't weigh in on strategy. Caleb rarely speaks, but when he does, people listen.

And Marcellus, he's the one who challenges Maximus most directly. Tests ideas, pokes holes in plans. It's not disrespect; it's how they work together. Maximus seems to value the pushback.

As the meeting winds down, Maximus assigns tasks. Julian is to coordinate with security teams on defensive positions. Nadia will reach out to her contacts in the eastern territories, gauge sentiment. Isabelle will secure additional resources for extended siege conditions. Ethan will focus on mapping Konstantin's fighting ring operations.

"Celeste," Maximus says, and I straighten slightly. "Tomorrow night, I want you to do a field assessment. There's a potential new donor in Decatur, restaurant worker, night shift, already aware of the supernatural community through a friend. Elena has done the preliminary vetting, but I need someone to meet them in person, verify their story, and assess whether they're viable for the network."

My first real assignment. Not training, not shadowing someone else, actual operational work.

"You'll go alone," Marcellus adds, his tone making it clear this is non-negotiable. "Consider it a test of your ability to operate independently in the field."

Alone. First solo mission. Either they trust me, or they're testing whether I'll run.

Probably both.

"I understand," I say. "What's the threat assessment for the location?"

"Neutral territory," Maximus answers. "No known Konstantin presence. Low risk, but stay alert. Things can change quickly."

"I'll brief you on the full details tomorrow evening," Marcellus says. "Meet me in my office at 8 p.m. You leave at 9."

I nod, trying to project confidence I don't entirely feel. This is what I wanted, a chance to prove myself beyond just training and fighting. But now that it's happening, the reality of operating alone in a city full of hostile vampires feels heavier.

The meeting breaks up, people filing out in small groups, still discussing defensive preparations and contingencies. I stand and move toward the door, but Marcellus catches my eye.

"A moment," he says.

I wait while the others leave, until it's just me, Marcellus, and Maximus in the conference room.

"Tomorrow night's assignment is straightforward," Marcellus says, his tone businesslike. "But don't underestimate it. Vetting potential donors requires judgment, reading people, identifying deception, assessing risk. You'll need to determine if this person is genuinely interested in joining our network or if they're a plant."

"What if they're a plant?" I ask.

"Then you walk away and report back. You don't engage, you don't confront, you don't try to be a hero." His eyes are hard. "Your job is assessment and intelligence gathering. Nothing more."

"Understood."

"The donor's name is Clara Ellis. She's twenty-six, works night shift at a diner in Decatur, has a friend who's a donor in our network. That friend vouched for her, said Clara was asking questions, seemed interested."

"That could be genuine or suspicious," I observe.

"Exactly. Which is why you need to meet her and make a judgment call." Marcellus pulls out his phone and sends me something. "I just sent you her file. Study it tonight. Know her background, her story, what to look for."

My phone buzzes. I glance at it, a detailed file on Clara Ellis. Work history, residence, known associates. They've already done significant background work.

"Questions?" Maximus asks. It's the first time he's spoken since giving me the assignment.

"How much autonomy do I have in making the assessment?" I ask. "If I think she's genuine, do I make the offer on the spot, or do I report back first?"

"Report back first," Maximus says. "You're not authorized to bring anyone into the network yet. Your job tomorrow is purely assessment."

That makes sense. They're testing my judgment, not giving me recruiting authority.

"Anything else?" Marcellus asks.

"No. I'll study the file tonight and meet you at 8 p.m. tomorrow."

Marcellus nods and leaves, his footsteps echoing down the corridor.

I turn to follow, but Maximus's voice stops me.

"Celeste."

I turn back. He's still standing by the conference table, his expression unreadable.

"You contributed well tonight," he says. "The intelligence about the fighting rings, that's exactly the kind of insight we need. Different perspective, different knowledge base."

"Thank you."

"Tomorrow night's assignment may seem simple, but it matters. Donor vetting is critical to maintaining the network's integrity. One bad actor can compromise everything."

"I understand."

He holds my gaze for a moment longer, like he's weighing whether to say something else. Then he just nods. "Get some rest. Study the file. Be ready."

"I will be."

I leave the conference room and make my way back to my quarters, my mind already spinning through what I learned tonight.

The inner circle is larger than I realized, seven core members plus Maximus and Marcellus, with Elena managing the human side of operations. Everyone has their role, their specialty. And they work together with the kind of efficiency that comes from years, maybe centuries, of practice.

Marcellus is still suspicious of me. That was clear in how he phrased the assignment, the warnings about not trying to be a hero. He's testing me, watching for any sign I might be compromised.

But the others seemed more accepting. Nadia acknowledged my honesty. Julian approved of my directness. And Maximus...

I push that thought away. He's my employer. My leader. The ancient vampire who saved my life and is now testing whether I'm worth the investment.

Nothing more complicated than that.

I reach my room and pull up the file Marcellus sent. Clara Ellis's information fills the screen: photos, employment records, and background check results. I settle onto the bed and start read-ing, committing details to memory.

Tomorrow night, I will prove I can handle solo operations.

Tomorrow night, I will show them I'm more than just a fighter who got lucky.

Tomorrow night, I will take the first real step toward earning my place in this world.

I study until dawn pulls me toward dormancy, Clara Ellis's face and story burned into my memory.

Time to show them what I can do.

MAXIMUS

I am not watching the security feed.

I am reviewing tactical reports at my desk, as I do every night. The fact that one of the monitors happens to display a tracker moving through East Atlanta is coincidental. Routine. The kind of standard oversight any commander would maintain for a solo operative in neutral territory.

The lie tastes bitter even in my own mind.

Celeste left the compound at precisely 9 p.m. Dark jeans, leather jacket, hair pulled back in a way that exposes the line of her neck. I watched her cross the grounds from this very window, her stride confident, her shoulders squared against whatever the night might bring.

She looked like a warrior going to war. She looked like she belonged here.

She looked like something I have no right to want.

I force my attention back to the supply reports. Donor reten-
tion rates. Blood quality metrics. The endless administrative

machinery that keeps my network running. Numbers and logistics and problems I know how to solve.

Not like the problem currently moving through the Decatur streets, her tracker blinking steadily on my screen, a rhythm I'd memorized without meaning to.

My phone buzzes. I reach for it too quickly, and the eagerness of the motion irritates me.

CELESTE

On site. No issues.

Her words are professional. Efficient. Exactly what I'd expect from any operative reporting in. There's no reason for my shoulders to loosen at the sight of them, no reason for the knot in my chest to ease.

I type back:

Understood. Report any concerns immediately.

Three dots appear. Disappear. Appear again.

CELESTE

Will do.

I set the phone down and stare at it like it might offer more. Like she might send another message just because. Like I'm a lovesick fool instead of a six-hundred-year-old vampire who has survived wars and betrayals and centuries of solitude.

This is beneath me.

I stand abruptly and move to the window, putting distance between myself and the screen. The grounds are quiet, security patrols moving in their established patterns, everything functioning exactly as it should. I built this. Every safeguard, every protocol, every layer of protection. An empire of control that has kept my people alive for decades.

And none of it matters if she doesn't come back.

The thought surfaces before I can stop it, and I let out a breath that's closer to a growl than I'd like to admit.

When did this happen? When did a fledgling vampire with eight months of experience and a talent for insulting me become the axis around which my thoughts revolve?

I know the answer. I just don't want to examine it.

It was the alley. The first moment I saw her, dying and defiant, while she mustered the strength to call me a CEO vampire. To say I didn't look scary. Something cracked open in my chest that night. Something I'd kept sealed for three hundred years.

I thought I could contain it. Train her, use her skills, maintain appropriate distance. I am excellent at distance. I have made distance into an art form, a fortress, a way of life.

But she keeps slipping through the walls.

The way she challenged me in the training room, refusing to back down even when I pushed too hard. The way she fought beside me during the attack, moving like she'd been born for battle. The way she sees through every mask I wear and doesn't flinch at what's underneath.

I press my palm flat against the cold glass of the window and watch the fog of my unnecessary breath cloud the surface.

Catherine, I think, and the name is a wound that never fully healed.

Three hundred years ago, I loved a woman. Turned her to save her life. Watched her go feral from contaminated blood. Killed her with my own hands when she attacked innocent humans.

I swore I would never feel that way again. Never let anyone close enough to hurt me, or to be hurt because of me. The walls I built after Catherine were meant to be permanent. Unbreachable.

Celeste breached them without even trying.

My phone buzzes again, and I'm across the room before the second vibration ends.

CELESTE

Complication. Guy at the counter watching us. Too interested. Might be nothing.

My entire body goes rigid. I can feel my fangs pressing against my gums, an instinctive response to perceived threat. To someone watching her.

Describe him.

The seconds between my message and her response stretch into small eternities.

CELESTE

White male, early 30s, hasn't touched his coffee in 15 minutes. Keeps glancing over.

Can you get a photo without being obvious?

The image arrives moments later. Casual angle, her phone positioned like she's just scrolling, but the man at the counter is clearly visible in frame.

I pull up the file on Clara's referral. David Preston, the donor who vouched for her. The photo matches.

The relief that floods through me is disproportionate. Absurd. He's not a threat. Just an overprotective friend who should have notified Elena but didn't. A minor breach of protocol, nothing more.

My hands are shaking.

I stare at them, these hands that have killed hundreds, that have held power over life and death for six centuries. Shaking. Because for thirty seconds, I thought someone might be watching her with hostile intent.

David Preston. The referring donor. He's in our network. Not a threat, but find out why he's there.

I set the phone down and grip the edge of my desk hard enough that the wood creaks in protest.

This is a problem.

Not her. She's not the problem. She's capable, intelligent, learning faster than anyone I've trained in decades. She held her own against attackers her first week here. She provides tactical insights that my inner circle, with their centuries of experience, had missed entirely.

The problem is me.

The problem is that I can't think clearly when she's involved. Can't calculate risks objectively. Can't maintain the cold detachment that has kept me alive and kept my people safe for longer than most vampires have existed.

I've sent operatives on dangerous missions hundreds of times. Watched them leave, knowing some might not return, and accepted that calculus as the cost of leadership. I've made hard choices, sacrificed pieces to protect the whole, and done what needed to be done without letting sentiment cloud my judgment.

But I can't do that with her. The very thought of her in danger makes something feral rise up in my chest, something that doesn't care about strategy or acceptable losses or the greater good. Something that would burn the entire city to ash if it meant keeping her safe.

That terrifies me more than Konstantin ever could.

My phone buzzes.

CELESTE

Confirmed. Clara was nervous about meeting alone, asked him to come. He should have notified Elena but didn't think of it. Not a setup, he actually verified her story from his end.

I exhale slowly. Read the message twice. Let the professional tone of her report anchor me back to something like rationality.

She's fine. She handled the complication perfectly. Identified the anomaly, reported it properly, waited for intelligence before acting. Good instincts. Sound judgment.

She doesn't need me hovering over her like a protective shadow.

But I want to be there anyway.

Another message arrives.

CELESTE

Clara checks out. Genuine interest, understands the terms, has reasonable motivation (needs money for nursing school). David confirmed his original referral. No red flags. Recommend bringing her into vetting pipeline.

Professional. Concise. Solid assessment.

I should feel satisfaction. Pride, even. I'm training her well, and she's exceeding expectations. This is exactly what I wanted when I brought her into the inner circle.

Except it's not what I wanted at all. What I wanted was to keep her close. What I wanted was an excuse to spend hours in the training room with her, correcting her stance, my hands on her body under the guise of instruction. What I wanted was to watch her grow stronger and know that I was part of it.

What I want is her.

The admission settles into my bones like poison, or perhaps like medicine. I've been denying it for days, constructing elaborate justifications for my behavior, telling myself that my interest is strategic, protective, professionally appropriate.

It's none of those things.

I want her in ways I haven't wanted anyone in three centuries. I want to know what sounds she makes when she comes undone. I want to trace every scar on her body and learn the story behind each one. I want to wake beside her at sunset and see her face before I see anything else.

I want to tell her about the weight I've carried alone for six hundred years. I want her to know me. The real me, not the vampire lord or the gatekeeper or the mask I wear to survive.

And that wanting is exactly why I should stay away from her.

I've already shown her too much. The way I watched her fight. The way I growled at Julian for touching her. The cracks in my control that everyone in that room saw, even if she didn't understand what they meant.

That makes her dangerous. Not to my network or my position or my strategic interests.

To me.

CELESTE

ETA 30 minutes. Going for a walk. Need to clear my head.

She needs to clear her head. After a successful mission, after proving herself capable and competent, she needs time to decompress. To process. To exist as something other than an operative completing an objective.

I understand that need. I've felt it myself, though I stopped indulging it centuries ago.

Be careful.

CELESTE

Always am.

Always am. Like safety is a habit she's cultivated. Like danger is something she navigates daily without thinking about it.

She does. She has been. For eight months, alone, surviving a world that wanted to kill her long before I found her dying in that alley.

She doesn't need my protection. She's been protecting herself just fine.

But I want to protect her anyway. Want to stand between her and every threat, want to bare my fangs at anyone who looks at her wrong, want to wrap her in the safety of my power and never let anything touch her.

The intensity of the wanting should alarm me.

Instead, it just feels inevitable. Like something I've been walking toward my entire existence without knowing it. Every battle, every loss, every century of isolation. All of it leading to a woman with dark eyes and a sharp tongue who looks at me like I'm worth seeing.

I close the security feed before I can talk myself out of it.

If I'm going to understand what's happening to me, what she's doing to me, I can't do it from behind a screen. Can't analyze this from a safe distance like it's a tactical problem to be solved.

I need to face her. Talk to her. See if whatever I'm feeling survives actual proximity or if it dissolves into nothing when confronted with reality.

I leave my study and head toward the compound entrance.

The night air is cold against my skin as I step outside. I don't feel temperature the way humans do, but I register it, file it away as sensory data. The chill of autumn settling into winter. The smell of fallen leaves and distant rain.

The tracker on my phone shows her approaching the gate. Seven minutes out. Six.

I should go back inside. Wait for her report through proper channels. Maintain the professional distance that a commander should maintain with an operative.

I don't move.

Five minutes. Four.

I stand in the shadows near the main entrance, hands clasped behind my back, and wait for her like a man awaiting judgment. Like a condemned prisoner who walked willingly to the gallows.

Whatever this is, whatever is building between us, I need to understand it before I act on it. Need to know if it's real or just the desperate reaching of a man who's been alone too long.

But standing here in the dark, counting down the minutes until she appears, I'm starting to suspect that understanding won't matter.

ELEVEN

CELESTE

I'm halfway across the grounds when I see him.

Maximus stands near the main entrance, hands clasped behind his back, watching me approach. The security lights cast sharp shadows across his features, highlighting the angles of his face, the stillness of his posture. He looks like a statue someone carved from marble and moonlight.

I slow my pace without meaning to. Something about seeing him here, waiting, makes my chest tighten in a way I don't want to examine.

"You didn't have to meet me," I say when I'm close enough to speak without raising my voice. "I was going to report in."

"I know." He falls into step beside me as I continue toward the entrance. "How do you feel?"

The question catches me off guard. Not "how did it go" or "what did you learn" but how do I feel.

"Fine. Good, actually." I glance at him, trying to read his expression in the dim light. "The mission was straightforward.

Clara Ellis checks out, the complication was minor. I can give you the full debrief."

"Tomorrow is soon enough for the official report." He holds the door open for me, a gesture so old-fashioned it almost makes me smile. "I meant how do you feel about operating alone. First solo mission. That's significant."

We step into the entrance hall together, and I'm suddenly aware of how close he is. The way his presence seems to fill the space around him. I catch a hint of something, not cologne, exactly, but something distinctly him. Old paper and sandalwood and something darker underneath.

"I felt..." I search for the right word. "Capable. Like I knew what I was doing, even when the situation shifted."

"Good. That confidence will serve you well."

We're walking through the compound now, and I realize I don't know where we're going. My room is in the opposite direction. But Maximus moves with purpose, and I find myself following without question.

"Where are we headed?"

"My study. I thought a drink might be in order. First solo mission completed successfully."

The invitation surprises me more than it should. Maximus doesn't strike me as someone who celebrates anything, let alone with drinks in his private study. But I don't question it. The silence between us isn't uncomfortable, it's weighted, expectant. Like the air before a storm.

I watch him from the corner of my eye as we walk. The way he moves is economical, precise, every step deliberate. Centuries of existence have stripped away any wasted motion. He's wearing the same dark clothes he always wears, but tonight his collar is slightly loosened, his sleeves pushed up to reveal forearms that are lean and corded with muscle.

I look away, irritated at myself for noticing.

His study is warm when we enter, a fire crackling in the hearth despite the fact that vampires don't need heat. Old habits, maybe. Or perhaps he just likes the ambiance. The flames cast dancing shadows across the walls, across the leather furniture, across...

A leather portfolio lies open on his desk. Through plastic archival sleeves, I can see yellowed documents, handwriting faded but still legible. Something old.

Maximus stops when he sees it, and I watch his posture change. A slight tension in his shoulders. Like he'd forgotten he left it out.

"What is that?" I ask before I can stop myself.

He moves to the desk, and for a moment I think he's going to close the portfolio, hide whatever I've glimpsed. Instead, he stands there looking down at it, his back to me.

"Letters," he says finally. " From my human life. My mother. Men I served with. A few others."

The words land strangely. His human life. Before he was turned. I remember the rumors I heard when I was searching for him, five hundred years, six hundred, maybe older. A world so different from this one that it might as well be another planet.

"How long have you had these?" I ask.

"Since I was human." He turns to face me, and I see something in his expression I've never seen before. Vulnerability. Rawness. Like a wound that never quite healed. "Over six centuries now."

Six centuries. The number is almost impossible to comprehend.

"And they've survived all that time?"

"I buried them before my life changed. Hid them where no one would find them." Something dark passes across his face. "When I was finally able to go back for them, a very long time later, they were damaged but intact. I had them properly preserved about a hundred years ago, when conservation techniques improved."

I move closer, drawn by curiosity. "Who were they from?"

For a long moment, I think he won't answer. Then he turns to a page near the front of the portfolio. Through the protective sleeve, I can see cramped handwriting on yellowed parchment.

"This one is from my mother. She wrote it the year before she died, before I was turned. Asking when I would come home. Whether I'd found a wife yet. Whether I was eating enough." A ghost of a smile crosses his face. "Mothers, apparently, are the same across centuries."

"What did you tell her?"

"That I would visit soon. That I was too busy for a wife. That I was eating plenty." He turns to another sleeve, not touching the document itself. "I never saw her again. I was turned three months later."

The grief in his voice is old but not gone. Buried, maybe, but still there underneath six centuries of control.

"I'm sorry," I say, because I don't know what else to say.

"It was a long time ago." He closes the portfolio gently and moves to the sidebar, pouring two glasses of whiskey. Offers one to me.

I take the glass, our fingers brushing briefly during the exchange. His skin is cool, smooth, and the contact sends a small shock through my system that I pretend not to notice.

"You're not what I expected," I say, taking a sip. The whiskey burns pleasantly, familiar despite my changed physiology. "When I first heard about you, the gatekeeper, the one who controls the blood supply, I imagined someone colder. More ruthless."

"I am cold. I am ruthless." He takes a drink from his own glass. "When necessary."

"But not always."

"No." His eyes meet mine, dark and unreadable in the firelight. "Not always."

I move to one of the leather chairs near the fire and sit, suddenly needing the distance. He remains standing, leaning against his desk, watching me with that intense focus that makes me feel like he's seeing more than I want to show.

"The letters," I say, gesturing toward the closed portfolio. "You said some were from men you served with. Your soldiers."

"Yes." He glances back at the leather case. "Fifty-three men under my command. We fought together for twelve years before Luciano took me."

"What were they like?"

The question seems to catch him off guard. He's quiet for a long moment, and I wonder if I've overstepped. But then he begins to speak, and his voice is different, softer, more distant, like he's reaching back through centuries to touch something long buried.

"They were young, mostly. Farmers' sons who'd never held a sword before I trained them. Merchants' sons looking for glory. A few younger sons of nobility with no inheritance, trying to make their own way." He takes another drink. "They were scared at first. Green. Didn't know how to hold a formation or read terrain or keep their heads when arrows started flying."

"But you taught them."

"I taught them. Drilled them until they could fight in their sleep. Learned their names, their families, their fears." His expression shifts, something painful flickering across it. "By the time we'd been together a few years, they weren't just soldiers. They were brothers. Family."

I think about my own found family, the fighters I trained with, the contacts I trusted, the world I built for myself in the underground circuit. All of it gone now. All of it unreachable.

"I understand that," I say quietly. "Finding family in unexpected places."

His eyes meet mine again, and something passes between us.

"You had that in the fighting world," he says. It's not a question.

"Yes. Not the same as what you're describing, but, yes. People who knew me, trusted me, had my back." I look down at my glass. "I can't contact any of them now. They think I'm dead or disappeared. And even if I could reach out, what would I say? 'Hey, remember me? I'm a vampire now. Want to grab coffee?'"

"The isolation is one of the hardest parts of this existence." He moves from the desk to the chair across from me, settling into it with the unconscious grace of someone who's had centuries to perfect every movement. "Humans age, die, move on. Vampires remain. The connections we form are either fleeting or complicated by power dynamics."

"Is that why you keep everyone at a distance?"

The question is more direct than I intended. I see him tense slightly, then force himself to relax.

"Partly." He swirls the whiskey in his glass, watching the firelight refract through the amber liquid. "I've learned that caring about people creates vulnerability. Weaknesses that can be exploited."

"You sound as if you've learned that the hard way."

"Yes." The word is clipped, hard. "Luciano. The vampire who turned me." He takes a drink. "Among other things he taught me."

I want to ask more, but I can feel the wall going up. So I offer something instead, a trade. Vulnerability for vulnerability.

"You know the facts about my mother," I say. "The overdose. When it happened. But you don't know..." I stop, surprised by the tightness in my throat. "You don't know what I've never told anyone."

He waits, not pushing, just... present.

"I was supposed to have dinner with her that night. She'd been asking for weeks. But I told her I had to work late, and I told myself I'd see her the following week." The words come out flat, controlled. "I didn't have to work. I just didn't want to go."

"You couldn't have known."

"That's what people say. What I tell myself." I look up at him, and something about the firelight, the whiskey, the late hour makes honesty easier. "But the truth is worse than just not knowing. The truth is I didn't even need an excuse. I just didn't want to see her."

His expression doesn't change, doesn't judge. Just listens.

"She'd been struggling for years. Relapses, broken promises, the constant waiting for a phone call telling me she was dead. I was exhausted by it. Exhausted by her." My voice drops. "She died alone. And the worst part is that underneath the guilt, there was relief. Relief that I didn't have to watch her destroy herself anymore."

The silence stretches between us. The fire crackles. Somewhere in the distance, I hear footsteps in the corridor, but they fade without stopping.

"When Luciano took me," Maximus says finally, "I was returning to camp alone. I could have sent a messenger. Should have. It was dangerous to travel without escort, and I knew it. But I was tired of the weight of fifty-three men depending on my every decision. I wanted an hour to myself. Just one hour without being responsible for everyone else's survival."

I look at him, surprised by the parallel.

"He found me on that road. Alone, vulnerable, exactly where I shouldn't have been. And because of that moment of selfishness, my men lost their commander." His jaw tightens. "I don't know what happened to them. Whether they died in the battles that followed, or survived, or...anything. I've spent six centuries not knowing, because knowing would make it real."

"You can't blame yourself for being taken."

"Can't I?" His eyes meet mine. "You blame yourself for your mother's death, and you couldn't have saved her. I blame myself for abandoning my men, and I couldn't have prevented being taken. The guilt doesn't respond to logic."

He's right. I know he's right. But knowing doesn't change the feeling.

"One of my soldiers wrote poetry," Maximus continues, his voice softer now. "Marco. Terrible poetry, objectively speaking. He wrote a poem for his wife and asked me to critique it before he sent it."

"What did you tell him?"

"That it was beautiful. That she would treasure it." The ghost of a smile crosses his face again. "It truly was awful. Rhymes that didn't quite work, metaphors that made no sense. But he was so proud of it, so hopeful that she would love it."

"Did she?"

"I don't know. I never saw him again to ask." The smile fades. "That's what I think about sometimes. Not the battles, not the glory, not even the men who died. I think about Marco's terrible poem, and whether his wife ever received it, and whether it made her smile."

Something shifts in my chest. A loosening, maybe. The realization that this powerful vampire carries the same kind of weight I do. The small losses. The unanswered questions. The guilt that doesn't respond to logic.

"I only contacted my sister once, and that was via text, since I was turned," I hear myself say. "To tell her that I took a job in Miami."

"Why?"

"Because she'll know." I stare into the fire, avoiding his eyes. "She'll hear something different in me, and she'll push, and I'll either have to lie or tell her that her sister is dead. That the person she's talking to is something else now."

"You're not something else. You're still you."

"Am I?" The question comes out sharper than I intended. "I drink blood to survive. I sleep through daylight. I can hear heartbeats from across a room and sometimes..." I stop, shaking my head.

"Sometimes what?"

"Sometimes they sound like food." The admission costs me something. "I hear humans talking, laughing, living their lives, and part of me is cataloging them. Which ones are healthy. Which ones smell clean. Which ones would be easy to take." I finally look at him. "That's not who I was. That's something else."

"That's the predator," Maximus says quietly. "It's part of you now, yes. But it doesn't have to define you. The fact that you're troubled by those thoughts means you're still Celeste. A true monster wouldn't question it."

"How do you know? Maybe I'm just a monster who hasn't accepted it yet."

"Because I've met true monsters." His voice is dark, heavy with memory. "Luciano was a true monster. He didn't question his nature; he reveled in it. Made art of cruelty. Enjoyed breaking people the way a child enjoys breaking toys." He leans forward slightly. "You are nothing like him."

The intensity in his voice makes me look away. It's too much, the firelight, the intimacy, the way he's looking at me like I matter.

"Luciano," I say, redirecting. "You said he turned you. But there's more, isn't there? The way you talk about him..."

He's quiet for a long moment. "He enslaved me for one hundred and fifty years."

The number hits me like a physical blow. "One hundred and fifty..."

"Years." He finishes his whiskey and sets the glass aside. "He turned me against my will and kept me as his... possession. Plaything. Weapon. Whatever he needed at any given moment."

I can't imagine it. Eight months of being a vampire alone has been hard enough. One hundred and fifty years of being controlled by someone who saw you as property...

"How did you survive that?"

"I buried the part of me that cared about survival. The part that hoped, that planned, that wanted things." His voice is matter-of-fact, like he's describing someone else. "I became exactly what he wanted me to be, until I wasn't anymore. Until I found a chance to escape and took it."

"And then what?"

"And then I spent a very long time being... not good." He stands, moving to the fire, his back to me. "I did things I'm not proud of. Became something I'm not proud of. It took centuries to build myself into someone I could tolerate being."

I watch the firelight play across his shoulders, the tension in his spine. The words come slowly, carefully, like they cost him something.

"The blood network," I say. "That's part of rebuilding yourself."

"Part of it." Something flickers across his face, there and gone. "Giving vampires access to clean blood, reducing the need for random attacks on humans, it's not absolution, but it's something. A way to create order instead of chaos." He turns to face me. "A way to protect people instead of destroying them."

"Like you wanted to protect your soldiers."

Something flickers across his face, surprise, maybe, at being understood. "Yes. Like that."

I stand without making a conscious decision to, drawn toward him like gravity. We're only a few feet apart now, close enough that I can see the reflection of the flames in his eyes.

"I don't know what I want to build," I admit. "I'm still just trying to survive. To figure out what I am, what I'm becoming. But I understand wanting to create something meaningful. To be more than just a predator."

"You already are more than that." His voice is lower now, rougher. "You've been a vampire for eight months, and you're fighting to hold onto your humanity. That's rare. Valuable."

"Or stupid."

"Perhaps both." He almost smiles. "They're not mutually exclusive."

We stand there in the firelight, not speaking. The silence is different now, charged, heavy with something I can't name. I'm aware of every inch of space between us. Aware of his stillness, his attention, the way his eyes haven't left my face.

"Why did you meet me at the gate?" I ask. "You didn't have to."

"No." He doesn't look away. "I didn't have to."

"Then why?"

The question hangs in the air. I watch him struggle with the answer, watch the careful control waver and resettle.

"Because I was..." He stops, starts again. "Because I wanted to see for myself that you were safe."

"The tracker told you I was safe."

"Yes. It did."

"But you needed to see me anyway."

He doesn't answer. Doesn't have to. The admission is there in his silence, in the way he's looking at me, in the tension radiating from his perfectly controlled posture.

He takes a step toward me. Just one, but it closes half the distance between us. I can feel the coolness of him now, the strange absence of heat that marks him as something other than human.

"I've spent centuries making sure I don't care about anyone," he says, his voice barely above a whisper. "It's safer. Simpler. Caring creates weakness, and weakness gets people killed."

"And me?" I ask. "Am I a weakness?"

His jaw tightens. "You're something worse."

"What?"

"A reason."

"Maybe..." I start, but I don't know how to finish after that statement that leaves my knees feeling weak. Maybe what? Maybe we're both broken in compatible ways? Maybe trauma recognizes trauma? Maybe this is just proximity and stress, and I'm reading something into nothing?

He reaches toward me. Slowly, like he's fighting himself with every inch. His fingers brush my jaw, feather-light, barely there.

A small gasp escapes me.

His hand hovers near my face, not quite touching, close enough that I can feel the ghost of contact. His eyes search mine, looking for something, permission, maybe. Or warning. Or both.

"I don't know what this is," he says quietly.

"Neither do I."

"That should concern me more than it does."

His thumb traces my cheekbone, still so light I might be imagining it. The touch sends electricity down my spine, pools heat in places I've been ignoring for eight months. I lean into his hand without meaning to, just slightly, just enough that my skin presses against his palm.

Something shifts in his expression. Wanting. Conflict. Fear.

Then he pulls back like he's been burned.

"You should rest." His voice is rough, strained, completely different from the controlled tones I'm used to. "Training tomorrow."

The whiplash leaves me dizzy. "Maximus..."

But he's already moving toward the door. Putting distance between us with every step.

"Good night, Celeste."

He leaves. Walks out of his own study, leaving me standing by the fire with my skin still tingling where he touched me.

I stare at the empty doorway, trying to process what just happened.

He touched me. Actually touched me, not the professional contact of training or the accidental brush of passing something between us. He reached for me deliberately, looked at me like I mattered, and then he ran away.

In his own house. From his own study.

I sink back into the chair, my legs suddenly unreliable. The fire crackles. The leather portfolio sits closed on his desk, secrets preserved behind plastic and leather. And I'm here alone, with the ghost of his touch on my skin and absolutely no idea what any of it means.

Does he want me? It felt like wanting. The way he looked at me, the way his voice changed, the way his hand trembled slightly when he touched my face.

But then why pull away? Why run?

Because he's scared, some part of me answers. Scared of wanting something. Scared of the vulnerability that comes with caring.

But that's just speculation. I don't actually know what he's thinking. I barely know him, five nights of training and strategy meetings, and moments like this one, weighted with things neither of us is saying.

I should go to my room. Should sleep. Should stop thinking about the way his fingers felt against my jaw.

Instead, I stay in his study, watching the fire burn down, trying to untangle the knot of confusion and want and uncertainty in my chest.

I told him things tonight I've never told anyone. About the fight, about my mother, about the relief mixed with the guilt. He told me things too, about his soldiers, about Marco's terrible poetry, about the century and a half he spent as someone's prisoner.

We traded vulnerabilities like secrets, and then he touched me, and then he ran.

What do I want from this?

The question surfaces unbidden, and I don't have an answer. I came here to survive.

I didn't come here to develop complicated feelings for a six-hundred-year-old vampire lord who looks at me like I'm simultaneously the answer to something and a problem he doesn't know how to solve.

But here I am anyway. Sitting in his study, surrounded by his things, thinking about his hands.

This is dangerous. I know it's dangerous. Getting emotionally entangled with someone this powerful, this complicated, this fundamentally broken, it's the kind of mistake that gets people hurt.

But knowing something is dangerous and being able to stop yourself from doing it are two very different things.

I finally stand, forcing myself to move. The fire has burned low, embers glowing orange in the grate. The portfolio on his desk draws my eye. I could open it, look through the protected pages, and learn more about who he was before everything went wrong.

I don't. Whatever's in those letters, he'll share them when he's ready. Or he won't. But that's his choice, not something I should take.

I leave his study, closing the door softly behind me, and make my way back to my room.

The compound is quiet at this hour. My footsteps echo in the empty corridors, a reminder of how alone I am here.

Except I'm not alone. Not really. There's Maximus, with his preserved letters and his careful walls. There's Marcellus, suspicious but teaching me anyway. There's Elena, human and warm and somehow surviving in this world of predators.

There's a place for me here, if I want it. A role. A purpose.

But is that all there is? Is that all I want?

I reach my room and close the door behind me, leaning against it for a moment. The darkness is complete, blackout curtains doing their job, but I can see perfectly. Another change. Another reminder.

I touch my jaw where his fingers rested. The skin feels exactly the same as it did before, cool, smooth. But something underneath has shifted. Some awareness I can't undo.

He wanted to keep touching me. I saw it in his eyes, felt it in the hesitation before he pulled away. He wanted more than that fleeting contact.

So did I.

The admission surprises me. I've been so focused on survival, on learning, on not dying, that I haven't let myself think about wanting. But there it is, undeniable. I wanted him to keep touching me. Wanted to know what would happen if neither of us pulled away.

And I have no idea what to do with that.

I change for bed and lie down in the darkness, staring at nothing.

Tomorrow there will be training. Strategy meetings. The

endless work of preparing for Konstantin's attack. I'll see Maximus, and we'll both pretend tonight didn't happen, because that's what people do when they're too scared to acknowledge what's building between them.

But tonight, in the dark, I let myself feel it.

The confusion. The wanting. The terrifying possibility that this might be real.

Whatever this is.

CHAPTER
TWELVE

I've been avoiding her.

Not obviously, I'm too disciplined for that. I still attend training sessions, still review intelligence reports with the inner circle, still move through my compound with the same controlled efficiency I've maintained for centuries. But I've arranged my schedule so our paths cross only when others are present. Only when there's structure. Safety in numbers.

Because three nights ago, I touched her face and nearly lost myself entirely.

The memory surfaces unbidden as I stand in the training room, watching Marcellus run Celeste through defensive formations. She moves well, better than she did a week ago. Her vampire instincts are finally integrating with her fighter's training, creating something fluid and dangerous.

She blocks a strike, counters, almost lands a hit on Marcellus before he redirects her momentum.

"Better," he says grudgingly. "Again."

I should leave. I have reports to review, messages to answer, a network to maintain. Instead, I watch her reset her stance, watch the focus settle into her expression, watch the way her body coils before she moves.

She glances toward me. Just a flicker, barely a second. But I see something in that look, awareness, uncertainty, a question she's not asking.

I look away first.

"Your footwork is still telegraphing," I say, my voice carefully neutral. "You shift your weight before you commit. Against an experienced opponent, that's a death sentence."

"Then show me."

The challenge in her voice makes something tighten in my chest. Three nights ago, that same voice told me about her mother, about guilt, about the relief she's never admitted to anyone else.

"Marcellus can demonstrate," I say. "I have matters to attend to."

I leave before she can respond. Before I can see whatever crosses her face.

Coward, some part of me whispers. *Over six hundred years old, and you're running from a woman you've known for a week.*

But that's precisely the problem. A week. And already she's slipped past defenses I spent centuries building. I've survived wars, betrayals, a hundred and fifty years of enslavement. I've outlived everyone I ever loved and learned to want nothing, need no one.

Now I find myself listening for her footsteps in the corridor. Catching her scent in rooms she left hours ago. Remembering the exact pressure of her cheek against my palm.

This is how empires fall. Not to armies, but to moments of weakness dressed as something softer.

In my study, I force myself to focus on the intelligence reports Ethan delivered this morning.

The news is not good.

Konstantin has accelerated his timeline. Three smaller blood operations in the southeastern territories have been hit in the past week, not destroyed, but disrupted. Donors frightened. Supply chains interrupted. The attacks are surgical, designed to create pressure without triggering full retaliation.

He's testing. Probing. Looking for weaknesses in the network.

And according to our sources, he's paying particular attention to reports about Celeste.

I set down the report and stare at the wall.

Word has spread faster than I anticipated. The vampire community thrives on gossip, and apparently the gatekeeper bringing an unknown fledgling into his sanctuary, training her personally, giving her access to the inner circle, is the most interesting thing to happen in Atlanta in decades.

THE DAYS BLUR TOGETHER. Training sessions. Strategy meetings. Intelligence briefings. I maintain my distance, and Celeste maintains hers, and the space between us fills with all the things we're not saying.

But distance doesn't stop me from noticing.

The way she laughs at something Elena says, her whole face transforming. The way she argues with Marcellus about technique, refusing to back down even when he's clearly right. The way she moves through my compound like she belongs here, like she's always been here, like the walls themselves have rearranged to accommodate her presence.

I catch myself smiling at one of her comments during a briefing, just a small observation about Konstantin's tactics, delivered with that dry wit I'm learning to anticipate. The smile is there before I can stop it.

I kill it immediately. But Nadia notices. I see her notice.

Nadia lingers at the door. "Be careful," she says quietly. "Not with Konstantin. With yourself."

She leaves before I can respond. Which is probably wise. I'm not sure what I would have said.

"You've been different."

Celeste's voice catches me off guard. We're alone in the training room, Marcellus stepped out to take a message, and I was too slow to invent an excuse to leave.

"Since the other night," she continues. "In your study."

"I've been busy. Konstantin's movements require attention."

"That's not why."

I meet her eyes, and for a moment, the careful distance I've maintained wavers. I see her as she was that night, firelight on her skin, vulnerability in her voice, leaning into my touch like it meant something.

It did mean something. That's the problem.

"You're avoiding being alone with me," she says.

"This isn't the time for..."

"When is?" She steps closer, and I have to force myself not to step back. "You touched me. You looked at me like..." She shakes her head. "And then you ran. Out of your own study. And now you're acting like it didn't happen."

"It shouldn't have happened."

The words land harder than I intended. I see them hit, see the flash of hurt she tries to hide.

"Fine," she says, her voice cooling. "Good to know where I stand."

She turns to leave, and the words escape before I can stop them.

"Shouldn't and didn't want to are very different things."

She stops. Turns back. The hurt in her expression shifts to something more complicated.

"Then which is it?"

Why does she have to be so direct? I should lie. Should maintain the distance. Should protect us both from whatever this is becoming.

Instead, I tell her the truth.

"I've spent three centuries making sure I don't want anything. It's safer that way. Wanting things means losing them, and I've lost enough for several lifetimes." I hold her gaze, letting her see more than I should. "And then you appeared in that alley, half-dead and insulting me, and I wanted something. For the first time in longer than I can remember. I wanted you to live. I wanted to know you. I wanted..."

I stop myself. Too much. Too honest.

"Wanted what?" she asks softly.

Wanted to touch you. Wanted to keep touching you. Wanted to know what would happen if I stopped running from this, I think.

"It doesn't matter," I say to her. "What I want isn't relevant. What matters is keeping you alive, keeping this network functioning, defeating Konstantin."

"So I'm just a tactical consideration."

"No." The word comes out rougher than I intended. "That's the problem. You're not. You should be. It would be simpler if you were. But you're not, and I don't know what to do with that."

She's quiet for a long moment. "Maybe you don't have to know. Maybe we just... figure it out as we go."

"I've had six hundred years of life. I don't 'figure it out as I go.'"

"Maybe that's the problem." She takes a step toward me, close enough that I can see the flecks of gold in her brown eyes. "Maybe six hundred years of planning for everything means you've forgotten how to just... let things happen."

"Letting things happen gets people killed."

"Controlling everything doesn't keep them alive. It just keeps them alone."

The words land somewhere deep, in a place I don't examine. Because she's not wrong. Six centuries of control, and what do I have? An empire of blood and logistics. A compound full of people who follow my orders. And an emptiness so profound I'd stopped noticing it until she arrived.

Marcellus returns before I can respond. The moment breaks. Celeste steps back, her expression closing off.

"Let's continue," Marcellus says, oblivious to what he interrupted. Or perhaps not oblivious at all.

I should stay. Should observe, assess, and critique her form.

Instead, I leave. And for the rest of the night, her words follow me.

Controlling everything doesn't keep them alive. It just keeps them alone.

THE INTELLIGENCE REPORTS pile up over the next two days. Each one is worse than the last.

Konstantin hits another operation in Decatur. Then one near the airport. His people are getting bolder, probing closer to our territory, and we're running out of ways to respond.

I spend hours in my study, staring at the map, looking for an advantage. We're outmanned. Konstantin has been recruiting for months while I've been focused on maintaining the network. A direct confrontation would be costly, and he knows it. He's content to bleed us slowly, waiting for us to make a mistake.

Unless we force him to overreach first.

The thought surfaces unbidden, and I try to dismiss it. But it keeps returning, each time more fully formed. Konstantin thinks Celeste is a weakness. His people have been watching her, asking questions, trying to understand why I've taken such interest in a fledgling.

If he believes she's vulnerable, he'll move on her.

And if we know he's coming...

I pour myself a whiskey and stand at the window, hating the cold logic assembling itself in my mind. There are other options. There have to be other options. But the more I examine them, the more they fall apart. We don't have the numbers for a direct assault. We can't keep playing defense while he chips away at our allies. And we can't wait for him to choose the time and place of engagement.

But we could choose it for him. We could give him exactly what he's looking for and make him pay for taking it.

The whiskey burns going down.

I tell myself I'm still considering. That I haven't decided anything yet. That when I call the briefing tomorrow, I'll present it as one option among many and let the inner circle weigh in.

But I already know what I'm going to do. I've known since the idea first surfaced.

And I hate myself for it.

When she finds the danger I'm putting her in, she'll never trust me again. Whatever fragile thing is building between us will shatter, and she'll look at me the way everyone eventually does. As a monster. As someone who uses people and discards them when they're no longer useful.

Perhaps that's for the best. Easier to kill something before it takes root than to watch it die slowly.

THE INTELLIGENCE BRIEFING confirms what I already suspected.

Ethan presents his findings to the core group: me, Marcellus, Nadia, and Julian. Celeste is conspicuously absent. I assigned her to shadow Elena in donor coordination, a legitimate task that also keeps her away while we discuss what I've been contemplating.

"Konstantin hit another operation last night," Ethan says, pulling up surveillance footage on the conference room screen. "Small donor collective in Decatur. Non-affiliated, but they'd been negotiating with us for protection."

"Casualties?" Nadia asks.

"Two vampires dead. Three donors hospitalized. The rest scattered." Ethan switches to a map showing attack patterns. "He's working inward. Started at the periphery, now moving toward our core territories. At this rate, he'll be testing our borders within days."

"He's trying to isolate us," Julian observes. "Cut off potential allies before the main assault."

"And it's working," Marcellus adds grimly. "I've had three inquiries today from smaller operations asking if we can guarantee their safety. I couldn't."

I study the map, tracking the pattern of attacks. Surgical. Strategic. Konstantin isn't trying to destroy, not yet. He's trying to destabilize. Create fear. Make vampires choose sides before they're forced to.

"What about his interest in Celeste?" I ask, keeping my voice neutral.

"Still active," Ethan confirms. "His people are watching. Asking questions."

The room is very quiet.

"Then we use that," I say.

Marcellus's head comes up sharply. "Use it how?"

"If Konstantin believes Celeste is a vulnerability, he'll try to exploit her. Target her specifically. We can use that. Set a trap. Let him think he's found an opening, then close it around him."

"You want to use her as bait," Nadia says flatly.

"She's not helpless bait. She's a skilled fighter with forty-three wins in underground combat, and she's adapted to vampire abilities faster than anyone I've trained in decades. If Konstantin's people underestimate her, that's their mistake."

I stand, moving to the map. "The neutral territory near Midtown. We have a donor meet scheduled for tomorrow. Low priority, routine. If Celeste handles it alone, with minimal visible backup..."

"Konstantin's people will see an opportunity," Julian finishes. "The gatekeeper's new protégé, exposed. Vulnerable."

"Exactly. We position teams nearby, out of sight. When they move on her, we take them."

The plan is tactically sound. Strategically elegant. Konstantin wants to find our weaknesses, so we give him a false one and make him pay for taking it.

But Nadia is watching me. "Does she know?"

"Not yet."

"Are you going to tell her?"

The honest answer is no. If she knows it's a trap, her behavior might change. She might be too cautious, too prepared. The deception needs to be complete.

"She'll be briefed on the mission parameters," I say carefully. "Routine donor meet."

"That's not what I asked."

"I know what you asked. The tactical advantage of her not knowing outweighs the alternative."

"And if something goes wrong? If we're wrong about their numbers, or their timing?"

"Then I'll get her out myself."

Nadia holds my gaze for a moment, then nods. Whatever she's thinking, she keeps it to herself.

"The plan proceeds," I say. "Marcellus, coordinate with Julian on team positioning. Nadia, I want intelligence on likely approach vectors. Ethan, keep monitoring Konstantin's communications."

They file out. Marcellus lingers.

"You know this could go wrong," he says quietly.

"I know."

"And you're doing it anyway."

"It's the right tactical decision."

"Is it?" He moves closer, lowering his voice. "Or are you trying to prove something to yourself? That you can still make the cold calculation? That she hasn't changed anything?"

I don't have an answer for that.

"Just make sure the teams are in position," I say. "I want zero margin for error."

Marcellus nods slowly. "And if she finds out? If she realizes you used her as bait without telling her?"

I think about her face in the firelight. The trust in her eyes when she shared her secrets. The way she leaned into my touch.

"I'll deal with it."

"That's not an answer."

"It's the only one I have."

I BRIEF CELESTE the next evening, keeping my voice neutral and professional.

"You'll be vetting a potential donor tomorrow night. She works at a restaurant in Midtown. Meet her at the location, assess her suitability, and report back."

Celeste nods, absorbing the details. She's been cooler since our conversation in the training room. Not cold, but careful. The easy rapport we'd been building has hardened into something more guarded.

I did that. And now I'm compounding it by sending her into danger she doesn't know is coming.

"Questions?" I ask.

"What's my backup if something goes wrong?"

"Julian will have a team positioned nearby. You'll check in every fifteen minutes, and if anything feels off, you get out immediately."

"Understood."

She turns to leave, and I should let her go. I should let her walk out without adding to the deception.

"Celeste."

She pauses at the door.

I want to tell her the truth. I want to warn her, to call off the operation, to find another way. But the part of my mind that's kept me alive for six centuries won't allow it. This is the right tactical play, even if everything else in me knows it's a betrayal.

"Be careful," I say.

Something flickers across her face. "I always am."

She leaves, and I stand there staring at the empty doorway longer than I should.

The tactical plan is sound. The teams are in position. Every variable has been accounted for. But as I return to my study to monitor communications, I can't escape the feeling that I've set something in motion I won't be able to control.

I'm sending her into an ambush because strategy demands it, and because I'm trying to prove to myself that she hasn't changed anything. But she has. I know it in the way my hands won't stay still while I watch the communications feed. I know it in the way every minute stretches into an hour even though she hasn't reached the location yet. I've sent dozens of operatives into dangerous situations over the centuries, and I've never once had to fight the urge to abandon the plan and follow them myself.

Controlling everything doesn't keep them alive. It just keeps them alone.

She was right. I've been alone for so long that I forgot it was a choice. Somewhere along the way, the walls I built to protect myself became a prison, and I stopped noticing the difference between surviving and living.

After tonight, she'll know what I did. She'll understand that I used her as bait without telling her, and whatever fragile trust existed between us will shatter. Part of me thinks that's for the best. Safe. Uncomplicated. Back to the way things were before she stumbled into that alley and looked at me like I was just a man.

The communications feed crackles. She's approaching the meeting point.

I watch the tracker move across the screen, and I wait.

Strange, how quickly safety has started to feel like a cage.

The restaurant is called Mireille's, a French bistro tucked into a quiet corner of Midtown where the streetlights cast warm pools on rain-slicked pavement. I arrive fifteen minutes early.

The potential donor's name is Tessa Whitaker, according to the briefing. Late twenties, server at Mireille's for three years, referred through a friend of a friend who's already in the network. Routine vetting. Meet her after her shift ends at ten, assess her suitability, report back.

Simple. Straightforward. The kind of mission designed to build my confidence without putting me at real risk.

I find a spot in the shadows across the street where I can watch the restaurant's entrance and side door. The dinner rush is winding down, couples lingering over wine and dessert, waitstaff moving between tables with practiced efficiency. Through the windows, I can see a blonde-haired woman who matches Tessa's description clearing plates from a table near the back.

I text Julian to let him know I've arrived.

On site. No issues.

His response comes quickly.

JULIAN

Copy. Team is positioned.

I pocket my phone and settle in to wait.

The night air carries the smell of rain and car exhaust and something cooking at the Thai place down the block. A couple walks past my position, arms linked, laughing at something on one of their phones. They don't notice me in the shadows.

Not long ago, I was one of them. Walking through the world without knowing what lurked in the shadows. Now I'm what lurks there.

Tessa emerges from the side door at 10:07, pulling on a jacket against the November chill. She's pretty in an understated way, with delicate features and blonde hair pulled back in a practical ponytail. She looks tired but not unhappy, the kind of tired that comes from honest work rather than despair.

I step out of the shadows as she approaches. "Tessa Whitaker?"

She startles slightly, then recovers. "You're from the network?"

"Celeste. I'm here to talk with you about the program, answer any questions you might have."

"Right. They said someone would come." She glances around the empty street. "There's a coffee shop around the corner that's open late. We could..."

"Here is fine." I gesture toward a bench near the bus stop, visible but not exposed. "It won't take long."

She hesitates, and I can see her weighing the situation. Meeting a stranger at night. The promise of money that sounds too good to be true. Every instinct telling her to be careful.

Smart woman. She should trust those instincts.

"Okay," she says finally, and we walk to the bench together.

I run through the standard screening questions. Health history. Lifestyle. Why she's interested in the program. Tessa answers carefully, honestly, as far as I can tell. She's got credit card debt and her car needs repairs she can't afford; she's been taking the bus for three months. She's not desperate, not yet, but she's tired of barely scraping by.

"The money is good," I tell her. "Better than anything else you'll find for this level of commitment. But you need to understand what you're agreeing to. Regular blood draws. Health monitoring. Complete discretion about who you're working for and why."

"The friend who referred me said it's like being a plasma donor, but more exclusive."

"Something like that."

She nods slowly, processing. "And the people I'd be... donating to. They're not going to hurt me?"

"No. The program exists specifically to prevent that kind of thing." I think about Elena's explanations, about the careful systems Maximus has built. "You'd be protected. Compensated. Treated well."

"It sounds almost too good to be true."

"It's not charity," I say. "It's a mutual benefit. You have something we need. We have resources you need. The arrangement works because both sides get something valuable."

Tessa is quiet for a moment, staring at her hands. "Can I think about it? I don't want to make a decision this big on the spot."

"Of course. Take a few days. If you're interested, call this number." I hand her a card with a generic business name and a phone number that routes to Elena's office. "If you're not interested, forget we ever met. No pressure either way."

She takes the card and tucks it into her jacket pocket. "Thank you. For being straight with me. Some of the other offers I've gotten felt... predatory."

"Those are the ones to avoid."

She almost smiles. "I figured that out. Eventually."

We stand, and I'm about to say goodbye when I feel it.

A shift in the air. A prickle at the back of my neck. The sudden, instinctive awareness that we're not alone anymore.

I scan the street without moving my head. The shadows between buildings. The parked cars. The alley that runs behind the restaurant.

There. Movement in the darkness near the Thai place. And there, across the street, a figure that wasn't standing in that doorway thirty seconds ago.

Two. No, three. Four.

My stomach drops.

"Tessa." I keep my voice calm, conversational. "I need you to go back inside the restaurant. Right now. Don't run, don't look around, just walk to the side door and go in."

"What? Why?"

"Because something's wrong, and I need you safe before I can deal with it."

She hears the tension under my controlled tone. To her credit, she doesn't argue or ask more questions. She just turns and walks toward Mireille's side door with the forced casualness of someone trying very hard not to look afraid.

I count the figures again. Five now. Six. They're emerging from the shadows like they were always there, just waiting for the right moment.

Six against one.

I reach for my phone to send an emergency signal, but I already know it's too late. They're moving, circling, cutting off escape routes with the coordination of predators who've done this before.

The first one steps into the light. Male, maybe thirty when he was turned, with a shaved head and the kind of bulk that comes from either serious weight training or serious violence. His smile shows too many teeth.

"Celeste Moreau," he says. "The gatekeeper's new pet. We've been wanting to meet you."

"Funny. I don't remember asking for introductions."

"Konstantin sends his regards."

They're all visible now. Six vampires spread in a loose circle around me, close enough to strike but far enough to make me work for any escape. They're dressed for combat, dark clothes and practical boots, and at least two of them are carrying weapons I can see. Which means the others are carrying weapons I can't.

I settle into a fighting stance without conscious thought, my body remembering thousands of hours of training. Underground rings. Maximus's brutal sessions. Every fight I've ever survived.

Forty-three wins. Zero losses.

But those were one-on-one matches against humans, or sparring sessions with rules and boundaries. This is six vampires with probably centuries of combined experience and every intention of killing me.

"You can come with us willingly," the bald one says. "Konstantin has questions. He's a civilized man. He'll make it quick once he has his answers."

"Or?"

"Or we take you in pieces. Your choice."

I think about Tessa inside the restaurant. About Julian's team, positioned nearby. About Maximus in his study, monitoring communications, trusting that his plan would work.

But where is my backup?

"I'll take option three," I say.

"There is no option three."

"There's always an option three."

I move.

The first rule of fighting multiple opponents is simple: don't. If you can run, run. If you can't run, make sure you're never surrounded. Keep moving, keep them in front of you, never let them coordinate.

I launch myself at the two on my left, the smallest gap in their circle. The bald one is already moving to intercept, but I'm faster than he expected. Eight months of vampire speed is still vampire speed, and I've been training with someone who doesn't believe in gentle learning curves.

My fist connects with the first one's throat, a strike that would have crushed a human's windpipe. He staggers, choking, and I'm already past him, spinning to put a parked car between me and the rest.

One down temporarily. Five are still coming.

They're fast. Faster than me, some of them. The bald one closes the distance in a blur, and I barely dodge the knife he's pulled from somewhere. The blade catches my arm, a line of fire that I ignore because I can't afford to acknowledge it.

I grab his wrist, twist, and use his momentum to throw him into the vampire coming up behind him. They go down in a tangle of limbs, and I have maybe two seconds before the others reach me.

Two seconds. I use them.

I vault over the hood of the car, putting more distance between us, and almost run directly into another attacker. Female, small but wiry, with eyes that have seen centuries of violence. She moves like water, slipping past my defenses, and her fist connects with my ribs hard enough that I feel something crack.

The pain is sharp, immediate, and I use it. Let the anger rise, the fighter's focus that turns pain into fuel. I catch her next strike, redirect it, and drive my elbow into her temple with everything I have.

She drops.

Two down. Four still standing. And I'm hurt now, my left side screaming with every breath, blood running down my arm from the knife wound.

The bald one is up again, circling with the others, that predator's smile still in place.

"Not bad," he says. "Konstantin was right about you. You've got fire."

I don't waste breath on a response. I'm calculating distances, angles, trying to find another gap in their formation. But they're learning now, adjusting. They won't let me break through again.

The next attack comes from two directions at once. I block one strike, take another to the shoulder, spin away from a third. Fighting on instinct, letting my body do what it's been trained to do while my mind races for solutions.

Julian's team should be here by now. The emergency signal should have triggered the moment I was surrounded. Where are they? Where is my backup?

The bald one sees me glance toward the street. His smile widens.

"Looking for your friends?" He laughs. "They're a little busy right now. Konstantin sent a welcoming party for them, too."

How did they know about Julian's team? How did they know any of this?

A kick catches me in the back, sends me stumbling forward into a fist that connects with my jaw hard enough to blur my vision.

No. Not like this.

I plant my feet, channel everything into one massive strike that catches the nearest attacker in the chest. I feel his ribs give way under my fist, feel the shock travel up my arm, hear his grunt of surprise and pain as he folds.

Three down. Three left. But I'm slowing now, the damage accumulating faster than I can compensate.

The bald one comes at me again, and this time I can't dodge fast enough. His fist catches my wounded side, and the pain is so intense that my vision goes white for a second. I hit the ground hard, asphalt scraping my palms, and I'm rolling before I can think, pure instinct saving me from the boot that comes down where my head was.

I get my feet under me, but barely. My left arm isn't working right, something grinding in my shoulder that shouldn't be grinding. Blood is dripping into my eye from a cut I don't remember getting.

Three of them left. All of them fresh. All of them between me and any escape.

"Enough," the bald one says. "You've made your point. Now stop making this harder than it needs to be."

I spit blood onto the pavement. "I'm just getting started."

It's a lie. We both know it's a lie. But I'll die before I kneel to Konstantin's people. I'll die standing, fighting, proving that I'm not the vulnerability they think I am.

I'll die like a warrior.

The bald one sighs. "Have it your way."

They come at me together this time, coordinated, no gaps to exploit. I take one more down with a strike to the knee that shatters bone, but then they're on me, too many hands grabbing, too much weight bearing down.

I fight. God, I fight. Every dirty trick I learned in the underground. Every technique Maximus and Marcellus drilled into me.

I break fingers, gouge eyes, bite down on an arm until I taste someone else's blood.

But there are still two of them, and I can barely stand. The bald one has my throat now, lifting me off the ground with casual strength, and his smile has turned ugly.

"Konstantin wanted you alive," he says. "But he didn't say anything about undamaged."

His fist draws back, and I brace for impact.

The blow never lands.

One moment he's there, solid and sneering and triumphant. The next, he's simply gone, ripped away from me with such force that I collapse to the ground, my legs unable to hold me.

I hear screaming. Not mine. Someone else, high and terrified, cut short by a sound like wet fabric tearing.

I blink blood out of my eyes and try to make sense of what I'm seeing.

Maximus.

He's not fighting. Fighting implies effort, contest, some question about the outcome. What he's doing is executing. The remaining attacker doesn't even have time to raise his hands before Maximus tears his throat out with his bare fingers.

The silence that follows is absolute.

Maximus stands in the middle of the carnage, surrounded by bodies, his chest heaving with unnecessary breaths. Blood covers his hands, his shirt, his face. His eyes are black, completely black, and there's nothing human left in his expression.

For the first time since I became a vampire, I understand why humans are afraid of us.

Then his gaze finds me, crumpled on the ground, and something shifts. The blackness recedes. The monster retreats. What's left is something almost worse: naked terror.

"Celeste."

He's beside me before I can blink, hands hovering over my injuries like he's afraid to touch me, afraid of causing more damage. The contrast between the violence of a moment ago and the gentleness now makes my head spin.

"I'm okay," I manage.

"You're not okay. You're bleeding. Your shoulder is dislocated. You have at least three broken ribs, possibly more." His voice is ragged, barely controlled. "I should have been here sooner. I should have..."

"Maximus."

He stops. Looks at me. Really looks at me, past the blood and the bruises, to something underneath.

"I'm alive," I say. "That's what matters."

For a long moment, he doesn't speak. His hand comes up to cup my face, impossibly gentle, his thumb brushing blood from my cheekbone. The touch sends warmth through me despite everything, despite the pain, despite the corpses on the pavement around us.

"I thought I'd lost you," he whispers, and his voice cracks on the words. "I was monitoring the feed, and I heard them surround you and I..." He stops, swallows.

"What about Julian's team?"

"Coming. I passed them on the way. I couldn't wait."

He couldn't wait. The man who plans everything, controls everything, calculates every variable. He couldn't wait.

Something in my chest cracks open at that. Something that has nothing to do with broken ribs.

"Can you stand?" he asks.

"I don't know."

"I'm going to lift you. It's going to hurt."

"Everything hurts. A little more won't make a difference."

He slides one arm under my knees, the other behind my back,

and lifts me as if I weigh nothing. The movement jars my shoulder, and I can't stop the gasp of pain that escapes. His arms tighten around me in response, pulling me closer to his chest.

"I'm sorry," he murmurs against my hair. "I'm so sorry."

I let my head rest against his shoulder, breathing through the pain, surrounded by his scent and his strength and the steady rhythm of movement as he carries me away from the carnage. For this one moment, I let myself feel safe. Protected. Cared for.

***

JULIAN and his team meet us halfway back to the compound. I'm dimly aware of their shocked expressions, of hushed voices discussing what happened, of someone offering to take me from Maximus so he can deal with the aftermath.

"No." His voice is ice. "I've got her."

No one argues.

He carries me through the compound entrance, past guards who stare and servants who scatter, all the way to the medical wing. Dr. Dalton is already waiting, alerted somehow, with equipment prepared and assistants standing by.

"Set her down here," Dalton says, gesturing to the examination table.

Maximus doesn't move.

"Maximus." Dalton's voice is gentle but firm. "I need to examine her. I can't do that while you're holding her."

For a moment, I think he's going to refuse. His arms tighten around me, his jaw clenching with something that looks like pain. Then, slowly, carefully, he lowers me onto the table.

His hand doesn't leave mine.

"Three broken ribs," Dalton says after a quick examination. "Dislocated shoulder. Multiple lacerations, none life-threatening.

Significant blood loss, but vampire healing is already working on the worst of it." He looks at Maximus. "She needs rest and blood. She'll be fine in a few days."

"Fine." Maximus's voice is hollow. "She'll be fine."

"I'll need to set the shoulder," Dalton continues. "It's going to hurt."

"Do it," I say.

Dalton positions himself, and Maximus moves to block my view. "Look at me," he says quietly. "Just look at me."

I look at him. At the blood still drying on his face, at the fear still lingering in his eyes, at the way his hand grips mine like I'm the only thing keeping him anchored.

Dalton moves. My shoulder screams. I don't look away from Maximus's face.

"Done," Dalton says. "I'll get blood and bandages. She should rest."

He leaves, and it's just the two of us. Maximus and I, in the harsh light of the medical wing, surrounded by the antiseptic smell of healing.

His free hand comes up to brush hair from my face. The gesture is tender, reverent, completely at odds with the violence I witnessed less than an hour ago.

"You're shaking," I say.

He looks down at his hands like he's never seen them before. They're still covered in blood, and yes, they're trembling.

"I killed them." His voice is strange, distant. "I didn't try to capture them. Didn't question them. I just... saw you on the ground, and I killed them."

"Maximus..."

"I haven't lost control like that in centuries." He meets my eyes, and what I see there isn't the cold strategist or the vampire lord. It's fear. Raw, undisguised fear. "The thought of losing you..."

He stops. Swallows hard.

"I can't," he says quietly. "I can't lose you."

He's quiet for a long moment. When he speaks, his voice is rough with something I can't name.

"Because the thought of losing you was worse than any tactical consideration." He looks down at our joined hands. "I've spent centuries learning to sacrifice anyone and anything for the greater good. And the moment I heard them close in on you, none of it mattered. Just you. Getting to you."

I want to reach for him. Want to let this moment be what it feels like, a confession, a turning point, the beginning of something real.

But something the bald vampire said keeps echoing.

"They knew about Julian's team," I say slowly. "How is that possible?"

Maximus's jaw tightens. "Konstantin has informants. We're still trying to determine..."

"But it was a routine donor meet. That's what you told me." I watch his face, pieces clicking together. "Except you've been avoiding me for days. And then suddenly, you're sending a team as backup when you didn't before. You told me to 'be careful' with more weight than a routine mission should need."

He doesn't answer.

"And there was a strategy meeting yesterday that I wasn't invited to. Elena mentioned it by accident." I watch something shift in his expression. Something that looks like dread. "What was discussed at that meeting, Maximus?"

"The situation required..."

"What situation? You told me it was routine."

Silence.

Somewhere down the hall, footsteps pass and fade. I wait.

"It wasn't routine," he finally says. His voice is barely a whisper.

"We had intelligence that Konstantin's people were watching you. Looking for an opportunity."

The words take a moment to land.

"You knew they might come for me tonight."

He closes his eyes. "Yes."

"And you sent me anyway."

"I had teams positioned."

"You *sent me anyway*. Without telling me." My voice cracks. "I was bait."

He doesn't deny it.

"We had backup in position."

"Not close enough. Not fast enough." I pull my hand from his, and the loss of contact feels like tearing. "You used me."

"I was trying to..."

"What? Protect the network? Gain tactical advantage?" I push myself up despite the pain, needing distance, needing to not be touching him. "Did you even consider telling me the truth?"

"If you knew, your reactions wouldn't have been genuine. They might have suspected."

"So you let me walk in blind. Let me think it was routine. Let me..." My voice breaks, and I hate myself for it. "I trusted you."

The words hit him like physical blows. I watch his face crumble, watch the walls he's been rebuilding since we left the street finally give way.

"Celeste."

"No." I hold up a hand, and he stops. "I can't do this right now. I can't look at you and reconcile the person who just killed six vampires to save me with the person who put me in danger in the first place."

"I will spend the rest of my existence making this right."

"I don't know if you can."

The words hang between us, heavy and final. His face is a

landscape of devastation, guilt, and grief, and something that looks like his heart breaking in real time.

Good, some petty part of me thinks. Let him feel it.

But another part, the part that remembers how gently he touched my face, how his voice cracked when he said he thought he'd lost me, that part wants to take the words back. Wants to reach for him. Wants to pretend I don't know what I know.

I don't reach for him.

"Leave," I say quietly. "Please."

For a moment, I think he'll argue. The Maximus I've come to know doesn't accept dismissal, doesn't cede ground, doesn't give up control.

But this Maximus, the one covered in blood and stripped of defenses, just nods.

"I'll send Dalton back in," he says.

He stands. He walks to the door. He pauses with his hand on the frame, his back to me, every line of his body speaking of words he wants to say and can't.

Then he's gone.

I sit alone in the medical wing, surrounded by the smell of blood and antiseptic, and I allow myself to feel.

CHAPTER
FOURTEEN

I make it three steps down the corridor before my legs stop working.

I don't collapse. I'm too old, too disciplined, too aware of the guards stationed at the end of the hall who would see their invincible leader crumble like a man made of ash. Instead, I stop walking. I put my hand against the wall. And I stand there, breathing, while something inside me comes apart.

I don't know if you can.

Her words keep replaying. Each time, they cut deeper.

The wall is cool and solid beneath my palm. I focus on that sensation, try to anchor myself in something physical and real, the way I've done a thousand times when emotion threatened to overwhelm discipline.

It doesn't work.

When I pull my hand away, I leave a smear of red on the white paint. Their blood. Still on my hands. I stare at the mark for a long moment, this visible evidence of what I did, what I became, and then I keep walking.

I should send someone to clean it. I don't.

I look down at my hands. Blood under my fingernails. Blood dried into the creases of my knuckles. Not hers, theirs. The vampires I tore apart in that alley. I can still feel the give of flesh, the crack of bone, the wet heat of it. I killed them with my bare hands because weapons would have been too slow, too clean, too merciful.

I don't remember making the decision to kill. I remember seeing her on the ground, blood pooling beneath her, and then I remember standing in silence surrounded by bodies. Everything between is red and rage and the sound of my own snarling.

I haven't lost control like that since I was a fledgling. Since the early years when the hunger was new and overwhelming, and I hadn't yet learned to leash the monster inside me.

Behind me, I hear Dalton enter the medical room. Hear his quiet voice asking Celeste questions about her pain levels. Hear her responses, steady despite everything, because she's stronger than anyone I've ever met.

Stronger than me, certainly.

I push off the wall and force myself to walk. One step. Another. My body knows how to do this even when my mind has abandoned the effort.

I find myself in the security center without remembering the journey there. Julian is already present, his arm in a sling, dried blood still flaking from a cut above his eye. Three of his team members are with him, all of them bearing wounds in various stages of healing. The fourth is in the medical wing, unconscious. The fifth didn't survive.

"Sir." Julian straightens when he sees me, then stops. Something in my expression makes him pause. "The attackers who hit our position, we killed two. The others escaped before we could pursue. We were too focused on getting to Celeste's location."

"How many escaped?"

"Three, maybe four. They scattered when they realized we'd broken through." His jaw tightens with frustration. "We should have captured at least one. But when we heard the fighting from her location, we..."

"You made the right call."

He nods, but I can see he doesn't believe it. A commander's instinct, always questioning, always finding fault with his own decisions. I understand that instinct intimately.

"Casualties?" I ask.

"Archer is dead. Patricia is critical but stable. The rest of us will heal."

Archer is dead. Twelve years in my service. Somewhere in Savannah, a wife and daughter who haven't seen him since he was turned will never know what happened to him.

"And the attackers who went after Celeste?" Julian asks. "How many did we capture?"

The question hits like a blade between the ribs.

Capture. That was the point. The entire reason for tonight. Use Celeste to draw them out, capture Konstantin's operatives, extract intelligence about his plans, his timeline, his network. Trade her safety for information that could save dozens of lives.

"None," I say.

Julian frowns. "None? They all escaped?"

"They're all dead."

"Dead." He processes this. "All six."

"All six."

The silence stretches. I watch understanding dawn on his face. The plan had been precise. Specific. Capture, don't kill. We needed what they knew. And between my team and his, we have nothing. The ones who attacked Julian scattered into the night. The ones who attacked Celeste are in pieces in an alley.

"So we have no intelligence," Julian says slowly. "No information about Konstantin's operations. No way to identify other operatives."

"No."

"The entire point of tonight..."

"Was wasted. Yes."

I betrayed her trust for nothing. Put her in danger, let her believe it was routine, watched her fight for her life against six attackers. And when the moment came to salvage something from the wreckage, to at least gain the tactical advantage that was supposed to justify all of it, I threw it away.

I killed them because I couldn't stop myself. Because seeing her hurt broke something in me that strategy couldn't reach. Because in that moment, nothing mattered except ending the things that had touched her.

And now I have nothing. No intelligence. No advantage. No justification.

Just blood on my hands in more ways than one.

"Sir?" Julian's voice cuts through the silence. "What are your orders?"

Orders. He wants orders. Because I'm the one in charge, the one who makes decisions, the one who's supposed to know what to do.

"Double the security on the compound," I hear myself say. "Konstantin knows his assault failed. He'll be assessing, regrouping. I want to know the moment any of his people move. And pull Celeste from all field operations until further notice."

Julian hesitates. "She won't like that."

"I'm aware."

"She's amazing, sir. What she did tonight, holding off six of them alone until you arrived, most vampires her age would have been dead in the first thirty seconds."

"I know exactly how good she is." My voice comes out sharper than intended. "That's not the point. She's off field duty until I say otherwise."

He nods, wisely choosing not to argue further. "Understood. I'll coordinate the security increase."

I leave before he can ask more questions.

I MAKE it to my study before Marcellus finds me.

He doesn't knock. Just opens the door and walks in, closing it behind him with a quiet click. His expression is carefully neutral, but I've known him long enough to read the concern beneath the control.

"She's stable," he says. "Dalton says she'll be fully healed in two or three days."

"I know."

"Julian lost a man. Archer."

"I know."

"And you killed all six attackers instead of capturing any for questioning."

I don't respond. There's nothing to say.

He crosses to the sidebar and pours two glasses of whiskey. Sets one in front of me without asking. Takes the chair across from my desk.

"Your hands are shaking," he observes.

I look down. He's right. A fine tremor runs through my fingers, visible even in the low light. I curl them into fists, but that only makes the shaking more obvious. My whole body feels wrong, depleted in a way that goes beyond physical exhaustion. I moved faster tonight than I have in decades, burned through reserves I didn't know I was still capable of accessing. And for what?

"You're not reacting like a commander who lost control of an operation," Marcellus says quietly. "You're reacting like this was personal. Like she was personal."

"She could have died." The words tear out of me, raw and jagged. "He had her by the throat, feet off the ground, and I wasn't fast enough. If I'd been a few seconds later..."

"But you weren't."

"But I could have been." I meet his eyes. "I sent her in there knowing what might happen. I calculated the risks, positioned the teams, accounted for variables. And then I stood in my study watching a screen while six vampires tried to kill her."

"You got there. You saved her."

"I'm the reason she needed saving. And then I threw away the only thing that could have justified it." I stare at the whiskey I haven't touched. "I was supposed to capture them. That was the plan. Get intelligence, make it mean something. Instead, I killed every single one of them without a thought."

"Why?"

"Because I saw her bleeding, and I stopped thinking. All my discipline. All my careful control. Gone the moment she was in danger."

The admission costs me something. I've spent my entire existence cultivating control, building walls, learning to make the cold calculation, even when everything in me screamed against it. Tonight proved that all of it was an illusion. One woman bleeding in an alley, and I became the monster I've spent lifetimes trying to bury.

Marcellus is quiet for a moment. "What did she say? When you told her?"

"I didn't have to tell her. She figured it out." The memory of her face cuts through me. "She asked me to leave."

"And?"

"And I left. What else could I do?"

He leans back in his chair, studying me. "I've known you a long time. I've seen you lose battles, lose territory, lose people you valued. I've never seen you like this."

"Like what?"

"Lost."

The word settles between us. He's not wrong. I am lost. For the first time in longer than I can remember, I have no plan, no strategy, no careful calculation to guide me. There's only the wreckage of what I've done and the look in her eyes when she told me she didn't know if I could make it right.

"She trusted me," I say. "That's what she said. She trusted me."

"Did you trust her?"

The question catches me off guard. "What?"

"Did you trust her? If you had, you would have told her the truth. Let her decide whether to take the risk. Instead, you made the choice for her." He leans forward. "You didn't just use her as bait. You decided she couldn't handle the truth."

I want to argue. Want to explain that I was protecting her, that I needed her reactions to be genuine, that it was tactically necessary.

But he's right. Underneath all the justifications, I didn't trust her enough to give her the choice.

"I've taken her off field duty," I say. "Until she's fully healed."

Marcellus raises an eyebrow. "She'll be furious."

"I know."

"She'll see it as you controlling her again. Making decisions for her without asking."

"I know." I finally pick up the whiskey, though I don't drink it. Just hold it, feeling the weight of the glass in my hand. "But I can't send her back out there. Not yet. Maybe not ever. The thought of her in danger again..."

"That's not strategy. That's fear."

"Yes." There's no point denying it. "It's fear. I'm afraid for her. I'm afraid of what I'll become if something happens to her."

The words hang in the air between us. I've never admitted to fear. Not to Marcellus, not to anyone. Fear is weakness, and weakness gets you killed.

But tonight I watched her fight for her life, and I felt something I haven't felt since Catherine.

That helpless, drowning terror of watching someone you care about slip away while you're powerless to stop it.

I turned Catherine to save her. She was dying of consumption, and I couldn't let her go, so I made her immortal. Then I watched the turning go wrong, watched her mind fracture into something feral and violent. And I had to end her myself. My choice to save her became my hand on the blade that killed her.

I swore I'd never feel that way again. Built my entire existence around making sure I never would.

And then Celeste appeared in that alley, and all my careful defenses meant nothing.

"What do I do?" The question comes out before I can stop it. "How do I fix this?"

"I don't know if you can." Marcellus echoes her words, and they hit just as hard coming from him. "But if there's any chance, it starts with honesty. Real honesty. Not strategic truth-telling. Not calculated vulnerability. The kind of honesty that costs you something."

"And if that's not enough?"

"Then at least you'll have given her what you should have given her from the start. The choice you took away."

He stands, finishes his whiskey, and moves toward the door. Then he pauses.

"She's strong," he says. "Stronger than you give her credit for.

But strength isn't the same as invulnerability. What you did tonight hurt her. Not the ambush. The lie. Remember that when you talk to her."

"And the field duty restriction?"

"Tell her the truth about that, too. That you're scared. That you can't think straight when she's in danger. Let her decide what to do with that information." He shakes his head. "You might be surprised. Or she might tell you to go to hell. Either way, at least you'll have been honest."

Then he's gone, and I'm alone.

I SHOULD REST. The hours before dawn are slipping away, and I've depleted more strength tonight than I have in years. My body aches in ways I'd forgotten were possible, muscles strained from moving at speeds I haven't attempted in decades, hands bruised from the violence I unleashed in that alley.

But instead of going to my chambers, I pull up the security feed from the medical wing.

Celeste is still awake. She's sitting up in the bed now, staring at nothing. Her injuries are healing, I can see the bruises fading, the cuts closing, but there's something in her expression that has nothing to do with physical pain.

I did that. That hollowness in her eyes. That stillness that speaks of trust broken and faith shattered.

I watch her for longer than I should. Watch her reach up to touch her shoulder where Dalton reset the joint. Watch her flex her fingers, testing her healing. Watch her finally lie back against the pillows and close her eyes, though I can tell from the tension in her body that she's not sleeping.

What would I even say to her?

I'm sorry seems laughably inadequate. *I was trying to protect the network* is true but irrelevant, she doesn't care about my strategic reasoning, and she shouldn't. *I was afraid of what I feel for you, so I tried to prove I could still make the cold calculation* is honest but damning.

Maybe that's what I need to tell her. The damning truth.

I close the security feed and stare at the fire in the fireplace instead.

The plan had been sound. Use Konstantin's interest in Celeste against him. Draw out his operatives. Capture them. Extract intelligence. A calculated risk with positioned backup and acceptable parameters.

Except the parameters weren't acceptable. Not to me. Not when it was her.

I think about what Marcellus said. About trust. About honesty.

I've built my entire existence on control. It's how I survived Luciano. How I built my network. How I became someone that other vampires fear and respect. Control is safety. Control is power.

But control is also a cage.

Celeste said that. In the training room, when I was trying to push her away. She said controlling everything doesn't keep people alive. It just keeps them alone.

She was right. I've been alone for so long that I stopped noticing. Stopped feeling the weight of it. Built walls so high that no one could reach me, and told myself it was strength.

Then she appeared in that alley. Dying, defiant, insulting me with her last breaths. And something cracked.

I wanted to save her. Not for strategic reasons. Not because she was useful. I wanted to save her because she looked at me like I was a person, not a monster or a myth. Because she didn't beg. Because even facing death, she was still herself.

And I've been running from wanting her ever since.

I go to the bathroom and finally wash my hands. Watch the dried blood turn the water pink as it swirls down the drain. Their blood, the vampires I killed. I try to remember their faces and can't. They were just obstacles between me and Celeste. Just things that needed to be destroyed so I could reach her.

That's what frightens me most. Not the violence itself, but the complete absence of thought behind it. I didn't decide to kill them. I simply did, the way a predator kills prey, without hesitation or consideration or mercy.

Is that who I am beneath all the careful control? Just a monster wearing the mask of civilization?

Or is that who I become when someone threatens the people I care about?

I dry my hands and return to my chair. The fire has burned low, embers glowing orange in the darkness.

Tomorrow night, I'll face her. I'll tell her the truth, all of it. About the plan. About why I made the choice I made. About the fact that I killed six vampires instead of capturing them because seeing her hurt made me lose every shred of the control I've spent my whole existence building.

I'll tell her about the field duty restriction, and I'll be honest about why. Not because she's incapable, she proved tonight just how capable she is. But because *I'm* not capable. Not of watching her walk into danger. Not of maintaining the cold detachment that command requires when she's the one at risk.

I'll tell her that I don't know how to do this. That I don't have a strategy for earning back trust I never deserved in the first place. That the great master tactician is completely lost when it comes to something as simple as being honest with someone he cares about.

Maybe it won't be enough. Maybe she'll never look at me the way she did before.

But at least I'll have given her the truth. And maybe that's where it has to start.

The first gray light of dawn creeps around the edges of the blackout curtains. I feel the pull toward dormancy.

I don't fight it. I let consciousness slip away.

My last thought before sleep takes me is her face. Not the betrayal. Not the anger.

The moment in my study when she leaned into my touch and looked at me like I might be worth believing in.

I don't know if I can earn that look again.

But I have to try.

FIFTEEN

CELESTE

I wake with the sunset, my body pulling me from dormancy the moment darkness falls.

For a moment, I don't remember where I am. The ceiling is wrong, too high, too white. The bed is too soft. The sheets smell like lavender and something antiseptic.

Then it all comes rushing back.

The alley. Six vampires emerging from shadows. The fight, brutal, desperate, knowing I was outmatched but refusing to go down easy. The bald one's hand around my throat, lifting me off my feet, the world starting to gray at the edges.

And then Maximus.

I close my eyes, and the memories sharpen. The sound of him arriving, not footsteps, just sudden violence, the bald vampire ripped away from me so fast I didn't see it happen. The screaming that wasn't mine. The wet, tearing sounds that I understood on some primal level without wanting to examine too closely.

Then silence. And him standing in the middle of it,

surrounded by bodies, his eyes completely black and nothing human left in his expression.

For a moment, I'd been afraid of him. Truly afraid, in a way I hadn't been since I was human. This wasn't the controlled, aristocratic vampire who'd saved me in an alley or trained me in his compound. This was something savage, a predator wearing a man's skin.

Then his eyes found mine, and the blackness receded. What replaced it was almost worse, naked terror. Like *he* was the one who'd almost died.

I remember him lifting me. The impossible gentleness of it, cradling me against his chest like I weighed nothing, like I was something fragile and precious. His voice in my ear, rough and broken: *I thought I'd lost you. I couldn't wait. I heard them surround you, and I, I've never moved that fast.*

The way his hands shook while Dalton examined me. The way he wouldn't let go of my hand when they set my shoulder. The way he brushed the hair from my face with fingers that trembled, his touch so tender it made my chest ache.

And then the realization. The questions I asked that led to answers I didn't want.

You knew they might come for me tonight.

Yes.

And you sent me anyway.

I open my eyes and stare at the ceiling.

How can someone hold you like you're the most important thing in the world and also use you as bait without telling you? How can tenderness and betrayal exist in the same person, the same hands, the same voice?

I don't understand him. I'm not sure I ever will.

I sit up slowly, testing my body. The ribs that were broken last night have knitted back together, tender when I press them, but solid. My shoulder rotates smoothly, only a ghost of stiffness where the joint was dislocated. The cuts and bruises have faded to nothing.

Vampire healing. At least something about this existence is useful.

The medical wing is quiet. Through the window, I can see full darkness; night has fallen. I slept through the entire day, my body demanding the dormancy it needed to repair itself.

I swing my legs over the side of the bed and stand. A little unsteady, but functional. Someone left clean clothes folded on the chair, my clothes, from my room. Black leggings, a soft gray sweater. Someone was thinking about my comfort.

I try not to wonder if it was him.

I'm pulling the sweater over my head when I hear footsteps in the corridor. Measured. Deliberate. I know that cadence.

Something tightens in my chest despite everything. My body hasn't caught up with my anger yet.

The door opens before I can finish dressing.

Maximus steps inside and stops dead.

I'm standing there with the sweater bunched around my shoulders, arms tangled in the fabric, wearing nothing but a bra from the waist up. For a frozen moment, neither of us moves.

His eyes drop. And stay.

I watch it happen, the way his gaze traces the line of my collarbone, slides down to the swell of my breasts against black lace, lingers on the curve of my waist, the bare skin of my stomach. There's nothing controlled about it. Nothing measured or deliberate. He looks at me like a man dying of thirst looks at water, like he's forgotten every rule he's ever made for himself.

His lips part. His hands curl into fists at his sides.

Then he seems to remember himself. He turns his head sharply to the side, jaw tight, a muscle feathering in his cheek.

"I should have knocked." His voice is rough. Wrecked.

"Yes. You should have."

I take my time pulling the sweater down, smoothing the fabric over my hips. I don't rush. Let him stand there, uncomfortable, not looking at me. After everything he's done, this small moment of power feels earned.

"You can turn around now."

He does, but something has shifted. The hollowness is still there, the exhaustion, but he won't meet my eyes directly. His control is back in place, but I saw what was underneath. Just for a moment.

I hate that it affects me. Hate the heat that curled through my stomach when he looked at me like that. I'm supposed to be angry.

I am angry. Both things can be true.

"You're awake," he says.

"Obviously."

He closes the door behind him and stands there, hands at his sides. Not approaching. Giving me space. Or maybe just afraid to come closer.

"How do you feel?" he asks.

"Healed. Mostly."

"Good. That's... good."

The silence stretches between us. He's the one who came here, but he doesn't seem to know what to say. I watch him struggle with it, this vampire who always has a plan, always knows the right move. Right now, he looks lost.

Part of me wants to help him. The part that remembers his face when he found me, the raw terror in his eyes, the way he whispered *I thought I'd lost you* like the words were being torn out of him. The part that remembers his letters, preserved for centuries, and the grief in his voice when he talked about his men.

The part that leaned into his touch in that firelit study and wanted more.

But then I remember the rest of it.

He takes a breath. "I came to apologize."

"Did you."

"What I did was wrong. Using you as bait without telling you, without giving you the choice, it was a betrayal of your trust. I knew the risks, and I didn't warn you. I told myself it was strategy, that your reactions needed to be genuine, that the tactical advantage outweighed..." He stops. Shakes his head. "None of that matters. I was wrong. I'm sorry."

Something shifts in my chest. He means it. I can hear it in his voice, see it in the way he's standing, not defensive, not making excuses. Just owning what he did.

He takes a step closer. Not much, just enough that I can see the details I was trying to ignore. The tension in his jaw. The way his hands flex at his sides like he wants to reach for me, but doesn't dare. The exhaustion carved into his features, deeper than one day could account for.

"I should have told you," he says quietly. "I should have trusted you with the truth and let you decide. Instead, I made the choice for you, and you almost died because of it. I'll carry that for the rest of my existence."

I want to stay angry. Want to hold onto the betrayal like armor. But looking at him now, seeing the weight of what he's carrying, I feel something loosen in my chest.

Maybe we can get past this. Maybe.

"There's something else," he says.

The loosening stops. "What?"

"I've taken you off field operations. Until further notice."

The words don't register at first. "What?"

"No more missions outside the compound. No donor vetting, no intelligence gathering, no..."

"You benched me."

"I'm keeping you safe."

"You *benched* me." I tighten my hands into fists. The softening I felt moments ago hardens into something sharp and brittle. "I just proved I could hold my own against six attackers. I kept them busy long enough for backup to arrive. And your response is to sideline me?"

"My response is to make sure you're never in that position again."

"That's not your decision to make!"

"It is, actually." His voice is calm. Controlled. The voice of someone who's used to giving orders and having them followed. "I'm responsible for everyone in this compound. That includes you."

"I'm not one of your subordinates. I'm not one of your soldiers. We had a deal: I work for you, you help me find Valentina. That deal included me being useful, not being locked up like some..."

"This isn't about the deal."

"Then what is it about?"

He's quiet for a moment. He steps closer, close enough now that I can smell him, that familiar scent of whiskey and old books and something darker underneath. My body responds without my permission, awareness prickling along my skin.

When he speaks again, his voice is lower. Rougher. "I can't watch you get hurt again. I won't."

"So you're going to control what I do instead."

"I'm going to protect you."

"I didn't ask for your protection!"

"You don't have to ask. It's not optional."

The words hit me like a slap. I stare at him, this man who held me so gently last night, who looked at me like I was something precious, something worth saving. And I see it now, the thing I should have seen from the beginning.

He doesn't see me as a partner. He sees me as something to manage. Something to keep safe in a box where nothing can touch me.

Just like Valentina saw me as something to use.

Different methods. Same result. My choices taken away by someone who decided they knew better.

"Valentina turned me without my consent," I say, and my voice is shaking now. "She took my life, my future, my family, everything I had. And the one thing I had left, the only thing, was deciding what to do with my existence. Who I would be. What I would fight for."

"Celeste."

"And now you're taking that too." I step toward him, anger burning through me, close enough now that I have to tilt my head back to meet his eyes. Close enough to see the way his throat moves when he swallows, the way his pupils dilate when I move into his space. "You get to decide where I go. What I do. Whether I'm allowed to take risks. You made yourself my gatekeeper, just like you're the gatekeeper for everyone else in this city."

"That's not..."

"Do you know what the worst part is?" My voice drops, and I watch him flinch like I've struck him. "You told me about Luciano. About what he did to you. How he controlled you, used you, treated you like property instead of a person. You told me that, and then you turned around and did the same thing to me."

He goes very still.

"I am not your property." The words come out hard and sharp. "I am not yours to command. And I am not going to let you lock me away because you're afraid. I've spent my whole life fighting for the right to make my own choices. I won't stop now."

The mask cracks. Whatever he uses to hold himself together, I just shattered it. His eyes are fixed on me, but not seeing me, like he's looking at something far away. Something terrible. The room seems to darken for a moment.

The silence stretches. I wait for him to argue, to defend himself, to tell me I'm being unreasonable.

He doesn't.

Instead, he turns and walks out of the room without a word.

The door closes behind him with a soft click, and I'm alone.

I stand there for a long moment, staring at the door, waiting for him to come back.

He doesn't.

"What the hell?" I say to the empty room.

I expected a fight. Expected him to push back, to explain himself, to give me something to rage against. Instead, he just... left. Like I'd struck him, and he didn't know how to respond.

I replay the conversation in my head. The apology that almost landed. The moment I felt myself softening, wanting to believe we could fix this. Then the benching, like my autonomy, was something he could grant or revoke at will.

And then...

You told me about Luciano. About what he did to you. How he controlled you, used you, treated you like property. You told me that, and then you turned around and did the same thing to me.

His face when I said that. The way he looked at me, but didn't see me.

I hit something. Something deep.

Good.

He deserved it. He *did* do the same thing. Maybe not as brutal, maybe not as cruel, but the pattern is the same. Control disguised as protection. Decisions made for me instead of with me. My autonomy sacrificed on the altar of his fear.

I won't apologize for pointing that out.

A knock at the door makes me jump.

"Celeste?" Elena's voice, hesitant. "Can I come in?"

I take a breath and try to smooth my expression into something neutral. "Yes."

She opens the door slowly, like she's expecting to find something broken. When she sees me standing by the window, she relaxes slightly, but concern still creases her forehead.

"I saw Maximus leave," she says carefully. "He looked... I've never seen him look like that."

"Like what?"

"Like someone had just put a stake through his chest." She steps into the room and closes the door behind her. "What happened?"

"He benched me. Took me off all field operations because he can't handle the idea of me being in danger." The words come out bitter. "After apologizing for using me as bait. Like taking away my choices is somehow better if he feels bad about it."

Elena is quiet for a moment. She moves to the chair by the bed and sits, her posture careful and contained.

"He told the security team this morning," she says. "Julian argued with him for twenty minutes. Said you'd proven yourself, that sidelining you was a waste of your skills. Maximus wouldn't budge."

"Of course he wouldn't."

"Julian said he's never seen Maximus like this." She pauses. "He said Maximus looked like a man who was terrified of his own decisions but couldn't stop making them."

I don't want to hear this. Don't want to think about what

Maximus is feeling, don't want to consider his perspective when he refuses to consider mine.

"He doesn't get to be terrified and controlling," I say. "He doesn't get to use his fear as an excuse to take away my autonomy."

"No, he doesn't." Elena's voice is steady. "You're right about that. What he's doing isn't fair, and you have every right to be angry."

I look at her sharply, surprised by the validation.

"But," she continues, "I've known him for eight years. I've seen him make hard decisions, ruthless decisions, calculated decisions. I've never seen him make a panicked one. Until now."

"What's your point?"

"My point is that something broke in him. I don't know what, and I don't know if it can be fixed. But the man who walked out of this room just now? That wasn't the Maximus I know. That was someone drowning."

"He's drowning because I told him the truth."

"Maybe the truth was something he needed to hear." She stands, smoothing her clothes. "I'm not here to defend him. I'm here because I care about both of you, and I can see that you're both in pain. What you do with that is your choice. It should be your choice."

She moves toward the door, then pauses with her hand on the frame.

"For what it's worth," she says quietly, "I've never seen him care about anyone the way he cares about you. That doesn't make what he did right. But it might help explain why he's doing it so badly."

Then she's gone, and I'm alone again.

I sink onto the edge of the bed, suddenly exhausted despite having slept all day. My body is healed, but everything else feels raw and wounded.

Elena's words circle through my mind.

I think about the study. The firelight. The letters he'd kept for centuries, preserved because they were all he had left of who he used to be. The way he'd looked at me when I talked about my sister, like he understood loss in a way that went beyond words.

The way he'd touched my face. The way he'd pulled back, afraid of something I couldn't name.

We were building something in those stolen moments between training sessions and strategy meetings. Something fragile and undefined, but real. I felt it when he looked at me. Felt it when he leaned close during sparring and his breath ghosted across my neck. Felt it when he said *I haven't been interested in anything for a very long time* and looked at me like I was the exception to centuries of emptiness.

And now it's shattered.

Not because of the ambush. I could have forgiven that, eventually. Could have understood the tactical reasoning, even if I hated the execution. Could have found my way back to trusting him if he'd shown me that he trusted me in return.

But he didn't. Instead of treating me like a partner, he treated me like something to protect. Something fragile. Something that couldn't be trusted to make her own decisions about her own life.

I stand up and move to the window. The grounds are dark, lit only by security lights along the paths. Somewhere out there, Konstantin is planning his next move. The blood crisis is getting worse. Vampires are going feral from contaminated blood, and Maximus is executing them one by one in that room with the drain in the floor.

And I'm supposed to just sit here, safe and useless, while everyone else fights.

No.

I don't care what Maximus decided. I'm not going to be sidelined. I'll find a way to be useful, with or without his permission. I didn't survive eight months alone, didn't claw my way through the underground to find clean blood, didn't survive six of Konstantin's vampires just to become someone's protected pet.

If he wants to control me, he'll have to do better than walking away.

But even as I think it, even as the anger hardens into resolve, there's something underneath it. Something that aches.

I think about his face in the firelight. The vulnerability he showed me, rare and precious. The way he said *I wanted to know you* like it was a confession he'd never intended to make.

I think about what we might have been in a different world. One where he trusted me as much as I had started to trust him.

No, I don't feel guilty for what I said. He needed to hear it. But I feel the loss of something that never quite existed, the possibility of us, crushed under the weight of his fear and my fury.

Maybe it was always going to end like this. Maybe two broken people can't build something whole.

I head for the door.

Whatever we were, whatever we could have been, I can't think about it now. I have work to do.

Time to find out exactly what "benched" means around here.

CHAPTER
SIXTEEN

I don't remember leaving the medical wing.

One moment I'm standing in that room, her words echoing through me. The next I'm in the east corridor, then the north wing, then somewhere else entirely, moving through my own compound without direction or purpose, just the desperate need to be elsewhere.

You told me about Luciano. How he controlled you, used you, treated you like property. You told me that, and then you turned around and did the same thing to me.

My legs carry me to the training room.

I don't realize where I'm going until I'm there, standing in the doorway, staring at the mats where I first tested her. Where she moved with that fierce precision, adapting to my attacks, refusing to be intimidated by my age or power. Where I first understood that she was something extraordinary.

The room is empty now. Silent. But I can see her everywhere, ducking under my strike, countering with that sharp elbow, the flash of satisfaction in her eyes when she almost took me down.

I walk to the center of the mats and stop.

My hands are shaking. I notice it distantly, the way you notice weather through a window. A fine tremor that starts in my fingers and radiates up through my arms. I curl them into fists, but it doesn't help.

I am not your property. I am not yours to command.

Her voice. But underneath it, another voice. Older. Colder.

You belong to me now, Massimo. Every choice you make, I allow.

The memory slices through me without warning. Not a gradual recollection but a violent intrusion, Luciano's face swimming up from the depths where I've buried it, his cold smile, his elegant hands that could break bones without effort.

I start pacing. Can't stop.

The training room is large, but it feels too small. I walk the perimeter like a caged animal, my footsteps silent on the mats, my mind churning through fragments I've spent centuries trying to forget.

A stone room. Chains on my wrists. Luciano circling me slowly, explaining in that patient, reasonable voice why I needed to submit.

"I'm not punishing you, Massimo. I'm teaching you. You'll thank me eventually. They all do."

I pace faster.

My foot catches the edge of a mat, and I stumble. Catch myself against the wall. Stay there, palm flat against the cool surface, breathing hard despite not needing air.

How long have I been in here? Minutes? Hours? The compound is silent around me, the deep silence of late night.

"You're learning," Luciano said, after I stopped fighting. After I'd been broken so thoroughly I couldn't remember what defiance felt like. "This is what caring gets you. Weapons to be used against you. Weaknesses to be exploited. Love is a leash, Massimo. The sooner you accept that, the less you'll suffer."

Massimo. A name I haven't heard in centuries since I'd chosen a more modern version of my name.

I push off from the wall and resume pacing. The shaking has spread from my hands to my whole body now, a fine vibration, like I'm coming apart at the seams.

I trusted her with that story. Trusted her with the worst thing that ever happened to me. And then I proved myself no better than the monster I described.

It's not optional.

My own words, less than an hour ago.

You don't have to ask. It's not optional.

You belong to me now. Every choice you make, I allow.

The parallel is so clear I don't know how I missed it. The same assumption underneath both statements: *I know better than you. Your autonomy is mine to grant or revoke. Submit, and I'll call it protection.*

I've become him.

The realization buckles my knees. I sink onto the mat, head in my hands.

"Maximus?"

The voice comes from the doorway. I jerk upright, instinctively reaching for composure, for the mask I've worn so long it feels like my real face.

Marcellus stands at the threshold, his expression shifting from concern to alarm as he takes in whatever he sees on my face.

"I've been looking for you for two hours," he says carefully. "You weren't in your study. Weren't answering comms."

Two hours. I've been in here for two hours.

"I'm fine," I say, and my voice comes out rough. Scraped raw.

"You're not." He steps into the room, moving slowly, like approaching a wounded animal. "What happened with Celeste?"

I laugh, and the sound is hollow. "She told me the truth. I didn't want to hear it."

He stops a few feet away, close enough to talk but not crowding. He knows me well enough for that.

"What truth?"

"That I've been treating her the way Luciano treated me." The words come out flat. Dead. "Control disguised as protection. Choices taken away for her own good. The same justifications, the same assumptions, just wrapped in prettier language."

Marcellus is quiet for a long moment. I can feel him studying me, assessing the damage.

"She said that?"

"She didn't have to say it in those exact words. She compared me to him. Said I told her about what he did, then turned around and did the same thing." I stare at my hands, still trembling. "She's right."

"Maximus."

"She's right, Marcellus. I benched her because I was afraid of losing her. I took away her autonomy because my fear mattered more to me than her choices. That's exactly what he did. Exactly. I've become him."

Marcellus is quiet for a moment. "No. You haven't."

I look up sharply.

"Luciano enslaved you for a hundred and fifty years," he says. "Tortured you. Forced you to do unspeakable things. You benched a woman from field duty because you were scared for her safety." His voice is flat, unsparing. "Those aren't the same, and calling them the same insults what you survived."

"But the pattern."

"The pattern is there," he agrees. "You took her choices. Used protection as justification. That's real, and it's a problem. But you're not a monster for being afraid. You're a man who learned the wrong lessons from his trauma and is applying them badly." He holds my gaze. "The question isn't whether you're Luciano. You're not. The question is whether you're going to keep repeating the one part of him that stuck."

I let his words wash over me, weighing them.

"What are you going to do?" he finally asks.

"I don't know." I drag my hands through my hair. "Words won't fix this. I already apologized for the bait situation, and then I made it worse. Another apology would be meaningless."

"So don't apologize. Do something."

I look up at him. "What?"

"You took something from her. Give it back." He crosses his arms. "Not with words. With action. Reinstate her field status. Give her the access you've been withholding. Show her you meant what you said about respecting her choices."

"And if she doesn't believe me? If she thinks it's just another manipulation?"

"Then you keep proving it. Day after day, choice after choice, until she sees the pattern change." He pauses. "Or you give up and let her go. Those are your options."

The thought of letting her go sends a spike of pain through my chest.

"I can't." I stop. Start again. "I don't want to lose her."

"Then stop holding on so tight you crush her." His voice softens slightly. "I've watched you for two centuries. I've seen you control everything around you because control feels safe. But control isn't love, Maximus. It's fear wearing a mask. And she sees through it."

Before I can respond, his comm unit buzzes. He glances at it, and his expression hardens.

"What?" I ask.

"Konstantin. His people hit the Decatur supply depot twenty

minutes ago. Burned it to the ground. No casualties, the staff evacuated in time, but we lost the entire stock."

The Decatur depot. One of our secondary distribution points. A significant loss, but not crippling.

But the timing, while I've been in here falling apart, Konstantin has been moving.

"He's testing us," I say, my mind shifting gears despite itself. The strategic part of my brain waking up, analyzing patterns. "Probing our defenses while we're distracted."

His people who escaped will have reported back by now. He knows we're destabilized.

"Or he's just opportunistic." I stand, muscle memory taking over even as the rest of me still feels shattered. "What's our response capability?"

"Julian is still recovering. I can mobilize a team, but if we retaliate tonight, we're doing it short-handed."

The old instinct surges, take control, make decisions, issue orders. Keep everything locked down tight so nothing else can hurt me.

But that's the same instinct that made me bench Celeste. The same fear dressed up as strategy.

"Don't retaliate tonight," I say. "Secure our remaining assets, increase patrols, but don't engage. I want a full assessment before we act."

Marcellus raises an eyebrow. "That's... measured. For you."

"I'm trying something new."

He studies me for a moment, then nods. "I'll coordinate the response. But Maximus, whatever you're going to do about Celeste, do it tonight. We need everyone to be functional when Konstantin escalates. And right now, neither of you is functional."

He's right. We're compromised, both of us, and Konstantin won't wait for us to sort ourselves out.

"I know," I say. "I'm going to talk to her."

"Talk?" He sounds skeptical.

"Show her. Talk to her. Whatever it takes." I meet his eyes. "You were right. Actions, not words. I'm going to start with the security center."

THE NIGHT SHIFT guards snap to attention when I enter.

"Sir. We heard about Decatur. Marcellus has already issued..."

"I'm not here about Decatur." I move to the primary console. "I need to modify an operational restriction. Celeste Moreau. I placed her on inactive field status earlier today."

"Yes, sir. It's logged."

"Remove it. She's reinstated to full active status, effective immediately."

The guard hesitates, glancing at his colleague. "Reinstated, sir?"

"That's what I said."

His fingers move over the keyboard. "Done. She's cleared for all field operations."

I turn to leave, then pause. "Log the change under my authorization. If anyone questions it, they answer to me."

"Yes, sir."

The walk to her room feels longer than it should. Each step is a choice, a choice to keep moving forward instead of retreating to the safety of control and distance. By the time I reach her corridor, my hands have steadied. The trembling has stopped.

But underneath the calm, something fragile and terrified still pulses.

I stop outside her door. Listen.

Movement inside. The soft pad of footsteps. She's awake, probably pacing the way I was pacing earlier. Two damaged people wearing paths in their respective floors.

I raise my hand to knock, and freeze.

What if she doesn't open the door? What if she opens it and slams it in my face? What if I've destroyed this beyond any possibility of repair?

The fear is a living thing, coiling in my chest. The same fear that made me bench her. The same fear that's driven every terrible choice I've made since I realized I cared about her.

Luciano would be proud. He spent decades teaching me that caring was weakness. I escaped him, killed him, built an empire on his ashes, and I'm still letting him win.

No more.

I knock. Two deliberate raps against the wood.

The footsteps inside stop. A pause. Then they approach the door.

It opens.

Celeste stands in the doorway, still in the black leggings and gray sweater from before. Her dark hair is loose around her shoulders, slightly disheveled, like she's been running her hands through it. Her eyes are guarded, her body tense, braced for another blow.

The sight of her hits me like a physical force. Even now, even with everything broken between us, I want to reach for her. Want to pull her close and promise that I'll never hurt her again.

But promises are just words. And words aren't enough anymore.

"I'm not here to apologize," I say.

Something flickers across her face, surprise, maybe, or suspicion. "Then why are you here?"

"To show you something." I keep my voice steady, though it

costs me. "You've been reinstated. Full active status, effective immediately. I removed the restriction myself."

She stares at me. The guardedness is still there, but underneath it, I see confusion. Like she's waiting for the catch, the condition, the way this will turn into another cage.

"Why?" she asks finally.

"Because you were right. About the pattern." I hold her gaze, refusing to look away despite how exposed I feel. "When you compared me to Luciano, I'm not going to pretend that didn't hit hard. What he did to me... a hundred and fifty years of enslavement isn't the same as benching you from field duty. I know that."

I pause, forcing myself to continue.

"But the pattern is there. Taking your choices away. Using protection as justification. Deciding I knew better than you what you needed." My voice roughens. "That's what he did to me, at the core of it. Wrapped chains in silk and called them safety. I learned that from him, learned it so well I didn't even recognize when I was doing it to someone else."

She's watching me, expression unreadable.

"I'm not him," I say. "But I was using his playbook. And that stops now."

The words hang in the air between us. She's close enough that I can see the faint shadows under her eyes, the tension in her shoulders. Close enough to smell the lavender from the medical wing sheets still clinging to her skin.

Close enough to touch, if I dared.

I don't.

"Konstantin hit our Decatur depot tonight," I continue. "Burned it down while I was..." *Falling apart.* "Dealing with this. He's escalating. We need everyone functional, which means I need you in the field, making decisions, using that tactical mind of yours. Not because I'm over my fear, but because the work matters more than my comfort."

Something shifts in her expression. Not softening, not yet.

"You're serious," she says slowly.

"I'm serious."

"And if I make a choice you don't like? If I take a risk you think is too dangerous?"

"Then I'll tell you my concerns. And then I'll respect whatever you decide." The words feel like swallowing glass, but I mean them. "Your life, your choices. I don't get to override that just because I'm afraid."

She's quiet for a long moment. I can see her processing, weighing, deciding whether to believe me. The silence stretches until it feels like it might snap.

"Okay," she finally says.

My chest loosens slightly. "Okay?"

"I'll watch what you do. That's all I can promise right now." Her chin lifts, that familiar defiance surfacing. "But if you pull something like this again, if you make decisions about my life without my input, I'm gone. No more chances."

"Understood."

We stand there, neither of us moving. The air between us feels charged, electric with everything that's been said and everything that hasn't. I'm acutely aware of the curve of her collarbone above her sweater, the way her lips part slightly.

She notices me looking. Something flickers in her eyes, awareness, maybe.

The pull toward her is almost gravitational. Every instinct screams to close the distance, to cup her face in my hands, to show her with actions what words can't convey.

But I don't get to make that decision for her. What I can do is step back. Give her the space to choose whether she wants me closer.

I step back.

"Goodnight, Celeste."

Something shifts in her expression at the retreat. Surprise, maybe. Or something else I can't name.

"Goodnight," she says. "Maximus."

She closes the door slowly. Not a slam. Just a quiet click, like a sentence ending with a period instead of an exclamation point.

I stand in the corridor for a moment, breathing through the ache in my chest.

It's not fixed. We're not fixed. I may never fully earn back what I destroyed.

But I've started. And for the first time since she told me to leave, I feel like something other than a monster.

I turn and walk toward the security center. There's work to do, Konstantin to counter, networks to protect, a war to fight.

But underneath all of it, a small flame flickers.

Hope.

Fragile, uncertain, but alive.

I'll try to be worthy of it.

SEVENTEEN

CELESTE

The conference room is already half-full when I arrive. Julian stands near the windows, tablet in hand, his expression tight with barely contained +frustration. Marcellus has claimed his usual position near the head of the table, arms crossed, radiating the kind of controlled tension that makes lesser vampires find somewhere else to be. Nadia sits with perfect posture, reviewing something on her phone. Two security officers I recognize from patrol rotations, Ethan and Victor, are murmuring over a spread of maps.

And Maximus.

He's at the head of the table, leaning over documents, one hand braced against the polished wood. The position pulls his jacket tight across his shoulders, emphasizing the breadth of them, the lean strength he usually hides beneath perfect tailoring. He's changed since I saw him at my door. Fresh shirt, dark jacket, every inch the commander his people need him to be. But the shadows under his eyes haven't faded, and when he shifts his weight, I catch the slightest tension in his jaw. A muscle feathering beneath the skin. The kind of tell that comes from holding yourself together through sheer force of will.

He looks up when I enter.

Our eyes meet across the room. Everything else falls away for a single, suspended moment. The other vampires. The crisis. The anger still coiled tight beneath my ribs. There's just him, looking at me like I'm the only fixed point in a spinning room. Those storm-gray eyes holding mine with an intensity that makes my skin prickle, makes me aware of every inch of space between us.

Then he blinks, and the commander is back. A small nod, nothing more, and he returns to the maps.

I take a seat near the end of the table. Not at his right hand. Not claiming authority I haven't earned. Just present. Included.

The room notices.

Ethan glances at me, then away too quickly. Victor's eyebrows rise a fraction of an inch. Julian studies his tablet with sudden, intense focus.

"Now that everyone's here." Maximus's voice cuts through the tension, low and commanding, the kind of voice that makes you want to lean closer even when you're trying to keep your distance. "Let's discuss our response."

He runs through what they know. Timeline of the attack. Damage assessment. Resources lost. His voice is controlled, precise, carrying the weight of centuries of command. This is who he is with them. The strategist. The leader. The vampire who built an empire out of blood and careful planning.

I force myself to focus on the maps instead of the way his hands move when he gestures. Long fingers, elegant but strong. The kind of hands that could snap a neck or cradle a face with equal ease. I'd felt them on my back when he carried me through the compound that first night. Cool and steady and impossibly gentle.

I look away.

"Konstantin hit the depot at 2:47 a.m.," Julian reports. "Incendiary devices, professionally placed. Staff evacuated with three minutes to spare, but we lost the entire stock. Two weeks minimum to rebuild supply lines."

Marcellus outlines defensive adjustments. Nadia reports on redistribution logistics. The discussion flows with the efficiency of people who have worked together for decades, maybe centuries.

I listen. Absorb. Try to understand the shape of what Maximus has built.

But my attention keeps snagging on him. The way he listens when his people speak, actually listens, his head tilted slightly, those gray eyes focused with absolute attention. The way his fingers tap against the table when he's thinking, a slow rhythm, the only tell that his mind is working faster than the conversation. The way the low light catches the sharp line of his cheekbone, the strong column of his throat where it disappears into his collar.

I'm watching too closely. I know I am.

"The attack pattern suggests probing behavior," Marcellus says. "Testing response times, identifying weaknesses. Standard reconnaissance tactics."

"Agreed." Julian pulls up a new screen. "He's gathering intelligence for a larger strike. Question is where he'll hit next."

"Reinforce the remaining depots," Victor suggests. "Increase patrol frequency on supply routes."

Everyone nods. Sound strategy. Protect the assets.

But something bothers me.

I watch them discuss patrol schedules and security protocols, and the itch grows stronger. They're focused on infrastructure. Depots. Routes. Storage facilities. Physical assets.

Konstantin didn't just destroy blood storage tonight. He destroyed a sense of safety. Proved he could reach them when and where he wanted.

What if that's the point?

"The eastern corridor needs double coverage," Maximus is saying. "And I want a full security review of all depot locations by tomorrow night."

"What about the donors?"

The words leave my mouth before I can stop them. Every head in the room turns toward me.

I feel the weight of their attention. Centuries of experience staring at a fledgling who's been here barely more than a week. But I've started now, and retreating would be worse than being wrong.

"Everyone's focused on infrastructure," I say, keeping my voice steady. "Depots. Supply routes. But the network isn't just buildings and blood bags. It's people. And Konstantin didn't just destroy storage tonight. He sent a message."

Maximus is watching me. His expression reveals nothing, but he hasn't interrupted. His body has gone very still, that predator stillness that means he's paying absolute attention.

"If I wanted to break a network like this, I wouldn't just go after buildings. I'd go after people's sense of security. Make them wonder if anywhere is safe. The donors trust you to protect them. What happens to that trust if Konstantin starts targeting them directly?"

Silence.

I'm suddenly aware of how presumptuous this must sound. Eight days here, and I'm questioning the strategy of vampires who've been doing this since before my grandmother was born.

"I could be completely wrong," I add. "I don't know enough to say where he'll hit next. But buildings can be rebuilt. Fear is harder to fix."

More silence. Julian exchanges a glance with Nadia. Victor shifts uncomfortably.

Then Maximus speaks.

"Ethan. Pull the donor residence list. I want a vulnerability assessment on every location by tomorrow night. Cross-reference with Konstantin's known operational patterns." He straightens, and I try not to notice the way the movement draws attention to his height, the lean lines of his body beneath that perfectly tailored jacket. "We've been thinking about this as a supply chain problem. Celeste is right. It's a psychological operation. Konstantin isn't just trying to cut our resources. He's trying to make everyone in this network feel hunted."

Julian leans toward me. "He's never changed strategy mid-briefing based on a fledgling's suggestion," he murmurs. "Just so you know."

I don't respond. Don't trust myself to.

Maximus didn't praise me. Didn't acknowledge what I'd said with anything more than immediate action. He just incorporated it, like my perspective was always supposed to be part of the equation.

That means more than any compliment could have.

The meeting continues for another twenty minutes. Assignments distributed, timelines established, contingencies planned. I follow the discussion, but my awareness has narrowed to a single point. Every time he moves, I track it. Every time he speaks, something tightens low in my stomach. I catalog details I shouldn't be noticing. The way his dark hair falls across his forehead when he leans over the maps. The faint hollow at the base of his throat. The curve of his lower lip when he's considering a problem.

I catch him glancing at me. Just once. A flicker of gray eyes meeting mine across the table, holding for half a second too long before he looks away.

The place where his gaze touched feels warm.

"We reconvene tomorrow night with preliminary assessments," Maximus says finally. "Questions?"

None.

"Then we're done."

Chairs scrape against the floor. The inner circle gathers tablets and documents, conversations splintering into smaller clusters as people file toward the door. Nadia leaves first, already on her phone. Ethan and Victor follow, still debating patrol routes.

Julian pauses near my chair. "Good call on the donors," he says quietly. "Not many people would challenge the room's assumptions their second week in."

"Seemed obvious."

"Obvious things are the easiest to miss when you've been staring at the same problems for a hundred years." He glances toward Maximus, then back at me. Something knowing flickers in his expression. "Get some rest. Tomorrow's going to be long."

Then he's gone, and the room is emptying, and I should stand up and leave with the others.

I don't.

Marcellus is the last to reach the door. He pauses with his hand on the frame, looking back at Maximus. Then at me. Then, at the shrinking distance between us that neither of us has acknowledged.

"I'll make sure you're not disturbed," he says.

The door closes behind him with a soft click.

The silence that follows is deafening.

We're alone. The realization settles into my bones, spreads through me like heat, makes my skin prickle with awareness. The conference room suddenly feels too small, the air too thick, the distance between us both too vast and not nearly enough.

Maximus is still standing at the head of the table, hands braced against its surface. The position makes the tendons in his forearms stand out beneath his rolled sleeves. I hadn't noticed when he'd pushed them up. I notice now. I notice everything now.

He's not looking at the maps anymore.

He's looking at me.

Neither of us moves.

"You were quiet." His voice is different now. Lower. Rougher. The commander stripped away, leaving something rawer underneath.

"I was listening."

"And what did you hear?"

"People who know what they're doing. People who care about protecting what you've built."

"But?"

He sees too much. Always has.

"I already said my piece."

"You held back. I could see you thinking through half the meeting, deciding whether to speak." He pushes off from the table. Takes a step toward me. "What else?"

"Nothing that can't wait."

"I'm asking now."

The distance between us shrinks with each word. He moves around the table slowly, deliberately, like a predator who doesn't need to rush because he knows his prey isn't going anywhere. I should stand. Should put the chair between us, maintain some barrier.

I stand. But I don't retreat.

Now we're on equal footing. Barely three feet apart. Close enough that his scent reaches me. Old books and whiskey and something darker underneath, something that belongs to him alone. I breathed it in when he carried me that first night. I've been trying to forget it ever since.

My body doesn't care about what I'm trying to forget. My body remembers everything.

"You were exactly who you needed to be tonight," I say, and I'm surprised my voice comes out steady. "In the meeting. With them."

"That's who I am with them." His eyes search my face, lingering on my mouth for a fraction of a second before meeting my gaze again. "It's not who I am with you."

"Which version is real?"

"Both." The word is quiet. Heavy. "But only one of them terrifies me."

The admission hangs between us.

"Why?"

"Because I don't know how to do this." He gestures vaguely at the space between us, and I track the movement of his hand, imagine it touching me instead of air. "I know how to command. How to strategize. How to build systems and maintain control. But this?" His jaw tightens. "I don't have a playbook. I can't calculate the right move or anticipate every outcome. You make me feel things I don't know how to manage."

He stops. His throat moves as he swallows.

"And that's terrifying," I finish.

"Yes."

He takes another step. The distance between us shrinks to two feet. I can see every detail now. The individual strands of dark hair that have fallen across his forehead. The fine lines at the corners of his eyes, the only evidence of age on a face frozen at thirty. The way his lips have parted slightly, like he's having trouble remembering he doesn't need to breathe.

Everything in me is drawn toward him. Gravitational.

Inevitable. The space between us feels charged, electric, like the air before a storm.

"I'm still angry," I whisper.

"I know."

"I don't know if I can trust you yet."

"I know that too."

"But watching you tonight. In the meeting. At my door before." My hands are trembling. I curl them into fists at my sides, nails digging into my palms. "You're trying. I can see you trying."

"Is it enough?"

"I don't know yet. But I want it to be."

Something shifts in his expression. Not hope. He's too careful for that. But something adjacent to it. Something raw and wanting that makes the ache in my chest spread lower, settling into places I'm trying not to think about.

He takes another step.

One foot of space between us now. I can feel the cool energy radiating off his body. Can see the faint silver threads in his gray eyes. Can smell that scent, stronger now, making my head swim.

His hand rises. Slowly. Trembling slightly.

It stops an inch from my face.

I can feel the proximity like a phantom touch. The ghost of his fingertips against my cheek. The almost sensation of his palm cradling my jaw. My skin tingles with the anticipation of contact that hasn't happened yet, might never happen, and the wanting is so intense it nearly buckles my knees.

His fingers hover there, trembling. This close, I can see the restraint costing him. The way his whole body has gone rigid with the effort of not closing that final inch. His eyes are locked on mine, searching, waiting.

"Tell me to step back." His voice is strained. Barely controlled. The words seem to scrape out of him. "Tell me and I will."

I should tell him to stay.

Part of me wants to. The part that remembers his face when he found me in that alley, the raw terror in his eyes, the way he whispered *I thought I'd lost you* like the words were being torn out of him. The part that remembers the firelit study and his centuries-old letters and the vulnerability he showed me that night. The part that leaned into his touch and wanted more, wanted everything, wanted him in ways I've never wanted anyone.

His fingertips drift closer. A hair's breadth from my skin. I can almost feel them. Almost.

My whole body aches toward that touch. Every nerve ending screaming for contact. The want is a living thing inside me, clawing at my resolve, demanding I close the distance and take what we both need.

But I need to know something first.

Not whether he would kiss me.

Whether he would stop.

"Step back."

He flinches. Just barely. A fracture in the marble.

But he does it. Immediately. No argument, no negotiation, no pleading. His hand drops to his side, and he takes one step backward, then another, until there's a proper distance between us again.

Three feet of space that feels like miles.

The absence of his almost-touch leaves me cold. My skin aches where his fingers should have been. I want to call the words back, want to close the distance and press myself against him, and forget all the reasons this is complicated.

I don't.

I watch what it costs him instead. The tight jaw. The careful breathing he doesn't need but does anyway. The way his hands curl into fists at his sides, knuckles white with the force of his restraint. The way his whole body seems to strain toward me even as he holds himself still.

Everything in him wants to close that distance. I can see it. Feel it. The wanting between us is a tangible thing, a thread pulled taut, vibrating with tension.

But he doesn't move toward me.

"Goodnight, Celeste."

His voice is rough. Wrecked. Like I've destroyed something in him just by asking him to stop.

I don't trust my voice. I just nod.

I make it to the door before I hear him exhale. A shattered sound. Something breaking apart in the silence behind me.

I don't look back. If I look back, I'll go to him. If I go to him, I'll never know if he could have let me leave.

The corridor is empty. My footsteps echo against the marble as I walk, too fast, toward my room. My whole body is trembling. My skin feels too tight, too sensitive, like every nerve has been scraped raw by what almost happened.

I told him to step back to see if he would.

He did.

Part of me wanted him to refuse. To close the distance anyway, to take the choice out of my hands so I wouldn't have to make it myself. That would have been easier. Simpler. I could have stayed angry, could have pointed to his inability to respect my boundaries as proof that nothing had changed.

Instead, he gave me exactly what I asked for. Stepped back. Let me go.

Proved that my choices matter more to him than his wanting.

I reach my room and close the door behind me, leaning against it, breathing hard even though I don't need air. The phantom sensation of his almost-touch still lingers on my cheek.

The space where his fingers should have landed burns with absence.

I press my hand to my face, covering the skin he didn't touch, and close my eyes.

Leaving was the hardest thing I've done since I died.

But I needed to know he could let me go.

Now I just have to figure out if I can stay away.

EIGHTEEN

I don't go to training.

I wait in my study, not the training room, because I'm not sure my presence there would be welcome. The clock on my desk marks the hour we usually begin. Then the hour after.

She doesn't come looking for me either.

This is what she asked for. Space. Distance. Time to decide if I'm worth trusting again.

I should be patient.

Instead, I'm pacing my study like a caged animal, fighting the urge to go to her door and beg for another chance.

I don't go.

The briefing that evening is torture.

She's there, taking the same seat as before, near the end of the table. Not at my right hand. Not claiming anything. Just present. Her dark hair is pulled back from her face, exposing the elegant line of her neck, the sharp cut of her jaw. She's wearing something simple, black and fitted, and I hate that I notice. Hate that I catalog every detail like a man memorizing something precious before it's taken away.

I force myself to focus on the agenda. On the reports. On the strategic adjustments we need to make.

But I'm aware of her in a way that borders on painful. Every shift of her body. Every time she pushes a strand of hair behind her ear. The way her fingers tap against the table when she's thinking.

I present the updated donor protection strategy. Credit her analysis publicly, because she deserves the recognition, and because I need her to see that I listened.

"Based on the intelligence review, we're reallocating resources to donor protection. The infrastructure can be rebuilt, but Celeste was right. Fear is the real weapon. We need to address that first."

I say her name without looking at her.

If I look at her, I'll lose the thread of whatever I'm saying. I'll forget there are other people in this room.

The briefing ends. I gather my documents. Speak briefly with Marcellus about patrol schedules.

Walk out without looking back.

Every step away from her feels like walking through water. Heavy. Wrong.

I make it to the corridor before I have to stop and press my hand against the wall.

This is what she asked for.

I repeat it like a prayer.

I ROUND a corner near the library, and there she is.

Twenty feet of marble and shadow between us. She's changed since the briefing, wearing something softer now, a gray sweater that looks like it would be warm beneath my hands. Her hair is loose around her shoulders, dark waves catching the low light.

She sees me. Stops.

For a long moment, neither of us moves.

I could close the distance. Could find something to say, some excuse to hear her voice. The wanting is a physical thing, pulling at my chest, urging me forward.

I nod instead. A small inclination of my head, formal and distant.

Then I turn down a different corridor and walk away.

It takes everything I have.

I HAVEN'T BEEN FEEDING PROPERLY.

The hunger is there, a persistent ache beneath my ribs, but it feels muted compared to the other ache that's consumed me. I'm sitting in my study, staring at reports I've already read three times, when the door opens without a knock.

Marcellus takes one look at me and stops.

"You look like hell."

"So I've been told."

"Have you fed? Properly?"

The silence answers for him.

"Maximus." He crosses the room and drops into the chair across from my desk. "She told you to give her space. Not to starve yourself into uselessness."

"I'm giving her what she asked for."

"Are you?" He leans forward. "There's a difference between respecting her boundaries and disappearing entirely. One is what she asked for. The other is avoidance."

"I don't know where the line is."

"Then figure it out. You can be present without being pushy. Available without being demanding." He pauses. "You credited her in the briefing. That was good. But one gesture doesn't rebuild trust. You need consistency. Night after night, choice after choice."

"And if it's not enough?"

"Then you accept that and let her go." His voice softens slightly. "But you're not there yet. She asked for space, not for you to vanish. There's still something worth fighting for."

He stands.

"Feed. And stop hiding in your study." He pauses at the threshold. "You told her you'd prove yourself with actions. Hard to do that when she never sees you."

Then he's gone, and I'm alone with the silence.

He's right. Hiding isn't proving anything. It's just another form of control, deciding for her that she's better off without my presence instead of letting her make that choice herself.

I need to find the middle ground. Present but not pushing. Available but not demanding.

I need to stop disappearing.

I FIND myself outside her door without meaning to go there.

The wood is solid oak, heavy enough to muffle sound. But I can sense her presence on the other side. That awareness of her that's developed over these weeks, tuned to her proximity like a compass finding north.

She's awake. Moving. I hear the soft pad of footsteps, the rustle of fabric.

My hand rises toward the door.

I imagine knocking. Imagine her opening it, her dark hair

loose, her brown eyes wary but not closed. Imagine finding the words to explain what I feel.

I lower my hand.

She asked for space. And I will keep giving it to her, keep proving that her choices matter more to me than my wanting.

Even when my wanting feels like it might hollow me out entirely.

I walk to the training room instead.

It's empty at this hour. Good. I don't want witnesses for what I'm about to do.

I strip off my jacket and push my sleeves past my elbows. The first punching bag hangs from its chain, worn leather waiting to absorb whatever I need to pour into it.

I hit it.

The impact shudders up my arm, satisfying in a way nothing else has been. I hit it again. Again. Finding a rhythm, letting my body take over.

For a few minutes, there's nothing but the strike and the impact. No thoughts of her. No memory of holding my hand an inch from her face. No phantom sensation of almost touching her cheek.

The bag splits on the forty-seventh hit.

Sand pours onto the mats. I stand there, watching my knuckles heal.

It's not enough.

I move to the next bag.

ANOTHER BRIEFING.

I make myself engage this time. Not just present the information and leave, but stay. Be visible. Let her see that I'm here, that I'm not running, that I can exist in her orbit without pushing.

She asks a question about the northeastern sector coverage. Her voice is professional, steady, but I hear the slight hesitation underneath.

I answer her question. Meet her eyes for the first time since the conference room.

Two seconds. Maybe three. Long enough to see the wariness there. Long enough to see something else underneath it, something that might be curiosity or might be hope.

I look away first.

After the briefing, I linger. Not obviously. Just taking my time with the documents, giving her the opportunity to approach if she wants to.

She doesn't.

She gathers her things and leaves with the others, and I watch her go.

But she glanced back once before she reached the door.

That's something.

I spend the following nights in the war room, refining the donor protection protocols. Making notes in the margins. Improving the system she identified as flawed.

If I can't show her who I am with words, I'll show her with work.

I'm deep in the northeastern sector analysis when I feel her.

That pull. That awareness. Like gravity redirecting itself.

I turn and open the door.

She's standing in the doorway, one hand raised like she was about to knock. Her dark hair is loose, falling past her shoulders in waves that catch the low light. Her eyes are uncertain but determined. She's wearing the gray sweater again, soft and fitted, and my fingers ache to know if it feels as warm as it looks.

"Celeste." My voice comes out rough. "Is something wrong?"

"No. I just..." She steps into the room. The distance between us shrinks. "I wanted to look at the donor protection updates. Elena mentioned there were adjustments."

A lie. We both know it.

I don't call her on it.

"Of course." I gesture toward the table, trying not to notice the way my hand wants to reach for her instead. "The files are there. The northeastern sector still has some gaps."

She moves closer. Stops at the edge of the table and looks down at the files. I don't think she's seeing them.

"You've been thorough," she says quietly.

"It's important. You were right to flag it."

She looks up. Our eyes meet across the scattered papers.

The shadows under her eyes match mine. She hasn't been resting well either. Some selfish part of me is glad. The rest of me wants to fix it, to make everything easier for her, even if that means staying away.

"Why didn't you come to training?" she asks.

The question lands like a blow. She noticed. She cared.

"I wasn't sure if you wanted me there."

"I didn't say I didn't want you there. I said step back. In that moment. That room."

"I know." I struggle to find the words. "But I didn't want to assume. Didn't want to push into spaces where you might not want me."

"I needed to know you could respect my choices. That doesn't mean I needed you to disappear."

Something cracks in my chest.

"I'm sorry. I'm not good at this. At knowing where the line is."

"Neither am I."

The admission hangs between us. An offering.

I move around the table before I can stop myself. Slowly. Carefully. Giving her every chance to tell me to stop.

She doesn't.

I stop two feet away.

Close enough to smell her, that scent that's been haunting me, something floral and warm underneath the compound's antiseptic air. Close enough to see the slight tremor in her hands. Close enough to count her eyelashes if I wanted to, dark against her pale skin, framing those eyes that see too much.

"I've thought about you constantly." The words escape before I can catch them. "Every hour. I kept walking to your door and stopping myself. Kept reaching for you in rooms where you weren't."

Her breath catches. The small sound undoes something in me.

"Maximus."

"I know I'm not supposed to say this. I know you asked for space." I stop. Force myself to breathe even though I don't need to. "But you're here. And I can't pretend I don't want you closer. I can't pretend these past nights haven't been the longest of my existence."

"Don't." Her voice is barely a whisper. "Don't say anything else."

I go still.

We stand there, two feet apart, the space between us thick with everything we're not doing. I can feel the pull toward her. Can see her feeling it too. The wanting is a living thing, straining against the leash I've wrapped around it.

My hands flex at my sides. Every instinct screams to close the distance, to cup her face in my palms, to kiss her until neither of us can think.

I don't move.

She asked me to stop. And I will keep stopping, keep stepping back, keep proving myself, for as long as she needs.

"I should go," I say. The words feel like swallowing glass.

"Yes."

I don't move.

"Maximus."

"I know." The breath I release is ragged. "I know."

I make myself turn. Make myself walk toward the door. Every step is an act of will. Every inch of distance feels like something tearing.

I'm almost there when I hear her move.

Footsteps. Quick. Determined.

"Maximus. Wait."

I stop. Turn.

She's standing in the middle of the room, her hands curled into fists at her sides, her eyes blazing with something I'm afraid to name.

"I'm done waiting," she says. "I'm done hiding. I'm done using my freedom to build walls against the one person I actually want to let in."

I don't move. Don't breathe.

"Celeste..."

"You stepped back when I asked you to. You gave me space. You proved that my choices matter more to you than your wanting." She takes a step toward me. Then another. "So now I'm making a choice."

"What choice?"

She crosses the remaining distance. Stops close enough that her scent floods my senses.

"Don't step back this time." Her voice is low. Certain. "Don't walk away. Don't give me space."

My control shatters.

CHAPTER
NINETEEN

CELESTE

I watch the words land.

Don't step back this time.

Something shifts in his expression. The careful control he's been wearing like armor cracks down the middle, and what's underneath steals the breath I don't need.

Want. Raw and desperate and barely contained. The same want I've been fighting for days, reflected back at me in those storm-gray eyes.

He moves.

Not slow this time. Not careful. He closes the distance between us in one stride, and then his hands are on my face, cupping my jaw, tilting my head back. His palms are cool against my cheeks, his fingers threading into my hair, and the touch I've been dreaming about is nothing compared to the reality.

"Tell me to stop." His voice is wrecked. Scraped raw. "Tell me and I will."

"I don't want you to stop."

Something breaks behind his eyes.

His mouth crashes into mine.

The kiss is nothing like I imagined. I thought it would be tentative. Careful. Two people testing boundaries, negotiating terms.

This is none of those things.

This is hunger. This is days of distance collapsing into a single point of contact. This is every almost and every not yet, and every time he walked away when he wanted to stay, all of it pouring out of him and into me.

His lips are cool and firm, moving against mine with an urgency that makes my knees weak. One hand slides from my face to the back of my neck, fingers tangling in my hair, angling my head for better access. The other drops to my waist, pulling me closer until there's no space left between us.

I grab the front of his shirt to anchor myself. The fabric bunches in my fists, and I feel the solid wall of his chest beneath it, the lean muscle I've watched during training sessions, the body I've tried not to think about late at night in my room.

He makes a sound against my mouth. Low and rough and desperate. It vibrates through me, settles somewhere deep in my core, and I want to hear it again. Want to know every sound he's capable of making.

I kiss him harder.

His restraint shatters completely.

He walks me backward until my spine hits the wall, and the impact barely registers because his mouth is on my jaw now, my neck, the sensitive spot below my ear. His lips trace a path of fire across my skin. His hands grip my hips like he's afraid I'll disappear if he lets go.

"Celeste." My name in his mouth, reverent and ruined. He breathes it against my throat like a prayer. "I've wanted this.

Wanted you. Since that first night in the alley. Since you looked at me like I was just a man."

I pull his mouth back to mine because I can't stand another second without it.

The second kiss is deeper. Slower. He takes his time now, learning the shape of me, the taste. His tongue slides against my lower lip and I open for him, and the sound he makes when I do is something I want to remember forever.

My hands find their way to his hair. It's softer than I expected, thick and dark, and when I drag my fingers through it, he groans into my mouth. His hips press me harder against the wall. I feel every inch of him, solid and cool and wanting.

This is what I was afraid of.

This is what I was waiting for.

His mouth moves to my jaw again, my neck, the curve of my shoulder. Each kiss leaves a trail of sensation that lingers long after his lips have moved on. My head falls back against the wall, and I don't try to stop the sounds escaping me.

"Do you have any idea," he murmurs against my collarbone, "what these past nights have been like? Knowing you were here. Wanting you. Unable to reach for you."

"I know." I tug his head up, force him to meet my eyes. "I know exactly what it was like."

Something flickers in his gaze. Understanding. Recognition. Two people who have been drowning in the same ocean, finally finding each other.

He lifts me.

My back slides up the wall, and I wrap my legs around his waist on instinct, pulling him closer. The position changes every-thing. Now I'm looking down at him, my hands braced on his shoulders, my hair falling like a curtain around both our faces.

His eyes are fixed on mine. Dark and wanting and absolutely certain.

"Beautiful," he breathes. "You're so beautiful."

I kiss him before he can say anything else. Before the words can make me feel things I'm not ready to examine. His hands grip my thighs, holding me steady, and his mouth moves against mine with a thoroughness that makes me forget everything else.

There is only this. Only him. Only the way our bodies fit together like they were designed for it.

But it's not enough.

The wanting has been building for too long, through too many nights of distance and denial. Now that I've let myself have this, have him, I need more. Need everything.

"Maximus." His name comes out breathless. Pleading.

He pulls back just enough to look at me. His eyes are dark, pupils blown wide, and his lips are swollen from my mouth. He looks wrecked. He looks beautiful.

"What do you need?" His voice is rough. Strained. "Tell me what you need."

"More." The word escapes before I can stop it. "I need more."

Something shifts in his expression. The hunger that's been simmering beneath the surface rises up, hot and undeniable.

"Are you sure?"

I answer by rolling my hips against him.

He groans, low and deep, and his forehead drops to my shoulder. I feel him shudder against me, feel the effort it takes for him to hold still.

"Celeste." My name is a warning. A plea. "If you keep doing that, I'm not going to be able to stop."

"I don't want you to stop."

His head comes up. His eyes search mine, looking for doubt, for hesitation.

He finds none.

"Hold on to me," he says.

I tighten my arms around his neck, and he shifts his grip. One hand stays under my thigh, holding me against the wall with effortless strength. The other slides up, trailing fire across my hip, my waist, the curve of my ribs.

He pauses at the hem of my sweater.

"Yes?" he asks.

"Yes."

His hand slips beneath the fabric. Cool fingers against my skin. I gasp at the contact, at the sensation of him touching me. His palm flattens against my stomach, and I feel myself tremble beneath it.

"So perfect," he murmurs against my throat.

His hand moves higher. His fingertips trace the ladder of my ribs one by one, counting them, mapping them, learning the architecture of my body. Each brush of his touch sends shivers radiating outward, building anticipation for where he might go next.

He reaches the underside of my breast and pauses.

My breath catches. My whole body goes taut with waiting.

"Don't stop," I breathe.

He doesn't.

His palm curves over me, cupping me through the thin fabric of my bra, and the contact drags a moan from somewhere deep in my chest. His thumb traces a slow circle, finding the peak through the lace, and the sensation shoots through me like lightning. I arch into his touch, pressing myself more firmly into his hand, wanting more pressure, more friction, more of him.

"So responsive," he murmurs against my ear. "Every little sound you make. Every way your body moves. I want to learn all of it."

His thumb continues its lazy circles, and I can feel myself growing desperate beneath his touch. The lace of my bra creates friction against the sensitive peak, amplifying every movement of his fingers. He rolls the hardened nub between his thumb and forefinger, a gentle pressure that makes my hips jerk against him involuntarily.

"That's it," he breathes. "Show me what you like."

I'm beyond words. Can only clutch at his shoulders as his hand works me through the fabric, as the heat builds low in my belly, spreading outward with every stroke of his fingers.

But it's still not enough.

"Please." I don't recognize my own voice. Desperate. Needy. "Please, Maximus."

"Please, what?" His lips brush my ear, his breath cool against my skin. "Tell me exactly what you want. I need to hear you say it."

"Touch me." The words come out ragged, torn from somewhere I didn't know existed. "Lower. I need you to touch me lower."

He goes still. For one agonizing moment, I think he's going to pull back, going to be noble and restrained, going to make me wait.

Then his hand begins its descent.

Slowly. So slowly it makes me want to scream. His fingers trail down over my ribs, my stomach, tracing the waistband of my leggings like he's memorizing the boundary. His touch is feather-light, teasing, and I squirm against him, trying to guide his hand where I need it.

"Patience," he murmurs, and there's a dark amusement in his voice that makes me shiver. "I've waited days for this. I intend to savor it."

"I can't wait." The confession escapes before I can stop it. "I've been thinking about this. About you. Every night alone in my room, I've been thinking about your hands."

His fingers pause at my waistband. I feel the tremor that runs through him at my words.

"Tell me." His voice has dropped to something rough and urgent. "Tell me what you thought about."

"Your fingers." I'm past the point of embarrassment, past caring how desperate I sound. "I thought about your fingers inside me. Thought about what it would feel like to have you touch me. To make me come."

He makes a sound that's almost a growl, and his hand slips beneath the fabric of my leggings.

The first brush of his fingers over my underwear makes me gasp. Even through the thin barrier, I can feel the cool pressure of him, the deliberate way he traces the shape of me. He explores slowly, mapping the territory, learning what makes me twitch and shudder.

"You're soaked," he breathes against my neck, and the rawness in his voice makes me clench. "I can feel how much you want this. How much you want me."

I can only nod, my fingers digging into his shoulders as he continues his exploration. His fingers press more firmly, finding the bundle of nerves at the apex of my thighs through the fabric, and my whole body jerks.

"There," I gasp. "Right there."

He circles the spot slowly, watching my face, cataloging every reaction. The pressure is perfect and not enough all at once. I need more. Need him closer.

"Please," I whisper. "I need to feel you. Really feel you."

He pulls back just enough to meet my eyes. The storm gray has darkened to something closer to midnight, and the intensity in his gaze makes my breath catch.

"Are you certain?"

"Yes." The word comes out steady. Certain. "I want your fingers inside me. I want to feel you."

He holds my gaze as his hand shifts, as his fingers hook into the waistband of my underwear and slide beneath. The first touch of his bare fingers against my slick flesh makes us both groan.

"God," he breathes. "You're so wet. So ready for me."

His fingers glide through my arousal, spreading it, exploring the terrain with devastating thoroughness. He traces every fold, every ridge, learning my body with the same focused attention he brings to everything else. When his fingertip grazes my entrance, I whimper.

"Here?" he asks, circling the opening with agonizing slowness.

"Yes. Please. Yes."

He presses inside.

One finger, sliding in slowly, giving me time to adjust to the intrusion. The sensation of being filled, even by just this small part of him, makes my inner walls clench. He pauses when he's buried to the knuckle, letting me feel the fullness, the stretch.

"More," I breathe.

He withdraws almost completely, then presses back in with two fingers this time. The additional stretch burns for a moment before melting into pleasure. He sets a slow rhythm, pumping in and out, curling his fingers with each stroke to press against a spot inside me that makes sparks dance behind my eyes.

"You feel incredible," he murmurs against my throat. "So tight. I could do this forever. Could spend hours just learning what makes you moan."

His thumb finds my clit, circling in counterpoint to the thrust of his fingers, and the dual sensation rips a cry from my throat. He swallows the sound with a kiss, his tongue mimicking the rhythm of his hand.

The pressure builds. Each stroke of his fingers, each circle of his thumb, winds the coil tighter in my core. I'm trembling now, my thighs shaking where they grip his waist, my fingers clawing at his shoulders.

"That's it," he breathes against my lips. "I can feel you getting close. Feel the way you're tightening around my fingers."

He increases the pace. His fingers pump faster, deeper, curling on each thrust to hit that spot that makes me see stars. His thumb presses harder against my clit, the circles tighter, more focused.

"I've imagined this," he says, his voice rough velvet in my ear. "Every night since I met you. Imagined what you'd look like when you came apart for me. Imagined the sounds you'd make. The way you'd feel."

His words push me higher. The tension is unbearable now, a wave about to crest.

"I've imagined it too," I manage, my voice barely recognizable. "Thought about your hands. Your mouth. Thought about you when I was alone."

He groans, and his fingers move faster. A third finger presses at my entrance, a question.

"Yes," I gasp. "Please. More."

He slides the third finger in alongside the others, and the fullness is overwhelming. He stretches me perfectly, fills me completely, and when he curls all three fingers against that sensitive spot inside me, I shatter.

The climax crashes through me like nothing I've ever felt. Wave after wave of pleasure radiates from where his fingers are buried inside me, pulsing through my core, my thighs, my entire body. I cry out his name, and he catches the sound with his mouth, kissing me through the peak, his fingers continuing to move, drawing out every last tremor.

"That's it," he murmurs against my lips. "Let go for me. I've got you. I've got you."

His thumb gentles on my clit as the aftershocks roll through me, his fingers slowing their rhythm, easing me down from the high. But he doesn't withdraw. He keeps his fingers inside me, letting me feel him there, a constant presence as my body slowly stops shaking.

I sag against the wall, boneless, and he holds me up with one arm, his other hand still buried between my thighs. His forehead presses against mine. His breath mingles with mine.

"That," he says quietly, reverently, "was the most beautiful thing I've ever witnessed."

I laugh, shaky and breathless. "You're six hundred years old. You've seen a lot of things."

"None of them compare to you." He pulls back just enough to look at me, and the tenderness in his expression makes my chest ache. "Nothing compares to you."

I kiss him. Soft. Sweet. A thank you and a promise all at once.

His fingers slide out of me slowly, and I shiver at the loss, at the sudden emptiness where he was. He brings his hand up between us, and I watch, transfixed, as he examines his glistening fingers in the low light.

He holds my gaze.

And slowly, deliberately, brings them to his lips.

His tongue traces along each finger, licking them clean, and the sight of it sends a fresh wave of heat through my already spent body. His eyes never leave mine as he tastes me, as he savors me like I'm something rare and precious.

"Oh," I breathe.

"I intend to taste you properly," he says when he's finished, his voice dark with promise. "When we have more time. When I can spread you out beneath me and take my time and make you come apart on my tongue. Again and again until you're begging me to stop."

The words send another pulse of want through me. I'm already thinking about it, already craving it, imagining his dark head between my thighs, his mouth where his fingers were.

"I'm going to hold you to that," I manage.

"I'm counting on it."

He kisses me again, and I taste myself on his lips, a strange intimacy that makes something warm unfurl in my chest. His arms wrap around me, holding me close, and for a moment there's nothing but this. Nothing but him.

The door bangs open.

We wrench apart. He sets me down so fast the room spins, one hand shooting out to steady me as I find my footing. I'm acutely aware of how I must look, flushed and disheveled, my sweater askew, my leggings twisted.

Marcellus stands in the doorway.

His expression is grim. Whatever he sees on our faces, the swollen lips, the obvious evidence of what we were doing, doesn't change it.

"We have a problem," he says. "A big one."

Maximus's commander mask slides into place. The transformation is instant, jarring. One second he's the man who was inside me, who tasted me on his fingers, who looked at me like I was everything. The next he's the vampire lord who's survived six centuries by being harder and colder than everyone else.

But his hand lingers on my waist for half a second before it falls away.

"What happened?"

"Konstantin didn't hit another depot." Marcellus's jaw tightens. "He hit donors. Six of them. Coordinated strikes at their homes across the city. All within the last hour."

The words are ice water.

Six donors. Not infrastructure. People. People who trusted the network to keep them safe.

"He has their addresses," I say, the realization churning my stomach. "He knows who they are."

"Which means he has access to information he shouldn't have." Maximus's voice is flat. Controlled. But I can feel the tension radiating off him. "We have a leak."

I think about what I said in the briefing. About Konstantin targeting people instead of buildings. About making them feel unsafe.

I was right.

It doesn't feel like a victory.

"It gets worse." Marcellus holds out a piece of paper. "He left a message. Same note at every location. Pinned to the bodies."

Maximus takes it. Reads it. His expression empties.

"What does it say?" I ask.

He hands me the paper. Five words, written in elegant script:

This is just the beginning.

The chill that runs through me has nothing to do with temperature.

"There's one more thing." Marcellus's voice is careful now. Gentler than I've ever heard it. "One of the donors who was killed. It was Clara Ellis."

The name hits me like a physical blow.

Clara Ellis. The woman I vetted on my first solo mission. The woman who asked good questions and wanted to know exactly what she was getting into. The woman who trusted me when I told her she'd be safe.

I vetted her. I brought her into the network.

And now she's dead.

"Celeste." Maximus's voice cuts through the spiral. His hand finds mine. Squeezes. "This isn't your fault."

"I vetted her. A week ago."

"And Konstantin has been planning this for months. He didn't kill her because of anything you did."

I know he's right. Logically, I know it.

But the guilt sits heavy in my chest anyway, a stone I don't know how to put down.

Marcellus disappears to coordinate the response. The door closes behind him, and for a moment it's just the two of us again, standing in the war room with the taste of each other still on our lips and the weight of six deaths pressing down.

Maximus turns to me. The commander slips, just for a second, revealing the man beneath.

"I'm sorry," he says quietly. "For the interruption. For all of this."

"Don't apologize for a crisis."

"I'm not apologizing for the crisis." His thumb brushes across my knuckles, a small gesture that shouldn't make my chest ache the way it does. "I'm apologizing because I know what that moment meant. What it cost you to let me that close. And now..."

"Now we have work to do."

"Yes." He doesn't let go of my hand. "But this isn't over. What's between us. It isn't over."

"I know."

"Whatever comes next, whatever we're walking into, I need you to know something first." He steps closer. Cups my face with his free hand, his thumb tracing along my cheekbone. "I don't regret a single second of what just happened. And when this is over, when we've dealt with Konstantin and the leak and whatever else he throws at us, I intend to pick up exactly where we left off."

My breath catches at the promise in his voice.

"Is that a threat?"

"It's a guarantee." He leans down and presses a kiss to my forehead. Soft. Reverent. "Now let's go find out who betrayed us."

He releases me and moves toward the door, and I take a moment to collect myself. To straighten my clothes. To smooth my hair. To try to look like a professional instead of a woman who just came apart on the most powerful vampire in the city's fingers.

I fail. I don't care.

He pauses at the door, looking back at me. Something warm flickers in those gray eyes.

"Together?" he asks.

The question means more than just walking into a meeting.

"Together," I answer.

We walk out of that room side by side.

Everything is falling apart. Donors dead, a traitor in our midst, Konstantin circling closer with every strike.

But his hand brushes mine as we move through the corridor. Just barely. A secret between us.

And for the first time since I died, I'm not facing the darkness alone.

TWENTY

The next hour is controlled chaos.

I move through it on autopilot, issuing orders, coordinating responses, managing the crisis with the part of my brain that's been doing this for centuries. The other part is still standing in that conference room, her taste on my lips, her hands gripping my forearms, the soft sound she made when I deepened the kiss.

Focus. Six people are dead. There will be time for everything else later.

The inner circle assembles in the security center rather than the conference room. Screens cover the walls, showing feeds from across the city. Red markers indicate the six locations where donors were killed. Six homes. Six families destroyed.

Julian runs point on coordinating with our people in the field. Nadia manages communications with the surviving donors, those we can still reach, those who haven't already fled. Marcellus stands at my shoulder, a solid presence I've relied on for two centuries.

And Celeste.

She's positioned near the back of the room, watching everything with those sharp eyes. Learning. Absorbing. She hasn't spoken since we left the war room, but I can see her processing the information, fitting pieces together.

When our eyes meet, something passes between us.

"Confirmed kills at all six locations," Julian reports. "Clean strikes. Professional. They were in and out within minutes."

"Security footage?"

"Disabled at each site before the attacks. They knew exactly where the cameras were."

The implication hangs heavy in the room. They had inside information. Not just donor addresses, specific security details.

"Pull the access logs," I say. "I want to know everyone who's had access to donor files in the last month."

"That's a significant list," Nadia says carefully. "Anyone in coordination, security, medical."

"Then we check every name."

The tension in the room thickens. I'm asking them to investigate each other. To look at colleagues, friends, as potential traitors.

It's necessary. That doesn't make it pleasant.

"Sir." Ethan steps forward, and for once the restless energy has focused into something sharp. "You need to see this. It was delivered to the main gate five minutes ago. I've already pulled security footage of the delivery and started a trace on the courier service."

He hands me the tablet. On the screen is a photograph of an envelope, formal, cream-colored, sealed with red wax. The kind of thing Konstantin would find amusing.

"Courier was human. Paid cash. Said a man gave him the envelope outside a coffee shop in Midtown, but the description is useless. Average height, average build, hat, and sunglasses. I've got people checking camera footage in the area, but I'm not optimistic. It's been scanned for threats. Clean."

"Bring it to me."

Two minutes later, I'm holding the envelope. The wax seal bears Konstantin's mark, a serpent eating its own tail. Pretentious bastard.

I break the seal and remove the letter inside. Heavy paper, elegant script. He always did have expensive taste.

Maximus,

By now, you've discovered that your network is not as secure as you believed. Six donors tonight. How many tomorrow? How many the night after?

This war of attrition serves neither of us. You will lose eventually, we both know this. The only question is how much you're willing to sacrifice before you accept the inevitable.

Surrender the network. Swear fealty. Do this, and I will be merciful. Your people will be absorbed into my organization with their positions intact. Even your new pet, the fighter you've been keeping so close, will be spared, provided she learns her proper place.

Refuse, and I will burn everything you've built. Starting with her.

You have until dawn to decide.

—K

I read it twice. The first time for content. The second time for the rage to settle into something cold and useful.

He knows that Celeste matters to me. That she's become something worth threatening.

"What does it say?" Marcellus asks.

I hand him the letter without comment. Watch his expression darken as he reads.

"He's making it personal," Marcellus says.

"He's trying to. He thinks threatening her will make me careless." I take the letter back, fold it precisely. "He's wrong."

But my hands aren't quite steady, and Marcellus notices.

"What do you want to do?" he asks quietly.

"I want to tear his throat out with my bare hands. What I'm going to do is find his leak, cut it off, and make him regret ever speaking her name." I turn to the room. "Continue the investigation. I want preliminary findings within the hour. No one leaves the compound until we've identified how Konstantin got his information."

The others scatter to their tasks. I catch Celeste's eye and nod toward the door.

She follows me into the corridor.

We walk in silence through the compound, away from the chaos of the security center. I don't have a destination in mind, I just need to move, to think, to process everything that's happened in the last two hours.

The kiss. The attack. The letter.

Even your new pet, the fighter you've been keeping so close, will be spared.

The words burn in my chest like acid.

"What did the letter say?" Celeste asks.

I consider lying. Consider protecting her from the knowledge that she's become a target.

But I promised her honesty. I promised her choices.

"Konstantin is offering terms. Surrender the network, swear

fealty, and he'll spare everyone." I pause. "He mentioned you specifically."

She stops walking. "Me?"

"He knows you're important to me. He's using that as leverage."

I watch her process this. The fear that flickers across her face, quickly suppressed. The anger that replaces it.

"He threatened me to get to you."

"Yes."

"And you're telling me this because..."

"Because you deserve to know. Because I promised I wouldn't make decisions about your life without your input." I turn to face her fully. "And because I need you to understand what we're dealing with. This isn't just about territory or blood supply anymore. He's going to come after you specifically. Use you to hurt me."

"Then maybe I should leave." The words are flat, pragmatic. "Remove the leverage."

"No." The word comes out sharper than I intended. I force myself to soften. "That's your choice, if you want to make it. But running won't protect you; it'll just make you an easier target. Here, at least, I can..."

I stop myself.

"You can what?" she asks. "Protect me?"

"I was going to say that. Then I remembered I'm trying not to do that."

Something shifts in her expression. Not quite a smile, but close.

"You can say it," she says quietly. "The instinct isn't the problem. It's whether you let it override my choices."

"Then yes. Here, I can help protect you. If you want to stay."

"I want to stay."

The relief that floods through me is embarrassing in its intensity. I nod, not trusting my voice.

We walk a bit further, ending up in one of the smaller sitting rooms. Empty at this hour, quiet, lit only by the security lights outside the windows.

Celeste sinks onto a couch and stares at nothing. The exhaustion shows on her face now, not physical, but emotional. The weight of everything that's happened pressing down on her.

"Clara Ellis," she says quietly. "She trusted us."

"I know."

"She asked good questions. Wanted to know exactly what she was getting into before she committed. I told her we'd keep her safe." Her voice cracks slightly. "I gave her my word."

I sit beside her. Not touching, but close.

"You didn't kill her."

"No. But I was part of the system that failed her."

"We all were."

She's quiet for a moment. Then: "Does it get easier? Losing people?"

The question cuts deeper than she knows. I think of all the faces over the centuries, humans I cared about, vampires I trusted, people who died because of me or despite me.

"No," I say honestly. "But you learn to carry it differently. The weight doesn't get lighter. You just get stronger."

She looks at me then, and I see the grief in her eyes. The guilt. The overwhelming sense of responsibility for something she couldn't have prevented.

I want to fix it. Want to say the right words that will make her pain disappear. But some things can't be fixed with words.

So instead, I do something I haven't done in a very long time.

I open my arms.

She doesn't move at first. Just looks at me with something

fragile and uncertain in her expression. Then she leans into me, her head against my shoulder, her body fitting against mine.

I hold her. Not with passion; there will be time for that later. Just hold her, the way I should have held people centuries ago instead of pushing them away. The way I'm learning to be with her.

"I'm sorry," I murmur against her hair. "About Clara. About all of this."

She doesn't respond with words. Just presses closer, her fingers curling into the fabric of my shirt.

We stay like that for several minutes. The silence isn't uncomfortable, it's necessary. Sometimes presence matters more than words.

Eventually, she pulls back slightly. Her eyes are dry, but there's a rawness to her expression that tells me the grief isn't finished. It's just been set aside for now.

"What are you going to do?" she asks. "About Konstantin's ultimatum?"

"Refuse it. Obviously."

"And then?"

"Find his leak. Cut off his intelligence. Make him fight blind." I pause. "Beyond that, I'm still strategizing."

She's quiet for a moment, something working behind her eyes. "I want to do something. I can't just sit here while people die."

"You're not sitting here. You're part of this." I hold her gaze.

She exhales, the frustration not gone but tempered by acceptance. "Fine. Then let's focus on what I can do. The leak."

"What about it?"

"I've been thinking about it since Julian mentioned the security footage. Konstantin's people knew exactly where the cameras were at six different locations. That's not something you learn from a single source."

I lean back slightly, giving her space to work through it. "Go on."

"Nadia said the access list would include coordination, security, and medical. But camera positions aren't in donor files. Those are in security files. Separate system, right?"

"Correct."

"So either the leak has access to both systems..." She pauses, something sharpening in her expression. "Or there's more than one leak."

The thought has occurred to me. I've been hoping I was wrong.

"It's possible," I admit. "But two traitors operating independently? The odds are..."

"What if they're not independent?" She sits up straighter, the grief pushed aside as her tactical mind engages. "What if they're connected? Family, friends, something that would explain why two people would both betray you?"

"We vet for those connections."

"How thoroughly? And how recently?"

Our vetting process is extensive, but it focuses on the initial screening. Ongoing relationships, new ones formed after someone joins the network, those are harder to track.

"You're suggesting someone was turned after they started working for us."

"Or compromised. Threatened. Bribed." She meets my eyes. "I'm new here. I don't know your people. But I know that loyalty can be bought or broken. What changed in the last few months? New staff? Someone with money problems? Someone with family outside the compound who could be leveraged?"

I stand, pacing toward the window. She's right; we've been looking at who had access, not what might have changed to make someone willing to share it.

"There are a few with family," I say slowly. "Their families are human and live outside the compound."

"Could Konstantin have gotten to them?"

"It's possible." The thought sickens me. "But I don't want to accuse anyone without evidence."

"I'm not saying it's anyone specific. I'm saying it's a vulnerability."

I turn back to face her. "You're good at this."

"I spent three years in the underground. You learn to read people. Figure out who's reliable and who'll sell you out for the right price." A shadow crosses her face. "I didn't always get it right. But I learned."

"What else do you see?"

She considers. "The timing. Konstantin's attacks have been escalating: the scrying, the depot, and now the donors. But his intelligence has been perfect. Every strike exactly where it hurts most." She pauses. "That's not luck. That's someone who knows your priorities. Who knows what matters to you."

"Someone close."

"Maybe. Or someone who's been watching for a long time."

The thought chills me. How long has Konstantin had eyes inside my operation? Weeks? Months? Longer?

"There's something else," Celeste says. "The letter. He mentioned me specifically."

"I told you..."

"I know what you told me. But think about it. How did he know I mattered to you? I've been here eight days. I've been on two missions. Most of that time I've spent training or in the medical wing."

The question stops me cold.

She's right. To an outside observer, Celeste should look like any other new recruit. Useful, perhaps, but not significant. Not someone worth naming in an ultimatum.

Unless someone told Konstantin otherwise.

"The leak isn't just sharing logistics," I say slowly. "They're sharing observations. Personal ones."

"Someone who's seen us together. Who noticed that you're..." She trails off.

"Different with you."

"Yes."

The circle of suspects narrows dramatically. Not just anyone with file access, someone close enough to observe my behavior. Someone in the inner circle itself.

"That limits the possibilities," I say.

"It also raises the stakes. If the leak is someone close to you..."

My comm buzzes before she can finish. Marcellus's voice: "We found something. You need to see this."

I meet Celeste's eyes. Whatever we've discovered here, it will have to wait.

"On my way."

I stand, offer her my hand. She takes it, lets me pull her to her feet. For a moment we're standing too close, her hand still in mine, the weight of everything between us, the kiss, the grief, the danger, the growing understanding that whoever is betraying us knows exactly what she means to me.

"This isn't over," I say quietly. "What you figured out matters. You matter."

"I know." Her fingers squeeze mine briefly before releasing. "Let's go see what they found."

THE SECURITY CENTER has transformed in our absence.

Maps cover every available surface. Data streams across multiple screens. Julian and Nadia are huddled over a tablet while Marcellus stands at the main display, his expression carved from stone.

"Report," I say.

Marcellus pulls up a series of timestamps. "We traced the access logs for donor addresses and security camera positions. Two separate systems, two separate access points, but the queries happened within minutes of each other."

"Two people?"

"One terminal. The access credentials belong to Cyrus Knight."

The name hits like a physical blow. Cyrus Knight, my security coordinator. Something cold settles in my stomach. "Security coordinator. He has access to camera feeds."

"All of them," Marcellus confirms. "Internal and external. It's part of his job."

I think about every corridor we've walked together. The training room. The conference room.

Cyrus saw all of it. Reported all of it.

That's how Konstantin knew Celeste mattered. Not because someone in my inner circle talked, but because someone was watching us through my own security system.

"He's been watching," Celeste says quietly. She's made the same connection. "That's how Konstantin knew about me. Footage."

"Where is he now?" I ask.

"That's the problem." Marcellus's jaw tightens. "He's gone. Left the compound approximately two hours ago, right before the donor attacks began. Security footage shows him exiting through the east gate."

"Alone?"

"Yes. He told the gate guard he was running an errand. Standard protocol for senior staff."

Which means he walked out freely, with whatever information he'd gathered, and delivered it directly to Konstantin.

"Find him," I say. "Quietly. I want him brought back alive."

"Already deployed teams. But Maximus," Marcellus hesitates. "There's something else. We pulled his communication logs. He's been in contact with an outside number for the past three months. The calls are encrypted, but we traced the number to a burner phone purchased in Konstantin's territory."

Three months. Cyrus has been feeding information to Konstantin for three months.

"His family," I say slowly. The pieces are falling into place. "Before he was turned."

Marcellus nods grimly. "Wife and daughter. He was turned forty years ago, but he never stopped watching them. The wife has since passed, but his daughter has children now, grandchildren he's never met. They live in Decatur."

"And Konstantin found out."

"They weren't at their residence when we sent someone to check."

So Konstantin has them. A family who probably doesn't even know Cyrus is still alive, that the husband and father they buried decades ago has been watching over them from the shadows. And now they're leverage.

The rage is cold now, focused. Konstantin didn't just attack my network; he destroyed a family to do it. Took a good man and forced him into an impossible choice.

I feel Celeste's presence beside me before I see her. She's been quiet, listening, absorbing. When I glance at her, I see understanding in her eyes.

She knows what I'm thinking. What I'm feeling. The guilt

that's already starting to settle in my chest, because Cyrus's family is in danger, and that's at least partially my fault for not seeing the threat sooner.

"We'll find them," she says quietly. "His family. We'll get them back."

I don't know if that's possible. But I nod anyway.

"Increase compound security to maximum," I tell Marcellus. "No one leaves without my explicit authorization. And start a full review of everyone's external contacts. If Cyrus was compromised through his family, others might be vulnerable too."

"Understood."

The others disperse to execute orders. I stand in the center of the room, surrounded by maps and data and the evidence of my failure.

Celeste hasn't moved.

"You should rest," I tell her. "Tomorrow will be worse."

"Probably." She doesn't leave. "What are you going to do?"

"Plan. Prepare. Figure out how to respond to Konstantin's ultimatum without getting more people killed."

"That's not what I meant." She steps closer, lowering her voice. "What are you going to do right now? Tonight? For the next few hours?"

I don't have an answer. The honest truth is that I'll probably stand here running scenarios until dawn, trying to find a path forward that doesn't end in disaster.

"I don't know," I admit.

"Then let me stay." Her hand finds mine again, a small gesture, hidden from anyone who might be watching. "You don't have to do this alone anymore."

The words crack something in my chest that I didn't know was still intact.

"Celeste."

"I know the timing is terrible. But you just found out someone you trusted for years betrayed you, and I'm not leaving you alone with that."

She's not offering passion. Not offering distraction. She's offering presence. The same thing I offered her when she was grieving Clara.

Learning from each other. Growing together.

"Okay," I say quietly. "Stay."

We stand there in the security center, hands clasped, watching the screens track the search for a man who used to be my friend.

Dawn is coming. Konstantin's deadline approaches. And everything I've built is more fragile than I knew.

But for the first time in a very long while, I don't feel I'm facing it alone.

CHAPTER
TWENTY-ONE

Dawn approaches like a held breath.

We've been in the security center for hours; Maximus coordinating the search for Cyrus, Marcellus managing compound lockdown, Julian and Nadia running communications with our remaining donors. I've done what I can, which isn't much. Mostly I watch. Learn. Try to be useful without getting in the way.

The screens show the city lightening from black to gray. Konstantin's deadline expires with the sunrise.

"Nothing," Julian reports, frustration bleeding through his professional tone. "Cyrus knows our search patterns. He's avoiding them."

"Keep looking," Maximus says. His voice is steady, but I can see the tension in his shoulders, the tightness around his eyes. He hasn't rested. Neither have I.

"Sir." Nadia looks up from her console. "Dawn in four minutes. We need to seal the compound."

The blackout protocols. Vampires can't function in daylight;

we go dormant whether we want to or not. The compound will lock down, and whatever happens next will have to wait until sunset.

Maximus nods. "Seal it. Skeleton crew on monitoring, humans only. Everyone else, rest while you can."

The others move to execute his orders. The screens flicker as external cameras switch to automated recording. Heavy shutters begin closing over windows throughout the compound.

I feel the pull of dawn like a weight settling into my bones. Eight months of this, and I still hate the loss of control, my body deciding when I sleep, whether I agree or not.

"You should rest," Maximus says. He's beside me suddenly, close enough that I can smell him. "Tomorrow will be worse."

"You keep saying that."

"It keeps being true."

I want to argue. Want to insist I can push through, stay awake, be useful. But the dawn pull is already dragging at me, making my thoughts sluggish.

"What happens when Konstantin realizes you've refused his ultimatum?"

"He escalates. Hits us again, harder. Tries to force compliance through attrition." Maximus's jaw tightens. "Or he does something unexpected. With three months of intelligence, he knows us well enough to improvise."

"That's not reassuring."

"It's not meant to be."

The last of the shutters close. The compound is sealed, a fortress against the sun. Around us, vampires are retreating to their quarters, surrendering to the biological imperative that makes us vulnerable during the day.

"Come on," Maximus says quietly. "I'll walk you to your room."

We move through corridors that are emptying quickly. The

humans on staff: Elena, Dr. Dalton, and the security personnel who can function in daylight, will maintain operations while we sleep.

At my door, we stop. The hallway is empty now; everyone else already in their quarters.

"Get some rest," he says.

"You too."

Neither of us moves.

What happened in the war room hours ago hangs between us, unfinished, interrupted, still burning under my skin. More than a kiss. So much more. The memory of his hands on me, inside me. The way he watched me fall apart. The dark promises he whispered against my throat.

I want to reach for him. Want to pull him into my room and finish what we started. Want to give him what he gave me, want to learn every sound he makes when he's the one coming undone.

But we're both exhausted, both frayed from crisis, and whatever this is between us deserves better than desperation.

His eyes drop to my mouth. Just for a second. But I see it.

"After," I say quietly. "When this is over."

"After," he agrees.

His hand comes up, brushes my cheek once, a whisper of contact that sends warmth spreading through my chest. Then he steps back.

"Sleep well, Celeste."

"You too."

I watch him walk away until he turns the corner. Then I go inside, close the door, and let the dawn take me.

I WAKE TO CHAOS.

The sun has barely set, I can feel it in the heaviness still clinging to my limbs, but someone is pounding on my door.

"Celeste!" Nadia's voice. "Security center. Now."

I'm dressed and moving in under a minute, vampire speed carrying me through corridors that are already filling with activity. Something happened while we slept. Something bad.

The security center is crowded when I arrive. Maximus stands at the central display, Marcellus at his shoulder. Julian is running through data on a tablet, his expression grim.

And in the corner, restrained by two security vampires, is Cyrus Knight.

He looks terrible. Clothes torn, face bruised, the defeated posture of a man who's lost everything. When his eyes meet mine, I see no defiance. Just exhaustion and something that might be relief.

They found him.

"Report," Maximus says. His voice is ice.

"Teams located him at a motel in Brookhaven," Marcellus says. "He didn't resist. Came willingly once we explained we weren't going to kill him immediately."

"That remains to be seen." Maximus turns to face Cyrus fully. "Forty years. Forty years you've served me. And for the last three months, you've been feeding information to Konstantin."

Cyrus doesn't deny it. "Yes."

"Why?"

The single word hangs in the air. I watch Cyrus's face, the way his jaw works, the struggle to find words that might matter.

"He has them," Cyrus says finally. "My family. My daughter is fifty-three now. Has two kids of her own. They don't know I exist. Don't know, I've been watching over them since I was turned. But Konstantin found out." His voice cracks. "He sent me photos. My granddaughter at her school. My grandson at soccer practice. My daughter getting groceries. And then he sent me a video of his people standing outside their house."

The room is silent.

"He said if I didn't cooperate, he'd turn them. All of them. Let them wake up as vampires with no guidance, no support. Let them go feral." Cyrus's hands are shaking despite the restraints. "What was I supposed to do?"

I think about my sister Simone in Savannah. About the trust fund Maximus set up to take care of her. About what I would do if someone threatened her life.

I'm not sure my answer would be different from Cyrus's.

"You could have come to me," Maximus says. "Told me what was happening. We could have protected them."

"Could you?" Cyrus looks up, and there's something raw in his eyes. "Konstantin has people everywhere. He knew things about my family that even I didn't know. Where my granddaughter takes dance lessons. Which coffee shop my daughter goes to every morning. He's been watching them for months. Maybe years." He shakes his head. "If I told you, he would have known. And he would have killed them."

"So instead, you betrayed everyone here. Got six donors killed. Gave Konstantin three months of intelligence on our operations."

"I know." Cyrus's voice is barely a whisper. "I know what I did. I'm not asking for forgiveness. I'm just telling you why."

Maximus is silent for a long moment. I can't read his expression; it's locked down, controlled, revealing nothing.

"Where are they now?" he asks finally. "Your family."

"I don't know. Konstantin moved them after I left the compound. Insurance, he said. To make sure I didn't talk." Cyrus's laugh is bitter. "But I'm talking now. Because he's going to kill them anyway. I've served my purpose. They're just loose ends."

"You don't know that."

"I know him. I've been listening to his communications for three months. I know how he thinks." Cyrus looks at Maximus directly. "He doesn't leave loose ends. Ever."

The weight of that settles over the room.

"What do you know?" Maximus asks. "About his operations. His plans."

"I know where some of his safe houses are. I know the names of three other people he's tried to turn inside your organization; they refused, so he had them killed. Made it look like accidents." Cyrus swallows. "And I know what he's planning next."

"Tell me."

"He's not going to wait for you to surrender. He knew you'd refuse. The ultimatum didn't matter. He just needed you to refuse it publicly so he'd have justification for what comes next.

"Which is?"

"He's planning to expose the full scope of your network. Not to humans, not yet. But to the other vampire lords in Atlanta."

"They already know I have a network," Maximus says.

"They know you have a network. They don't know how big it's become." Cyrus's voice is hollow. "He has documentation of everything. Every donor, every safe house, every vampire who answers to you. The full map of your operations across the entire city. He's going to show them you control more of Atlanta than all of them combined."

I watch Maximus absorb this. His expression doesn't change, but something shifts behind his eyes.

"When?" he asks.

"Soon. Within the week. He's already sent messages to the other lords. Requesting a gathering to discuss 'matters of mutual concern.'" Cyrus swallows. "Once they see the full picture, how much power you've consolidated, they'll view you as the threat, not him. By the time it's over, you'll have the entire city against you. And then he'll take everything."

The silence stretches.

Maximus turns to Marcellus. "Contact our people in the neutral territories to have them prepared. I'm going to set up a meeting with the other lords on neutral ground, following formal protocols. The meeting will be within forty-eight hours."

"They're not going to want to meet," Marcellus says. "Not if Konstantin's already been talking to them."

"They'll meet. Because if they don't, it confirms they've already sided with him. And that becomes its own problem." Maximus looks at Julian. "Pull all intelligence on Konstantin's safe houses. Cross-reference with Cyrus's information. I want possibilities for where he's holding the family."

"Sir?" Julian sounds uncertain.

"Separate operation. Marcellus, pull together a team. Small, fast, capable of extraction. We find where Konstantin is holding them, and we get them out."

Marcellus's expression tightens. "That's a significant risk for a traitor's family."

"It's leverage Konstantin shouldn't have. And it's the right thing to do." Maximus's voice is flat. "Cyrus made his choices. His family didn't."

I watch this exchange, seeing the calculation behind Maximus's decisions. He's not doing this out of forgiveness. He's doing it because it weakens Konstantin's position and because innocent people shouldn't be pawns.

Maximus turns back to face Cyrus. "Anything else?"

"The gathering he's calling, it's not just to expose you. He's going to offer the other lords a deal. Join him in containing your expansion, and he'll share the network once he takes it. Everyone gets access to clean blood, and you're isolated." Cyrus's voice cracks. "I'm sorry. I didn't want any of this."

"But you did it anyway." Maximus's voice is cold. "Take him to a holding cell. Comfortable, but secure. No communications. We'll deal with him after I handle the other lords."

The security vampires escort Cyrus out. The room is still crowded, but people are moving to their assignments. Marcellus heads toward the communications station. Julian pulls up data on his tablet.

For a moment, no one is standing close enough to hear.

I step near Maximus, keeping my voice low. "I'm not sure I would have done differently. If someone had Simone."

He doesn't look at me. Just keeps his eyes on the screens. But his jaw tightens.

"You would have come to me first," he says quietly.

"Maybe." I pause. "Or maybe I would have been too scared they'd find out."

He's silent for a long moment. Then nods once, barely perceptible.

People start moving, assignments are distributed, and the machinery of response is grinding into motion. I hang back, waiting until the others have dispersed.

"Are you taking me with you?" I ask. "To meet the other lords?"

"Yes."

"Why?"

Maximus considers the question. "Because Konstantin has been telling them stories about you. The fighter I've been keeping close. My new weakness. If I show up without you, it looks like I'm hiding something. If I show up with you, they can see for themselves that you're an asset, not a liability."

"So I'm a prop."

"You're a statement." He meets my eyes. "And I trust you to make a good impression."

There's more in that sentence than the surface meaning. He trusts me. After eight days, after everything that's happened, he trusts me.

"What if I make things worse?"

"You won't."

"How do you know?"

"Because I've watched you. In training, in crisis, in the quiet moments between. You read situations. You adapt. You know when to speak and when to listen." Something softens in his expression. "And you don't back down from things that scare you. The other lords will respect that, even if they don't like it."

I don't know what to say to that. The faith he's placing in me feels heavier than any assignment.

"When do we leave?" I ask instead.

"Tomorrow night. I need to arrange the meetings first, send messages, call in favors, make sure we're received as guests rather than threats." He pauses. "Tonight, we prepare. And you rest."

"I just woke up."

"Then eat. Train. Do whatever you need to do to be ready." His hand brushes mine, a brief contact hidden from the others still moving around the room. "We'll talk more later. Alone."

The promise in those words sends heat through my chest.

"I'll be ready," I say.

I turn to leave, but his voice stops me.

"Celeste."

I look back.

"What you said earlier. About Cyrus, what you would have done in his position." He's watching me with an intensity that makes my breath catch. "I've been thinking about it."

"And?"

"And I understand why you said it. Because you're thinking about your sister. About what you'd sacrifice to protect her."

I don't deny it.

"But here's what I can't reconcile," he continues, his voice quiet but hard. "Cyrus chose to save three people, his daughter and two grandchildren, by putting hundreds of lives at risk. Six donors are already dead. The network that keeps those hundreds of vampires from going feral, from starving, from becoming the monsters humans fear, he compromised all of it. For three people."

The words settle like stones in my chest.

"I understand the instinct," Maximus says. "I even understand the choice. But understanding doesn't make it right. He valued three lives he loved over hundreds of lives that depended on him. And now I have to clean up the damage while those three are probably already dead anyway."

It's brutal. Cold. But it's also true.

"I saw how you reacted to Clara Ellis's death," he says quietly. "The guilt you carried even though you weren't responsible. You understood that her life mattered, not just to you, but in itself. That's the difference." He pauses. "If someone threatened Simone, you'd come to me. We'd find another way. Because you wouldn't be able to live with yourself if you saved her by sacrificing people who trusted you."

"I would have come to you," I say.

"I know." Something eases in his expression.

He turns back to the displays before I can respond, already focused on the next crisis.

I leave the security center with his words echoing in my head.

Trust. That's what this comes down to. Not just attraction, not just convenience. He's trusting me with his operation, his reputation, his future. And I'm trusting him with mine.

Whatever happens next, we're in it together.

TWENTY-TWO

I wake at sunset.

The screen in front of me is dark, my hand still resting on the keyboard where dawn pulled me under mid-sentence. Vampire dormancy doesn't care about convenience. When the sun rises, consciousness simply stops, like a switch being flipped. No dreams, no awareness, just forced shutdown until darkness returns.

I went down in the middle of composing a message to Lord Dmitri.

I complete it now, choosing each word with the precision of someone defusing a bomb. Because that's what this is. Political explosives that could detonate in my face if I'm not careful.

Lord Dmitri, I request a formal audience at your earliest convenience. Recent developments require discussion among Atlanta's established powers. I propose neutral ground within 48 hours. The matter concerns us all.

Professional. Urgent without seeming desperate. The phrase "established powers" is deliberate, a reminder that Dmitri and I have been here longer than Konstantin, that we built this city's vampire infrastructure before he arrived with his ambitions and his army.

I send it. Then I compose similar messages to the others:

Lady Vivienne in Buckhead. Lord Chen in East Atlanta. Lord Okonkwo in West End. Lady Santos in Midtown.

Five lords total, not counting myself or Konstantin. Five potential allies, or five potential enemies, depending on how convincingly Konstantin has been whispering in their ears.

Cyrus's confession echoes in my mind. Konstantin requested a gathering to discuss "matters of mutual concern." That gathering hasn't happened yet. I would have heard. Which means I have a narrow window to reach them first. To present my side before Konstantin poisons the well.

My phone buzzes. Dmitri's response arrives in under three minutes:

LORD DMITRI

Lord Maximus. Tomorrow. 9 PM. The Whitley. Bring no more than two. —Dmitri

The Whitley. An abandoned hotel in neutral territory, maintained by all of us for exactly this purpose. Formal meetings, treaty negotiations, the rare occasions when Atlanta's vampire lords need to sit across from each other without the home advantage. Lord Dmitri's use of my full title even in a text message is characteristic. The man hasn't relaxed his formality in four centuries.

Agreed.

One down. Four to go.

Lady Vivienne responds next, then Lord Chen. Both agree to tomorrow night, same location, same terms. Lord Okonkwo takes an hour but eventually confirms. Lady Santos doesn't respond at all, which is its own kind of answer. She's either already committed to Konstantin or staying out of it entirely.

Four lords are willing to meet. That's enough.

I forward the confirmations to Marcellus with instructions: Full security detail. Compound on lockdown while we're gone. If this is a trap, I want everyone here protected.

MARCELLUS

Already arranged. Celeste?

She's coming with me.

Three dots appear. Disappear. Appear again. Finally:

MARCELLUS

Good. You'll need her.

I stare at that message longer than I should. Marcellus has gone from openly distrusting Celeste to endorsing her presence at the most critical political meeting I've had in decades. The shift happened somewhere between watching her fight off six attackers and seeing her tactical mind at work during the crisis meetings.

I find her in the training room.

She's alone, which surprises me. The space is empty except for her, moving through combat forms with the fluid precision of someone who's been fighting her whole life. Her dark hair is pulled back, and she's wearing simple training clothes. Black tank top, dark pants, bare feet on the mat.

I stop in the doorway and watch.

I shouldn't. I should announce myself, discuss the meeting, and maintain the professional distance I've been desperately clinging to since Marcellus interrupted us two nights ago. But instead, I stand here like a fool, watching the way she moves. The economy of motion. The controlled power in every strike.

I had my fingers inside her. I felt her come apart against me, watched her face as pleasure shattered her, tasted her on my fingers while she watched with those dark eyes gone wide.

I haven't been able to think about anything else since.

She executes a spinning kick, and her tank top rides up, exposing a strip of pale skin at her waist. The same skin I touched in the war room. The same skin that trembled beneath my palm as I slid my hand lower, lower, until I found where she was slick and wanting.

My hands curl into fists at my sides.

"Are you going to stand there all night, or are you going to tell me why you're here?"

She hasn't turned around. Hasn't broken her form. But she knew I was watching. Of course she did.

"We need to talk," I say, stepping into the room. My voice comes out rougher than intended. "The meeting is set. Tomorrow night, nine o'clock."

Now she turns. Her eyes find mine across the training room, and something shifts in the air between us. The same electricity that's been crackling since our interrupted moment. The same tension I can't seem to escape, no matter how hard I try.

She's flushed from exertion, the telltale sign that she's fed recently. A faint pink blooms across her cheekbones, her throat. I remember pressing my lips there. Remember the sounds she made when I did.

"That's fast," she says.

"I rarely make requests. That probably means something." I move closer, stopping at the edge of the mat. Maintaining distance. If I get too close, I don't trust myself. "Four of the five lords agreed to meet. Santos didn't respond, which likely means she's either with Konstantin already or staying neutral."

"So we need to convince the other four."

"Three of the four. Chen will likely follow Dmitri's lead. They have history. If we can get Dmitri and either Vivienne or Okonkwo, we have a majority."

She nods, appearing to process. "What do I need to know?"

This is why she's valuable. No panic, no hesitation. Just immediate focus on what needs to be done.

And yet I can't stop noticing the way her chest rises and falls with each unnecessary breath. The way her lips part slightly as she listens. The way her tongue darts out to wet them, and I remember those lips opening for me, remember the taste of her mouth, remember the sounds she made against my tongue while my fingers worked inside her.

"Maximus?"

I blink. She's watching me with raised eyebrows, waiting.

"Lord Dmitri is formal," I say, forcing my mind back to the task at hand. "Russian aristocracy, turned in the 1600s. He values tradition, protocol, respect for hierarchy. Address him as 'Lord Dmitri,' never just 'Dmitri.' Don't speak unless spoken to first. And never interrupt him."

"Got it. What about Vivienne?"

"The opposite. French court, turned during the Revolution. She despises formality, considers it a mask for weakness. She'll try to provoke you, test whether you can think on your feet. If you're too deferential, she'll dismiss you. If you push back intelligently, she'll respect you."

"And Chen?"

"Careful. Patient. He thinks in terms of centuries, not years, and he won't commit to anything without considering long-term implications. But if he does commit, he's absolutely loyal."

Celeste nods, filing it away. "Okonkwo?"

"West African nobility, turned in the 1700s. He values honesty above everything else, considers deception beneath him. Don't try to manipulate him. Don't dance around the truth. Just tell him what you need and why."

"Four ancient vampires with completely different approaches to politics." She almost smiles. "Should be fun."

"It's not a game, Celeste."

"I know." Her expression sobers. "I also know that walking into that room scared is the fastest way to get eaten alive. So I'm choosing not to be scared."

"It's not that simple."

"Isn't it?" She tilts her head, studying me. "You taught me that. In the training room, my second day here. Fear is a choice. You can acknowledge danger without letting it control you."

She's quoting my own words back at me. I'm not sure whether to be impressed or annoyed.

"This is different," I say. "These aren't Konstantin's soldiers. These are vampires who've been playing power games longer than most civilizations have existed. One wrong word, one moment of weakness, and they'll..."

"They'll what? Kill me?" She steps closer, and I force myself not to step back. "It's not like I haven't almost died since I met you, Maximus. I'm getting used to it."

"That's not funny."

"It's not meant to be." She's close now. Close enough that I can smell her. The same scent that filled my lungs in the war room when I had her pressed against the wall, when her head fell back, and she gasped my name.

I've been trying not to think about it for two days. I'm failing spectacularly.

"I'm going into that room tomorrow, whether you think I'm

ready or not," she says. "So instead of trying to talk me out of it, maybe focus on making sure I'm prepared."

She's right. I know she's right. But every instinct I have screams to keep her here, to lock her in the compound where Konstantin can't touch her, where ancient vampires with centuries of political cunning can't destroy her with a well-placed word.

I've already tried controlling her. I've already tried protecting her by taking away her choices.

I won't make that mistake again. Even if watching her walk into danger might kill me.

"There's one more thing," I say. "Wait here."

I go to my private quarters and retrieve a small leather box from my desk drawer. It's nothing special to look at. Worn leather, brass hinges, no ornamentation. But what's inside has been with me for over six hundred years.

When I return to the training room, Celeste is watching me with curiosity.

"What is that?"

"A statement." I open the box.

Inside, nested in black velvet, is my signet ring.

Heavy gold, wide band, engraved with my family's mark. A stylized M intertwined with symbols that marked my family in fourteenth-century Italy, when I had a name that mattered.

"It's beautiful," Celeste says quietly.

"It's mine. Was my father's before, and his father's before that." I lift the ring from the box. The gold catches the light, gleaming against my fingers. "Luciano took it when he turned me. I took it back when I killed him."

Her expression shifts. She understands what I'm not saying. That this ring represents everything I lost and everything I fought to reclaim.

"Every vampire in that room will know what it means when they see it on you."

Her eyes snap to mine. "Maximus."

"It's a claiming gesture," I say. The words come out rougher than I intended. "Everyone in that room will see it and understand exactly what it signifies. That you're mine. That you act with my authority. That anyone who threatens you answers to me."

Mine. The word settles into my chest, and I remember the possessive surge that flooded through me in the war room. The primal satisfaction of feeling her clench around my fingers, of hearing her cry out my name, of watching her face as she shattered for me.

She's quiet for a long moment, her gaze moving between my face and the ring in my hand.

"Every vampire in that room will look at me and know exactly what I am to you," she says slowly. "What am I to you?"

The question hangs between us. I should have an answer. A political answer, a strategic answer, something that explains this in terms of alliances and assets and tactical advantages.

But when I open my mouth, nothing comes out.

Because the truth is too much. The truth is something I haven't let myself name, haven't let myself examine too closely, because if I do, I'll have to acknowledge that I'm falling. That I've been falling since the moment she looked at me in that alley and saw a person instead of a monster. That what happened in the war room only accelerated a descent that was already inevitable.

"You're trusting me with more than my own safety," she says when I don't answer. "You're asking me to carry your reputation into that room. Your name. Your legacy."

"Yes."

"And if I fail? If I say the wrong thing, show weakness, make a mistake?"

"You won't."

"But if I do. It damages you. Maybe permanently."

"I know."

She studies me, searching for something in my expression. I don't know if she finds it.

"Why?" she asks. "Why trust me with that much?"

Because I can't imagine walking into that room without you beside me. Because somewhere in the last two weeks, you became essential, and I don't know how to undo it. Because I'm terrified of what I feel for you and even more terrified of losing you. Because two nights ago I had my fingers inside you and I've thought of nothing else since, and I want more, want everything, want to spend hours learning every way to make you fall apart.

"Because you've earned it," I say instead. It's true, even if it's not the whole truth.

She holds my gaze for a long moment. Then she extends her hand, palm up.

Something in my chest tightens.

I take her hand before I can second-guess myself. Her fingers are cool in mine, slender, scarred across the knuckles from years of fighting. I remember these fingers gripping my shoulders in the war room. Remember her nails digging into my skin through my shirt as she came.

I slide the ring onto her finger. Too large. It slips loosely past her knuckle.

"Wait here."

I return a moment later with a gold chain. Not delicate, but solid links with weight to them, the kind that won't break if someone grabs it in a fight.

Without asking permission, I thread the ring through the chain and step closer to fasten it around her neck. My fingers brush the nape of her neck, and she goes very still.

Her skin is cool beneath my touch. Soft. I remember tracing this same skin, remember the way she shivered when my lips found the spot just below her ear.

I take longer than necessary to fasten the clasp. Let my fingers linger against her neck, her shoulders, the top of her spine. She doesn't move. Doesn't breathe.

The ring settles against her chest, just below her collarbone. Right over her heart.

My ring. Against her skin.

Something primal settles in my chest. Something possessive that I thought I'd buried centuries ago.

Mine.

She looks down at the ring resting against her, then back up at me. We're standing too close. I can see the flecks of amber in her dark eyes, the faint scar at her temple, the curve of her lower lip. I can see the way her breath has quickened.

Two nights ago, I touched her. Two nights ago, I learned what sounds she makes when she's close, when she's desperate, when she shatters. Two nights ago, I tasted her on my fingers and promised her more.

We haven't had more. There hasn't been time, not with the crisis consuming every waking hour, not with six donors dead and a traitor unmasked and Konstantin's threat growing by the day.

But standing here now, with my ring against her heart and her scent filling my lungs, I can't remember why any of that matters.

"Maximus." Her voice is barely above a whisper.

"I know." I force myself to step back, to put distance between us before I do something inadvisable. "We need to focus on tomorrow. On what's coming."

"And after?"

The words hang between us. Loaded. Dangerous.

I remember what I promised her in the war room. *When we*

have more time. When I can spread you out beneath me and take my time and make you come apart on my tongue.

I've been thinking about that promise constantly. Imagining it. Wanting it so badly it's become a physical ache.

"After," I say, and my voice comes out rough, barely controlled, "I intend to make good on every promise I made you in that war room."

Her breath catches. I watch her throat move as she swallows.

"Every promise?"

"Every single one." I hold her gaze, letting her see exactly what I mean. "I told you I wanted to taste you properly. I told you I wanted to take my time. I meant it."

Her lips part slightly. I can see her remembering, can see the heat building in her eyes.

"That sounds like a threat," she says, but her voice is unsteady.

"It's a promise."

The tension between us is unbearable. Every instinct I have screams to close the distance, to back her against the nearest wall, to finish what we started. My hands ache to touch her. My mouth aches to taste her.

But tomorrow matters. The meeting matters. If I touch her now, I won't stop. And we both need to be sharp for what's coming.

"You should prepare," I say, and the words cost me more than I want to admit. "Review the files again. Make sure you have all of this straight in your head."

She nods, but she doesn't move. Neither do I.

The moment stretches. The air between us grows thicker. I watch her fingers drift up to touch the ring at her chest, tracing the engraved M, and the sight of it does something to me that I don't have words for.

"I won't let you down," she says finally, and there's something raw beneath the confidence. "I know what you're risking by bringing me. I know what it costs you to trust anyone."

"You're not just anyone."

The words are out before I can stop them. She goes still. I don't take them back.

The silence stretches between us, charged and dangerous. I should say something. Clarify. Retreat behind professionalism and strategy. But I'm tired of retreating. I'm tired of pretending that every moment in her presence doesn't feel like the first time I've been alive in centuries.

"I should go," she says. Her voice is strained. "If I stay here much longer, I'm going to do something that will make both of us useless for tomorrow."

"That would be inadvisable."

"Very inadvisable."

Neither of us moves.

"Celeste."

"I know." She takes a deliberate step backward. Then another. Putting distance between us that feels like miles. "Tomorrow. We focus on tomorrow."

"Yes."

She's at the door now, her hand on the frame, her body half-turned toward the corridor. The ring glints against her chest.

"Maximus?"

"Yes?"

"We're going to win tomorrow. You know that, right?"

I want to believe her. Want to have her confidence, her certainty that we can walk into a room of ancient vampires and convince them to side with us over Konstantin.

"I hope you're right," I say.

"I am." She almost smiles. "Because we're not going in there asking them to save us. We're going in there showing them we're the better bet. That we're strong, united, and more valuable as allies than enemies."

She lifts the ring from her chest, letting it catch the light one more time.

"Besides," she adds, "I'm wearing your ring now. Which means I'm part of you. And you don't lose."

She leaves before I can respond.

I stand alone in the training room, staring at the empty doorway. My body is still humming with want. My mind is still full of her. The scent of her lingers in the air, and I breathe it in, knowing I shouldn't, unable to stop myself.

Tomorrow, Celeste will walk into a room full of predators wearing a ring that marks her as mine. She'll stand beside me, and she'll hold her ground, because that's who she is.

And I'll watch her do it. Terrified. Proud.

Falling.

The word catches in my mind, and I can't shake it loose.

I close the empty box and return to my quarters to prepare for tomorrow. Because she's right about one thing. I don't lose.

I just never expected winning to feel this much like surrender.

TWENTY-THREE

The dress is waiting on my bed when I awake.

Black. Floor-length. Nothing like the soft, pretty things human women wear to galas and weddings. This is structured, architectural, a gown that looks like it was designed by someone who understood that beauty and danger aren't opposites.

I run my fingers along the fabric. Heavy, matte, with a subtle texture that catches the light. The bodice is fitted, boned like a corset but flexible enough to move in. The neckline cuts low enough to display the ring resting against my chest. The back is open nearly to my waist. And the skirt, fitted through the hips, then falling to the floor with slits up both sides that would let me kick, run, fight if I needed to.

There's no note. There doesn't need to be.

Beside the dress: boots. Black leather, heeled but sturdy, rising to mid-calf. Not decorative. Functional.

He thought of everything.

I pick up the dress and hold it against my body, studying my reflection in the mirror. The neckline plunges in a deep V, and I imagine his eyes following that line. Imagine his gaze tracing the exposed skin, remembering what his hands felt like there. What his fingers felt like lower.

Heat coils in my stomach.

I shouldn't be thinking about this. Not now, not with everything at stake tonight. But my body doesn't seem to care about political alliances and vampire lords. My body remembers the war room. The wall against my back. His hand sliding beneath my clothes.

A knock at my door. Elena slips in without waiting for an answer, takes one look at the dress, and stops dead.

"Holy shit."

"Yeah."

"He gave you that?"

"It was waiting when I woke up."

She crosses the room and touches the fabric with something like reverence. "This is... Celeste, this is serious. I've never seen him do anything like this for anyone."

Her eyes drop to the ring at my chest. She goes still. She reaches out and lifts it gently, turning it to catch the light. "His signet ring," she says quietly. "Do you know what this means?"

"He explained."

"Did he explain that I've worked here for eight years and I've never seen him give anyone anything?" She lets the ring fall back against my skin. "Not a gift, not a token, not a single personal possession. He doesn't... he doesn't do this, Celeste."

I don't know what to say to that. So I don't say anything.

Elena studies my face for a long moment, then seems to make a decision. "Okay. We need to get you ready. Sit down."

"Elena."

"Sit."

I sit.

She disappears into my bathroom and comes back with supplies I didn't know I had. Makeup, brushes, hairpins. Either she brought them, or someone stocked the room without my knowledge. Given how this household operates, probably the latter.

"I'm going to do your hair and makeup," she says, positioning herself behind me. "You're going to sit there and let me. And while I work, you're going to tell me how nervous you actually are, because I know you're not as calm as you're pretending to be."

"I'm not ner—"

"Celeste." Her hands are gentle in my hair, starting to twist and pin. "I saw you come back from that bait mission covered in blood. Marcellus told me you fought off six vampires without flinching. But right now, your hands are shaking."

I look down. She's right. They are.

"I'm terrified," I admit. The words come out quieter than I intended. "Not of dying. I've made peace with that. But of... failing him. Embarrassing him. Making him regret trusting me."

"You won't."

"You don't know that."

"I do." She meets my eyes in the mirror. "And I know him. If he's bringing you into that room, it's because he knows you belong there."

She goes back to my hair, fingers deft and sure. I watch her work in the mirror, the concentration on her face, the care she's taking. It hits me suddenly that this is what having a friend feels like. I'd almost forgotten.

"Elena?"

"Hmm?"

"Thank you."

She smiles. "Thank me by making those bastards choke on their own arrogance."

Despite everything, I laugh.

Twenty minutes later, I barely recognize myself.

My hair is swept into a low, sleek twist at the nape of my neck, elegant but secure, nothing that could be grabbed in a fight. My eyes are dark and smoky, dramatic in a way I've never bothered with. My lips are painted deep burgundy, almost black in certain light.

I look dangerous. I look like I belong at Maximus's side.

"One more thing." Elena holds up a small bottle of nail polish. "Hold out your hands."

I do. She looks at them, the short nails, the scarred knuckles, the calluses from years of fighting, and puts the bottle away.

"Never mind. Leave them. It's better."

"Better?"

"It tells them who you really are." She squeezes my fingers. "Not a lady. A warrior."

The dress fits like it was made for me. Probably because it was.

I stand in front of the mirror, and the woman looking back at me is a stranger. She's pale and sharp and beautiful in a way that has nothing to do with softness. The dress hugs her body like armor. The ring glints gold against her chest. Her eyes are dark, unreadable.

His ring. His dress. His world.

But I'm still me underneath it.

The fabric whispers against my skin as I move, testing the range of motion. The slits in the skirt reveal flashes of pale thigh with each step. I think about him seeing me like this. Think about his eyes tracing the exposed skin of my back, the curve of my waist, the way the bodice frames my breasts.

I think about his promise. *When we have more time.*

We don't have more time. Not yet. But soon.

"Ready?" Elena asks.

No.

"Yes."

I find him waiting in the foyer, dressed in a dark suit that probably costs more than everything I owned in my human life combined. He turns when he hears my footsteps on the stairs.

He goes still.

For a long moment, he just looks at me. His gaze starts at my face and travels down, slowly, deliberately. Over the plunge of the neckline. The ring resting against my chest. The way the fabric clings to my waist, my hips. The slits that reveal my legs with each step down the staircase.

His expression doesn't change, not exactly, but something in his eyes does. Something heated and possessive and barely controlled. I recognize that look. I saw it in the war room, right before he pressed me against the wall and slid his hand between my thighs.

My body responds without my permission. A flush of warmth spreading through me. An ache building in places he touched.

"It fits," he says finally. His voice is rougher than usual. Strained.

"Yes." I stop in front of him, close enough to see the tension in his jaw. The way his hands have curled into fists at his sides. "Thank you."

"Don't thank me." He reaches out and adjusts the chain at my neck, an unnecessary gesture, an excuse to touch me. His fingers brush my collarbone, and I feel the contact everywhere. My skin prickles with awareness. My breath catches.

His eyes drop to my lips. Linger there.

"Thank me by making every vampire in that room understand exactly who you are," he says quietly.

"And who am I?"

His hand drops. But slowly. His fingers trail along my collarbone, down over the swell of my breast, before falling away. The touch is so light it might have been accidental.

It wasn't.

His eyes hold mine.

"Someone they should be afraid of."

The car is a black sedan with tinted windows, driven by a vampire I don't recognize. Marcellus wanted to come, but Maximus insisted he stay and oversee the compound's security. "If this is a trap," he'd said, "I need someone I trust protecting what we've built."

So it's just us in the back seat. Close enough that I can feel the tension radiating off him. Close enough that his knee almost touches mine when the car takes a turn.

Close enough that I can smell him. That scent I've become addicted to. Old books and whiskey and something darker underneath.

"Last chance to go over anything," he says, eyes forward.

"Dmitri: formal, never interrupt, address as Lord Dmitri. Vivienne: will provoke me, push back intelligently. Chen: patient, long-term thinker, follows Dmitri's lead. Okonkwo: values honesty above all else." I tick them off on my fingers. "Santos: wild card, probably won't show."

"Good."

"You've told me this."

"I want to make sure."

"Maximus." I turn to face him. "I've got it. Either I'm ready, or I'm not, and going over it again twon't change anything."

He's quiet for a moment. His jaw works. "You're right."

"I usually am."

The corner of his mouth twitches. Not quite a smile, but close.

The car takes another turn, and my knee brushes against his thigh. The contact sends a jolt through me. I don't move away. Neither does he.

We ride in silence for a few minutes. The city slides past the tinted windows, lights, buildings, humans going about their evening without any idea that monsters move among them. That monsters are driving past them right now, on their way to a political negotiation that could determine the fate of Atlanta's vampire population.

I'm acutely aware of his body beside me. The way he's sitting, angled slightly toward me. The way his hands rest on his thighs, those elegant fingers that I know so intimately now.

"When we walk in," Maximus says, and his voice is tighter than before, "stay close to me. Not behind me, beside me. They need to see you as my equal, not my subordinate."

"I thought the ring already tells them I'm yours."

The word hangs in the air between us. *Yours.*

His eyes cut to me. Dark. Hungry.

"It tells them you're under my protection. Your bearing tells them whether you deserve it."

I absorb that. "And if someone challenges me directly?"

"Then you handle it. I won't intervene unless there's a physical threat." His jaw tightens. "Which I don't expect. These are civilized vampires. They use words as weapons, not fists."

He turns to look at me fully. His gaze drops to my lips, then lower, to the neckline of the dress, to the ring resting between my breasts. When his eyes return to mine, they're burning.

The air in the car feels thick. Charged. I want to close the distance between us. Want to climb into his lap and finish what we started in the war room.

"After this is over," I say quietly, "you owe me a debt."

His eyebrow rises slightly. "A debt?"

"You made me promises." I hold his gaze. "I intend to collect."

Something flares in his expression. Hot and possessive and barely leashed.

"I remember exactly what I promised you." His voice has dropped to something low and rough that makes my skin prickle. "I remember every word. Every sound you made. Every way you felt around my fingers."

My breath catches. My thighs press together involuntarily.

"And I intend to deliver." He turns back to the window, but I can see the tension in his shoulders. The effort it's taking to maintain control. "After."

The word is a promise and a threat all at once.

I spend the rest of the ride trying to remember how to breathe.

The Whitley Hotel looks like it's been abandoned for decades.

The facade is crumbling, windows are dark, and weeds are pushing through cracks in the circular driveway. A human passing by would see nothing worth investigating, just another relic of a city that builds faster than it maintains.

But I'm not human anymore. And I can see the subtle signs of maintenance beneath the decay. The strategic sight lines. The shadows that move in ways shadows shouldn't.

"Neutral territory," Maximus murmurs as the car pulls to a stop. "Maintained by all of us, controlled by none."

"Clever."

"It's worked for seventy years." He opens his door, then pauses. "Ready?"

No. Yes. Does it matter?

"Let's go."

He rounds the car and opens my door before I can reach for the handle. Old-fashioned. Deliberate. When I step out, he offers his hand to help me rise, and I take it even though I don't need the assistance. His fingers close around mine, cool and strong, and for a moment we're just standing there in the dark, connected.

His thumb strokes across my knuckles once.

Then he releases me and places his hand on the small of my back. The dress is open there, and his palm presses directly against my bare skin. Cool fingers against my spine. The contact sends shivers radiating outward, settling low in my belly.

We walk toward the entrance together.

The interior of the Whitley is nothing like the exterior. The moment we cross the threshold, decay gives way to dark elegance. Restored woodwork, gleaming marble floors, chandeliers that cast warm light across everything. It's like stepping through a portal into another century.

"Impressive," I say quietly.

"We've had time to cultivate our tastes."

His hand is still on my bare back. His thumb traces a small circle against my spine, and I have to fight to keep my expression neutral. To not lean into the touch, to not let my body respond the way it wants to.

A vampire I don't recognize meets us in the foyer, young-looking, professionally blank expression. "Lord Maximus. They're waiting in the east parlor."

"Thank you."

We follow him through corridors lined with art that belongs in museums, past rooms that hint at luxury I can barely imagine. The whole place smells of old wood and something else, something darker. Power, maybe. Or just decades of vampire presence seeping into the walls.

Maximus's fingers flex against my back. A silent message. *We're almost there.*

The east parlor is announced by massive double doors, already standing open.

I take one breath. Square my shoulders. Remember who I am beneath this dress, beneath the ring, beneath everything he's draped over me.

I'm a fighter.

This is just another fight.

We walk in.

Four vampires wait inside. I catalog them instantly, fighter's instinct, assessing threats before my conscious mind has finished processing the room.

Maximus's hand presses slightly firmer against my back. His voice is barely a breath near my ear, his lips close enough that I feel the words against my skin.

"Dmitri, by the fire. Vivienne, on the chaise. Chen at the window. Okonkwo in blue."

Four names. Four predators. I file them away and keep my expression neutral, despite the goosebumps rising where his breath touched me.

Lord Dmitri sits in a high-backed chair near the fireplace, positioned like a throne. Pale, sharp-featured, with silver-streaked dark hair and the bearing of someone who was born to rule. His eyes are pale blue, cold as winter. He wears a suit that looks like it was sewn onto his body, every line perfect.

Lady Vivienne lounges on a velvet chaise like she owns it, and everything else in the room. Red hair, porcelain skin, lips painted the color of old blood. Her dress is green silk that clings and flows in equal measure. She looks like a predator pretending to be bored, and her eyes find me the moment I enter.

Lord Chen stands near the window, hands clasped behind his back. A man in his fifties when he was turned, perhaps. There's a stillness to him that makes the air around him feel heavier. His expression gives away nothing.

Lord Okonkwo is the largest of them, broad-shouldered and

imposing, with dark skin and close-cropped hair. He wears traditional robes in deep blue, and his presence fills space in a way that has nothing to do with physical size. His eyes are the warmest in the room, which isn't saying much.

No Lady Santos. Not surprising.

"Lord Maximus." Dmitri's voice is accented, formal, exactly as described. He doesn't rise, but he inclines his head, a greeting between equals. "Thank you for arranging this gathering on such short notice."

"Lord Dmitri." Maximus matches his formality. "I appreciate you making time. These are urgent matters."

"So your message implied." Dmitri's pale eyes slide to me. "And this is...?"

"Celeste Moreau. Of my inner circle."

A beat of silence. I feel them all reassessing, not just looking at me, but at what my presence means. A vampire less than a year old, standing beside the most powerful lord in Atlanta, wearing his ring around her neck.

Vivienne is the first to speak.

"My, my." She sits up slowly, a smile curving her red lips. "Maximus's new pet, wearing his collar for all to see." Her eyes drop to the ring at my chest. "How delightfully medieval of you."

A soft laugh from the corner of the room.

The sound slithers across my skin like a warning. One of Vivienne's guards, a tall vampire with a cruel mouth who's been standing near the window. He doesn't step forward, doesn't need to. His voice carries just fine.

"A pet's still a pet, even with a pretty collar." He smirks at me, teeth flashing. "Though I suppose the gatekeeper's little blood whore has to earn her keep somehow."

The room goes still.

Not quiet. Still. The way prey goes still when a predator's shadow passes overhead.

Behind me, the hand on my back disappears.

I feel the displacement of air before I register movement. A rush of cold where Maximus was standing. The whisper of fabric. Then a sound, sharp and wet, like meat hitting marble.

The guard is against the wall.

Maximus has him pinned, forearm crushed against his throat, other hand gripping his jaw at an angle that's one twist away from snapping his spine. The impact cracked the plaster behind them. Dust drifts down like snow.

It happened in less than a second. I didn't even see him move.

"What." Maximus's voice is soft. Conversational. The voice of someone discussing the weather while holding a man's life in his hands. "Did you just call her?"

The guard's eyes are wild, whites showing all around. His hands claw uselessly at Maximus's arm, nails scraping against the suit jacket without gaining purchase. His feet dangle three inches off the floor. He can't move his head, can't do anything but stare into those flat gray eyes.

I've seen Maximus fight. I've seen him kill. But I've never seen him like this. No rage on his face. No heat. Just cold, absolute stillness, like something terrible wearing a human mask.

Something dark and hot unfurls in my chest. Watching him like this, violent and lethal and utterly controlled, defending my honor without a moment's hesitation.

I should be horrified. Should be afraid of the monster I'm seeing. Instead, I'm aroused.

The realization shocks me. But I can't deny it. Watching him pin that guard to the wall, watching the absolute certainty in his movements, the deadly grace, the possessive rage simmering beneath that calm exterior... it's doing something to me. Something primal and undeniable.

The fire crackles. Someone's glass trembles faintly against a side table. Otherwise, silence.

No one moves to help him.

"Maximus." Lord Dmitri's voice cuts through the tension, calm but carrying the weight of centuries. "This is neutral ground."

"Then he shouldn't have spoken." Maximus doesn't look away from the guard. His grip doesn't loosen. "Neutral ground has rules. Respect is one of them."

I can smell fear now. Sharp and coppery, cutting through the woodsmoke and old leather. It's coming from the guard. His terror is a living thing, filling the space.

Vivienne hasn't moved from her chaise. If anything, she looks entertained. She swirls wine in her glass, watching the scene like it's theater performed for her amusement.

"Darling," she says to her guard, though he's clearly past hearing anything but his own terror, "I did try to warn you about Maximus. You really should have listened."

A small sound escapes the guard's throat. Not words. Just a thin, animal whine.

Maximus's fingers flex against his jaw. I hear the creak of bone under pressure. Not breaking. Not yet. A promise.

I watch the guard's face. Watch the moment understanding arrives. No one is coming to save him. His lady finds this amusing rather than offensive. He's about to die for a few words in a room full of vampires who won't lift a finger.

His eyes find mine. Pleading.

Part of me wants to let it happen. No one's ever defended me like this. No one's ever looked at someone who insulted me and decided they deserved to die for it. There's something dark and satisfied unfurling in my chest, something that likes watching this man learn the cost of his words.

But we're here for alliances, not enemies.

"Maximus."

He goes still at my voice. Completely, utterly still, like a predator interrupted mid-strike. His grip doesn't loosen, but the pressure stops increasing.

The room seems to lean in, waiting.

"I think he understands now."

For a long moment, nothing happens. The tension stretches until I can almost hear it humming, a wire pulled too tight. The fire pops. Sparks spiral upward. The guard's whimpering has stopped. He's gone silent with terror, eyes glazed, body limp in Maximus's grip.

Then Maximus opens his hand.

The guard drops. His legs don't catch him. He crumples against the wall, slides down it, lands in a heap on the floor. One hand goes to his throat. The other presses flat against the marble like he needs proof the ground is solid.

He doesn't try to stand. Doesn't try to speak. Just presses himself into the corner, making himself as small as possible, trembling so hard I can hear his teeth clicking together.

Maximus turns his back on him like he's already ceased to exist.

He walks back to my side. Steps unhurried, perfectly controlled. His hand finds the small of my back again, settling into the exact spot it occupied before, palm against bare skin. Like nothing happened. Like he didn't just cross a room in milliseconds and nearly tear a man's head off with his bare hands.

But when his eyes meet mine, there's something burning in them. Something that has nothing to do with the guard and everything to do with me. The mask hasn't slipped, not quite, but I can see what's behind it. Possession. Protection. Something older and fiercer than I have words for.

And desire. Raw, barely leashed desire.

My skin prickles where he's touching me. Heat spreading from that single point of contact, pooling low in my belly.

"I apologize for the interruption," he says to the room. "I believe we were making introductions."

Vivienne's smile has sharpened into something almost respectful. "We were. Though I think the introduction just got significantly more interesting." She looks at me with new calculation, new weight. "You stopped him."

"We're here to build alliances," I say, keeping my voice even despite the way my blood is still singing. Despite the ache building between my thighs. "Not body counts."

"Practical. I approve." She tilts her head, red hair catching the firelight. "And you didn't flinch. Not when my guard ran his mouth, not when Maximus moved. Most fledglings would have screamed or cowered or done something tedious."

"I'm not most fledglings."

"No." Her eyes flick to Maximus, to his hand on my back, then back to me. "You're clearly not."

I feel Maximus's fingers flex against my spine. A possessive gesture. A claim.

Vivienne settles back on her chaise, but her lazy posture doesn't fool me anymore. She's watching everything now. Reassessing. I can almost see the calculations happening behind those glittering eyes.

"I was going to make a clever comment about medieval craftsmanship," I say. "But I think the moment's passed."

She laughs, genuine and surprised, the sound ringing off the high ceiling. "Oh, I like this one." She looks at Maximus. "Where did you find her?"

"Dying in an alley. She insulted me instead of begging for her life. I found that interesting."

"I can see why." Vivienne's gaze slides to the corner where her guard is still pressed against the wall, still trembling. "I can see why indeed."

Dmitri clears his throat, a subtle but unmistakable signal. The room reorients toward him, grateful for the shift in focus.

"Perhaps we might proceed to the matter at hand," he says, his pale eyes revealing nothing of what he thought of the display. "Miss Moreau, you may sit."

It's not a request. It's a test. Will I wait for Maximus's permission, or act on my own?

"Thank you, Lord Dmitri." I move to an empty chair positioned slightly behind and to the right of where Maximus will sit. Close enough to participate, but not presumptuous.

As I settle into the chair, I feel Maximus's gaze on me.

Approval.

Maximus takes his seat, and the meeting begins.

The next hour is a masterclass in vampire politics.

Dmitri leads the discussion with formal precision, laying out what everyone already knows: Konstantin has been moving against Maximus's blood network. The attacks have been escalating. The contamination crisis has made clean blood more valuable than ever, and whoever controls the supply controls Atlanta's vampire population.

"What concerns me," Dmitri says, "is the instability this conflict creates. War between two lords affects us all."

"I'm not the one seeking war," Maximus replies. "Konstantin has attacked my operations, killed my donors, and sent spies into my compound. I'm seeking allies to help me end this before it escalates further."

"By 'end this,' you mean...?" Chen speaks for the first time, his voice soft and measured.

"Whatever is necessary. Ideally, a show of united opposition that convinces Konstantin to stand down. If not..." Maximus lets the implication hang.

"And if we refuse?" Vivienne asks, examining her nails. "If we stay out of your little war?"

"Then Konstantin picks us off one by one." Maximus's voice hardens. "He's not going to stop with me. Once he controls the blood network, he controls all of you. Every vampire in this city will be dependent on his goodwill for survival."

"That assumes he wins," Okonkwo says. His deep voice carries weight. "You have resources. Strength. Why do you need us?"

"Because I'd rather win cleanly than win bloody." Maximus leans forward. "I can fight Konstantin alone. I'll probably win. But the cost to my people, to the network, to the stability we've all benefited from, will be catastrophic. A united front prevents that. It tells Konstantin that moving against me means moving against all of you."

Silence. The lords exchange glances, calculations happening behind their eyes.

Then Dmitri looks at me.

"Miss Moreau. You've been quiet."

Every head turns. I feel the weight of their attention like a physical pressure.

"I was told not to speak unless spoken to, Lord Dmitri."

His lips twitch, the closest he's come to a smile. "Consider yourself spoken to. I'm curious about your perspective."

I take a moment to gather my thoughts. To think about the points Maximus and I discussed while we strategized.

"I know Konstantin's operation from a different angle than Lord Maximus does," I say. "Before I was turned, I fought in underground rings. Human and vampire. Konstantin sponsors those rings, uses them to recruit soldiers, identify talent, build loyalty among young vampires who have nowhere else to go."

Chen tilts his head slightly. "Go on."

"He's not just building an army. He's building a culture. A sense of belonging for vampires who've been abandoned by their makers, rejected by the establishment, left to figure out this life on their own." I keep my voice steady. "That's his real power. Not his soldiers or his resources. It's the fact that he offers something no one else does: a place to belong."

Okonkwo's eyes sharpen with interest. "And you know this how?"

"Because I was one of them. Abandoned. Alone. Surviving on contaminated blood because I didn't know any better." I glance at Maximus. "Lord Maximus offered me something different. But if he hadn't found me first, Konstantin might have."

The room is silent.

"What's your point?" Vivienne asks. Her voice has lost some of its laziness.

"My point is that you can't just defeat Konstantin militarily. Cut off the head, and another will grow back, because the problem isn't him, it's the void he fills. If you want lasting peace, you need to offer an alternative." I look around the room. "You need to give abandoned vampires a reason to choose you instead of him."

More silence. Longer this time.

Then Okonkwo nods slowly. "The girl speaks truth. I've seen it in my own territory, young ones turning to Konstantin because no one else will have them."

"That's a long-term problem," Dmitri says. "We're here to discuss the immediate threat."

"The immediate threat is a symptom," I reply. "Treating symptoms keeps you sick."

Dmitri studies me for a long moment. Something shifts in his expression, not warmth, exactly, but something closer to respect.

"You've chosen an interesting advisor," he says to Maximus.

"I've chosen a capable one."

Across the room, I catch Maximus watching me. His expression is controlled, neutral, but his eyes aren't. There's pride there.

The discussion continues. Alliances are weighed, terms proposed, conditions negotiated. Dmitri commits first, formally, precisely, with caveats and stipulations that will take lawyers to parse. Chen follows his lead, as Maximus predicted. Okonkwo takes longer, asking pointed questions about what support will look like in practice, but eventually nods his agreement.

Vivienne remains uncommitted.

"This is all very interesting," she says as the conversation winds down, "but I'm not convinced this is my fight. Konstantin has never moved against my territory."

"Yet," Maximus says.

"Yet," she agrees. "But 'yet' isn't 'now,' and I prefer to make decisions based on present realities."

"Suit yourself." Maximus's voice is carefully neutral. "When he does move against you, I hope you'll remember this conversation."

Vivienne smiles. "I always remember conversations, Lord Maximus. It's one of my many talents."

She turns her attention to me, and something in her expression shifts. Becomes sharper. More calculating.

"Tell me, Celeste Moreau. Do you know who made you?"

The question catches me off guard. "Valentina Russo."

"Yes. Konstantin's little pet." Vivienne's smile widens. "Do you know why she turned you?"

I feel Maximus tense beside me. "What does this have to do with..."

"I'm asking Miss Moreau, not you." Vivienne doesn't look away from me. "Do you know why?"

I force myself to hold her gaze. "No. I beat her in a fight. I assumed it was revenge."

"Revenge." Vivienne laughs softly. "Oh, my dear. Valentina Russo doesn't do anything out of emotion. She's far too calculating for that."

The room has gone very still. Even Dmitri is watching now, pale eyes sharp with interest.

"What are you implying?" I ask.

"I'm implying that it's a rather remarkable coincidence, don't you think? Konstantin's most trusted lieutenant just happens to turn a fighter with exceptional skills, then just happens to abandon her in Atlanta, where she just happens to end up in Maximus's inner circle within days." Vivienne tilts her head. "Almost as if it were planned."

Cold spreads through my chest.

"How do you know all of this?" My voice comes out steadier than I feel.

"I have my sources," she replies.

"You think I'm a spy?"

"I think you're something." Vivienne's eyes glitter. "I just haven't decided what yet. But I've lived long enough to know that coincidences are rarely coincidental. And you, Celeste Moreau, are a very interesting coincidence."

I want to argue. Want to defend myself, prove that I'm not some planted operative, that my loyalty to Maximus is real.

But the truth is, I don't know why Valentina turned me. I've never known. I assumed rage, wounded pride, the impulsive cruelty of a vampire who couldn't stand losing to a human.

What if I was wrong?

"Vivienne." Maximus's voice cuts through the room like a blade. "If you have evidence that Celeste is compromised, present it. Otherwise, I suggest you keep your conspiracy theories to yourself."

"No theories." Vivienne rises gracefully from her chaise. "Just observations. Take them as you will."

She glides toward the door, then pauses.

"I'll be watching with great interest to see how this all unfolds." She looks back at me one last time. "Especially you, Miss Moreau. Something tells me you're going to be very important before this is all over. I just can't decide if that's good news or bad."

She leaves.

The room is silent.

Dmitri rises, signaling the meeting's end. "Lord Maximus, you have my support. We'll discuss the specifics tomorrow."

"Thank you, Lord Dmitri."

Chen and Okonkwo offer similar farewells, formal, measured, alliance confirmed, but details pending. One by one, they file out, leaving Maximus and me alone in the parlor.

The fire crackles. Shadows dance across the walls.

I haven't moved from my chair.

"Celeste."

Maximus is standing in front of me. I don't know when he moved. His face is unreadable, but his voice is gentler than I've ever heard it.

"What she said..."

"What if she's right?" The words come out hollow. "What if Valentina turned me on purpose? What if I'm here because Konstantin wanted me here?"

"Then it doesn't matter."

I look up at him. "How can you say that?"

"Because I know who you are." He crouches in front of my chair, bringing himself to eye level. Close enough to touch. Close enough that I can smell him, that familiar scent that's become synonymous with safety and desire. "I know what you've done. I know where your loyalties lie. I've watched you fight beside me, bleed for my people, risk your life to protect what we've built."

"But..."

"Vivienne is a manipulator. She plants seeds of doubt because chaos benefits her. She wants you off-balance." His gray eyes hold mine. "Don't let her win."

"And if there's truth to it? If Valentina really did..."

"Then we'll find out what her plan was. And we'll destroy it." His hand comes up to cup my face. His palm is cool against my cheek, his thumb brushing along my cheekbone. The touch is tender. Possessive. "Whatever you were meant to be, you chose something different. That choice is yours. No one can take it from you."

My eyes burn. I don't understand the sensation. Vampires don't cry. But something aches behind them anyway.

"I didn't ask for any of this," I whisper.

"Neither did I." His voice is rough. "But here we are."

Here we are.

In a crumbling hotel that pretends to be beautiful, surrounded by vampires who play games with lives and loyalties, wearing a ring that belonged to a family I'll never know.

Here we are.

His hand is still on my face. His eyes are still on mine. And for a moment, everything else falls away. Vivienne's insinuations, Konstantin's shadow, the weight of a war I never chose.

There's just him. Just me. Just the impossible thing building between us.

"Maximus," I breathe.

Something shifts in his expression. The control he's been wearing all night cracks, just slightly, revealing the hunger beneath.

"I've been watching you all night," he says quietly. "Watching you hold your own against vampires over ten times your age. Watching you think on your feet, speak with authority, command respect from creatures who've existed for centuries."

His thumb traces my lower lip. The touch sends sparks cascading through me.

"Do you have any idea what it did to me?" His voice has dropped to something rough and intimate. "Watching you wear my ring, my dress, stand beside me as my equal? Watching every vampire in that room realize exactly what you are?"

"What am I?"

"Mine." The word comes out like a growl. "And theirs to fear."

He leans closer. I can feel the cool brush of his breath against my lips. Feel the tension thrumming through his body, the restraint.

"I wanted to touch you all night," he murmurs. "Every time you crossed your legs, and that slit revealed your thigh. Every time you spoke, and I remembered those same lips around my name in the war room. Every time you looked at me, and I knew you were remembering too."

"I was," I admit. My voice is barely a whisper. "I couldn't stop."

His fingers tighten against my jaw. A muscle feathers in his cheek.

"We should go," he says, but he doesn't move.

"We should."

Neither of us moves.

His thumb traces my lip again. His eyes drop to my mouth. The hunger in his expression makes my stomach clench.

"When we get back to the compound," he says, "I'm going to

take this dress off you. Slowly. And then I'm going to make good on every promise I made in that war room."

The words send a bolt of heat straight through me. I press my thighs together against the ache building there.

"Every promise?" My voice comes out breathless.

"Every single one." He stands abruptly, pulling his hand away like it burned him. But I see the effort it costs him. See the tension in every line of his body. "But not here. Not in this place."

He's right. We need to leave. We're still in hostile territory, still surrounded by potential enemies, still vulnerable.

I rise from my chair, smooth down the dress he gave me, touch the ring he placed around my neck. The weight of it feels different now. Heavier. More complicated.

But also more right.

We walk out of the Whitley together, side by side, not touching.

The night air hits my face as we step outside. Cool, damp, smelling of the city. Real. Grounding.

"Three out of four," I say quietly. "That's a victory."

"It's a start."

We get in the car. The driver pulls away.

Maximus's hand finds mine in the darkness of the back seat. His fingers intertwine with mine. His thumb strokes across my knuckles in slow, deliberate circles.

It's not enough. After everything tonight, after the tension and the fear and the desire simmering beneath every moment, I want more. I want his hands on me, his mouth on me. I want to finish what we started.

But Vivienne's words echo in my head:

Almost as if it were planned.

You're going to be very important before this is all over.

I just can't decide if that's good news or bad.

I stare out the window at the city lights, and I wonder if I'll ever know the truth about what I am.

Or if finding out will destroy everything I've built.

Maximus's hand tightens around mine. A silent message. *I'm here. Whatever comes.*

I hold on.

TWENTY-FOUR

The car stops in front of the compound, and Celeste hasn't spoken in twenty minutes.

Her hand is still in mine. Has been since we left the Whitley, my thumb tracing slow circles across her knuckles while the city slid past outside the windows. But somewhere in the last few miles, the charged silence between us shifted. I watched her retreat into herself, shoulders turning toward the window, gaze fixed on nothing, her other hand drifting to the ring at her chest. Processing.

Vivienne's words landed exactly where she intended them to.

But that's not all I'm thinking about as I watch her in the dim light of the car's interior. I'm also thinking about what I said to her at the Whitley. *When we get back to the compound, I'm going to take this dress off you. Slowly.* The words hang between us, a promise I fully intend to keep. But the woman beside me isn't the same fierce creature who made me say them. Something has dimmed in her since Vivienne's insinuations.

And yet I can't stop noticing the way she looks in that dress.

The way the fabric clings to her body. The exposed skin of her back that I've been touching all night. The ring glinting gold against her chest, rising and falling with each unnecessary breath.

I've been half-hard since she walked down those stairs hours ago. The ache has only intensified as the night wore on, watching her hold her own against vampires much older than her, watching every lord in that room realize exactly what she is. What she is to me.

And when I pinned that guard to the wall, when I nearly killed him for what he called her, I saw the way her eyes darkened. She wasn't afraid of what I'd done.

She was aroused by it.

The memory makes my grip tighten on her hand.

The driver opens my door, and I force myself to release her. Step out into the night air. The compound is quiet. Marcellus has the security teams on high alert, but they're positioned at the perimeter, out of sight. The main house looks almost peaceful, lights glowing warmly behind curtained windows.

I round the car and open Celeste's door before the driver can reach it.

She looks up at me, and something in my chest tightens. The smoky makeup around her eyes has smudged slightly. The fierce warrior who held her own against four ancient vampires looks younger now. Uncertain.

She takes my offered hand and steps out of the car. Her fingers are cool in mine, and she doesn't pull away immediately. Her other hand drifts to the ring at her chest, that unconscious gesture I've noticed her making throughout the night.

"Thank you, Kyle," I say to the driver without looking at him. "That will be all."

The car pulls away, leaving us standing in the circular drive. The night is quiet except for the soft rustle of wind through the gardens. The moon is nearly full, casting silver light across the manicured hedges and stone pathways.

"You should rest," I say, though the words feel inadequate. "It's been a long night."

"I'm not tired."

"Celeste."

"I don't want to be alone right now." She meets my eyes, and there's no pretense in her expression. No walls. Just raw honesty. "I know that's probably not what you want to hear, but I'm asking anyway."

What I want. She has no idea what I want.

I want to do exactly what I promised her at the Whitley. I want to take her inside and peel that dress off her body inch by inch. I want to make good on every promise I made in the war room. I want to spread her out beneath me and take my time and learn every sound she makes.

I've been wanting it for hours. Days. Weeks, if I'm honest with myself.

"Come with me," I say.

We walk into the compound together. The foyer is empty, the staff either at their posts or in their quarters. Our footsteps echo on the marble floor, hers steady despite the heeled boots, mine deliberately measured. The chandelier casts warm light across the space, but the house feels different at this hour. Quieter. More intimate.

I'm acutely aware of her beside me. The whisper of her dress against the marble. The scent of her, that indefinable something that's been driving me slowly insane. The heat still simmering between us despite Vivienne's poison.

I lead her to my study. A fire burns low in the hearth.

She's been here before. The night I offered her a place in my inner circle, with Marcellus standing guard in the corner. And again, alone, the night she returned from her first solo mission, when I'd carelessly left my letters out, and she saw more of my past than I intended. When I touched her face and then fled my own study like a coward.

But tonight is different. Tonight, there's nothing accidental about why we're here.

She moves to the fireplace, arms wrapped around herself. The same spot where she stood that night.

I pour two glasses of whiskey and hand her one. Our fingers brush during the exchange. The contact sends a jolt through me, and I see her breath catch. She feels it too. After everything tonight, after the promises and the tension and the hours of wanting, even this small touch feels electric.

She takes a sip, then sets the glass down on my desk. Studies the room with those sharp, observant eyes, lingering on the books, the maps, the fire.

"Vivienne was trying to destabilize me," she says finally. "I know that. I understand the tactic."

"But?"

"But what if she's right?" She turns to face me. The firelight catches the gold of the ring at her chest, makes it glow against the black fabric of her dress. "You told me Valentina was scouting for Konstantin. I made peace with that, being recruited instead of just revenge. But Vivienne's saying something different. She's saying I ended up here, with you, and that wasn't an accident either. That I'm not just a recruit. I'm a plant."

I watch her face as she speaks. Watch the doubt creeping in, the uncertainty that wasn't there an hour ago when she was trading barbs with ancient vampires and earning their respect.

This is what Vivienne does. Plants seeds and watches them grow into something poisonous.

"Then we find out what that plan was," I say. "And we destroy it."

"You make it sound simple."

"It's not simple. But it's manageable." I set down my own glass, move closer to her. "Whatever Valentina intended, whatever Konstantin hoped to gain, you're not their pawn anymore. You chose to be here. You chose to fight beside me. Those choices are yours, and nothing Vivienne says can take them from you."

"And if I was designed to be here? If everything I've chosen was somehow orchestrated?"

"Then you've exceeded your design." I stop in front of her, close enough to see the amber flecks in her dark eyes. Close enough to smell her, that scent that's been driving me slowly insane all night. "The woman who stood in that room tonight and made four vampires reassess their assumptions, that wasn't Konstantin's creation. That was you."

She's quiet for a moment, her gaze searching my face. "You really believe that?"

"I watched you tonight. The way you handled Vivienne's provocation, you didn't just survive it; you turned it back on her. She's been playing political games for years, and you made her laugh. Do you understand how rare that is?"

Celeste shakes her head slightly. "I was just..."

"You were magnificent." The word escapes before I can temper it. "When you spoke about the fighting rings, about Konstantin's recruitment strategy, Chen was taking mental notes. Okonkwo looked at you like you'd just solved a puzzle he'd been working on for decades. You earned their respect in an hour. Most vampires spend centuries trying and failing to do what you did tonight."

She stares at me. I've surprised her. Surprised myself, perhaps. I don't give compliments freely. Don't admit when I'm impressed. But she needs to hear this. Needs to understand that whatever

Vivienne planted in her mind, it doesn't diminish what she accomplished.

"Maximus."

"You asked me in the training room what you are to me." The words come out before I can stop them. "I didn't answer. I should have."

She goes still. The ring glints gold against the black fabric of her dress, rising and falling with each breath she chooses to take.

"What am I to you?" she asks softly.

Everything. The word surfaces unbidden, and I force it back down. Too much. Too fast. But something needs to be said, something true, something that acknowledges what's been building between us since that first night in the alley.

"You're the first person in centuries who's made me feel like I'm still alive," I say. "Not just existing. Not just maintaining an empire. Alive."

Her expression shifts. Something vulnerable and fierce all at once.

"That's terrifying," she says.

"Yes."

"For me too."

"I know." I take a breath I don't need. "The last time I felt this way..." I stop. Consider whether to continue. Decide she deserves the truth. "The last time I let myself care about someone this much, I lost her. I lost myself for a very long time afterward."

"What happened?"

"Her name was Catherine. Three hundred years ago. She was human, a donor. We fell in love, though I told myself we hadn't. When she became ill, I turned her to save her life." The words come slowly, dragged from a place I've kept locked for centuries. "She fed on a contaminated human for her first feeding. We didn't know about contaminated blood back then. It was probably opium. Who knows? She became feral, no recognition, no memory of who she'd been. Just hunger and violence. By the time I found her, she'd already killed."

Celeste's expression softens. "Maximus..."

"I had to kill her myself. The woman I loved, the woman I'd turned to save, I put a blade through her heart to stop her from killing more. She didn't even recognize me." I hold her gaze, let her see the old wound beneath the words. "After that, I swore I'd never let myself care that much again. Caring was weakness. Caring got people killed."

"And now?"

"Now I look at you, and all those walls I built feel like sand against the tide." I laugh, but there's no humor in it. "I've survived wars, betrayals, a hundred and fifty years of enslavement. I've outlived everyone I ever loved and learned to want nothing, need no one. And then you looked at me in an alley while you were dying and called me pathetic, and I haven't been the same since."

She laughs too, a small, surprised sound. "I was dying. My judgment was impaired."

"Your judgment was perfect. You saw exactly what I am. Ancient, controlled, terrified of anything I can't manage. And you weren't afraid of me."

"I was a little afraid."

"But you insulted me anyway."

"I've always had a problem with authority."

We're standing closer now. I don't remember moving, but the space between us has shrunk to something intimate, something charged. I can smell her, that indefinable scent that's purely her. I've been trying not to notice it for weeks. I'm done trying.

"I believe I made you a promise," I say, and my voice has dropped to something rougher. "At the Whitley. About what would happen when we got back here."

Her breath catches. "You said you were going to take this dress off me. Slowly."

"I remember." I reach out and trace my finger along the neckline of the dress, barely touching her skin. She shivers. "I remember every word I said. Just like I remember every word I said in the car. Every promise I made in the war room."

"You said you'd make good on all of them."

"I intend to."

I close the distance between us.

Her lips meet mine, and the world narrows to this single point of contact. She tastes like whiskey and something darker, something that's purely her. The kiss is tentative at first, a question. An invitation.

I answer it.

My hand slides to the back of her neck, fingers finding the sleek twist of her hair. The pins holding it in place press against my palm as I cup her head, angle her mouth more firmly against mine. She makes a small sound, not quite a gasp, not quite a moan, and something snaps loose in my chest.

All that control. All that discipline. All those carefully maintained walls. All the years of convincing myself that I didn't need anyone. All of it crumbling under the pressure of her lips moving against mine.

I back her against the desk, and she goes willingly, her hands fisting in the lapels of my jacket. The kiss deepens, hungrier now, more demanding. Her mouth opens under mine, and I take what she's offering, pouring centuries of loneliness into the space between us.

Her back hits the edge of the desk. Papers scatter. A pen rolls off and clatters to the floor. I don't care. My hands find her waist, the curve of her hip, the exposed skin of her lower back where the dress dips open. She's cool to the touch, smooth, perfect. I've been thinking about this skin all night. Touching it through the thin excuse of guiding her. Now I let myself feel it properly, spreading my palms across her bare back, pulling her closer.

The ring presses between us as she arches into me. I feel it against my chest, the hard circle of gold that marks her as mine. The sensation grounds me even as it inflames me. My ring. My ring against her skin, now pressed against mine. Something primitive and possessive roars to life in my chest.

She pulls at my jacket, and I shrug it off without breaking the kiss. It falls somewhere behind me, forgotten. Her fingers find the buttons of my shirt, work the first two open with efficiency that speaks to her practical nature, then slip inside to press against my chest.

"Maximus." My name on her lips, breathless and wanting. The sound of it nearly undoes me.

I kiss down the line of her jaw, the column of her throat, the place where the gold chain meets her collarbone. She tilts her head back to give me access, baring her throat with a trust that devastates me. In the vampire world, that gesture means something. It means everything.

My lips find the ring where it rests against her chest. I press a kiss to the cool metal, then to the skin around it, tracing the shape of my claim on her body. My mouth moves lower, following the plunge of the neckline, tasting the swell of her breast where the fabric barely contains it.

"You have no idea," I murmur against her skin, "what watching you tonight did to me."

"Tell me."

I lift my head to meet her eyes. They're dark, pupils blown wide, that same heated look I saw when I had the guard pinned to the wall.

"Every time you spoke, I thought about your mouth. Every

time you crossed your legs and that slit revealed your thigh, I thought about what's between them."

Her breath shudders out. "I was. I couldn't stop."

"Neither could I." I run my hands up her thighs, pushing the fabric of the dress aside. The slits allow me access, and I take it, feeling the lean muscle beneath her skin, the evidence of years of training and fighting. "I've been thinking about what I promised you. About tasting you properly. About taking my time."

"Then do it." Her voice is strained. "You said when we got back. We're back."

God, I want to. I want to drop to my knees right here and bury my face between her thighs. I want to find out if she tastes as good as I remember. I want to make her come on my tongue, then my fingers, then me. I want to spend hours learning every way to make her fall apart.

I lift her onto the desk, scattering more papers, positioning myself between her thighs. The dress falls away, baring her legs completely. She wraps them around me, pulls me closer, and the contact is so intense I have to break the kiss.

She's perfect like this. Wrecked and wanting, her careful hair coming undone, her lipstick smeared, her eyes dark with need. Mine. She's mine.

Her hands move to my belt.

Her fingers fumble. Just slightly. Just enough that I notice.

Celeste doesn't fumble. She's precise, controlled, a fighter's economy of movement in everything she does. But her hands are shaking now, just a little, and when I look at her face, I catch it. Her eyes are closed too tightly. Not the soft surrender of pleasure. Something harder. Like she's trying to block something out.

I still her hands with mine.

"Celeste. Look at me."

She does. And I see it. The want is there, but underneath it, something else. Something unsteady.

"Are you here with me?" I ask. "Or are you trying to prove something?"

She flinches. It's small, barely perceptible.

"I want this," she says.

"That's not what I asked."

She's quiet for a long moment. Her hands have gone still on my belt. When she finally speaks, her voice is smaller than I've ever heard it.

"I can't stop hearing her. Vivienne. What she said." She swallows. "What if she's right? Valentina turning me, me ending up here, with you. What if none of it was coincidence?"

There it is. The doubt I saw in the car. The poison Vivienne planted, still working its way through her.

I look at her. Really look. At the vulnerability she's letting me see, the fear underneath the want. Like she came here tonight trying to outrun the questions, bury them under sensation. And I almost let her.

If we do this now, if I take her on this desk the way every instinct is screaming at me to do, part of her will wonder.

I can't do that to her. I can't let our first time be shadowed by doubt.

I catch her wrists. Gently, but firmly.

She freezes. I see the flash of hurt in her eyes before she can hide it, the assumption that I'm about to push her away and call this a mistake.

And God, part of me wants to. Part of me, the part that's been running from this for weeks, the part that still hears Luciano's voice telling me that caring is weakness, is screaming at me to stop this now. To rebuild the walls. To protect myself and her from whatever destruction caring will inevitably bring.

But that's not why I'm stopping. Not this time.

"Not like this," I say, and my voice comes out ragged. Wrecked. "Not tonight."

"Why?" The word is sharp. Defensive. She's bracing for rejection, and I hate that I've taught her to expect it.

"Because of what Vivienne said."

She flinches. Tries to pull her hands back. I don't let her.

"Not because I believe it," I say quickly. "Because you do. Or part of you does. And I won't have that between us. Not for this."

She stills. Searches my face.

"I don't want the first time I'm inside you to be something you question afterward." I release her wrists, bring my hands up to frame her face instead. Force myself to meet her eyes even though every nerve in my body is screaming at me to stop talking and start touching. "I don't want you wondering if you're here because you wanted to be, or because someone else wanted you to be. I don't want Vivienne in this room with us."

"She's not."

"Isn't she?" I brush my thumb across her lower lip, swollen from kissing. "You were quiet for twenty minutes in the car. You've been somewhere else since she's said that, even when you were kissing me. Part of you is still in that parlor, listening to her tell you that none of your choices are really yours."

She's quiet. I watch her face, watch the emotions flickering across it. Frustration. Recognition. Something that might be relief.

"I hate that you're right," she says finally.

"I hate that I'm right, too." I let out a breath that's more frustration than anything else. "Do you have any idea how much I want you right now? How hard it is to stop?"

"I can feel how hard it is." She shifts her hips against me, and the friction makes me groan. "Literally."

"That's not helping."

"It's not meant to." But her expression has softened. The defensiveness is fading, replaced by something warmer. "You're really not pushing me away."

"No."

"You're not saying this is a mistake."

"It's the furthest thing from a mistake." I rest my forehead against hers. We're both breathing hard. "I'm saying I want it to matter. I'm saying I want you to be certain. Completely certain. Not because of Vivienne, not despite Vivienne, but because you chose this. Chose me."

"I have chosen you."

"Then choose me again. Tomorrow. When the poison has had time to fade. When you've had time to think, really think, about what she said and what it means and what it doesn't mean." I pull back enough to look at her properly. "I've waited centuries to feel this way again. I can wait another night to be sure you feel the same."

She stares at me for a long moment. I watch her process, that sharp mind working through the implications of what I've said and what I'm offering.

"That might be the most romantic thing anyone's ever said to me," she says finally.

"I'm over six hundred years old. I've had time to learn."

She laughs, a real laugh, surprised and warm. The sound loosens something in my chest.

"You're also infuriating," she says.

"I've been told."

"And arrogant."

"So I've heard."

"And you're going to leave me aching all night because you want to be noble."

"I'm going to be aching too, if that helps."

"It doesn't." But she's smiling now. Something real, something that reaches her eyes. "It really doesn't."

She pulls me down for another kiss, softer this time. Tender rather than demanding. A promise rather than a plea.

When she pulls back, her expression has changed. The uncertainty is still there, but it's tempered now by something warmer. Something that looks like trust.

"Later," she says.

"Later."

"And you'd better make good on those promises."

"Every single one." I press a kiss to her forehead. Her cheek. The corner of her mouth. "I told you in the car that I remembered every word. Every sound you made. Every way you felt around my fingers. I've been thinking about nothing else for days. When I finally have you, it won't be quick. It won't be desperate. It will be everything I've been imagining since the war room."

Her breath catches. "You're not making the waiting easier."

"Neither are you."

Footsteps in the hallway. We both freeze.

They pass by without stopping, someone on patrol, probably, or staff heading to their quarters. But the moment breaks the spell.

Celeste slides off the desk. Smooths her dress. Touches her hair and grimaces at the damage we've done to Elena's careful work.

I retrieve my jacket from the floor, shake out the wrinkles, don't put it back on. My shirt is still hanging open, and I catch her looking at the exposed skin with an expression that makes me want to forget everything I just said about waiting.

"I should go," she says. "Rest. Process. All the things you're supposed to do after a night like this."

"Celeste."

She pauses, one hand on the door.

"When you think about what Vivienne said," I tell her, "remember this too: whatever you were meant to be, whatever Valentina intended, it doesn't change what you've become. What you are to me."

"And what's that?"

I tell her the truth.

"Essential."

She's still for a moment. Then she crosses back to me, rises on her toes, and presses a kiss to the corner of my mouth. Soft. Brief. A promise.

"Goodnight, Maximus."

"Goodnight, Celeste."

She leaves. The door closes behind her with a soft click.

I stand alone in my study, surrounded by scattered papers and the lingering scent of her, and I try to remember the last time I felt this frustrated.

I move to the window, pushing aside the heavy curtain to look out at the grounds. The moon has shifted position, casting different shadows across the gardens. Somewhere out there, Konstantin is planning his next move. The other lords are weighing their options.

And none of it matters as much as it should.

My lips still feel the pressure of her kiss. My skin still remembers the path of her fingers. I haven't been this aroused and this frustrated in centuries.

But I meant what I said. When I finally have her, I want it to be clear. Uncomplicated by doubts and poison and the machinations of vampires who've been playing games since before she was born.

I want her to choose me. Really choose me. Not because she was designed to, not because she's running from fear, but because she wants to. Because she sees what I am and wants me anyway.

The ring box on my desk catches my eye. I pick it up, turn it over in my hands. A small leather box that held a ring for centuries. My father's ring. His father's before him. Generations of Marchetti men who lived and died and never imagined their legacy would end up around the neck of a vampire in twenty-first-century Atlanta.

Empty now because I gave it to a woman I've known for approximately two weeks.

A woman I'm falling in love with anyway.

I set the box back on the desk. Pour myself another whiskey, though I don't drink it. Just hold the glass, feel the weight of it, the coolness against my palm.

I don't know what Valentina intended. But I know this: whatever Celeste was meant to be, she's chosen to be something else. She's chosen to stand beside me. To fight with me. To trust me with her fear and her uncertainty and her hope.

I can do no less.

I set down the glass, untouched, and move toward the door. Dawn is still hours away. There's work to be done. Security reports to review, strategies to refine, a war to plan. And a cold shower to take, because there's no way I'm going to be able to concentrate on any of it in this state.

But as I walk through the quiet corridors of my compound, I find myself pausing outside her door. Listening. I can hear her moving inside, the soft pad of footsteps, the rustle of fabric. She's not sleeping either.

I raise my hand to knock. Hesitate. Lower it again.

Later. I promised her later.

I intend to keep that promise.

I walk away, heading for my quarters. Part of me is already counting the hours until I can stop waiting and start living.

CHAPTER
TWENTY-FIVE

I wake with my hand already at my chest.

The ring is cool from resting against my skin all day.

Essential.

The word surfaces before I'm fully conscious, dragging the memory of last night with it. His study. The scattered papers. His mouth on mine, his hands pushing aside the slits of my dress, the hard length of him pressing against me when I wrapped my legs around him.

And then: *Not like this. Not tonight.*

I press the ring against my sternum and stare at the ceiling.

He stopped us. Not because he didn't want me. That much was obvious. I felt exactly how much he wanted me when he positioned himself between my thighs. But because of what Vivienne said. Because he saw me retreat into myself during the car ride home and knew part of me was still in that parlor, listening to her poison.

I don't want the first time I'm inside you to be something you question afterward.

309

The memory of those words sends heat pooling low in my belly. The raw honesty of them. The way he looked at me when he said them, forehead pressed to mine, breathing hard, every line of his body screaming with the effort of holding back.

He said later. When I've had time to think, really think, about what Vivienne said and what it means.

I sit up slowly, letting the blackout curtains keep the room in darkness. My body aches in ways that have nothing to do with injury. My lips still feel swollen from his kisses. My skin still remembers the path of his hands, up my thighs, across my bare back, cupping my face like I was something precious.

I've had time to think. The hours before dawn, lying in my bed, staring at the ceiling. And now, waking, the first coherent thoughts forming around the same questions.

Did Valentina have some ulterior motive beyond wounded pride? Was my ending up here less coincidence than Vivienne implied?

And the conclusion I keep reaching: even if it's true, it doesn't change anything.

Valentina didn't make me fight my way into Maximus's inner circle. She didn't make me stand beside him in that room full of ancient vampires. She didn't make me fall for him. Whatever her reasons for turning me, whatever Konstantin might have hoped to gain, I'm the one who chose to be here. I'm the one who chose him.

That's mine. No one can take it from me.

My internal clock says it's just after sunset. The compound will be stirring to life, another night of preparations and strategy in the ongoing conflict with Konstantin.

I shower and dress in practical clothes. Dark pants, fitted top, boots I can fight in. The dress from last night hangs in my closet, a whisper of black fabric that still smells faintly of him. I touch it once, remembering the way he looked at me when I walked down those stairs. The way his eyes traced the neckline, the exposed skin of my back, the slits that revealed my thighs.

You have no idea what watching you tonight did to me.

I close the closet and head for the conference room.

The space is already half-full when I arrive.

Marcellus stands at the head of the table, reviewing something on a tablet. Julian and Nadia are deep in conversation near the window. Ethan is marking positions on a large map spread across the table's surface. Other members of the inner circle filter in, vampires I've come to know over the past weeks, faces that have shifted from suspicious to accepting to something approaching respect.

The atmosphere is tenser than usual. Something has happened.

I take a seat near the middle of the table and try not to watch the door.

I fail.

When Maximus enters, the room's energy shifts. Conversations pause. Attention reorients. He moves to the head of the table with the ease of someone who's commanded rooms for centuries, and I watch him because I can't seem to do anything else.

He's in dark clothes, practical, ready for combat if needed. His expression is controlled, focused. The commander, not the man who lifted me onto his desk and kissed down my throat while I wrapped my legs around him.

But then his eyes find me across the room.

Just for a moment. A flicker of contact that lasts maybe two seconds. His gaze drops to the ring at my chest, lingers there, then travels back to my face.

Something warm moves through his expression before the mask slides back into place.

Two seconds. That's all.

It's enough to make heat flood through me. Enough to make me press my thighs together under the table.

"Let's begin," he says, and the meeting starts.

The intelligence is grim.

"Lord Dmitri's people intercepted communications," Ethan says. "Konstantin's been coordinating with his forces since we left the Whitley. He's not waiting anymore."

He pulls up a display showing the city's perimeter. Konstantin's forces have been gathering at three locations. Movement patterns, estimated numbers, likely approach vectors. The picture he paints is one of coordinated assault, multiple breach points, overwhelming force.

"He's not testing us anymore," Marcellus says. "This is the real thing."

"Timeline?" Maximus asks.

"Best estimate: tonight. Tomorrow at the latest." Ethan pulls up another display. "He's moved too many pieces into position. Holding them there without acting risks exposure."

The room absorbs this in silence. I see the weight of it settle onto shoulders, tighten jaws, sharpen focus. These are vampires who've survived centuries, who've fought wars and weathered crises. But this is different. This is an assault on their home.

"Defensive positions," Maximus says. "Julian, take me through the compound's vulnerabilities."

Julian moves to the map and begins outlining entry points, sight lines, choke points. I listen, filing away information, building a mental picture of the battlefield. The compound is large. Multiple buildings, extensive grounds, too much perimeter to defend without spreading thin.

"The east wing is our weakest point," Julian says, indicating a section of the map. "Limited sight lines, multiple approach routes through the gardens. If they're smart, that's where they'll hit hardest."

"Then we reinforce the east wing," Nadia says. "Pull resources from..."

"From where?" Marcellus interrupts. "We're already stretched. Pulling from one position just weakens another."

The debate continues. I watch Maximus absorb the arguments, his expression revealing nothing. But I can see him calculating, weighing options, preparing to make the call that everyone will follow.

"What about the underground approach?"

The words are out of my mouth before I've fully decided to speak. Every head turns toward me.

"Explain," Maximus says. His voice is neutral.

"The underground fighting circuit. That's where I was for three years before I was turned." I stand, moving toward the map. "You've said Konstantin pulls soldiers from those rings. If that's who we're facing, I know how they think. Practical. Efficient. No glory, just winning. They don't care about dramatic entrances. They care about what works."

Julian frowns at the map. "So they wouldn't hit the obvious weak point..."

"They'd let you think that's where they're coming," I say. "Then hit somewhere that actually hurts."

"The medical wing," Maximus says quietly. His eyes meet mine across the table, and for a moment, the room falls away. "Less defended, higher impact."

"That's how I'd do it," I agree.

"The medical wing is secondary priority," Marcellus says. "Our main defensive line is..."

"The medical wing is where Elena coordinates the donor network," I interrupt. "It's where your clean blood supply is stored, where wounded would be treated. If Konstantin's smart, and he is, he knows that taking out your medical capability cripples you even if he doesn't breach the main compound."

Silence.

I feel the weight of their assessment. These are ancient vampires, warriors who've been strategizing since before I was born. And I'm a fledgling who's been part of this world for eight months.

But I know what I'm talking about. I spent three years in that underground world. I know how those fighters move, how they think, what they prioritize.

"She's right," Nadia says finally. "We've been thinking about this like a siege. They're not laying siege. They're running an operation. Different tactics."

Maximus hasn't looked away from me. The intensity of his gaze makes my skin prickle. "Recommendations?"

"Split the reinforcement. Make the east wing look fortified. Visible presence, obvious strength. But keep a mobile reserve near the medical wing. Fast response, minimal footprint. When they hit the service entrance, we're ready."

"And if you're wrong?" Marcellus asks.

"Then I'll be the first one at the east wing." I hold his gaze. "I'm not asking anyone to take risks I won't take myself."

Another silence. Then Marcellus nods slowly. "Acceptable."

Maximus's voice cuts through. "Implement those strategies. Julian, visible reinforcement on the east wing. Nadia, coordinate the mobile reserve. Celeste." Our eyes meet. "You'll lead the reserve team."

The weight of that lands on me. Lead a team. In combat. Against Konstantin's forces.

"Yes," I say. Because what else is there to say?

The meeting continues for another hour. Logistics, communications, contingencies. By the time it ends, my head is swimming with information, and my body is humming with pre-battle tension.

People file out, heading to their posts. The room empties gradually until only a few of us remain. I'm studying the map, committing the layout to memory, when I feel him approach.

He doesn't touch me. Doesn't need to. His presence is enough, that particular quality of attention that makes the air feel heavier.

"You handled that well," he says quietly.

"I told them what I knew."

"You told them what they needed to hear, in a way they could accept. That's leadership."

I look up at him. The room is nearly empty now. Just Nadia at the far end, gathering documents, and Marcellus lingering near the door. Not private, but close.

"I was scared," I admit quietly. "Telling a room full of ancient vampires they were thinking about this wrong."

"You didn't show it."

"I've had practice hiding fear."

Something shifts in his expression. His hand moves, and for a moment I think he's going to touch my face the way he did last night.

But Marcellus is watching. Others might return at any moment. So instead, his fingers brush against mine where my hand rests on the table. A light pressure. There and gone.

The brief contact sends electricity racing up my arm.

"This isn't how I wanted tonight to go," he says quietly. His voice is low, rough. Frustrated.

"I know." I hold his gaze. "But we survive this first. Then you can make good on those promises."

Something flares in his eyes. Hot. Hungry. Barely controlled.

"I haven't forgotten a single one." His voice drops even lower, meant only for me. "When this is over, Celeste. The moment it's over."

My breath catches. "I'm holding you to that."

He holds my gaze for a beat longer. I see the effort it's taking him to maintain distance. To be the commander instead of the man. But there's a battle coming, and we both know what's at stake.

He turns and walks toward Marcellus. The two of them fall into conversation about perimeter defenses, and I'm left standing at the map with the ghost of his touch still tingling against my fingers.

Nadia catches my eye from across the room. Her expression is carefully neutral, but there's something knowing in it. She doesn't say anything. Just nods once, then leaves.

The shift between Maximus and me isn't a secret. It's not announced either. It simply exists, visible in glances, in the space we do or don't leave between us, in the quality of attention we pay to each other when we think no one's watching.

Everyone sees it. No one comments.

That might be more unnerving than if they did.

The hours before battle pass in a strange blur.

I check weapons, review positions, meet with the vampires who'll form my reserve team. They fall into formation without complaint. Word has spread about my contribution in the strategy meeting. For now, at least, they're willing to follow my lead.

The compound transforms around me. Quiet hallways become staging areas. Elegant rooms are stripped of valuables and converted to defensive positions. The staff who remain, humans and vampires alike, move with focused efficiency, preparing for what's coming.

I find myself near the medical wing as the hours deepen, checking sight lines and approach routes. The service entrance is just as I described: unassuming, practical, exactly the kind of target underground fighters would choose.

"You really think they'll come this way?"

I turn. Elena stands in the doorway to the medical wing, arms crossed, expression tense.

"I think it's possible," I say. "Maybe probable."

"Great." She laughs, but there's no humor in it. "I'm coordinating emergency blood supplies in the most likely breach point. That's comforting."

"I won't let anything happen to you."

The words come out with more intensity than I intended. Elena's expression softens.

"I know." She studies me for a moment. "You seem different tonight."

"Do I?"

She tilts her head. "Settled. Like something clicked into place."

I think about last night. The study. His hands. *Essential.*

I think about the hours before dawn, turning Vivienne's words over in my mind. And the conclusion I reached: I'm the one who chose this. I'm the one who chose him.

"Maybe something did," I tell Elena.

She doesn't push. That's one of the things I appreciate about her. She knows when to let things be.

"I should get back inside," she says. "Blood supplies won't organize themselves."

"Elena."

She pauses.

"When this is over," I say, "when we've survived it, I want you to know how much it's meant. Having you here. Having a friend."

Her eyes glisten slightly. "God, don't get sentimental on me before a battle. That's bad luck."

"I don't believe in luck."

"Neither do I." She smiles. "But I believe in you. So don't die tonight, okay? I'm not training another vampire to understand how the donor coordination system works."

She disappears back into the medical wing, and I'm left alone.

The waiting is the worst part.

Teams are in position. Communications are active. Everyone is ready.

And nothing happens.

Minutes stretch into an hour. Then two. The tension that was sharp and focused begins to fray at the edges. Not fear, we're all too disciplined for that, but the particular exhaustion of sustained alertness. Watching shadows that don't move. Listening for sounds that don't come.

"Movement on the east perimeter."

The voice crackles through the communication system. My team snaps to attention around me.

"Hold position," I say. "Wait for confirmation."

Seconds tick by. Then:

"Confirmed. Multiple hostiles approaching through the gardens. East wing is under assault."

I feel ice settle into my veins.

"Stay sharp," I tell my team. "If I'm right, we're next."

We wait. Through the comms, I hear the sounds of combat. Shouts, impacts, the particular quality of violence that vampire-on-vampire fighting produces. The east wing is holding, but barely.

One minute. Two. Three.

"Service entrance! We have a breach at the service entrance!"

"Go," I say, and we move.

The attackers are exactly what I expected. Young vampires, hungry and vicious, fighting with the desperate efficiency I remember from the underground circuit. No finesse, no strategy, just overwhelming force directed at a single point.

There are eight of them. My team is five, plus me.

Not great odds. But not impossible either.

I take the first one myself, using speed and angle to catch him off-guard. He's strong but predictable. I've fought his type a hundred times. He goes down, and I'm already moving to the next.

My team fights well. I can't track everyone, can't coordinate perfectly in the chaos, but I hear them engaging, holding the line, doing exactly what they need to do.

Blood everywhere. Some mine, mostly theirs. A stake grazes my arm, and I spin away, taking the wielder's head with a blade I barely remember drawing. The world narrows to instinct and reaction, the same focused clarity I used to find in the underground ring.

Another attacker falls. Then another.

We're winning. We're actually winning.

And then the second wave hits.

Twelve more. They pour through the breached entrance like water through a crack, and suddenly the numbers shift from difficult to catastrophic.

"Fall back!" I shout. "Protect the medical wing!"

We retreat in formation, buying space with every step. I'm acutely aware of the door behind us. Elena behind that door. The blood supplies behind that door. Everything the attackers came for behind that door.

I can't let them through.

I won't let them through.

A vampire twice my size rushes me. I sidestep, but he's fast, faster than the others. His fist catches my shoulder, sends me spinning. Before I can recover, he's on me, stake in hand.

I catch his wrist. We struggle, strength against strength. He's older than the young ones, more experienced. His stake inches closer to my chest.

I wrench sideways at the last second. The stake misses my heart, but drives into my shoulder instead.

Pain explodes through me. White-hot, blinding. A scream tears out of my throat before I can stop it, raw and ragged. My grip falters.

Not like this.

I never got to tell him...

A blur of motion. The vampire is ripped away from me, the stake tearing free as he goes. His head snaps back, his body crumpling. Maximus stands where he was, eyes wild, fangs extended, more terrifying than I've ever seen him.

"Celeste." My name in his mouth sounds like a prayer. Like a curse.

"I'm fine," I manage.

"You almost..."

"I'm fine."

The battle isn't over. More attackers pressing forward. But he looks at me for one endless moment, and I see everything in his eyes. Fear, relief, rage.

"Later," I say.

"Later," he agrees.

And then we're fighting side by side, and there's no time for anything but survival.

TWENTY-SIX

The stake was in her shoulder thirty seconds ago.

Thirty seconds, and I'm still seeing it. Still feeling the moment my dead heart tried to restart in my chest. Still tasting the panic that flooded my mouth like copper.

Now I'm tasting blood. Theirs.

A vampire rushes her from the left. Before she can react, I'm there, catching him mid-lunge, driving my blade through his throat with enough force to nearly sever his head. He drops. I'm already moving to the next one.

"I had him," Celeste snaps.

I don't answer. Can't. The rage has swallowed everything else.

She ducks under a swing, drives her blade up through an attacker's ribs, spins away before his body hits the ground. Blood arcs through the air. Some of it hers, still seeping from the wound in her shoulder, mixing with the spray from her kills. She's fighting like the injury doesn't exist. Like she didn't almost die a minute ago.

I intercept another vampire angling for her blind side. This one I don't kill quickly. I break his arm first, then his knee, then I tear out his throat with my bare hands while he screams.

The sound satisfies something dark in my chest.

They made her scream. I heard the pain in it, and something in me snapped clean in half.

Now I want to hear all of theirs.

We fall into rhythm despite my fury. She goes low, I go high. She draws their attention. I come from behind. Two bodies moving as one. But I'm not fighting tactically anymore. I'm fighting to annihilate. Every vampire I kill is the one who drove that stake toward her heart.

Another comes at me with a stake, movements precise rather than frantic. He feints left, strikes right. I read the deception a half-second too late, and the stake grazes my ribs, tearing through shirt and skin. Pain flares, hot and sharp.

Before he can press the advantage, Celeste sweeps his legs from behind. He goes down hard, stake clattering away. I crush his skull beneath my heel. No hesitation. No restraint.

Our eyes meet across his body. Her face is streaked with blood. Hers and theirs, indistinguishable now. Her chest heaves with unnecessary breaths, her fangs fully extended. The wound on her shoulder seeps through her ruined shirt, a dark stain spreading with every movement.

She's still fighting. Still bleeding. Still here.

The rage doesn't fade. It sharpens.

She nods once. I nod back.

Then we're moving again, because the fight isn't over, and I have more killing to do.

Around us, the tide is turning. My people have rallied at the service entrance, reinforcements arriving from other positions now that the east wing attack has been revealed as the feint it was. Konstantin's soldiers are good. Underground fighters, just as

Celeste predicted. But they're outnumbered now, outmaneuvered.

And I am not showing mercy.

Julian takes down two attackers in rapid succession. Nadia guards the medical wing door with lethal focus. But I'm barely tracking them. My attention keeps snapping back to Celeste. To the way she favors her injured shoulder. To the pallor beneath the blood on her face. To the wound that should be healing faster than it is.

One by one, Konstantin's soldiers fall.

The last attacker, a scarred woman with close-cropped hair and wild eyes, realizes she's alone. She bolts for the breach point. Julian intercepts her three feet from the exit, his blade flashing once, twice. She crumples.

Silence settles like dust after an explosion.

The service entrance looks like a slaughterhouse. Bodies everywhere, some still twitching with the last echoes of undead life. Blood pools on the concrete, runs in rivulets toward the drain in the center of the floor. The walls are splattered with it.

Some of it is hers. The thought won't leave me.

Celeste stands in the middle of the carnage, blade still raised, turning slowly to scan for threats that are no longer there. Her ruined shirt clings to her body, soaked through with blood. The wound on her shoulder has slowed but hasn't closed. Raw flesh visible through the torn fabric.

Another inch to the left.

The thought hits me like a physical blow. Another inch, and the stake would have found her heart. Another inch, and she'd be one of the bodies on the floor.

The rage transmutes into something else. Something that makes my hands shake as I lower my weapon.

"Clear," Julian calls out. "Service entrance secure."

"East wing?" I ask without taking my eyes off her.

"Holding. Konstantin's forces are retreating across all positions."

Retreating. Not defeated. He'll regroup, reassess, and come back stronger.

But that's a problem for later. Right now, the only thing I can focus on is the woman standing ten feet away, slowly lowering her weapon, finally meeting my eyes.

The adrenaline is fading, and in its absence, I can feel every wound I collected during the fighting. The gash across my ribs pulses. Something in my shoulder grinds when I move. Torn muscle, maybe, or a joint knocked out of alignment. Smaller cuts sting across my arms, my face, my hands.

I ignore all of it.

"You're hurt," I say.

She glances down at her shoulder like she's forgotten about it. "It's nothing."

"You're bleeding."

"So are you."

I close the distance between us in three strides. "Medical wing. Now."

She opens her mouth to argue.

"Now, Celeste."

I guide her through the medical wing door.

Inside, it's controlled chaos.

Elena stands at the center of it, clipboard in hand, directing traffic with the calm efficiency of a general commanding troops. "Minor wounds to the left, serious to the right. Anyone who can walk, clear the beds for those who can't. You..." She points at a vampire cradling his arm. "That's a clean break. Set it and move on. We need the space."

The staff move around her, following orders without question.

The vampire healers work on the more serious cases, a woman with a stake wound to the abdomen, and others whose injuries I can't immediately identify.

"Shoulder wound needs cleaning," she says to Celeste. "Examination table three. I'll send someone."

"I've got it," I say.

Elena's eyebrows rise slightly, but she doesn't comment. Just nods and turns back to her coordination.

Celeste tries to wave off the treatment as we make our way to the indicated table. "I'm fine. There are others who need..."

"Sit down." I guide her to the table with a hand on her lower back, feeling the tension in her muscles.

"Maximus, I can—"

"You can sit down and let me look at you, or I can carry you to this table. Your choice." My voice comes out rougher than I intend. "I just watched a stake come within an inch of your heart. Give me this."

Something in her expression softens. "Okay."

"Let me see," I say, reaching for the medical supplies.

"You're not a healer."

"I've been treating wounds since before modern medicine existed. Since before this country existed." I gather supplies from a nearby cabinet: antiseptic, a clean cloth, and bandages. "Sit."

She sits. But her jaw is set, her eyes tracking my movements with wariness.

"Take off your shirt," I say.

One eyebrow arches. "Here?"

"I need to see the wound."

"I'm sure you do."

Despite everything, the battle, the blood, the fear that's still clenched around my heart like a fist, I almost smile. "Celeste."

"Fine." She reaches for the hem, then winces as the movement pulls at her shoulder. "Little help?"

I move closer. My fingers find the ruined fabric, sticky with drying blood. I work it up her body slowly, carefully, trying to minimize the strain on her wound. She raises her arms as much as she can, and I pull the shirt over her head.

Underneath, she's wearing a simple black undergarment. Functional, not decorative. Appropriate for battle. And yet the sight of her, the lean muscle, the pale skin, the scattered bruises already fading, makes something tighten in my chest.

The wound is worse than I thought.

The stake went deep, tearing through the muscle of her shoulder, scraping against bone. The edges are ragged, struggling to knit closed. Blood still seeps from the deepest part, welling up each time she moves.

"That bad?" she asks, watching my face.

I don't answer. Don't trust my voice.

Instead, I soak a cloth in antiseptic and begin to clean the wound. She hisses at the sting but doesn't pull away. Her hands grip the edge of the examination table, knuckles white.

"Sorry," I murmur.

"Don't be. Just do it."

I work methodically, carefully. The antiseptic clears away the dried blood and reveals the true extent of the damage. Deep, but clean. No fragments left behind, no signs of infection. It will heal. She will heal.

But the memory of watching her pinned beneath that vampire will take longer to fade. The stake driving into her shoulder. Her cry of pain. Knowing the next strike would find her heart if I didn't reach her in time.

"You're shaking," she says quietly.

I look down at my hands. She's right. A fine tremor runs through them, barely visible, but there.

"No, I'm not."

"You are." Her hand covers mine, stilling its movement. "Maximus. I'm okay."

"You almost weren't."

"But I am." Her fingers thread through mine, squeeze gently. "Because you got there in time. Because you came for me."

"Of course I came for you." The words come out rough, raw. "Did you think I wouldn't?"

"I didn't think anything. I saw the stake coming, and then you were there." She tugs at my hand, pulling me closer. "You're always there."

I'm standing between her knees now. One hand still holding the cloth, the other clasped in hers. Close enough to see the flecks of amber in her dark eyes. Close enough to count each individual eyelash. Close enough to feel the cool brush of her breath against my face.

"I should finish cleaning this," I say.

"Probably."

Neither of us moves.

"Maximus." Her free hand comes up, touches my face. Traces the line of my jaw, the corner of my mouth. Her fingers come away bloody; I didn't realize I was wounded there. "You're hurt too."

"It's nothing."

"Now who's minimizing?"

"I've had six centuries to practice."

"Show-off."

I laugh. The sound startles me.

She smiles, and something in my chest cracks open.

I finish cleaning her wound in silence. Apply pressure until the bleeding stops completely. Cover it with a clean bandage, my fingers lingering on her skin longer than strictly necessary.

"You should drink," I say. "Blood will speed the healing."

"Later."

"Celeste."

"I'll drink when you let someone look at your ribs." She nods toward my side, where my shirt is still soaked through with blood. "Deal?"

"I don't negotiate..."

"Deal or no deal?"

I sigh. "Deal."

She smiles again, and I realize I would agree to almost anything to keep that expression on her face.

"Sir."

Marcellus's voice cuts through the moment. I step back from Celeste, not far, not fast, but enough to establish some semblance of professional distance.

He stands in the doorway, his expression carefully blank. Blood streaks his face and arms, evidence of his own fighting, but he moves without obvious pain. Whatever wounds he took, they're already healing.

"Report," I say.

"All positions secure. Final count: six of ours dead, twelve wounded."

Six. The number lands like a blow. Six names to add to the list I carry. Six faces I'll see when I close my eyes.

"Who?"

Marcellus recites them. I listen to each name, commit them to memory. Victor, who'd been with me for seventy years. Maria, barely out of her first decade. Edward, Julian's protégé. Others whose lives stretched back decades, centuries, reduced now to bodies awaiting burial.

"Konstantin's casualties?" I ask.

"At least thirty confirmed. Possibly more, some retreated with wounds that may prove fatal." Marcellus pauses. "He wasn't present. Led the assault remotely."

Coward. Or strategist. The line between them has always been thin.

"That wasn't their real push," Celeste says. She's pulled her ruined shirt back on, holding it closed over her bandaged shoulder. "They pulled back too clean. Too organized."

"Reconnaissance," Marcellus agrees. "He wanted to test our defenses, see how we'd respond."

I nod slowly, processing. Konstantin is smart, always has been. He won't make the same approach twice. Whatever comes next will be different, unexpected, designed to exploit whatever vulnerabilities tonight revealed.

"Double the perimeter watch," I say. "Four-hour shifts, fresh rotations. I want damage assessments from all positions by dawn. And contact Lord Dmitri. His intelligence was accurate. I want to know if he has more."

"Already in progress." Marcellus hesitates, his eyes moving between me and Celeste in a way that suggests he sees more than I'd like. "Sir. You should rest. You took damage."

"I'll deal with it."

"You're bleeding through your shirt."

"I said I'll deal with it."

Another pause. Longer this time. Then Marcellus nods once.

"I'll handle the reports," he says. "Take the night. Both of you."

He leaves before I can respond to what is clearly not a suggestion.

The compound settles into the exhausted quiet that follows crisis.

I walk through the corridors with Celeste beside me, surveying the damage as we go. Broken windows, blood-streaked walls, furniture splintered from combat. My people move past us, some injured, some whole, all wearing the hollow expressions of survivors.

We should stop. I should talk to them, offer reassurance, be the leader they need me to be.

So I do. A hand on a shoulder. A nod of acknowledgment. Brief words to those who need them. "You fought well." "Get that looked at." "Rest while you can."

It takes longer than I'd like. Every moment, I'm aware of Celeste beside me, waiting. But these are my people. They bled for me tonight. They deserve more than my back as I walk past.

When I've done what I can, when the immediate needs have been addressed, I finally let myself keep walking.

Celeste matches my pace without comment. Her shoulder must be throbbing, vampire healing or not, a wound that deep takes time, but she doesn't slow, doesn't complain. Just walks beside me, close enough that our arms occasionally brush.

Each contact sends electricity through my skin.

We pass the conference room. Through the open door, I see Julian and Nadia bent over the maps, already planning for the next assault. They look up as we pass. Julian opens his mouth to speak.

I shake my head slightly, keep walking.

We climb the stairs to the residential wing. The sounds of the compound fade behind us: voices, movement, the organized chaos of aftermath. Up here, it's quiet. Private.

My quarters are at the end of the hall. I've walked this path thousands of times over the decades. Tonight, it feels different. Charged.

I stop in front of my door. Turn to face her.

She's watching me with those dark eyes, waiting. Patient. The ring glints at her chest, catching the dim light from the wall sconces.

"You should rest," I say.

"So should you."

"Celeste."

"If you're about to tell me to go to my room like a good soldier, don't."

Something shifts in my chest. A lock turning. A wall crumbling.

I tried to do this right. Tried to give us time, space, the opportunity to come together without fear or adrenaline clouding the decision. I wanted our first time to mean something. To be a choice, not a reaction.

But she almost died tonight. The memory of it hits me fresh. The stake buried in her shoulder. The blood soaking through her shirt. The split second where I thought the next blow would find her heart, and I wouldn't reach her in time.

I'm done waiting.

I close the distance between us. Her back meets the door, and I brace one hand beside her head, leaning in until my mouth is inches from hers. I can smell her. Blood and underneath it, something that's purely her. Something I want to drown in.

"I wasn't going to tell you to go to your room."

Her breath catches. I watch her pupils dilate, feel the subtle shift in her posture as she leans toward me.

"Then what were you going to say?"

I don't answer. I'm done talking.

I kiss her like I've been starving for it. Because I have. Weeks of restraint, of pulling back, of telling myself I was being noble when really I was just terrified. All of it burns away the second her mouth opens under mine.

She gasps against my lips, and I swallow the sound, my hand

fisting in her hair, tilting her head back to deepen the kiss. She tastes like blood. Hers and mine and theirs, all mixed together, and I don't care. I want more of it. More of her.

Her hands grab my ruined shirt, yanking me closer. The movement pulls at my wound, and I don't care about that either. Pain is nothing. Pain is background noise. The only thing that exists is her mouth and her hands and the sounds she's making against my lips.

I reach behind her and shove the door open.

We stumble through together, still kissing, her fingers working the buttons of my shirt with desperate urgency. She gets three open before she gives up and just tears. Buttons scatter across the floor. The sound of them hitting wood is obscenely loud in the quiet room.

"That was expensive," I manage against her mouth.

"Bill me."

I laugh.

She pushes the shirt off my shoulders, and her hands find bare skin. I shudder. Her touch is cool, but it burns everywhere it lands, tracing the planes of my chest, the ridges of my stomach, the edges of the wound across my ribs.

"Does it hurt?" she asks.

"Yes."

She kisses it.

Something snaps in my chest. The last thread of control I was clinging to.

I walk her toward the bed, my mouth never leaving hers. Her knees hit the mattress, and she falls back, pulling me down with her. I catch myself on my forearms, hovering over her, looking down at her face in the darkness.

Blood on her cheek. Fire in her eyes. The ring glinting gold at her throat.

Mine.

I tear her shirt open the same way she did mine. The fabric gives easily, already weakened from battle. Underneath, just a simple black undergarment and the bandage on her shoulder, spotted with blood.

I should be careful with her. She's wounded. She almost died.

I can't be careful. Not tonight. Not after everything.

I lower my mouth to her throat and bite. Not to feed. Just to mark. Just to taste the salt of her skin, to hear the sound she makes when my fangs graze the spot where her neck meets her shoulder.

She arches into me, her nails raking down my back hard enough to draw blood. The pain lights up my nerve endings. I growl against her throat and bite harder.

"Maximus." My name comes out broken. Desperate. "Please."

"Please, what?"

"More. Everything. I don't care, just don't stop."

I drag my mouth down her body. The undergarment disappears. I'm not sure if I unclasped it or tore it. Doesn't matter. My lips find the swell of her breast, the peak of her nipple, and I suck hard enough to make her cry out. Her hands fist in my hair, holding me there, her hips rolling up against mine.

I want to take my time. Want to taste every inch of her, learn every sound she makes, find every spot that makes her shake.

I can't. The need is too sharp. Too many years of loneliness compressed into this single moment, this single woman, and I can't wait another second.

I work my way back up her body, kissing and biting as I go. She's writhing beneath me now, her hands everywhere, tugging at my belt, shoving at my pants, making frustrated sounds when the fabric doesn't cooperate.

I help her. Clothes disappear. And then there's nothing

between us, just skin against skin, cool against cool, her body pressed along the length of mine.

She wraps her legs around my waist and pulls me closer. The pressure of her against me makes my vision blur.

"Now," she says. "I need you now."

I should ask if she's sure. Should give her one more chance to stop this.

But I look at her face, and I see the same desperation I'm feeling. The same hunger. The same need that goes beyond want into something closer to survival.

I stop thinking.

I push into her in one long stroke, and the world whites out.

She's tight. Perfect. Her body grips me like she was made for this, made for me. I don't care about anything except the way she feels around me, the sounds she's making, the way her nails dig crescents into my shoulders as I start to move.

"God." The word tears out of her. "Maximus."

I set a brutal pace. Can't help it. Can't slow down. Every thrust drives us both higher, the headboard slamming against the wall, the bed groaning beneath us. She meets me stroke for stroke, her hips rising to take me deeper, her teeth finding my shoulder and biting down hard enough to break skin.

The pain mixes with pleasure until I can't separate them. Don't want to separate them. This is what I needed. This is what I've been denying myself. Not just sex but this. This rawness. This loss of control. This feeling of being consumed and consuming in equal measure.

"Harder," she gasps. "I won't break."

I grab her thigh, hitch it higher on my hip, and drive into her with everything I have. The new angle makes her scream. Her walls clench around me, and I feel her getting close, feel the tension building in her body.

My control is slipping. I can feel it fraying with every thrust, every sound she makes, every drag of her nails down my back. My fangs have extended fully, aching with a hunger that has nothing to do with sustenance. My gaze keeps dropping to her throat, to the pulse point where her blood would flow if she still had a heartbeat.

I want to taste her. Need to taste her. The urge is primal, overwhelming, tangled up with the pleasure until I can't separate them.

"Celeste." Her name comes out rough, strained. I drag my fangs along the curve of her neck, feeling her shiver beneath me. "I need... Can I?"

She understands what I'm asking. I see it in her eyes, the flash of surprise followed by something darker. Hunger of her own.

"Yes." She tilts her head back, baring her throat to me. "God, yes."

The trust in that gesture undoes me.

I lower my mouth to her neck. Press a kiss to the sensitive skin first. Then I let my fangs graze the spot, testing, giving her one last chance to change her mind.

"Do it," she breathes. "I want to feel you everywhere."

I bite.

Her blood floods my mouth, and the world fractures.

She tastes like fire. Like lightning captured in liquid form. I feel her strength, her defiance, her stubborn refusal to break no matter what the world throws at her. I taste her fear and her hope tangled together. Her desire, sharp and urgent, matching my own. The trust she's placed in me, terrifying in its completeness.

And underneath it all, something else. Something that makes my chest crack open.

She cares for me. Not just wants me, cares. Deeply. Fiercely.

The taste of it overwhelms me.

Celeste cries out beneath me, her body arching off the bed. The bite has intensified everything for her, too. I can feel it in the way her walls clench around me, the way her nails score my back, the way she's shaking apart.

"Maximus." My name tears out of her, broken and desperate. "I'm going to..."

"Let go." I seal my mouth over the wound, drinking deep, feeling her pleasure echo through her blood. "I've got you."

She shatters.

Her release rips through her with a cry she doesn't bother to muffle. Her body clamps down on mine, pulsing, pulling, and I follow her over the edge with a groan that sounds like it's been ripped from somewhere deep. I bury myself as deep as I can go and let it take me.

For a long moment, neither of us moves.

Then she laughs. Soft and surprised and thoroughly wrecked.

"I think you broke something."

I lift my head to look at her. "What?"

"I don't know. My brain. My ability to form sentences." She grins up at me, and the sight of it, her hair a disaster, bite marks blooming on her throat, makes something warm bloom in my chest. "That was..."

"Not enough."

Her grin widens. "Not even close."

I'm still inside her. Still hard, or hard again. Vampire stamina has its benefits.

I pull out slowly, watching her face, the way her eyes flutter, the way she bites her lip. Then I flip her onto her stomach.

"Maximus, what..."

I pull her hips up, positioning her on her hands and knees. She looks back at me over her shoulder, eyes dark with renewed hunger.

"We have all night," I say. "I intend to use every second of it."

I push back into her and start again.

The second time is slower. Deeper. I grip her hips hard enough to bruise, watching myself disappear into her body, watching the way her back arches, listening to the sounds she makes with each thrust. She drops to her elbows, changing the angle, and we both groan at the difference.

I lean over her, my chest against her back, my mouth at her ear. "You're mine," I tell her. "Say it."

"I'm yours."

"Again."

"I'm yours." She pushes back against me, taking me deeper. "I'm yours, Maximus."

The words undo me. I wrap one arm around her waist, my other hand sliding between her thighs to touch her where we're joined. She comes again, harder this time, her whole body shaking, and I follow her with a groan that echoes off the walls.

We collapse together onto the sheets. I gather her against my chest, pressing my face into her hair, breathing her in.

"We should clean up," she mumbles.

"No."

"I'm covered in blood. You're covered in blood. Your sheets are..."

"I don't care." I roll her onto her back, settling my weight between her thighs again. She blinks up at me, surprised. "I told you. All night."

"We just..."

"And we're going to again." I lower my mouth to her breast, swirling my tongue around her nipple until she gasps. "And again. Until neither of us can move."

Her laugh dissolves into a moan as I work my way down her body.

I take my time now. The desperate edge has dulled, replaced by something deeper. Something that wants to learn her. Memorize her. Every curve. Every scar. Every spot that makes her gasp or shiver or moan my name.

I kiss the bruises on her hips, already fading. Press my lips to the scar on her thigh from some long-ago fight. Trace the line of her hip bone with my tongue.

"Maximus." Her voice is strained. "What are you..."

"Shh." I spread her thighs wider, settling between them. "Let me."

I lower my mouth to her center and taste her.

She cries out, her hands flying to my hair, gripping hard. I don't mind the sting. I want her holding onto me. Want her anchored to me while I take her apart.

I work her with my tongue, slow and thorough, learning what makes her gasp, what makes her moan, what makes her thighs tremble around my head. She tastes incredible. Sweet and salt and something darker underneath, something that's purely her.

"Please," she whimpers. "I can't, I need..."

I slide two fingers inside her, curling them just right, and suck hard on the bundle of nerves at her apex.

She comes with a scream that probably wakes half the compound. I don't stop. Keep working her through it, drawing out the pleasure until she's shaking, until she's pulling at my hair, trying to push me away.

"Too much," she gasps. "It's too much, I can't..."

"You can." I climb up her body, positioning myself at her entrance again. "One more. Give me one more."

I push inside her.

She's so sensitive now that she cries out at the first thrust. Her walls flutter around me, still pulsing from her last orgasm, and the sensation nearly undoes me.

This time I go slow. Rolling my hips instead of thrusting, grinding deep, keeping constant pressure on the spot inside her that makes her eyes roll back. Her legs wrap around my waist, her heels digging into my lower back, urging me deeper.

"Look at me," I say.

Her eyes open. Dark and dazed and full of something that makes my chest ache.

I brush the hair back from her face, still moving inside her, slow and deep. I want to tell her what I'm feeling. The words are right there, pressing against my teeth. Three words I haven't said to anyone in centuries.

But I'm not ready. Not yet. So I show her instead.

I lower my forehead to hers and let my body say what my mouth can't.

Her hands come up to frame my face, holding me there, her eyes locked on mine as we move together.

It builds slowly this time, a wave rather than a crash, rising and rising until we're both trembling with it.

"Together," she whispers. "I want to feel you."

"Together."

We shatter at the same moment. Her cry and my groan tangling in the air between us, her body clenching around mine as I spill into her. The pleasure whites out everything else, and for a long suspended moment, there's nothing but sensation and her.

We lie tangled together afterward, breathing hard out of habit rather than need. Her body is draped across mine, one leg thrown over my hips, her head on my chest. I trace lazy patterns on her bare back, feeling the smooth skin, the curve of her spine.

"My shoulder hurts," she admits after a while.

"I know. I've been avoiding it."

She laughs softly. "You were being careful. Even when you were being rough, you were being careful."

"Of course I was." I tilt her chin up so she meets my eyes. "You're mine now. That means your pain is mine to avoid making worse."

"That's very sweet for someone who just had me screaming loud enough to wake the compound."

"Three times."

"Four. You lost count."

I smile against her hair. "Your shoulder needs blood to heal properly."

"Later."

"Celeste."

"Later." She presses a kiss to my chest. "Right now, I just want to stay here. Like this."

I tighten my arms around her. "Then stay."

Silence settles over us. Comfortable. Full.

Outside the window, the first gray hints of dawn are beginning to lighten the sky. The pull of dormancy tugs at my consciousness.

"We should sleep," I say reluctantly.

"Probably." But she doesn't move. Her fingers trace idle patterns on my chest. "Maximus?"

"Yes?"

"When we wake up tonight..." She hesitates. "Will this still be real? Or will you go back to being the cold, distant lord who pretends he doesn't feel anything?"

The question cuts deeper than she knows.

"I spent centuries building walls," I admit. "It won't be easy to tear them down completely. There may be moments when I retreat. When old habits take over." I tilt her chin up so she's looking at me. "But I will never pretend this isn't real. I will never pretend you don't matter. You've carved yourself a place inside me, Celeste. That doesn't disappear with sunrise."

"Promise?"

"Promise."

She kisses me. Soft and sweet.

"Then I can sleep," she says.

She's asleep before I am. I can tell by the way her body relaxes against mine, the way her breathing evens out.

I stay awake a little longer. Watching her. Memorizing the way she looks in my arms, in my bed.

There are words I want to say. Words I'm not ready to say. Words that feel too big, too terrifying, too much like handing someone a weapon and hoping they won't use it.

But looking at her now, I think maybe I'll find the courage. Soon. When the time is right.

The sun pulls at me, and I let my eyes close.

The last thing I feel before dormancy takes me is her breath against my chest, steady and even.

Mine.

TWENTY-SEVEN

I wake slowly.

That's unusual. Since I was turned, waking has been instant. One moment dormant, the next alert. No transition. No gradual drift toward consciousness.

But tonight is different. Tonight I surface in stages, awareness seeping in like water through sand. First, the weight of blankets. Then the coolness of sheets against my bare skin. Then the solid presence of a body pressed against my back, an arm draped over my waist, breath stirring my hair.

Maximus.

The memories flood back. His mouth on mine. His hands everywhere. The desperate, consuming need that drove us both past the point of control. The things we did to each other, the sounds we made, the way he looked at me like I was the only thing in the universe that mattered.

I'm in his bed. In his arms. Naked and sore in ways that make me want to smile.

I don't move. Don't want to break whatever spell is holding this moment together. Outside the blackout curtains, evening has fallen. I can feel it in my bones, that vampire awareness of the sun's position. We slept through the entire day, tangled together, dead to the world in the most literal sense.

His arm tightens around my waist. He's awake. I can tell by the shift in his breathing, the subtle tension in his muscles.

"Stop pretending to sleep," he murmurs against my hair.

"I wasn't pretending. I was savoring."

"Savoring what?"

"This." I press back against him, feeling every inch of his body against mine. "Waking up with you."

He makes a sound low in his throat. Something between a growl and a sigh. His hand splays across my stomach, pulling me closer, and I feel him hard against my lower back.

"Good evening," I say. "Or night. Whatever."

"Evening." His lips find the curve of my neck, press a soft kiss there. "How do you feel?"

"Like I was thoroughly wrecked by an ancient vampire lord."

"Wrecked." I can hear the smile in his voice. "That's the word you're going with?"

"Would you prefer ravished? Debauched? Absolutely ruined for anyone else?"

"I like that last one."

I turn in his arms, rolling to face him. The movement presses us together in new ways, and I watch his eyes darken.

He looks different in the dim light of evening. Softer, somehow. The hard edges that usually define him have blurred. His hair is mussed, falling across his forehead in a way I've never seen. There are scratches on his shoulders from my nails, already fading but still visible.

I did that. I marked him.

We stare at each other for a long moment. This close, I can see the gray of his eyes, the faint lines around them that suggest centuries of expression, even if his face hasn't aged. I can see the vulnerability he usually hides, the softness he buries under command and control.

"Last night was..." I trail off, not sure how to finish.

"Yes." He traces a finger along my jaw. "It was."

"Is it always like that?"

"No." His expression is serious now. "I've never had that."

"What was that?"

He considers the question. His thumb brushes across my lower lip, a gesture that's becoming familiar. "I think that was what happens when you stop holding back. When you let yourself feel everything instead of just the physical."

I understand what he means. Last night wasn't just bodies. It was everything we'd been denying, everything we'd been afraid of, finally given permission to exist.

"I want more," I tell him.

"More?"

"Not just..." I gesture vaguely between us. "I want to know you. Really know you. Everything you've been hiding behind those walls of yours."

Something flickers in his expression. Caution, maybe. Or hope. "That's a lot to ask."

"I know." I prop myself up on my elbow. "But I'm asking anyway."

He's quiet for a long moment. I watch him wrestle with something.

"There's a way," he says finally. "For you to know me. All of me. But it's... intimate. More intimate than what we did last night, in some ways."

"More intimate than sex?"

"For vampires, blood is..." He pauses, searching for words. "It's not just sustenance. It's connection. When you drink from someone, you taste everything they are. Their essence. Their history. Their emotions. Nothing is hidden."

I remember the way he bit me last night. The flood of sensation, the pleasure that bordered on pain.

"You drank from me," I say slowly. "What did you taste?"

His expression softens. "I tasted your strength. Your fire. Your fear and your hope and that stubborn defiance that made me notice you in the first place." His thumb traces my lower lip again. "I tasted how much you want me. How much you trust me, despite everything. It was... intoxicating."

"I want that." The words come out before I can second-guess them. "I want to taste you. Know you the way you know me now."

"Celeste." He cups my face in both hands, making sure I'm looking at him. "I need you to understand what you're asking. When you drink from me, you'll taste everything. All of it. The good and the bad. Over six hundred years of pain and violence and loneliness. I won't be able to hide any of it from you."

"I don't want you to hide from me." I turn my head, press a kiss to his palm. "I want to know all of you. Even the parts you think I won't like."

He's quiet for a long moment.

Then he tilts his head back, baring his throat.

The gesture steals my breath.

I understand its significance without being told. For a vampire of his age and power, with his history of enslavement, offering his throat is an act of profound trust. He's making himself vulnerable in a way he probably hasn't since before Luciano took him.

"You're sure?" I whisper.

"I'm sure." His voice is steady, but I can feel the tension in his body. "I want you to know me. All of me. I'm tired of hiding."

I move over him, straddling his hips, feeling him stir beneath me. That can wait. This first.

I lower my mouth to his throat.

His skin is cool against my lips, smooth over the taut muscle beneath. I can smell him. My fangs extend without conscious thought, responding to proximity and desire.

I press a kiss to his pulse point. Another to the hollow of his throat. Another to the place where his jaw meets his neck.

"Whenever you're ready," he says. His voice is steady, but his hands have come up to grip my hips, fingers digging in.

I bite.

His blood fills my mouth, and the world explodes.

It's nothing like drinking from a blood bag. Nothing like the stolen sips of contaminated blood that kept me alive before Maximus found me. This is something else entirely. This is drinking lightning. Drinking fire. Drinking centuries of existence compressed into liquid form.

I taste his age first. The sheer weight of six hundred years, each one leaving its mark. Layer upon layer of experience, of memory, of emotion. More than any human could ever contain.

Then the emotions hit me.

Grief, old and deep, like a river that's been flowing so long it's carved canyons into stone. Loneliness so profound it makes my chest ache, centuries of going through the motions of existence without ever truly living. The cold patience of survival, of endurance, of continuing forward simply because the alternative is unthinkable.

I taste his human life. A boy in medieval Italy, learning to fight, learning to lead. The men he trained, the battles he survived, the family he left behind. Letters he never got to send. A mother he never saw again.

I taste Luciano. The taking. The century and a half of enslavement. The violation of being used, controlled, broken down, and rebuilt into something he didn't recognize. The hatred that kept him alive when everything else had been stripped away. The moment he finally killed his maker and felt nothing but hollow silence where satisfaction should have been.

I taste Catherine. The first person he loved after Luciano. The hope she represented, the future he'd started to imagine. Then the horror of watching her go feral, of realizing he would have to kill her himself. The blade through her heart. The centuries of guilt that followed, the vow to never let himself care that much again.

I taste the walls he built. Brick by brick, year by year. The careful distance he maintained from everyone. The way he convinced himself that power was enough, that control was safety, that love was just another word for vulnerability.

And beneath all of it, running through everything like veins of gold through dark rock: warmth. New warmth. Tentative and fragile and fierce.

The warmth has a name.

Me.

I taste how he felt when he first saw me in that alley. Irritation mixed with curiosity mixed with something he couldn't name. The moment he decided to save me. The moment he realized he wanted to keep me.

I taste the night he watched me on the security feeds during my first solo mission. The way his chest tightened every time I moved out of frame. The realization that he was compromised, that he cared, that all his centuries of walls had been breached by a fledgling with eight months of experience and a stubborn streak a mile wide.

I taste his fear. Fear of losing me. Fear of caring. Fear of opening himself up to pain after so long being numb.

I taste his desire. The way he's wanted me, fought against

wanting me, surrendered to wanting me. The way every touch between us has burned itself into his memory.

And I taste, unmistakably, irrevocably, his love.

He loves me.

It's not just an emotion. It's a certainty. Bone-deep. Blood-deep. The truest thing he's felt in centuries. He loves me with a desperation that terrifies him and a tenderness that surprises him and a totality that has remade him from the inside out.

I pull back, licking the wound closed, and stare down at him.

My face is wet. Tears, I realize. I didn't know vampires could cry.

"Celeste?" He reaches up to touch my cheek, catching a tear on his fingertip. "What is it? What did you taste?"

I should tell him. Should say the words, let him know I felt it, that I feel it too. But the emotions are too big, too overwhelming. Language feels inadequate.

Instead, I kiss him.

He tastes like blood now. Like me and him and something new, something we've created together. His hands grip my hips and pull me down onto him, and I realize he's fully hard, ready for me, and I'm ready too, more than ready, my body responding to the intimacy of the blood with renewed hunger.

"Again?" I murmur against his mouth.

"Again," he agrees. "But slower this time. I want to savor you."

He rolls us so I'm beneath him, his weight pressing me into the mattress. But he doesn't rush. Doesn't claim. He kisses me soft and deep, taking his time, letting the heat build gradually instead of crashing over us all at once.

His mouth leaves mine, traces down my throat. Soft kisses. Gentle scrapes of teeth. Nothing like the biting hunger of last night. This is worship.

"Last night was about need," he says against my collarbone. "Tonight is about want. There's a difference."

"Show me."

He does.

He maps my body like he's charting unknown territory. Every curve, every scar, every sensitive spot I didn't know I had. He finds the place beneath my ribs that makes me gasp. The inside of my wrist that makes me shiver. The dip of my hip bone that makes me moan.

"You're sensitive here," he observes, running his tongue along the crease where my thigh meets my hip.

"I'm sensitive everywhere when you do that."

"Good." He looks up at me, eyes dark with desire. "I want you feeling everything."

He settles between my thighs, and I feel exposed. Vulnerable. Completely at his mercy.

His hands grip my hips, thumbs tracing circles on the sensitive skin of my inner thighs. So close to where I need him, but not close enough.

"Maximus. Please."

"Please, what?" He presses a kiss to my inner thigh. "Tell me what you want."

"Your mouth. I want your mouth on me."

His smile is slow and wicked. "As you wish."

The first touch of his tongue tears a cry from my throat. Pleasure explodes through me, and I fist my hands in his hair without conscious thought.

He groans against me, and the vibration adds another layer to the sensation. His tongue works in slow, devastating strokes, learning my body the way his hands learned it earlier. Finding the spots that make me gasp. The spots that make me moan. The spots that make my thighs tremble around his head.

"You taste incredible," he murmurs. "I could do this for hours."

"I won't last hours."

"Then I'll bring you to the edge and back. Again and again. Until you're begging."

He does exactly that. Every time I get close, he pulls back, gentles his touch, lets the wave recede before building it again. It's torture. The sweetest torture I've ever experienced.

"Maximus, please, I can't..."

"You can." He slides two fingers inside me, curling them perfectly. "One more time. Show me how beautiful you are when you fall apart."

I shatter with his name on my lips.

He works me through it, drawing out every tremor, and before I've fully recovered, he's rising over me, positioning himself at my entrance.

"Look at me," he says.

I open eyes I don't remember closing.

His face is inches from mine. Tender and fierce all at once. "I need you to know something before we do this again."

"What?"

"When you bit me..." He pauses, and I see him gathering courage. "You tasted what I feel. But I need to say it. Out loud. In words."

My breath catches.

"I never said it to Catherine," he continues. "I was working up the courage when she turned. When I had to... I never got to say the words. I've regretted it for three hundred years." His jaw tightens. "I've had lovers since. But never someone I actually loved. Not until you."

"Maximus..."

"Let me finish." He cups my face in his hands. "I love you. I love you, Celeste Moreau. I've loved you since you looked at me like I was worth saving when I'd stopped believing I was worth anything at all. I've loved you through every argument and every battle and every moment I pushed you away because I was too afraid to let you close."

Tears are streaming down my face now. Those impossible vampire tears.

"I love you," he continues, "and I'll spend the rest of eternity proving it if you'll let me. I'll fight beside you and protect you and drive you absolutely insane with my controlling tendencies, and I'll try every day to be worthy of what you've given me. Because you've given me something I thought I'd lost forever."

"What?" I whisper.

"Hope." He brushes a tear from my cheek. "You've given me hope."

I'm crying properly now. Tears streaming down my face, dripping onto the pillow beneath me. I didn't know I could feel this much. Didn't know there was room inside me for emotions this big.

"I love you too," I manage. "I think I've loved you since the training room, when you looked at me like I was actually worth something. I've just been too stubborn to say it first."

"Stubborn." He's smiling now, his own eyes bright. "I've noticed."

"You like it."

"I love it." He leans down, kisses me soft and deep. "I love everything about you. Even the things that drive me crazy."

"Good. Because I plan to keep driving you crazy."

"I'm counting on it."

He pushes inside me.

Slow. So slow. Inch by inch, giving me time to feel every moment of it. The stretch. The fullness. The intimacy of being joined with someone who just handed me his heart.

"Celeste." My name is a prayer on his lips. "You feel... I can't..."

"I know." I wrap my legs around him, pull him deeper. "I know."

He bottoms out and goes still.

For a moment, neither of us moves. We just exist in this moment, foreheads pressed together, bodies joined, connected in every way possible. The ring is caught between our chests, metal pressing into both our skins.

"Move," I whisper. "Please move."

He moves.

We find a rhythm together. Give and take. Push and pull. He rolls his hips against mine, and I rise to meet every thrust, our bodies speaking a language we're still learning. The pleasure builds slow, deep, amplified by everything we just shared.

"I felt it," I tell him between kisses. "In your blood. Everything you feel for me."

"And?"

"And I feel it too." I pull his face down to mine. "All of it. I feel all of it."

Something breaks open in his expression. The last wall. The final barrier.

He moves faster, but it's not desperate. It's purposeful. Like he's trying to fuse us together, to make us one thing that can never be separated.

"I want you to feel it," he says against my ear. "Every night. I want you in my bed, in my arms, in my life. I want to wake up to you. I want to fall asleep inside you. I want everything."

"You have it." My voice breaks. "You have all of it."

The pleasure crests. I feel myself starting to fall.

"Together," I gasp. "I want us to..."

"Together," he agrees.

We shatter at the same moment. His groan and my cry tangling in the air between us, our bodies pulsing in unison. The pleasure whites out everything else, and for one endless moment, there's nothing but sensation and connection and him.

We collapse together, still joined, neither willing to separate.

I run my fingers through his hair, feeling the silk of it, the way he shivers slightly at my touch.

"I want to taste you too," I say eventually.

He lifts his head. "You already did."

"No, I mean..." I gesture vaguely. "What you did to me. I want to do that. For you."

Understanding dawns. A smile curves his lips. "You want to worship me?"

"Don't get cocky about it."

"Too late." But he rolls onto his back, arms spread wide. "I'm yours. Do what you will."

I take my time.

I explore him the way he explored me. Kissing down his chest, tracing the lines of muscle with my tongue. He's built like a warrior, lean and hard, every inch honed by centuries of combat. Scars mark his skin in places, pale lines that have faded but never fully disappeared. I kiss each one.

"This one?" I press my lips to a jagged line across his ribs.

"Battle. Before I was turned."

"This one?" A smaller scar on his shoulder.

"Training accident. Luciano's training." His voice goes flat.

I kiss that one twice. Then move lower.

He tenses when I reach his hip. His breath catches when I trace the trail of dark hair that leads down his stomach.

"Celeste..."

"Let me." I look up at him. "You worshipped me. Let me return the favor."

I take him in my mouth.

The sound he makes is gratifying. A groan that seems to come from somewhere deep in his chest. His hands fist in the sheets, knuckles white with restraint.

I learn the taste of him, the feel of him, the sounds he makes when I do something he particularly likes. For all his control, all his centuries of discipline, he comes apart under my mouth with gratifying speed.

"Enough." His voice is strained. He pulls me up, flipping us so I'm beneath him. "I need to be inside you again."

"So romantic."

"I'll give you romantic later." He slides into me in one smooth thrust, and we both groan. "Right now I just need to feel you."

"Then feel me."

Afterward, we lie tangled in the ruins of his bed.

The sheets are destroyed. Torn in places where we gripped too hard. Neither of us cares.

My head rests on his chest. His arm wraps around me, fingers trailing lazy patterns on my shoulder. The silence between us is comfortable. Full of things that don't need to be said.

"Thank you," he says eventually.

I lift my head. "For what?"

"For not giving up on me. Even when I made it difficult."

"You were worth the fight." I settle back against him. "You still are."

His arms tighten around me. A shudder runs through him.

"I'll spend eternity proving you right."

"I'm counting on it."

He loves me. Really, truly loves me. I felt it in his blood, deeper than words could ever reach.

And I love him. Whatever comes next, whatever Konstantin throws at us, that doesn't change.

The last thing I feel is his arms around me, holding on like he'll never let go.

TWENTY-EIGHT

The knock comes sharp and insistent, cutting through the comfortable silence.

Marcellus. I'd recognize his knock anywhere.

Celeste tenses against me, her head lifting from my chest. "Trouble?"

"Probably." I press a kiss to her forehead before extracting myself from the tangled sheets. "Stay here. I'll see what he needs."

"I'm not hiding in your bedroom while you deal with a crisis."

"I wasn't suggesting hiding. I was suggesting you get dressed before facing my second-in-command."

She glances down at her naked body, then back at me. A smile tugs at her lips. "Fair point."

I pull on pants and cross to the door, opening it just enough to see Marcellus's face. His expression is grim, which tells me everything I need to know about how the rest of this night is going to go.

"What happened?"

"Intelligence from Dmitri's people." His eyes flick past me into the room. I don't bother pretending Celeste isn't there. He's not stupid, and I'm not interested in deception. Not about this. "You're going to want to see this. Both of you. Conference room in twenty minutes."

"That bad?"

"Worse."

He leaves without elaborating. That's unlike him, which means whatever he's learned has shaken him. Marcellus doesn't shake easily. In two centuries, I've seen him rattled exactly four times. Whatever this is, it's joining that list.

I close the door and turn to find Celeste already out of bed, gathering her scattered clothes from the floor. The sight of her moving naked through my room does things to my concentration that are entirely unhelpful given the circumstances.

"I need to go to my room," she says. "I can't show up to an emergency meeting in yesterday's blood-stained clothes."

"There's a shower through there." I nod toward the bathroom. "And I can have fresh clothes brought."

She pauses, considering. "That would require someone knowing I'm here."

"Celeste." I cross to her, take her hands. "Everyone already knows. Marcellus certainly does. Probably the entire inner circle. Vampires have excellent hearing, and we weren't exactly quiet."

"Oh god." She covers her face with her hands.

"I'm not interested in hiding what we are. I spent too long hiding from it myself." I bring her hands to my lips, kiss her knuckles. "Whatever happens when we walk into that room, we walk in together. As partners."

Something softens in her expression. The embarrassment fades, replaced by something fiercer. "And what are we? Officially, I mean. What do I call this?"

"Together." The word feels inadequate for the enormity of

what I feel, but it's the only one I have. "Whatever else happens, we're together now."

"I can work with that."

"Good." I kiss her once, quick but thorough. "Now shower. I'll handle the clothes."

Twenty-three minutes later, we walk into the conference room side by side.

The inner circle is already assembled. Marcellus at the head of the table, maps and documents spread before him. Julian and Nadia flanking him, their postures tense. Ethan near the door, arms crossed, face unreadable. Elena is there too, which is unusual; she rarely attends tactical meetings, preferring to focus on the donor coordination that keeps the network running.

Every eye in the room tracks our entrance.

I don't touch Celeste as we walk in. Don't need to. The way she takes the seat beside mine without hesitation, as if she's been sitting there for years. The way I angle my body toward hers without conscious thought, a gravitational pull I've stopped trying to resist.

Nadia's eyebrow rises almost imperceptibly. Her gaze moves from me to Celeste and back again, cataloging details. The faint mark on Celeste's neck that hasn't quite faded. The way my hand rests on the table between us, close enough to touch her if I choose to. The general air of two people who've recently been very thoroughly naked together.

Julian's expression remains neutral, but there's a knowing glint in his eyes.

Ethan shifts slightly by the door. His face stays blank, but I catch the subtle tension in his shoulders. Celeste is new here, still proving herself. Some will wonder if she's earned this position.

Elena simply smiles. Small, warm, genuinely pleased. She's

always had a soft heart, even after working with vampires for eight years.

Marcellus doesn't react at all, which is its own form of commentary. He knew before any of them. He's had time to process. And ultimately, Marcellus cares about one thing: what's best for the network. If I'm more effective with Celeste at my side, he'll support it. If I'm not, he'll tell me so directly, and I'll listen.

No one says anything about our obvious intimacy. Wise of them.

"Report," I say.

Marcellus slides a tablet across the table. "Dmitri's people intercepted communications between Konstantin and someone inside the city. Someone with access to information they shouldn't have."

I scan the intercepted messages. Most are coded, but Dmitri's cryptographers have cracked enough to paint a disturbing picture. Logistics. Timing. Target acquisition. The language of war, dressed up in euphemism.

"He's not targeting the compound again," I say slowly, pieces clicking into place. "He's targeting the blood supply directly."

"The central distribution hub," Marcellus confirms. "Where we process and store clean blood for the entire network. If he takes that out, we don't just lose supply, we lose the infrastructure to rebuild."

"When?"

"The communications reference 'the gathering.' We believe that means the quarterly meeting of the donor coordinators. Every hub supervisor in one location."

I look at Elena. Her face is pale, her hands gripping the edge of the table hard enough to whiten her knuckles.

"That's tomorrow night," she says quietly. "We have representatives coming from six states. If Konstantin hits that meeting..."

"He cripples the network across the Southeast," I finish. "One strike."

Silence settles over the room. The implications are staggering. Months of work, years of relationship-building, an entire infrastructure of trust and logistics, all of it vulnerable to a single coordinated assault.

"We cancel the meeting," Nadia says. "Postpone until we've dealt with the threat."

"And tell them what?" Julian counters. "That we can't protect our own people? That will do more damage than Konstantin could. Coordinators will panic. Donors will flee. The network collapses anyway."

"Better a collapsed network than dead coordinators."

"Is it? If the network collapses, vampires start feeding uncontrolled. Humans die anyway, just more of them, over a longer period." Julian's voice is tight. "There are no good options here."

"Then we fortify," Nadia says. "Bring everyone here, defend in force."

"We don't have the resources to protect both the meeting and the compound," Marcellus says. "If we concentrate our forces at the distribution hub, we leave the compound vulnerable. If he's smart, and he is, he hits both locations simultaneously."

"Split our forces," Ethan suggests from the door. "Half at each location."

"Then we're weak at both." Marcellus shakes his head. "Half-strength defense is barely better than no defense."

"What about Dmitri's forces?" Nadia asks. "He provided the intelligence. Surely he'd provide support as well."

"Sharing intelligence is one thing. Committing forces to another lord's war is something else entirely." I shake my head. "The political cost of asking, and the debt we'd owe if he said yes, could be worse than fighting alone."

The conversation circles, each option examined and found wanting. I listen, let them work through the possibilities, and file away the insights that emerge from the debate. This is how good strategy happens, not from a single brilliant mind but from multiple perspectives colliding until something useful emerges.

"He's trying to make us choose," Celeste says quietly.

Everyone turns to look at her.

She's been silent since we sat down, absorbing the information, processing. Now she leans forward, her expression focused.

"That's what he's doing," she continues. "He knows we can't protect everything. So he's forcing us to pick: the meeting or the compound. The network or our home. Either way, he wins something."

"She's right," I say. "This is classic siege warfare. Stretch the enemy thin, make them defend everywhere, then strike where they're weakest."

"So what do we do?" Elena asks. "We can't just let him slaughter our people."

"No," I agree. "We can't."

I lean back in my chair, mind racing through possibilities. Every option has costs. Every strategy has holes. Konstantin has been planning this for months, maybe years. He's had time to consider our responses, to prepare counters for our counters.

But he doesn't know everything.

"We don't play his game," I say finally. "He wants us to react. To scatter our forces trying to protect everything. Instead, we go on the offensive."

"Attack him?" Julian frowns. "We don't even know where his base of operations is."

"But we know where he'll be tomorrow night." I tap the tablet. "These communications go both ways. If he's coordinating an assault on the distribution hub, he'll need to be close enough to direct it. He won't trust lieutenants with something this important."

"You want to draw him out," Marcellus says slowly. "Use the meeting as bait."

"I want to end this." I look around the table, meeting each pair of eyes in turn. "We've been defensive for too long. Reacting to his moves, cleaning up his damage, mourning our losses. It's time to take the fight to him."

"And the coordinators?" Elena's voice is tight with barely controlled fear. "The donors? They're not soldiers. If we use them as bait..."

"We're not using them as bait. We're giving Konstantin what he thinks he wants while positioning ourselves to take him down when he reaches for it."

"Explain," Nadia says.

I stand, move to the map on the wall. The distribution hub is marked in blue, the compound in green, the suspected locations of Konstantin's forces in red.

"The meeting goes forward as planned," I say. "But we change the venue. Move it here, to the compound, under the pretense of additional security given recent attacks."

"That concentrates our vulnerabilities," Julian objects. "If he hits the compound while everyone's here..."

"He won't. Because we're going to leak information suggesting the meeting is still at the distribution hub." I trace a line on the map. "We leave a skeleton force there, enough to sell the illusion. Meanwhile, our main strength is here, protecting the coordinators while a strike team positions near the hub."

"You want him to attack an empty building," Celeste says, understanding dawning.

"I want him to attack a building he thinks is full. When his forces engage, they'll find minimal resistance. They'll call for reinforcement, and Konstantin will come to see his victory firsthand." I tap the map. "That's when we hit him."

"It's risky," Nadia says.

"Everything is risky. But this gives us a chance to end the war instead of just surviving another battle."

"How do we plant false information convincingly?" Marcellus asks.

"We don't plant it. We let it leak naturally." I gesture at the room. "We make a show of fortifying the distribution hub. Increased patrols, visible security. Konstantin's scouts will report what they see. He'll draw his own conclusions."

Silence falls over the room again. I can see them processing, weighing the options, calculating odds. These are people I've worked with for decades, some for centuries. They know me. They trust me.

But trust only goes so far when lives are on the line.

"I'm in," Celeste says.

Everyone looks at her again. Some expressions show surprise. She's new, still proving herself, speaking up in a room full of vampires who've been doing this longer than she's been alive. Others show something closer to respect.

"He's right," she continues. "We can't keep playing defense forever. Konstantin will wear us down eventually. If we have a chance to take him out, we have to take it."

"Easy for you to say," Julian mutters. "You've been here five minutes."

"Which means I'm not tired yet." She holds his gaze steadily, unflinching. "I haven't spent years losing people, watching the network shrink, feeling the noose tighten. I can see this clearly because I'm not exhausted. And what I see is that we're running out of time. If we don't act now, we won't get another chance."

Julian holds her stare for a long moment. Something passes

between them, not hostility, exactly, but assessment. Testing. Then he nods slowly.

"She's got a point."

"I agree," Nadia says. "It's our best option."

"Ethan?" I ask.

He pushes off from the wall, uncrossing his arms. "I don't love the risk to the coordinators. But I love the alternative less. I'm in."

"Elena?"

She takes a shaky breath. "I trust you. All of you. If you think this is the way, I'll make sure my people are ready."

Marcellus looks at me. "What do you need?"

The next two hours are a blur of planning.

We work through scenarios, contingencies, backup plans for backup plans. The distribution hub has to look vulnerable enough to tempt Konstantin but defended enough to survive the initial assault. Our strike team needs to be positioned close enough to respond when he shows himself, but hidden well enough that his scouts don't spot them.

Nadia takes point on the false intelligence, working out how to plant information that will seem credible without being obviously fed. Julian coordinates the actual defense of the compound, calculating sight lines and choke points. Ethan begins assembling the strike team, selecting vampires who can move fast and hit hard.

Marcellus oversees all of it, his centuries of experience showing in every suggestion, every correction, every insight that sharpens our plan from rough concept to precision instrument.

Through it all, Celeste is at my side. Not just physically, though she is, her chair close enough that our shoulders occasionally brush, but mentally. She asks questions that challenge assumptions, offers perspectives the rest of us miss, pushes back when she thinks we're wrong.

"The approach from the east is too obvious," she says at one point, pointing to the map. "It's the logical route, best cover, clearest path. Which means it's exactly where they'll be watching."

"Then we approach from the west," Julian suggests.

"No. We approach from the east, but we make noise about it first. Let them think they've spotted us, let them feel clever. Meanwhile, the real strike team comes from here." She traces a route through the industrial district. "There's an old tunnel system, storm drains, I think. I used to use them when I was fighting. They're not on any official maps."

Julian and Nadia exchange looks. Impressed looks.

"You know this area," Nadia says.

"I know this area." Celeste traces the route on the map. "I spent three years in the underground circuit. I know which routes people don't watch."

No one has a response to that.

The others notice the shift in how she operates, how I operate around her. I see it in the subtle glances, the way conversations pause when we lean close to examine the same document. Nadia's earlier curiosity has evolved into something more thoughtful. Julian's skepticism has faded, replaced by grudging respect.

Elena catches my eye across the table at one point and smiles. A small, private smile that says she's happy for me.

I nod slightly in acknowledgment. Then I turn back to the plans, because we don't have time for sentiment. Not yet.

When the planning finally winds down, the others filter out to begin preparations. Celeste stays behind, lingering by the window as I gather the scattered documents.

"You're thinking about something," I say.

"I'm thinking about Vivienne."

The name lands like a stone. I'd almost forgotten, in the chaos of the battle and everything that came after. Almost. But not quite. Some things you can't forget, no matter how much you want to.

"Her claim about your turning."

Celeste turns from the window to face me. The evening light catches her features, highlighting the worry lines around her eyes. "I've tried to make peace with it, I really have, but what if she's right? What if Konstantin orchestrated all of this? Valentina turning me, me finding my way to your network, all of it?"

"To what end?"

"I don't know. That's what scares me." She wraps her arms around herself, a gesture of vulnerability I've rarely seen from her.

I cross to her, take her hands, and make her look at me.

"I don't care."

"Maximus."

"I don't care if Konstantin himself arranged for you to be here. What matters is what we choose to do now. What we choose to be to each other."

"But really, what if none of this was a coincidence?"

"Then we'll deal with it." I squeeze her hands. "Whatever he planned, whatever he intended, he didn't count on one thing."

"What?"

"That I would fall in love with you," I say the words simply, directly. No hesitation. They're true, and she deserves to hear them as many times as I can say them. "That changes everything. Whatever purpose you were supposed to serve, it's gone now. You're not his tool. You're mine. And I protect what's mine."

Her eyes glisten. "That's very possessive."

"Yes."

"I should probably object to being called yours."

"Probably."

"I don't want to."

I pull her into my arms and hold her tight against my chest. She fits there perfectly, like she was designed for exactly this space.

"When this is over," I murmur into her hair, "when we've dealt with Konstantin and secured the network and stopped running from crisis to crisis, we're going to find out the truth. About Valentina, about your turning, about all of it. I promise you that."

"And if we don't like what we find?"

"Then we face it. Together."

She pulls back to look at me. Whatever she sees in my face must satisfy her, because she nods slowly.

"Together," she agrees.

The door opens. Marcellus stands in the doorway, his expression tight.

"We have a problem."

Of course we do. The universe has a sense of humor, and it's not a kind one.

"What now?"

"Konstantin sent a message." Marcellus holds up a small envelope, sealed with dark red wax pressed with an elaborate K. "Hand-delivered to the compound gates. By Valentina. Security has already cleared it, no contaminants, no traps. Just paper."

Celeste goes rigid beside me.

"She's here?" Her voice is barely a whisper.

"Was here. She left before our people could intercept her." Marcellus crosses the room and hands me the envelope. "She said to tell Celeste that they'll see each other soon. She was smiling when she said it."

I open the envelope. Inside is a single card, thick cream paper, elegant script.

My dear Maximus,

I believe you have something that belongs to me. I'd like her back.

Tomorrow night, at the gathering your people have so carefully planned, we can discuss terms. Bring Celeste. Come alone.

Refuse, and I'll burn your network to ash and scatter the remains.

Your old friend, Konstantin

P.S. Ask her about Rome. She'll understand.

I hand the card to Celeste. Watch her read it. Watch her go completely still as she reaches the postscript.

"Rome," she breathes. "I was never in Rome."

"So, what does he mean?"

"I don't... " She stops. Frowns. Presses a hand to her temple like she's fighting a headache. "I don't remember. But the word means something. Something important. I can feel it, like it's right at the edge of my memory, but I can't quite..."

"Valentina," Marcellus says grimly. "Makers can manipulate their progeny's memories. Especially in the first year, before the bond fully settles. It's one of the darker aspects of our kind."

Celeste looks at me, and for the first time since I've known her, I see real fear in her eyes. Not the fear of battle or death, she's faced both without flinching. This is deeper. The fear of not knowing yourself. Of having pieces of your own mind locked away where you can't reach them.

"What did she do to me?" she whispers. "What don't I remember?"

I don't have an answer.

But I'm going to find one.

Whatever it takes.

TWENTY-NINE

Rome.

The word circles through my mind like a vulture, patient and relentless. I'm sitting in Maximus's study, trying to reach for something that keeps slipping away.

Rome. Rome. Rome.

What happened in Rome?

I close my eyes and push inward, searching for the memory. It has to be there. Somewhere in the dark corners of my mind, locked away where I can't reach it.

Nothing. Just darkness, and the frustrating sense of something hovering just beyond my grasp.

"Anything?"

Maximus's voice is gentle. He's been watching me for the past hour, patient as only an immortal can be. Not pushing. Just present.

"Shadows." I open my eyes and rub my temples. "When I focus on the word, I get flashes. Light on water. The smell of old stone. Fear." I shake my head. "Nothing concrete."

He moves from his chair to kneel in front of me, taking my hands in his. "Memory manipulation is complex. The harder you push, the more the barriers resist. It's designed that way."

"Then how do I break through?"

"Time. Triggers. Sometimes blood from the maker can unlock what they sealed." His jaw tightens. "Though that would require access to Valentina."

"Which we might have tomorrow night."

"Which we might have," he agrees. "If we go."

If. Such a small word to carry so much weight.

I look down at our joined hands. His are larger than mine, scarred in places from centuries of violence. Strong hands. Capable hands.

"What if Rome is the reason I'm here?" I ask quietly.

"Then we'll deal with it."

"How can you be so calm about this?"

"Because I've survived centuries by preparing for the worst while hoping for the best." He squeezes my hands. "And because I refuse to let fear of what might be poison what actually is."

"What actually is?"

"You. Me. This." He brings my hands to his lips, kisses my knuckles.

I want to believe him. I do believe him, mostly. But ever since I've seen the word Rome, the shadows in my mind whisper doubts.

"I want to try again," I say. "Help me try again."

"How?"

"You said blood can unlock memories. Not maker blood, but you've drunk from me..." I trail off, not sure where the instinct is coming from. "Maybe if you bite me again while I focus, the shared blood could... I don't know. Break through the barriers."

He's quiet for a moment, considering. "It's possible. Shared blood can create echoes between vampires. But it might also be painful. Forcing locked memories open isn't gentle."

"I don't need gentle. I need answers."

He studies my face, looking for doubt. He won't find any. Whatever's hidden in my mind, I need to know. Even if it hurts.

"Alright." He rises, drawing me up with him. "Come here."

He guides me to the leather couch by the fire, positions me so I'm sitting with my back against his chest. His arms wrap around me, holding me secure. Safe.

"Focus on Rome," he murmurs against my ear. "Let the word fill your mind. Don't push, just hold it there."

I close my eyes. Rome. I think of the word, the shape of it, the sound. Let it expand until it's all I can see in the darkness behind my eyelids.

His lips brush my throat, feather-light. "Now let me in."

His fangs pierce my skin.

The pain is brief, familiar now, immediately replaced by the rush of pleasure that comes with being fed upon by someone you love. I feel the pull of blood leaving my body, feel the intimacy of the connection between us.

And then he goes rigid against me.

His arms lock around me, muscles tensing. A sound escapes him, something between a gasp and a growl. He's seeing something. Through my blood, through whatever connection we share, he's seeing something that isn't in this room.

I wait, heart pounding, as he drinks. His body shudders once. Twice. Then he tears himself away from my throat, sealing the wound with a swipe of his tongue, but his hands are shaking.

"What?" I turn to face him, gripping his arms. "What did you see?"

His eyes are wild. Unfocused. Like he's still half in whatever vision the blood showed him. "Rome," he says hoarsely. "You were in Rome."

The word hits me like a physical blow. *Flash. Cobblestones. Rain. Running.*

"I saw you running," he continues, voice rough. "Through streets. Old stone. Someone chasing you..."

Flash. My feet slapping against stone, lungs burning. Behind me, footsteps. Faster than mine. Gaining.

"...and then a room. Small, dark. You were bleeding. Someone standing over you..."

Flash. The smell of blood, my blood. A woman's voice, speaking words I can't quite hear. My body won't move. I try to scream, but nothing comes out.

"Valentina," I whisper. The fragments are surfacing now, his words cracking open the locks she placed in my mind. "She was there. She turned me there, not here."

"There was pain." His jaw tightens. "So much pain. I felt it through your blood. What she did to you." He stops, swallows hard. "She was laughing."

Flash. My body remaking itself, dying, and being reborn. The taste of blood in my mouth, not mine. Hers. Valentina's. She's laughing.

I'm shaking now. Can't seem to stop. "What else?"

He hesitates. Whatever he saw next is worse.

"Tell me."

"Daylight," he says slowly. "You were standing in daylight. Through a window. The sun was on your skin, and you weren't burning."

Flash. Light pouring through glass. Warmth on my face. Wrong, daylight is death now. But I'm standing in it, and it doesn't burn.

"That's not possible," I breathe.

"There was a man watching you." Maximus's voice is strained. "He was in the sunlight too."

Flash. A man across the room. I know him. I know his face. Cruel smile, eyes that have seen centuries.

"Konstantin," I say. The name tastes like poison.

Maximus nods grimly. "Konstantin."

For a long moment, neither of us speaks.

Maximus's hands are still shaking.

"The pain," he says finally, his voice raw. "What she did to you, I felt it. Every moment of it." His jaw works. "I've been tortured, Celeste. I know what agony feels like. But experiencing yours..." He breaks off, and I see something in his eyes I've never seen before.

Helpless rage.

"It's over now," I say, though we both know that's not entirely true.

"It's not over. It's *in* you. What they did, whatever they did, it's still there. Those memories, that pain, locked away inside you where you couldn't even access it." His hands frame my face, thumbs brushing my cheekbones. "You've been carrying this alone. For months. Not even knowing you were carrying it."

"I didn't know."

"I know. That makes it worse." He pulls me against his chest, arms wrapping around me so tight it would hurt if I were still human. "I want to kill her. Valentina. I want to tear her apart for what she did to you."

I press my face into his shoulder, breathing in the scent of him. "You might get your chance tomorrow."

"It won't be enough. A thousand deaths wouldn't be enough." His hand cradles the back of my head, fingers threading through my hair. "I saw you running. Terrified. And I couldn't do anything. I couldn't reach you, couldn't help you, I could only watch."

"That wasn't real. It was a memory."

"It felt real." His voice cracks on the word. "Feeling your fear, your pain, and being powerless to stop it. That's a particular kind of hell."

I pull back enough to look at him. His eyes are bright with emotion, ancient eyes that have seen centuries, now stripped raw by what he witnessed in my blood.

"Now you know," I say quietly. "Everything she did to me. Everything I couldn't remember."

"Not everything. There are still gaps. Shadows." His thumb traces my lower lip. "But I know enough. I know what she took from you. And I know..." He swallows hard. "I know you survived it. That you're still here, still fighting, still *you* despite what they tried to make you."

"You sound surprised."

"I'm in awe." He says it simply, without embellishment. "What you endured would have broken most vampires. It nearly broke you, I felt that too, in the blood. The moment where you almost gave up. And then you didn't."

I hadn't known that. Hadn't remembered that there was a moment where I'd wanted to let go, to stop fighting. The knowledge sits heavy in my chest.

"I don't remember deciding to keep fighting."

"Your body does. Your blood does." He kisses my forehead, lingering there. "You chose to survive, Celeste. Even when you didn't know what you were surviving for. That's who you are."

I close my eyes, letting his words wash over me. Being known like this, truly known, down to the blood and bone and buried memories, should feel like violation. Like exposure. Instead, it feels like relief. Like setting down a weight I didn't know I was carrying.

"Thank you," I whisper.

"For what?"

"For seeing it. For carrying it with me now." I look up at him. "I'm not alone in it anymore."

His expression shifts, something fierce and tender all at once. "You're never alone. Not anymore. Whatever else they locked in your mind, whatever else we discover, we face it together. Understood?"

"Understood."

He kisses me then, soft and slow. A seal on a promise. When he pulls back, the trembling in his hands has stilled.

But his expression remains troubled.

"The daylight," he says quietly. "That's what I can't stop thinking about. You and Konstantin, standing in sunlight. Not burning."

"It shouldn't be possible."

"No. It shouldn't." He's quiet for a moment, and I can see him turning something over in his mind.

"There are legends," he says slowly. "Old stories. About vampires who found ways to walk in sunlight. The methods were always considered too dangerous, too costly. Most dismissed them as myths."

"But you don't think they're myths."

"I think Konstantin has been alive for over a thousand years, and he hasn't survived that long by being ordinary." His jaw tightens. "But I don't know what we actually saw. Whether he's found some way to withstand sunlight, whether it only works temporarily, whether you survived because of something he did or something you are."

The implication settles over me like cold water. "And there's no way to test it."

"No." His voice is rough. "If you step into sunlight and you can't withstand it, you burn. There's no halfway. No safe experiment."

So I might be able to walk in daylight. Or I might die the

instant I try. And we have no way of knowing which until it's too late.

He takes my hands, his grip tight. "We need to tell the others. If he's found a way to operate in daylight..."

"Then our plan is useless." The realization compounds what we've just discussed. "We're setting a trap for him at night. If he can move during the day, he could hit us while we're all sleeping. While we're helpless."

"The compound has human staff during daylight hours. Security measures that don't rely on vampires."

"Against Konstantin? Against someone with a thousand years of experience?" I shake my head. "We're not ready for this."

"We have to be." He stands, pulling me with him. "Come. We need to find Marcellus."

***

THE INNER CIRCLE assembles within the hour.

The mood in the conference room is tense as I recount what I saw. Fragmented as the memories are, the implications are clear. If Konstantin can walk in daylight, everything changes.

"It could be false," Nadia says when I finish. "Implanted memories designed to frighten us. Make us hesitate."

"To what end?" Julian counters. "If she hadn't had Maximus drink from her tonight, she wouldn't have remembered anything. Konstantin couldn't have planned for that."

"Unless he did." Marcellus's voice is grim. "Unless everything has been planned. Her turning, her arrival here, their relationship." He glances at Maximus. "All of it leading to this moment. To her, unlocking these memories right before we spring our trap."

"You think I'm compromised." I keep my voice level, though my hands are clenched at my sides. "You think these memories are a weapon."

"I think we'd be fools not to consider the possibility."

"Enough." Maximus's voice cuts through the tension. "We can debate the nature of her memories later. Right now, we need to focus on the practical question: do we still go to this meeting?"

Silence falls.

"His letter was clear," Julian says. "He wants both of you. If you don't show up..."

"He'll burn the network to ash," I finish. "He's made that threat before."

"Which doesn't mean he'll follow through," Nadia argues. "Threats are leverage. If he destroys the network, he has nothing left to bargain with."

"Unless destroying the network was always the goal," Marcellus says quietly. "And the bargaining is just entertainment."

We all consider that for a moment. The thought of Konstantin playing with us, drawing out our suffering for his own amusement, feels disturbingly plausible.

"We go," Maximus says finally. "As demanded. Both of us."

"That's exactly what he wants," Nadia protests.

"Yes. And if we don't give him what he wants, people die." Maximus's voice is hard. "The coordinators. The donors. Everyone who depends on this network. I won't sacrifice them because walking into a trap makes me uncomfortable."

"It's not about comfort. It's about survival."

"It's about both." He looks around the table, meeting each pair of eyes in turn. "We go. But we go prepared. Strike team positioned nearby, ready to extract us if things go wrong. Secondary forces at the distribution hub in case this meeting is a diversion. And everyone else here, defending the compound."

"That spreads us thin," Julian observes.

"We're already thin. We've been thin since this war started." Maximus's jaw tightens. "This is the best we can do with what we have."

"What about the daylight issue?" Elena asks. "If Konstantin can really walk in sunlight..."

"Then we deal with that when we have confirmation." Maximus stands, signaling the meeting's end. "Right now, it's a fragment of a memory from a mind that's been manipulated. We can't plan around something we're not sure is real."

The others file out, each to their assigned tasks. I stay behind, watching Maximus stare at the map on the wall. The weight on his shoulders is visible in every line of his body.

"You don't have to go," I say quietly. "I could meet with him alone. You're too important to risk."

He turns to look at me, something fierce in his eyes. "You think I'd let you face him alone?"

"I think you're the one holding this network together. If something happens to you..."

"If something happens to me, Marcellus takes over. He's been preparing for that possibility for two centuries." He crosses to me, takes my face in his hands. "I'm not sending you into that warehouse without me. We're partners. We face this together."

"Even if it's a trap?"

"Especially if it's a trap." He kisses me, brief but firm. "Now come. We have preparations to make."

The hours before the meeting pass too quickly.

Marcellus rigs trackers for both of us, small devices hidden in our clothing. Nadia provides panic signals, buttons that look innocuous but send an emergency alert to the strike team. Julian briefs the extraction squad on every possible approach to the warehouse, every exit, every contingency.

Through it all, Maximus and I work side by side. Checking

weapons. Reviewing plans. Preparing for every scenario we can imagine.

An hour before the meeting, we find ourselves alone in his quarters.

Maximus stands by the window, looking out through a gap in the blackout curtains. The moonlight casts faint illumination across the sharp planes of his face, softening them. He looks younger in this light. More human.

I cross to him, and he opens his arms without looking. I step into them like I've been doing it for centuries.

"I'm scared," I admit.

The vulnerability of the admission surprises me. I don't usually confess to fear. In the underground fighting circuit, fear was weakness. You swallowed it, buried it, used it as fuel. You never, ever named it out loud.

But I'm not in the ring anymore. And this man has seen my worst memories through my own blood. There's nothing left to hide.

"Good," he says, his voice rumbling through his chest where my ear presses against it. "Fear keeps you sharp."

"What if we can't get out? What if he's planned for everything?"

"Then we fight." He pulls back enough to look at me, hands sliding up to frame my face. "I've survived six centuries, Celeste. I've walked into more traps than I can count. I'm still here."

"You didn't have someone to worry about before."

"No." His thumb traces the line of my jaw. "I didn't. That's new. But it's also why I'm going to fight harder than I ever have. Because I have something worth fighting for now."

I turn my head, press a kiss to his palm. "I keep thinking about all the things I haven't told you yet. All the conversations we haven't had. What if..."

"Don't." His voice is firm but gentle. "Don't start cataloging regrets. We have time. We're going to have time."

"You can't promise that."

"No. But I can promise that I'll do everything in my power to make it true." He tilts my chin up, makes me meet his eyes. "I have centuries of experience in staying alive. Let me use it."

I want to argue. Want to point out that experience doesn't matter when you're walking into an ambush, that Konstantin has centuries of his own, that love is exactly the kind of weakness an ancient predator knows how to exploit.

But I don't. Because right now, in this moment, I need to believe him. Need to believe we're going to walk out of that warehouse together.

"Tell me something," I say. "Something about you I don't know. Something that has nothing to do with war or vampires or Konstantin."

He blinks, caught off guard by the request. Then something shifts in his expression, a softening, a remembering.

"I used to paint," he says. "In my human life. I wasn't good; the masters of the time would have laughed at my work. But I loved it. The way colors could capture light. The way a few strokes could make something feel alive."

"I didn't know that."

"I haven't painted since Luciano." He stops, shakes his head. "I stopped making beautiful things. It felt like a weakness. A vulnerability he could exploit."

"And now?"

His eyes meet mine, soft and fierce all at once. "Now I'm thinking I'd like to start again. When this is over. Maybe try to capture the way you look in firelight."

My heart clenches. "That's unfairly romantic."

"I have hundreds of years of unexpressed sentiment saved up. Consider yourself warned."

I laugh despite everything, despite the fear, the danger, the knowledge that we might be dead before sunrise. He smiles at the sound, and for a moment, we're just two people who found each other against impossible odds.

Then the smile fades, and reality reasserts itself.

"Come back to me," I say. "Whatever happens in there, come back to me."

"I will." He cups my face, holding my gaze. "And you come back to me. No heroics. No sacrificing yourself for some greater good. You stay alive, because I refuse to spend eternity without you."

"Even if it means other people die?"

The question hangs between us. It's the question we've both been avoiding.

"I would burn the world for you," he says quietly. "I'm not proud of that. It goes against everything I've tried to build, every principle I've held for centuries. But it's true. And I need you to know it's true, so you understand exactly how serious I am when I tell you to stay alive."

"Maximus."

"I know it's selfish. I know a good leader would say the mission matters more than any individual life, including yours. Including mine." His grip on my face tightens. "But I'm not a good leader right now. I'm a man who's finally found something he can't lose. So please. Please, Celeste. Stay alive."

I should argue. Should tell him that I'd make the same sacrifice he would, that I can't promise to put my life above others, that love doesn't trump duty.

Instead, I say, "I promise."

Because I want to believe it too. Want to believe we get to have the future he's painting in his words, a future with terrible paintings and firelight and centuries stretching out before us.

"Good." He kisses me, long and deep. When he pulls back, there's fire in his eyes. "Now let's go show Konstantin what happens when he threatens what's ours."

The meeting point is a warehouse on the edge of Konstantin's territory.

We approach together, as demanded. Just the two of us, walking into what we both know is likely a trap. But we're not entirely alone. Somewhere in the shadows, a strike team tracks our movement. The panic buttons rest secure in our pockets.

The warehouse door is open. Waiting for us.

I take a breath I don't need. Maximus's hand finds mine, squeezes once, then lets go. We need to be able to fight if this goes wrong.

We walk in together.

The interior is vast, empty, lit by industrial lights that cast harsh shadows across the concrete floor. Our footsteps echo as we move deeper into the space, every sense alert for threats.

At the far end, two figures wait.

Valentina. Beautiful and terrible, exactly as I remember her. She's smiling, that cat-with-cream smile that makes my stomach clench with a hatred so pure it surprises me.

And beside her...

Konstantin.

He's taller than I expected. Silver hair swept back from a face that might have been handsome once, before cruelty carved itself into every line. His eyes are ancient, patient, the eyes of a predator who's never had to hurry.

"Maximus." Konstantin's voice is cultured, warm. A gentleman greeting an old friend. "It's been too long. A century, at least."

"Not long enough," Maximus replies, his voice flat.

"Still holding grudges? How tedious." Konstantin's gaze slides to me, and I feel the weight of it like a physical touch. "And this must be Celeste. At last. I've been looking forward to meeting you properly."

"You've met me before." The words come out before I can stop them. "In Rome."

Something flickers in his expression.

"So you're beginning to remember." He glances at Valentina. "I told you the blocks wouldn't hold forever."

"What did you do to me?"

"I improved you." He spreads his hands. "Made you stronger. Faster. Better than any ordinary fledgling. I gave you gifts, Celeste. Gifts you haven't even begun to unwrap."

"What gifts?"

"All in good time." He steps closer, and I feel Maximus tense beside me. "But first, we have business to discuss. My offer stands. Come with me willingly, and this war ends. Your people live. The network survives."

"And Maximus?" I ask.

"Maximus..." Konstantin's smile widens. "Maximus and I have old scores to settle. That's between us."

"No deal," I say flatly. "I'm not leaving him."

"How touching." Konstantin's voice drips with false sentiment. "She loves you, Maximus. Truly loves you. Do you know how rare that is? How precious?" His expression hardens. "And how easily I could take it away?"

"Threaten her again," Maximus says quietly, "and this conversation ends with your head on the floor."

"So protective. So fierce." Konstantin laughs. "You've changed, old friend. The Maximus I knew didn't care about anyone. He was cold. Efficient. A perfect machine of survival." He tilts his head, studying us. "She's made you weak."

"She's made me strong."

"We'll see."

The silence stretches. I can feel the tension building, the moment balancing on a knife's edge. Any second now, this is going to explode into violence.

And then Konstantin smiles.

"But I didn't bring you here to fight. Not yet." He pulls out a phone, checks the screen. "I brought you here to watch."

A chill runs down my spine. "Watch what?"

"Did you think I didn't know about your little trap?" Konstantin's voice is almost gentle. "Your strike team in the shadows. Your forces at the distribution hub. Your compound, defended by a skeleton crew while you came to meet me."

No. No, no, no.

"Your people are scattered across the city, waiting for an attack that isn't coming." Konstantin tucks the phone away. "While my people, my main force, are approaching your compound right now."

Maximus goes rigid beside me. "You're lying."

"Am I?" Konstantin's smile is terrible. "Valentina, dear. Show them."

Valentina produces a tablet and turns it to face us. On the screen, security footage. Our compound. And approaching from multiple directions, dozens of vampires, moving fast, coordinated, overwhelming.

"They'll breach the walls in about..." Konstantin checks his watch. "Three minutes. Your people will fight, of course. Marcellus is there, isn't he? Loyal Marcellus. He'll die bravely." His eyes gleam. "So will the others. Julian. Nadia. That charming human coordinator, Elena. All of them."

I reach for the panic button...

Valentina moves faster than I can track, her hand closing around my wrist. "None of that."

Maximus lunges for Konstantin, but more vampires emerge from the shadows. Four, six, eight of them, surrounding us. We're outnumbered. Outmaneuvered. Exactly where Konstantin wanted us.

"You can try to fight your way out," Konstantin says pleasantly. "But by the time you reach your compound, there won't be anyone left to save. Or..." He holds up a hand. "You can listen to my alternative offer."

"What offer?" Maximus growls.

"Celeste comes with me. Now. Willingly." Konstantin's eyes lock onto mine. "And I call off the attack. Your people live. Your network survives. All it costs is her."

"No," Maximus says immediately.

"I wasn't asking you." Konstantin's gaze never leaves my face. "I was asking her."

The compound. Elena. Marcellus. Everyone we left behind, trusting us to keep them safe. They're going to die because we walked into this trap. Because we weren't smart enough to see what Konstantin was really planning.

Unless I stop it.

The calculation is cold and instant, the same part of my brain that used to assess opponents in the ring. Threat. Vulnerability. Leverage. Konstantin doesn't just want me; he wants to use me against Maximus.

So I give him what he wants.

"Celeste, don't." Maximus's voice is strained. He knows. Of course he knows. "Whatever you're thinking..."

"Call them off," I say to Konstantin, and my voice doesn't shake. I'm proud of that. "Call off the attack. Now. And I'll come with you."

"Celeste!"

Time slows down the way it used to before a fight. Every detail crystallizes: the dust motes floating in the warehouse light, the slight curl of Konstantin's satisfied smile, the desperate fury in Maximus's eyes.

I catalog what I'm giving up.

The compound that became home. The room where Maximus first kissed me. The training sessions where I finally started to feel competent in this new body. Elena's sharp humor and sharper compassion. Nadia's grudging respect. Julian's quiet mentorship.

Maximus.

I'm giving up Maximus.

The ring presses against my chest beneath my shirt. His signet ring, his father's ring, the one Luciano stole and Maximus killed to reclaim. Six hundred years of legacy given to me with shaking hands and a vulnerability I don't think he's ever shown anyone. I'm wearing his claim, his promise, his heart, and I'm walking away from him.

"Do we have a deal?" I ignore Maximus, keep my eyes on Konstantin. If I look at Maximus now, I'll break.

The vampire smiles. "We have a deal."

"NO!" Maximus tries to reach me, but the guards hold him back. I hear the sounds of struggle, of violence, of a six-hundred-year-old vampire fighting with desperate fury. "Celeste, you can't, I won't let you!"

"You don't get to let me." I finally look at him, and it takes everything I have to keep my voice steady.

His face.

I will remember his face for the rest of eternity, however long that turns out to be. The anguish. The rage. The helpless love that's tearing him apart because he can't protect me, can't save me, can't stop me from making this choice.

"This is my choice," I tell him. "My decision."

"You promised! Not like this. Not to save me!"

"Not just you. Everyone." I hold his gaze, trying to pour everything I feel into the look. Every moment we've shared. Every kiss, every touch, every whispered conversation in the dark. The future we were supposed to have, paintings by firelight, centuries together, a love that would outlast empires.

I'm giving it up. I'm giving it all up.

"I love you," I say. "That doesn't change. But I won't let them die when I can stop it."

"I'll come for you." His voice breaks, and the sound shatters something in my chest. I've never heard him sound like this. Desperate. Destroyed. "I'll find you. I'll burn down everything he has until I get you back."

"I know." I almost smile. Almost. "I'm counting on it."

Konstantin snaps his fingers. "Valentina. Make the call."

Valentina steps away, phone to her ear. A moment later: "It's done. Forces are pulling back."

The compound will survive. Marcellus will survive. Elena. Nadia. Julian. Everyone I've come to care about. They'll live because I made this choice.

It has to be worth it. It has to be.

"Excellent." Konstantin extends a hand to me. "Shall we?"

I don't take his hand. But I step toward him, away from Maximus, away from everything we've built together.

Each step feels like walking through water. My body doesn't want to go. Every instinct screams at me to turn around, to run back to Maximus, to fight our way out together, even if it means everyone at the compound dies.

But I keep walking. Because I'm not just a fighter anymore. I'm part of something larger. And the people I care about are depending on me to make the hard choice.

"Celeste." Maximus's voice is ragged. "Please."

I don't look back. I can't. If I look back, I'll see his face again, and I'll break, and I'll run to him, and people will die.

"Take care of them," I say instead. "Take care of the network. And don't stop looking for me."

"Never," he swears. "Never."

Konstantin's hand closes around my arm. His grip is proprietary. Possessive. Like I'm a prize he's finally won after a long campaign.

I suppose I am.

"Come," he says, voice silky with triumph. "We have so much to discuss. Starting with what really happened in Rome."

He leads me toward a back exit, Valentina falling into step behind us. I focus on the mechanics of movement. Left foot. Right foot. Don't think about what you're leaving behind. Don't think about the sound of Maximus's voice breaking. Don't think about the ring against your chest, the weight of his promise against your heart.

The last thing I hear before the door closes is Maximus's roar of rage, and the sound of fighting as he tears through Konstantin's guards to come after me.

Too late. He'll be too late.

But he'll come. I know he'll come. I hold onto that knowledge like a lifeline as Konstantin guides me into the night.

By the time he gets free, we'll be gone.

And I'll be exactly where Konstantin wants me.

But I won't stay there.

I'm coming back to you, I think, hoping somehow he can feel me the way I felt him when our blood mingled. *Wait for me. Fight for me. And when you find me, because you will find me, we'll make them pay for every second they kept us apart.*

The night swallows us whole.

I kill the first guard before he can raise his weapon.

My hands find his throat and twist. The crack of his spine is satisfying in a way I don't have time to examine. He drops, and I'm already moving, already reaching for the next one.

There are eight of them. Eight vampires between me and the door Celeste just walked through.

Eight obstacles.

The second guard swings a blade at my head. I duck under it, drive my fist through his chest, and rip out something vital. He screams. I don't care. The third and fourth come at me together, coordinated, trained. They last four seconds longer than the first two.

She's getting farther away with every second you waste.

The thought burns through me like silver in the blood. I grab the fifth guard by the skull and slam him into the sixth. Bones shatter. Bodies fall. The seventh tries to run, actually turns his back on me to flee toward the warehouse door.

Coward.

I catch him before he makes it three steps. My hand closes around the back of his neck, and I use his own momentum against him, driving his face into the concrete floor. The impact leaves a crater. He doesn't get up.

The eighth guard, the last one, is smarter than the others. He holds up his hands, backing away slowly, fear rolling off him in waves.

"Wait," he says. "I'm just hired muscle. I don't even know what..."

I don't let him finish.

His head hits the ground before his body realizes it's dead.

Eight guards. Maybe twenty seconds. An eternity when every second takes her farther from me.

I stand in the center of the carnage, breathing hard. Old habits. Human habits. The kind that surface when you're operating on pure instinct and rage.

Blood coats my hands. My shirt. My face. Some of it's mine, I took hits I didn't bother to dodge because dodging takes time, and time is something I don't have. The wounds are already healing, flesh knitting back together with the efficiency of six centuries of vampiric existence.

But the wound in my chest, the one that has nothing to do with physical damage, that one isn't healing at all.

She walked away from me.

I knew what she was doing the moment she opened her mouth. Saw the calculation in her eyes, the cold assessment of a fighter weighing odds and finding only one path to victory. She traded herself for everyone in that compound. For Marcellus. For Elena. For all the vampires and humans who depend on me.

For me.

And I couldn't stop her. Couldn't reach her. Could only watch as Konstantin's hand closed around her arm and led her away.

The memory of her face in that moment, the love and the anguish and the iron resolve, will haunt me for the rest of eternity. However long or short that turns out to be.

I reach for my phone, fingers slick with blood. The screen smears red as I dial.

Marcellus answers on the first ring. "Sir?"

"The meeting was a diversion." I'm moving as I talk, following the scent of her through the warehouse. "While we were here, Konstantin sent his main force to the compound. They were minutes away from breaching the walls."

Silence. I can hear him processing the horror of what almost happened.

"Celeste traded herself to stop it," I continue. "She agreed to go with Konstantin in exchange for calling off the attack."

More silence. When Marcellus speaks again, his voice is different. Heavier.

"She saved us." It's not a question.

"Yes."

"And now she's..."

"With him. With Konstantin and Valentina." I'm moving as I talk, following the scent of her through the warehouse. "I'm going after her."

"What do you need?"

"Compound on full lockdown. Konstantin may not honor the deal; the attack pulled back, but that doesn't mean it's over. Get everyone inside, seal the perimeter, trust no one who approaches without verification."

"Already in progress. The moment you said the assault was retreating, I initiated protocol seven." His voice is clipped, professional, but I can hear the tension underneath. "The strike team is three minutes out from your location."

"Tell them to stand down."

"Sir..."

"I'm not waiting three minutes, Marcellus. I'm not waiting three seconds." I find the back exit, the one Konstantin led her through. The door hangs open, night air rushing in. Her scent lingers here, blood and fear and underneath it, that indefinable something that's purely *her*. "I'm going after her now."

"Alone? Against Konstantin and, however many guards he has waiting?"

"Yes."

"That's suicide."

"Maybe." I step through the door into the alley beyond. The night is cool, the sky a muddy orange from the city's light pollution. Somewhere out there, Celeste is with a monster. "But she walked away from me to save everyone in that compound. I will not let that sacrifice mean nothing. I will not leave her with him."

"Maximus." There's something in his voice I rarely hear. Concern. Not for the mission or the compound, but for me. "She did what she did because she loves you. She'd want you to protect the compound. To protect yourself."

"I know what she'd want." My voice comes out colder than I intend. "And I know what I need. Those aren't the same thing."

"They could be. Wait for backup. Three minutes..."

"Every minute I wait is a minute he has to hurt her. To break her. To do whatever he's been planning since Rome." I start down the alley, following her scent. "I've spent years being patient, Marcellus. Being careful. Weighing every decision against potential consequences. And right now, the only consequence I care about is what happens to her if I don't move fast enough."

Another silence. Longer this time.

"I'll protect the compound," Marcellus says finally. "Go get her back."

"If I don't return..."

"You'll return. And so will she." A pause. "You don't get to die before I've had a chance to properly apologize for doubting her."

Something almost like a smile tugs at my mouth. Almost. "Hold me to that."

"I intend to." His voice softens, just slightly. "Many years I've followed you, sir. You've never once asked me to trust you blindly. You've always explained your reasoning and allowed me to question your decisions. So trust me now when I say: go. Find her. Bring her home. And let me handle everything else."

"Marcellus."

"That's an order. From your second-in-command to his lord." I can almost hear his dry smile. "I believe the protocols allow for that in cases of emotional compromise."

Emotional compromise. Is that what this is? This clawing desperation in my chest, this single-minded focus that's drowning out every other consideration?

Yes. Probably. Definitely.

I don't care.

"Keep them safe," I say.

"Always."

I end the call and focus on the hunt.

The alley behind the warehouse is narrow, littered with debris and the detritus of urban decay. Celeste's scent hangs in the air, faint but unmistakable. She's bleeding. Not much, but enough for me to track. Enough to leave a trail through the maze of backstreets and abandoned lots that make up this corner of Konstantin's territory.

She didn't go quietly.

The evidence is everywhere. Scuff marks on the concrete where someone struggled. A smear of blood on a brick wall, hers or Valentina's, I can't tell. A broken heel from a shoe, probably one of Konstantin's guards. A dent in a metal dumpster that looks like someone was thrown into it.

That's my girl.

The thought surfaces unbidden, and I don't push it away. She is. She's mine, and I'm going to get her back, and then I'm never letting her out of my sight again.

I move fast. The city blurs around me as I follow the trail. Left down the alley. Right onto a side street. Past abandoned buildings and shuttered storefronts, through the forgotten corners of a city that doesn't know monsters walk among them.

My mind races as I run. Where would Konstantin take her? Not far, he'd want to move quickly, get her somewhere secure before I could pursue.

Somewhere close. Somewhere defensible. Somewhere he could regroup and plan his next move.

I think about the territory. About the maps I've studied over decades of cold war with Konstantin. About the places he controls, the properties he owns, the locations he might use for something like this.

There's a parking structure three blocks from the warehouse. Industrial. Abandoned. Konstantin bought it through a shell company fifteen years ago, ostensibly for development that never materialized. I always assumed it was a safe house. A bolt hole. Somewhere to retreat if things went wrong.

The trail confirms it. The scent grows stronger as I approach, layered with others now, Valentina's sickly-sweet perfume, Konstantin's distinctive musk, the copper tang of fresh blood.

Fresh blood. More of it now.

Someone is hurt.

I slow as I approach, forcing myself to think strategically despite every instinct screaming at me to charge in blind. Konstantin has been alive for over a thousand years. He didn't survive this long by being careless. Whatever's waiting inside, it's not an accident. It's not a coincidence.

It's a trap.

But traps only work if you don't see them coming. And right now, I don't care about traps. I don't care about strategy or consequences or any of the things that have kept me alive for six centuries.

I care about her.

And then I hear it.

The clash of bodies. The grunt of impact. The unmistakable sound of combat.

She's fighting.

I abandon caution and run.

The parking structure is three levels of crumbling concrete and rusted support beams. Graffiti covers the lower walls, and broken glass crunches under my feet as I enter. The sounds are coming from the second level, echoing off the walls, bouncing through the empty space. I take the ramp at full speed, my footsteps silent despite my haste.

What I see when I reach the second level stops me cold.

Celeste, covered in blood, locked in combat with Valentina.

They're moving almost too fast to track, a blur of strikes and counters, two predators fighting with everything they have. Valentina is older, stronger, her movements carrying the fluid grace of centuries of practice. But Celeste is fury incarnate. She fights like she's got nothing left to lose, like she's already decided how this ends.

My ring glints at her chest, catching the dim light that filters through the broken windows. Still there. Still hers.

Pride swells in my chest even as terror grips my throat. She's magnificent. She never intended to go quietly. Never intended to be a passive prisoner waiting for rescue. The moment she saw an opportunity...

She took it.

That's who she is. That's who I fell for. A fighter. A survivor. Someone who doesn't wait to be saved.

Valentina snarls something I can't hear, driving Celeste back with a series of vicious strikes. Celeste blocks most of them, but one gets through, a slash across her shoulder that sprays blood across the concrete. She doesn't cry out. Doesn't falter. Just adjusts her stance and keeps fighting.

I move to help her.

"Not so fast, old friend."

Konstantin steps out of the shadows, blocking my path. He's immaculate despite the chaos around him, not a hair out of place, not a speck of blood on his tailored suit. His smile is the same one he's worn for centuries: amused, superior, utterly certain of his own invincibility.

I hate that smile. I've hated it for four hundred years.

"Let her fight her own battle," he says, gesturing toward Celeste and Valentina. "It's been a long time coming, don't you think? Maker and creation. Mother and daughter, in a sense. Very poetic."

"Get out of my way."

"Or what?" He spreads his hands, the gesture almost theatrical. "You'll kill me? You've been trying to do that for centuries, Maximus. It hasn't worked out well for you."

He's right. We've fought before, twice, in fact. The first time, in Prague in 1723, we destroyed an entire city block before his allies pulled him out. The second time, in Shanghai in 1891, I had him cornered in a burning warehouse before the roof collapsed and separated us.

Both times, I was the one left standing. Both times, he was the one who ran.

Not tonight.

I don't waste words on a response. I attack.

The first blow catches him off guard, a strike to his jaw that snaps his head back and sends him stumbling. Centuries of training and combat experience compressed into a single motion. He recovers quickly, but not quickly enough. My second strike opens a gash across his cheek. My third drives him back another step.

"Impressive," he says, touching his face where blood wells from the wound. "You've gotten faster."

I press the advantage, driving him away from Celeste, away from the fight I desperately want to be part of. Every strike is meant to kill. Every movement is designed to cause maximum damage. I'm not fighting to win, I'm fighting to end him, permanently, finally, after centuries of this cold war.

But Konstantin is faster than me. Stronger than me. A thousand years of existence has honed him into something beyond what most vampires can achieve. He weathers my assault with the patience of someone who's seen empires rise and fall, blocking and dodging and waiting for an opening.

"She's something special, isn't she?" He parries a strike, counters with one of his own. Pain blooms across my ribs where his fist connects. "I knew she would be. From the moment I saw her in that underground ring, I knew. A fighter. A survivor. Exactly the kind of weapon I needed."

"She's not a weapon."

"Everyone's a weapon, Maximus. The only question is who's holding the trigger." He ducks under my swing, lands a blow to my kidney that would have dropped a younger vampire. "I held it first. Made her. Shaped her. You just got the finished product."

I catch his wrist as he strikes again, twist until I hear bone crack. He hisses but doesn't scream. Doesn't retreat. Just smiles that infuriating smile and wrenches free, his wrist already healing.

"You know what the best part is?" he asks, circling me now, looking for weakness. "You fell for her exactly like I planned. The great Maximus, who hasn't cared about anything in centuries, brought low by a fledgling I designed specifically to destroy him."

"You didn't design her. You just turned her."

"Oh, I did much more than that." His eyes gleam in the darkness. "Rome was only the beginning. The turning, the memory blocks, the gifts lying dormant in her blood, that was all me. Valentina was just the instrument. A very eager instrument, I might add. She enjoyed her work."

Behind us, I hear Celeste cry out. Not in pain, in rage. The sound of impact, of bodies hitting concrete. I don't turn to look. Can't turn to look. Konstantin would use the distraction to kill me.

But I hear her. I hear her fighting. And I know, I *know*, she's going to win.

"What did you do to her?" I demand, pressing my attack. "In Rome?"

"Curious?" Konstantin parries my strike, dances back. "You should be. She's going to be extraordinary, Maximus. More than you can possibly imagine. The sunlight is just the beginning."

"The sunlight is a myth."

"Is it?" He grins. "Ask yourself why she adapted so quickly. Why she's stronger than she should be, faster than she should be." He spreads his arms wide, leaving himself open. Deliberately. Tauntingly. "She's evolving. And when she's done, when she's fully awakened..."

I take the opening. Drive forward with everything I have, my hand aimed at his chest, at his heart.

He sidesteps. Catches my arm. Uses my momentum against me.

I hit the ground hard, rolling to my feet immediately, but he's already there. His foot catches me in the ribs, sends me crashing into a concrete pillar. The impact cracks the structure. Dust rains down around us.

"Still so predictable," Konstantin says, advancing slowly.

I spit blood onto the concrete. Push myself upright. "And yet you're the one who keeps running."

His smile flickers. "Strategic withdrawal. There's a difference."

"Is that what tonight is? Strategy?" I step toward him. "You went to all this trouble, Rome, the memory blocks, Valentina, this entire war, because you're terrified of what Celeste might become without your control."

He stills. "I'm not afraid of anything."

"You're afraid of her. And you're afraid of us together." I step toward him, and for the first time, he doesn't immediately counter-advance. "That's why you need to separate us. That's why you couldn't just kill me and take her. You needed her to choose to leave. Needed to break what we have before you could use her."

"An interesting theory."

"It's not a theory. It's the truth." Another step. "You've spent a thousand years building power, accumulating strength, crushing anyone who might threaten you. And then a fledgling, a vampire less than a year old, became the one thing you couldn't control. The one variable you couldn't predict."

"She's a weapon. My weapon."

"She's not yours. She never was." I'm close enough to strike now. Close enough to see the uncertainty flickering behind his eyes. "And whatever you did to her in Rome, it's not going to work the way you planned. Because she's not fighting for you. She's fighting *against* you. With everything she has."

As if to punctuate my words, a scream echoes through the parking structure.

Valentina's scream.

Konstantin's head snaps toward the sound, and I see it, the first crack in his composure. The first moment of genuine concern.

Because Valentina isn't just his instrument. She's been with him for centuries. His most loyal servant. His most reliable tool.

And from the sound of that scream, she's losing.

I don't waste the opportunity. I drive forward, catching Konstantin with a strike to the throat that staggers him backward. Follow it with an elbow to the temple. A knee to the ribs. Every blow landing with satisfying impact.

He recovers, of course he recovers, but now there's something different in his eyes. Calculation. Reassessment.

He glances toward where Celeste and Valentina are fighting. Back at me. Weighing his options.

"This isn't over," he says.

"No," I agree. "It's just beginning."

We clash again, ancient vampire against ancient vampire, centuries of history and hatred compressed into every strike. The parking structure shakes with our impacts. Concrete cracks. Metal groans.

And through it all, I hear Celeste fighting. Hear the sounds of combat from the other side of the structure. Hear her grunts of effort and Valentina's increasingly desperate snarls.

Two battles raging simultaneously. Two outcomes hanging in the balance.

I don't know how this ends.

But I know one thing with absolute certainty: we're both fighting for our lives tonight.

And only one side is going to walk away.

THIRTY-ONE

Valentina's fist catches me in the jaw, snapping my head back.

I roll with the impact, using the momentum to create distance. Blood fills my mouth, my own. I spit it onto the concrete and circle, keeping my maker in my line of sight.

She's smiling. Of course she's smiling. That same cat-with-cream smile she wore the night she turned me, the night she ruined my life and walked away laughing.

"You should have stayed quiet," she says, advancing slowly. "Played the obedient prisoner. Konstantin would have treated you well, you know. He has plans for you."

"I don't care about his plans."

"No. You care about *him*."

She tilts her head toward where Maximus and Konstantin are fighting, the sounds of their combat echoing through the parking structure. I hear the crash of bodies against concrete, the grunt of impact, the unmistakable rhythm of two predators trying to destroy each other.

Every instinct screams at me to look. To find Maximus, make sure he's still standing, still fighting. But I can't take my eyes off Valentina. Not for a second.

"It's pathetic, really," she continues. "Eight months as a vampire and you've already made the oldest mistake in the book. Falling for someone who can't save you."

I don't respond. I'm watching her feet, her hips, the subtle shifts in her weight that telegraph her next move. Eight months isn't long for a vampire, but it's long enough to learn how to read an opponent. And I was reading opponents for three years before she ever sank her fangs into me.

A particularly loud crash echoes from across the structure. Maximus's voice, raised in fury. My chest tightens.

Valentina lunges, exploiting my distraction.

I sidestep, barely, and rake my nails across her arm as she passes. The wounds are shallow, already healing, but she hisses in annoyance.

"Lucky," she spits.

"Trained."

"And distracted." Her eyes gleam. "He's got you so twisted up you can't even focus on the enemy in front of you. That's exactly what Konstantin wanted, you know. A weakness. A blind spot. Something to make the great Maximus vulnerable."

I force myself to center. To push Maximus to the edge of my awareness, present but not consuming. I can hear him fighting. That has to be enough. If I let myself worry about him, Valentina will kill me. And if I die, I can't help him at all.

"Why me?" The question comes out before I can stop it. "Why go to all this trouble for one fledgling?"

Valentina circles me, predator assessing prey. "Because you were perfect. Konstantin has been searching for decades for someone with the right combination of strength, stubbornness, and fire. Someone who could survive what he needed to do."

"Which was?"

"Make you better." She feints left, strikes right. I block, but the impact rattles my bones. "The underground rings were his hunting ground. He had people at dozens of fights, watching, evaluating. Most fighters were too weak. Too broken. Too easily controlled." Her smile widens. "But you. You beat me that night, remember? A vampire. You didn't know what I was, and you still won."

The memory surfaces, the private match, the big payout, the woman who moved wrong and smiled wrong and looked at me like prey. I'd been so focused on the money. So sure of my own skill.

"That's when he knew," Valentina continues. "Watching you take down a vampire with nothing but human strength and sheer determination. He said, 'That one. She's the one.'"

"The one for what?"

"For the program." She circles closer. "He's been building an army, Celeste. Enhanced vampires. Stronger, faster, more resilient than anything that's ever existed. You were supposed to be his masterpiece."

"I'm no one's weapon."

"You already are. You just don't know it yet." She lunges again, and this time her fist catches me in the ribs. I feel something crack. "The turning was just the beginning. After that came the modifications."

"In Rome." The fragments Maximus unlocked flash through my mind, cobblestones, rain, a small dark room. Konstantin in daylight.

"Yes, he mentioned the blocks were failing faster than expected." Valentina circles me, looking amused rather than concerned.

"But knowing you were in Rome and understanding what happened there are two very different things."

"The fight was in Atlanta. The underground ring. I remember that clearly." I circle her, keeping my guard up. "So how did I end up in Rome?"

"The transformation takes three days. Your heart stops. Your brain goes dark. Your body is just meat waiting to be remade." She's enjoying this, the confusion on my face, the pieces not fitting together. "Three days is a long time, Celeste. Long enough to put your corpse on a private jet. Long enough to fly you across an ocean."

The realization hits like a punch to the gut. "You took me to Rome while I was transforming."

"You woke up there, your first true awakening as a vampire. Three weeks of modifications followed. Experiments. Konstantin remaking you cell by cell." Her eyes gleam. "And when he was finished, we blocked those memories, flew you back to Atlanta, and let you wake up in that warehouse thinking it was your first night. Thinking only three days had passed since I turned you."

Three weeks. Not three days.

My real first awakening happened in Rome, and I don't remember any of it. The fragments Maximus unlocked are just slivers of three weeks that were stolen from me.

"The note," I say slowly. "'Welcome to eternity, sweetheart.' You left it to make me think..."

"That I'd turned you and abandoned you on the spot. The confused fledgling narrative." Valentina laughs. "It was important that you believed you'd survived alone from the start. We just... gave you a head start first."

"What did he do to me?"

"Ask yourself why you survived the contaminated blood." She circles closer. "A fledgling, eight months old, with no maker to guide her. Yes, Maximus gave you clean blood, but I've seen vampires twice your age die even with intervention. The contamination had spread through your entire system. You should have been too far gone to save."

I remember those hours. The black veins spreading under my skin. The certainty that I was dying. The clean blood sliding down my throat. And then the recovery, faster than anyone expected.

"The others in his facility," Valentina continues. "The ones who went feral, who couldn't be saved, they had clean blood too. Medical care. Everything Maximus could offer." She smiles. "They still died. But you bounced back in hours. Doesn't that strike you as odd?"

I don't answer. Because I don't have one.

"That wasn't normal," Valentina confirms. "That was the modifications working. Your body adapting, evolving, becoming what Konstantin designed you to be."

"Which is what?"

"A weapon." Her eyes gleam in the darkness. "That was just the beginning. There are other gifts sleeping in your blood, waiting to wake up. Enhanced strength. Accelerated healing. Resistances that no other vampire has." She pauses, savoring the next words. "And a kill switch."

The words land like ice in my veins. "What?"

"You think Konstantin would build a weapon he couldn't control?" Valentina laughs. "There's a trigger buried in those modifications. A command phrase, a signal, something. When he activates it, you won't be Celeste anymore. You'll be exactly what he designed: a perfect killing machine with no will of its own."

"You're lying."

"Am I?" She tilts her head. "Ask yourself why he let you go. Why he let you wander Atlanta, let you find your way to Maximus, let you fall in love with his oldest enemy." Her smile turns cruel.

"Because it doesn't matter. When the time comes, when you're exactly where he wants you, he'll flip the switch. And you'll kill Maximus yourself. You won't be able to stop it. You won't even want to."

Across the structure, I hear Maximus roar, a sound of pure rage. The crash of bodies. A pillar cracking.

I take a step toward the sound before I can stop myself.

Valentina moves faster.

Her hand closes around my throat, slamming me back against a concrete pillar. Stars explode across my vision. Her face fills my sight, beautiful and terrible and utterly without mercy.

"He's fine," she says. "Konstantin won't kill him. Not yet. He wants to break him first, and you can't break someone by killing them quickly. It's like a game to him, his whole reason for existing. I guess you get bored when you're over a thousand years old." Her grip tightens. "But you... You, I can kill. And I think I will. You've outlived your usefulness to me."

"Konstantin won't..."

"Konstantin doesn't control me. Not anymore." Something dark flickers in her expression. "He promised me Atlanta if I delivered you. Promised me territory, power, everything I've wanted for three centuries. But watching you now, watching you pine for Maximus when you should be focused on the enemy about to kill you, I think I'd rather just watch you die."

Her free hand draws back, claws extended, aimed at my chest.

I have maybe half a second.

I use it.

My knee comes up hard, connecting with her stomach. It's not enough to hurt her, not really, but it's enough to loosen her grip. I twist free, gasping, and put distance between us.

"You'll have to do better than that," I manage.

"Oh, I intend to."

We circle each other again. Both wounded now. Both bleeding. The sounds of Maximus's fight continue in the background, crashes and grunts and the occasional word I can't quite make out.

Stay alive, I think at him, knowing he can't hear me. *Stay alive for me.*

"There's something else you should know," Valentina says. "Before I kill you. A parting gift from your loving maker."

"I don't want anything from you."

"You'll want this." She smiles. "The love you feel for Maximus? That's real. Completely, painfully real. Konstantin didn't manufacture it. He didn't have to."

I stare at her, waiting for the twist.

"That's what makes this so perfect," she continues. "You genuinely love him. And when Konstantin activates you, you'll be aware of every second of it. You'll watch yourself tear him apart, and you won't be able to stop. You'll feel your own hands killing the man you love, and there won't be a single thing you can do."

The horror of it washes over me.

"He could have made you a mindless drone," Valentina says. "But that's not what he wanted. He wanted you to suffer. Wanted Maximus to see the woman he loves become his executioner. Wanted you both to know, in those final moments, that your love was real and it didn't matter." Her smile widens. "That's the cruelty of it. If you didn't love him, it wouldn't hurt. But you do. And it will."

I think of every moment with Maximus. Every touch. Every word. The way he looked at me in the firelight. The way he chose me over and over again.

All of it real. All of it mine.

And all of it potentially the setup for his murder.

"You're a time bomb," Valentina purrs. "Ticking away in his bed, in his heart, in his life. And he doesn't even know it."

"He knows now," I say quietly. "And so do I. Which means we can stop it."

"Can you?" She laughs. "Konstantin has been perfecting this for centuries. You think you can just... decide not to be activated? Will yourself out of programming you don't even understand?"

"I think I can try. I think we can find a way." I meet her eyes. "And I think you're afraid of that. Afraid that your master's perfect plan might fail."

Something flickers in her expression. Uncertainty. Just for a second.

"And when you've served your purpose," she says, recovering, "when you've destroyed him completely, Konstantin will collect what's left. A broken lord. A broken weapon. Everything he's wanted for a thousand years."

"No."

"No?"

"You're wrong." I straighten, pushing down the fear, the horror, the sickening uncertainty. "I don't care what Konstantin built into me. I don't care what trigger he buried. I will find a way to rip it out. And until then, I will fight every single second against whatever he tries to make me do."

"You can't fight programming."

"Watch me." I meet her eyes. "I've been fighting my whole life. Fighting to survive. Fighting to matter. Fighting against people who told me I was nothing, that I'd never be anything. And I'm still here." I feel something shift inside me. Something that might be the weapon waking up, or might just be rage. "Konstantin thinks he built a bomb he can detonate whenever he wants. But bombs can be defused. Triggers can be removed. And I would rather die, *truly* die, than let him use me to hurt Maximus."

"Pretty words. Let's see if you mean them."

I attack before she can respond.

Not with technique, but with fury. All the rage I've been carrying since I woke up in that warehouse, alone and changed and abandoned. All the grief for the life that was stolen from me, the sister I can't see, the future that was ripped away. All the hatred for the woman who did the stealing and then walked away laughing.

I fight dirty. No rules. No referees. Just violence, pure and purposeful.

I grew up scrapping in back alleys before I ever learned proper form. I know how to fight someone who outmatches me. You don't try to win, you try to survive long enough for them to make a mistake.

We tear at each other. She opens a gash across my stomach; I rake my nails down her face. She breaks two more of my ribs; I dislocate her shoulder. Blood splatters across the concrete, mine and hers, mingling.

Through it all, I stay aware of the other fight. The rhythm of it. Maximus is still standing, I can tell by the sounds, by the way the combat ebbs and flows. He's hurt but holding. Matching Konstantin blow for blow.

Hold on, I think. *I'm coming.*

Valentina catches me with a strike to the temple. The world tilts. I stagger, and she presses the advantage, driving me back toward a concrete pillar.

"You can't win," she snarls. "I made you. I know every weakness you have."

"You didn't make me." I duck under her swing, spin behind her. "You just awakened me."

My elbow locks around her throat. She thrashes, but I hold on, tightening my grip until I feel her spine grinding against my forearm.

"Let me tell you what you actually gave me," I hiss in her ear.

"Eight months alone. Eight months of figuring out how to survive without a maker, without guidance, without anyone. Eight months of fighting every single night just to see the next sunset."

She claws at my arm. Blood wells up, but I don't let go.

"You thought you were breaking me. But you were training me. Every night I survived made me stronger. Every battle I won proved I could do this on my own." I tighten my grip. "You made a mistake, Valentina. You should have killed me when you had the chance."

"Konstantin will..."

"Konstantin isn't here. And even if he was, I don't care." I feel her struggles weakening. "You took everything from me. My life. My sister. My future. And now I'm taking something from you."

"What?"

"Your existence."

She makes one last desperate move, her hand diving into her jacket, pulling out something that gleams silver in the dim light. A blade. Short, sharp, designed for killing.

The blade catches me in the side, sliding between my ribs, burning as it goes. The pain is unlike anything I've felt, not just physical agony, but something deeper. Something fundamentally wrong, like my blood itself is screaming.

But I don't let go.

"That won't save you," I growl through gritted teeth.

"Silver to your original modification site." Valentina's voice is a rasp, barely audible. "Konstantin said that was your weakness. The place where he first changed you. Now the changes will come undone. You'll die, just slower than me."

"Then I better make this quick."

I wrench my arm sideways, snapping her neck. But that won't be enough, not for a vampire her age. Not for my maker.

So I don't stop.

I twist with everything I have left. The crack of her spine separating vibrates through my palms. She's still fighting, still clawing, so I keep going. I dig my fingers into the torn flesh of her throat and pull until muscle shreds and tendons snap like wet rope.

Her jaw is still working. Still trying to curse me.

I wrench her head free. The sound is wet and grinding, nothing clean about it. Her body spasms once, twice, then goes still.

I drop her head and watch it roll across the concrete until it comes to rest against a pillar. Eyes finally empty.

I stand over what's left of her, breathing hard despite not needing to breathe at all.

My maker. The woman who turned me, abandoned me, used me. Who watched me struggle and suffer and nearly die, and laughed about it. Who told me I was nothing but a weapon, a product, a thing designed for someone else's destruction.

She's dead. By my hand. With my strength.

I should feel triumphant. Instead, I feel... hollow. Empty. Like I've been running on rage for so long that without it, there's nothing left.

The silver blade is still lodged in my side. I wrap my hand around the hilt, grit my teeth, and pull.

The pain is blinding. I hear myself scream, distant, detached, like it's coming from someone else. The blade comes free with a wet sound, and I throw it away from me, watching it clatter across the concrete.

Blood pours from the wound. Too much blood. And something else, a wrongness spreading from the injury, radiating outward through my body.

The modifications will come undone, Valentina said. *You'll die, just slower than me.*

I can feel it starting. A destabilization deep in my core. My blood turning against itself, fighting some internal war I can't see or understand. The silver wound in my side burns with a wrongness that goes beyond pain, like it's unraveling something fundamental.

Silver to your original modification site, Valentina said. *The place where he first changed you. Now the changes will come undone.*

Whatever Konstantin built into me, the silver is tearing it apart.

I stumble. Catch myself on a concrete pillar. The parking structure spins around me, lights blurring into smears of white and gray.

The silver is still working its way deeper, I realize. Spreading from the wound site. Destroying whatever it touches.

I slide down the pillar, leaving a streak of blood on the concrete. My legs won't hold me. My vision is tunneling, darkness creeping in at the edges.

Through the haze, I see Maximus and Konstantin.

They're both bloodied now. Both moving slower than before. Maximus has a gash across his chest that hasn't fully healed; Konstantin favors his left side where something seems to be broken.

But they're still fighting. Still matched. Neither willing to give ground.

Then Konstantin sees me.

His gaze moves from me, to Valentina's headless corpse, back to me slumped against the pillar, blood pooling at my feet. I watch him calculate. Watch him reassess.

"It seems my fledgling has exceeded expectations," he says to Maximus, loud enough for me to hear. "Killing her own maker. Impressive."

Maximus doesn't take the bait. Doesn't look away from Konstantin. "Surrender. This is over."

"Is it?" Konstantin smiles. "Your woman is dying, old friend. I can smell it from here. The silver is in her modification site, Valentina's little insurance policy. Whatever's happening to her, it's not going to stop on its own."

Now Maximus does look. Just a glance, a fraction of a second, but I see his expression change. See the fear flash across his face.

"We'll continue this another time," Konstantin says. "Go save my weapon. See if you can defuse her before I decide to use her."

He moves before Maximus can stop him, a blur of motion toward the ramp, toward the exit. Maximus takes one step to follow.

Then he stops.

I watch him make the choice. Watch the war on his face, the fury and the fear, the need for vengeance battling against something stronger. He could chase Konstantin. Could finally end the enemy who's been hunting him for centuries.

Instead, he turns away.

He turns toward me.

He's running, crossing the distance between us in a blur, dropping to his knees at my side. His hands find my face, my shoulders, my wound, cataloging damage with desperate efficiency.

"Celeste. Look at me."

I try to focus on his face. It keeps blurring, splitting into doubles. "You let him go."

"I let him go."

"You've been hunting him for..."

"I don't care." His voice cracks. "I don't care about Konstantin. I don't care about the war or the network or any of it. I care about you."

"That's very poor strategic thinking."

He chokes out something that might be a laugh. "You're dying, and you're critiquing my strategy?"

"Someone has to."

His hands are shaking as they press against my wound, trying to slow the bleeding.

"Valentina's dead," I manage. "I killed her."

"I know. I saw." He smooths blood-matted hair from my face. "You were magnificent."

"She told me things. About Rome. About what Konstantin did to me." Another wave of pain washes through me, and I curl into him, gasping. "I'm a weapon, Maximus. A sleeper agent. He built a trigger into me, something that will make me... make me..."

"Make you what?"

"Kill you." The words come out broken. "When he activates it, I won't be able to stop myself. I'll be forced to... I'll watch myself..." I can't finish. The horror of it chokes me.

His hands frame my face, forcing me to meet his eyes. "I know."

"You... what?"

"Konstantin told me. While we were fighting." His jaw tightens. "He was very pleased with himself. Said he'd finally found a way to destroy me that I couldn't fight. That the woman I love would be my executioner."

"And you still came to me. You still..."

"Of course I did."

"Maximus, I'm dangerous. I'm a bomb he can set off whenever he wants. You should..."

"Should what? Leave you to die?" His voice is fierce. "Let you bleed out alone because you *might* be used against me someday?"

"Yes."

"No." The word is absolute. "I've spent six hundred years being strategic. Being careful. Keeping everyone at arm's length because attachment is weakness and love is a vulnerability." He leans closer. "And you know what it got me? Centuries of survival.

Centuries of emptiness. Centuries of being so alone I forgot what it felt like to want someone this much."

"I could kill you."

"You could." He doesn't look away. "And I would rather die by your hand than live another century without you."

"That's insane."

"Probably." His thumb brushes my cheek, wiping away blood or tears, I can't tell which. "But here's what I know: I love you. Not because Konstantin designed it. Not because of any modification or trigger or plan. I love you because you're stubborn and fierce, and you insult me when you should be afraid. Because you saved my compound and killed your maker and chose me over and over again."

"What if I can't fight it? What if he activates me and I..."

"Then we'll find a way to deactivate it. We'll tear out whatever he put in you. We'll burn his work out of your blood cell by cell if we have to." His forehead presses against mine. "But I am not letting you die tonight. I am not letting him win by making us afraid of each other."

The cold is spreading faster now. I can feel myself fading, pieces of my existence slipping away into the darkness.

But his words are warm. His hands are steady. His eyes, those beautiful eyes, are full of something I never expected to see from a six-hundred-year-old vampire lord.

Hope. Love. Defiance.

"Something's wrong," I whisper. "Inside. The silver, Valentina drove it into the original modification site. Whatever Konstantin built into me, it's coming apart."

His expression goes very still. "What do you mean?"

"I can feel it. Unraveling. Like I'm coming apart at the seams." Another wave of pain. I ride it out, gritting my teeth. "The silver is destroying whatever he did to me in Rome. I don't think vampire healing can fix this. I don't think anything can fix this."

"There's a way." His voice is rough. "A bond. Deeper than what we've done before, deeper than shared blood, deeper than anything. It would anchor you to me. Make my strength yours. Give you something to hold onto while your body stabilizes."

"What kind of bond?"

"A blood bond." He holds my gaze. "It's rare. Two vampires drinking from each other simultaneously, with intent. It links them permanently, what one feels, the other feels. What one knows, the other knows. It can't be undone, Celeste. Once it's done, we're bound for eternity."

The weight of what he's offering settles over me. Forever. Not just love, not just partnership, a permanent merging of two existences.

"You'd never be free of me," I whisper. "Every thought. Every feeling. Every dark corner of my mind, you'd have access to all of it."

"Yes."

"And I'd have access to yours."

"Yes."

"Including whatever Konstantin put in me. If there's a trigger, if he activates it..." I force myself to say it. "You'd feel me trying to kill you. You'd feel everything."

"Yes."

"And you still want this?"

"I want *you*." He says it like it's simple. Like it's obvious. "All of you. Even the parts Konstantin touched. Even the weapon he tried to make. Because that's not who you are. That's just what he did to you. And I will spend eternity helping you tear it out. I already wanted to have a blood bond with you, even before this."

My eyes are burning. From pain or emotion, I can't tell anymore. "You've thought about this."

"Yes. I've been trying to find the right time, the right way to ask you. I wanted to give you a choice." His voice cracks again. "I wanted it to be romantic. Candles or something. Not a parking structure. Not with you bleeding out in my arms."

"Candles would have been nice."

"I'll make it up to you. A thousand candles. A million. Every night for the rest of eternity."

"That's a lot of candles."

"I have a lot of time." His forehead presses against mine. "Please, Celeste. Let me save you. Let me bind myself to you. Not because you're dying, but because I love you. Because I want forever with you. Because the thought of existing without you is more terrifying than anything Konstantin could ever do to me."

His eyes, those beautiful eyes, are full of hope. Love. Need.

"Okay," I whisper.

"Okay?"

"Yes." I manage a smile, even though it hurts. "I choose you. I've been choosing you since the moment I arrived in your medical wing and decided to trust a vampire who could have killed me. I chose you when I stayed. When I fought for you. When I walked away with Konstantin to save your people."

"Celeste..."

"I'm not done." I find his hand, lace my fingers through his. The grip is weak, weaker than it should be, but I hold on anyway. "I don't care what Konstantin built into me. We'll find it. We'll rip it out. And until then, I will fight every second of every day to stay *me*. To stay yours."

"Ours," he corrects softly.

"Ours." I like the sound of that. "So do it. Save me. Bind yourself to me forever. And then..." Another wave of pain, worse than before. I gasp through it. "And then let's spend eternity making Konstantin regret ever touching me."

For a long moment, he just looks at me.

Then he nods.

"This will hurt," he says. "The bond, it's not gentle. It's going to feel like dying and being reborn all at once."

"I've done that before. Wasn't a fan."

"This is different. This is..." He struggles for words. "This is becoming part of each other. Permanently. Irrevocably."

"Maximus." I squeeze his hand. "I'm already dying. Whatever comes next can't be worse than this."

He looks at me for one more second. Then he lifts his wrist to his mouth and bites.

Blood wells up, rich and dark and smelling of power, of centuries, of him. He holds his wrist to my lips.

"Drink," he says. "And don't stop until I tell you."

I drink.

THIRTY-TWO

She drinks from my wrist, and I watch her throat move with each swallow.

Her eyes are closed. Her skin is too pale, the silver's poison visible in the dark lines spreading from the wound in her side. She's fading. I can see it, feel it in the way her grip on my arm weakens with each passing second.

This has to work. It has to.

I shift her in my arms, tilting her head back to expose her throat. The pulse point where I drank from her before. Where I saw her memories, felt her pain, witnessed fragments of what Valentina and Konstantin did to her in Rome.

This time will be different. This time, it won't be one-way.

"Don't stop drinking," I tell her. "No matter what happens. No matter what you feel. Don't stop until I tell you."

Her eyes flutter open. Dark and glazed with pain, but still her. Still that stubborn fire that made me fall for her in the first place.

She nods weakly and keeps drinking.

I lower my mouth to her throat and bite.

Her blood hits my tongue, and the world explodes.

Pain. Hers, flooding into me like a tidal wave. The silver burning through her veins, eating away at whatever Konstantin built into her. The cold spreading through her limbs, the numbness, the terrifying sense of coming undone at the seams.

I feel all of it. Every agonizing second.

But I don't stop. I drink deeper, pulling her into me, and I feel her doing the same at my wrist. Two currents flowing in opposite directions. Two rivers meeting, merging, becoming one.

Fear. Not of death, but of losing me. Of being used against me. Of becoming the weapon Konstantin designed and destroying the man she loves with her own hands.

And beneath that fear, love. So much of it. Overwhelming, terrifying, all-consuming. She loves me with a ferocity that I can't comprehend. Chose me. Keeps choosing me. Even knowing what she might become.

The bond begins to form.

I feel it like a thread of fire stretching between us, fragile at first, barely there. But with each pull of blood, each swallow, it grows stronger. Thicker. More real.

Her memories crash into me.

A little girl with scraped knees, learning to throw a punch from an older cousin. "You're small," he says, "so you gotta be fast."

A young woman standing over her mother's body, too numb to cry. Teenage Simone sobbing beside her. The smell of death and the knowledge that nothing will ever be the same.

The underground ring. Blood on her knuckles. The roar of the crowd. The only place she felt powerful, in control, alive.

Waking up in a warehouse, alone and changed and terrified. A note on a receipt: "Welcome to eternity, sweetheart."

Eight months of survival. Contaminated blood and desperate hunger and the constant, crushing loneliness of being something inhuman in a human world.

And then, me.

I see myself through her eyes.

The first time she saw me in that alley. A monster in an expensive suit, offering salvation or death. She couldn't tell which.

The first time I touched her, checking her wounds in the medical wing. The electricity that sparked between us, unexpected and undeniable.

The first time she realized she was falling for me. The terror of it. The impossibility.

I drink deeper, and she does the same, and the bond thickens into something unbreakable.

Her feelings pour into me, raw and unfiltered. Not just love, but everything. The anger she carries, hot and bright. The grief for the life that was stolen. The fierce protectiveness for her sister, for Elena, for the people she's come to care about. The terror of losing control, of becoming Konstantin's puppet, of hurting me. The desperate need to be enough. To be more than what he made her.

And beneath it all, running like a river through everything she is: strength. Pure, stubborn, relentless strength. The kind that doesn't know how to give up. The kind that fights back even when winning is impossible.

This is who she is. This is what I'm binding myself to. Not the weapon Konstantin tried to create. The woman who refuses to be controlled.

Yes, I think. Yes. All of it. I want all of it.

The bond snaps into place.

It's like nothing I've ever experienced. Six hundred years of existence, and nothing compares to this moment. One second I'm alone in my own head, the way I've been for centuries, the way I thought I'd always be.

And then I'm not.

She's there. Not just her blood in my veins or her body in my arms. Her. Her presence, her essence, woven into the fabric of my consciousness. I can feel her fear fading as my strength floods into her. Feel her pain dulling as the bond stabilizes whatever the silver was destroying.

I can feel her feeling me.

My centuries of loneliness. The endless nights. Luciano's cruelty, carved into my psyche like scars that never fully healed. The walls I built around my heart, so high and so thick, I thought nothing could ever breach them.

And then, her. The crack in those walls that became a door-way. The light that flooded in when I finally let someone see me.

She sees it all. Everything I am. Everything I've been. Every dark corner, every shameful memory, every moment of weakness I've hidden from the world.

And she doesn't pull away.

I feel her love. Not words, but something deeper. A truth that resonates through the bond like a bell being struck. I love all of it. Even the broken parts. Especially the broken parts.

Then I feel something else. Something strange, tangled in her blood where Konstantin's modifications live. The bond is touching it, wrapping around it, and I feel the shape of what he built into her. The trigger. The kill switch. It's there, buried deep, waiting for a signal that would turn her into a weapon.

The bond doesn't destroy it. But it does something else.

It anchors her. Wraps around the core of who she is and holds on. Whatever command Konstantin sends, it will have to go through me now. Through us. Through this connection that neither of us fully understands.

It's not a cure. But it's a shield.

Then I feel something else entirely. A burning sensation spreading across my chest, directly over my heart. Not painful. Warm. Insistent. Like something being written into my skin.

Celeste gasps against my wrist, and I know she feels it too. Her free hand claws at the fabric over her heart.

"What..." She pulls back just enough to look down at herself, tugging her torn shirt aside. Her eyes go wide.

A shape is forming on my chest. Deep crimson, the color of blood, etching itself into my skin like something being branded by invisible fire. A crescent moon, curving elegantly across my heart.

Through the bond, I feel Celeste's shock as she watches the same thing happen to her. The same mark, forming over her heart. A mirror image of mine.

What is this?

But even as I think the question, I know the answer. The bond isn't just internal anymore. It's marked us. Claimed us. Made us visible to each other in a way that can never be hidden or denied.

I seal the bite at her throat, and she releases my wrist. The blood exchange is complete. The bond is formed.

For a long moment, we just breathe. Her in my arms, both of us trembling with the aftermath of what we've done.

Then I feel it.

A flutter in my chest. Faint at first. So faint I think I'm imagining it.

But it comes again. And again. Steady. Rhythmic.

Impossible.

"Maximus." Celeste's voice is barely a whisper. Her hand presses against my chest, right over the place where the sensation is coming from. Right over the new crimson mark. "Do you feel that?"

I do. I feel it in my chest, and I feel it in hers, through the bond. Two flutters, perfectly synchronized.

"That's not possible," I say. "Vampires don't have..."

"Heartbeats." She finishes the word for me, wonder in her voice. Her hand moves to her own chest, pressing against the space beneath the ring I gave her, against her own new mark. "But I feel it. I feel yours. And mine. They're..."

"The same." I cover her hand with mine, pressing it harder against her chest. Beneath our joined hands, I feel it. The impossible rhythm. A heartbeat. Her heartbeat. Matching mine perfectly.

"How?" she breathes.

"I don't know." And I don't. In six hundred years, I've never heard of anything like this. Blood bonds are powerful, but they don't give vampires heartbeats. Nothing does. We're technically dead. Our hearts don't beat.

Except now they do.

"Maximus." Celeste's voice is strange. Wondering. "Your chest. The mark."

I look down again at the crimson design. In the dim light, it seems to pulse faintly, glowing with a soft luminescence that matches the rhythm of our shared heartbeat.

"You have one too," I say.

She pulls back enough to look at her own chest, at the crimson crescent now etched into her skin. Her fingers trace the curve of it, elegant and strange.

"They're the same," she breathes. "But mirrored."

I shift, turning to face her more fully, and she does the same. When our chests align, the crescents join together, forming one complete full moon. Two halves finally whole.

"I've never seen anything like this," I admit. "Blood bonds don't leave marks like this. Simple black lines, yes, barely visible. But this..."

"Apparently ours does." She touches her mark, then mine. Both pulse warmly at the contact. "Is this another Konstantin thing? Something he built into me?"

"No." I'm certain of that now. I felt his work during the bonding, and it felt nothing like this. Cold. Mechanical. Designed. This is something else entirely. "This feels ancient. Older than anything he could design. Older than me. Maybe older than him."

"How do you know?"

"Because it feels right." I pull her close again. "It feels like it was always supposed to be there."

"The trigger," she says quietly. "Konstantin's kill switch. I felt you touch it during the bond. What happened?"

"The bond wrapped around it. Around you. The core of who you are." I try to find words for what I sensed. "It didn't remove it. But it anchored you. Whatever signal he sends, it will have to fight through our connection to reach you."

"So I'm still dangerous."

"You were never dangerous to me. Not the real you." I press my forehead to hers. "And now we have time. Time to find it. Time to rip it out. Time to make sure he can never use you."

She's quiet for a moment, absorbing that. I feel her hope bloom through the bond, fragile but real.

"Does it hurt?" she asks, touching the mark on my chest.

"No. You'd feel it if it did." I press my hand flat against my chest, marveling at the sensation. A heartbeat. A mark. After six centuries of silence, my heart is beating again, and the proof of our bond is written on my skin. "It feels..."

"Alive," she finishes.

"Yes."

She laughs, a small sound, broken and exhausted, but real. "We have heartbeats. Vampires with heartbeats. And matching marks that glow. Konstantin is going to lose his mind when he finds out."

"Good." I pull her closer, adjusting her weight in my arms. She's still weak, still pale, but I can sense that the unraveling has stopped. The silver's damage has stabilized. She's going to survive. "Let him wonder what else we can do."

"What can we do?" She looks up at me, and I feel her curiosity bloom between us, bright and warm. "The bond. What does it mean?"

"It means we're connected. Permanently. What I feel, you feel. What you feel, I feel." I brush a strand of blood-matted hair from her face. "It means I'll always be able to find you. Always know if you're hurt, scared, or in danger. It means if Konstantin tries to activate you, I'll feel it. I can fight for you, even inside your own mind."

"You'd do that?"

"I'd burn the world down for you. Fighting a trigger in your head seems manageable by comparison."

She laughs again, and the sound warms something in my chest. Something that's been cold for centuries.

"It also means," I continue, my voice rougher now, "that I'll never be alone again."

"Neither will I." Her fingers find mine, lacing together. "Is that okay? Not being alone?"

"I think it's the best thing that's ever happened to me."

She's quiet for a moment, and her emotions wash over me unbidden. Wonder, exhaustion, love, and beneath it all, a flicker of something darker. Doubt.

"What is it?" I ask.

"You can feel that?"

"I can feel everything." I tilt her chin up, making her meet my eyes. "What's wrong?"

"I just..." She bites her lip. "Now you'll know. Everything. Every petty thought, every moment of jealousy or insecurity. Every time I'm scared or angry or..."

"Yes."

"That doesn't bother you?"

"Celeste." I press my forehead to hers. "I've spent six hundred years hiding what I feel. Burying every emotion, every weakness, every vulnerable moment. It was exhausting. It was lonely." I open myself fully, letting her feel the truth of my words. The weight of centuries, the desperate isolation, the relief of finally being known. "Having someone who sees all of it? Who feels all of it? That's not a burden. That's a gift."

She absorbs that for a moment. I feel her turning it over, examining it, testing it against her own fears.

Then something shifts in her. A release. A letting go.

"Okay," she says softly.

"Okay?"

"Okay, I believe you." She manages a small smile. "And for what it's worth, I feel the same way. Having access to all of you, even the dark parts? It doesn't scare me. It makes me feel..." She searches for the word. "Safe."

Safe. A six-hundred-year-old vampire, and she feels safe with me.

Something cracks in my chest. Not the heartbeat. Something deeper. Something that's been frozen for centuries, finally thawing.

Even the dark parts. She means it. I can feel that she means it through the bond. But there are shadows I've kept buried for three centuries, coiled so tight even Marcellus doesn't know about them. Seraphina's gift. The darkness that answers when I call.

The bond is wide open, but some things I've learned to bury deeper than feeling.

Someday I'll show her. When I'm sure it won't make her run.

"We should go," I say, my voice rougher than I intended. "Get you back to the compound. Elena will want to examine you, make sure the silver is fully neutralized."

"In a minute." She snuggles closer, despite the blood and the cold and the concrete floor beneath us. "Just let me feel this for a minute."

"Feel what?"

"You." She closes her eyes. "I've never felt anything like this. It's like you're everywhere. In my head, in my chest, in my blood. I can feel your heartbeat like it's my own."

"It is your own. They're the same."

"How is that possible?"

"I don't know." I tighten my arms around her. "But I'm not questioning it."

We sit in silence for a moment, just breathing together. Our hearts beat in perfect unison, a miracle neither of us expected, neither of us can explain.

Her exhaustion finally overtakes her. I feel it like a wave cresting and breaking. The adrenaline fading. The pain dulling to a manageable throb. She's crashing, hard, and she needs rest.

"Come on." I shift, gathering her more securely in my arms. "Time to go home."

"Home," she murmurs, her eyes already drifting shut. "I like the sound of that."

I stand, lifting her easily. She weighs nothing, less than nothing. But the weight of what we've done, what we've become, settles over me like a cloak.

Bonded. Permanently. Irrevocably.

I should be terrified. I've spent centuries avoiding exactly this.

Any connection that could be used against me, any vulnerability that could be exploited. And now I've bound myself to someone so completely that I'll feel it if she stubs her toe. Someone with a kill switch buried in her blood that her creator could activate at any moment.

But as I carry her out of the parking structure and into the night, all I feel is peace.

She's alive. She's mine. And whatever comes next, we'll face it together. Konstantin, the war, the trigger we need to find and destroy. All of it.

Our hearts beat in unison as I walk into the darkness.

THE COMPOUND IS in controlled chaos when I arrive.

Marcellus meets me at the gate, his expression shifting from relief to alarm when he sees Celeste in my arms. Then he goes very still.

"Sir." His voice is strange. "I can hear..."

"I know."

"That's not possible."

"I know."

He stares at me, at Celeste, at the space between us where two heartbeats pulse in perfect unison. For a moment, the unflappable Marcellus looks genuinely shaken.

"She's alive," I say before he can ask more questions I can't answer. "Injured, but alive."

"And Konstantin?"

"Escaped." The word tastes bitter. "But Valentina is dead. Celeste killed her."

Something flickers in Marcellus's expression. Surprise, respect, and concern are all tangled together. But his gaze keeps drifting to my chest, to the sound that shouldn't exist. "Elena is standing by in the medical wing."

"Good."

I carry Celeste through the compound, aware of the eyes on us. My people, watching their lord carry a bloody, unconscious woman through the halls. Some of them stop mid-step. Tilt their heads. Listen.

They can all hear it. Every vampire in this building can hear the rhythm coming from both of us.

Let them wonder. I don't have answers for them yet.

Elena is waiting when I reach the medical wing. She takes one look at Celeste and goes pale.

"Silver wound," I say. "Left side, between the ribs. It hit something Konstantin modified. She started destabilizing. I had to do something I've never done before."

Elena looks up from examining Celeste's wounds. "What do you mean?"

"A blood bond. We fed from each other simultaneously. It's rare." I watch her process this. "It anchored her to me. Stabilized whatever the silver was destroying."

"And that saved her?"

"It's the only reason she's still alive."

Elena nods slowly, filing the information away the way she does with all the vampire knowledge she's accumulated over eight years. "What does it mean? Long term?"

"It means we're connected. Permanently. What she feels, I feel. What I feel, she feels." I pause, considering how much to share. "And it means we have some protection against what Konstantin built into her."

Elena's hands still on Celeste's wound. "What he built into her?"

"A trigger. A kill switch. Something that would let him take control of her, turn her into a weapon." I watch Elena's face go pale. "The bond didn't remove it, but it created a barrier. Anchored her to me in a way that should make it harder for him to reach her."

"Should?"

"We don't know for certain. We need to find a way to remove it entirely. But for now, she's stable. She's herself."

Elena nods briskly, though I can see the fear she's trying to hide. "Put her on the table. Let me see what we're dealing with."

I lay Celeste down gently, reluctant to let her go even for a moment. The bond pulses between us. I can feel her even when I'm not touching her, a constant presence at the edge of my consciousness. But it's stronger when we're in contact. Brighter.

Elena examines the wound, her movements clinical and efficient. "The bleeding has stopped. The tissue around the wound is strange. Regenerating, but differently than normal vampire healing."

"Konstantin modified her. In Rome. We don't know exactly what he did, but we know some of it. Enhanced healing. Sunlight resistance. And the trigger."

"Wonderful," Elena says dryly as she reaches for Celeste's wrist. "Let me check if the silver damage has spread to the extremities."

She freezes.

Her fingers press harder against the inside of Celeste's wrist. She holds still for a long moment, disbelief written across her face.

"That's not possible," she whispers.

"What?"

"She has a pulse." Elena looks up at me, eyes wide. "Vampires don't have pulses. They don't have heartbeats. But she..."

"I know." I press my hand against my own chest. "I have one too. The same one. They beat together."

Elena stares at me. Then, hesitantly, she reaches for my wrist. Her fingers find the pulse point, and I watch her face go pale as she feels the rhythm, identical to the one still beating beneath her other hand on Celeste's wrist.

"The bond did this?"

"We don't know. Nothing like this has ever happened before."

Elena stares at us for a long moment, the scientist in her clearly warring with the impossibility of what she's feeling beneath her fingertips. Then she shakes her head and returns to her examination.

"Sir." Her voice is hesitant. "Your shirt. There's a mark on your chest."

I look down. My shirt is still torn open from earlier, and the crimson bond mark is clearly visible, still pulsing faintly with that soft glow.

"Yes. Another effect of the bond." I pull the fabric of Celeste's shirt aside slightly, revealing the matching mark over her heart. "She has one too."

Elena's eyes widen further. "I've read about bond marks in the archives. They're described as faint black lines, barely visible. But this is..."

"Different. Everything about this bond is different."

She stares at the marks for a long moment, watching them pulse in perfect synchronization. Then she shakes her head and returns to her examination with renewed focus.

"Whatever the modifications are, the bond seems to have stabilized them. She's healing faster than I'd expect given the blood loss and the silver exposure."

"She'll recover?"

"She'll need rest. A lot of it. And blood. Clean blood, as much as she can take." Elena straightens, wiping her hands on a cloth. "But yes. She'll recover."

Relief floods through me, so intense it's almost painful.

Celeste stirs on the table. Her eyes flutter open, unfocused at first, then finding mine.

"You're broadcasting," she murmurs, her voice barely a whisper.

"What?"

"Your relief. I can feel it." A small smile plays at her lips. "It's very loud."

The bond. She can feel my emotions as clearly as I felt hers during the forming.

"You're supposed to be resting," I say.

"Hard to rest when you're..." She winces, shifting on the table. "Actually, never mind. I'm exhausted. Wake me up when there's blood. I'm starving."

Her eyes drift closed, and within seconds, her breathing evens out. Her presence dims at the edge of my mind. Not disappearing, but quieting. Resting.

I stand by her bedside for a long moment, watching her sleep. The rise and fall of her chest. The heartbeat, our heartbeat, pulsing steadily beneath her skin. The crimson mark glowing softly in the dim light.

"Sir." Marcellus appears in the doorway. "Nadia is requesting a debrief. The others have questions."

Of course they do. The inner circle will want to know every-thing. About the trap, about Valentina, about Konstantin's escape. About the bond. About the weapon sleeping in her blood.

I should go. Should handle the political fallout, reassure my people, and start planning our next move.

Instead, I pull a chair next to Celeste's bed and sit down.

"Tell Nadia I'll brief everyone at sunset tomorrow," I say. "Tonight, I'm staying here."

Marcellus looks at me for a long moment. Then, for the first time in a long time, he smiles.

"Yes, sir," he says. And leaves us alone.

I take Celeste's hand in mine, feeling the pulse of our shared heartbeat through our joined fingers. My other hand rests against my chest, over the mark that proves what we've become.

Tomorrow, I'll deal with Konstantin. With the war. With the trigger buried in her blood that we need to find and destroy before he can use it.

But tonight, I'm exactly where I need to be.

With her.

THIRTY-THREE

I wake to the sound of a heartbeat.

Not just any heartbeat. Ours. The steady rhythm pulses through me, synchronized, a miracle neither of us can explain.

Before I open my eyes, I feel him.

Not his body, though I sense that too. The coolness of him beside me, the weight of his hand in mine. Something deeper. His emotions, bleeding into my awareness like ink in water. Relief, so profound it aches. Worry, still lingering at the edges. And love, vast and terrifying and certain.

He loves me. I've known it, heard him say it, but this is different. This is feeling the truth of it in my own chest, undeniable and overwhelming.

I open my eyes.

Maximus is beside me, sitting in a chair pulled close to my bed. He looks exhausted. Blood still streaked across his shirt, shadows under his eyes, his normally immaculate appearance wrecked from battle. But his gaze is fixed on my face, and when he sees me looking back, I feel his relief surge through the bond like a wave.

"You're awake." His voice is rough.

"You look terrible."

He laughs, a short, surprised sound. "You almost died."

"Don't remind me." I try to sit up and wince as pain flares in my side. The wound is still there, still healing, but the wrongness is gone. The unraveling has stopped.

"Careful." His hands are on me immediately, helping me upright, adjusting pillows behind my back. Through the bond, I feel his concern spike. "Elena says you need rest."

"How long was I out?"

"Through the day. It's evening now." His thumb traces circles on my wrist, right over the pulse point. I feel his wonder at the sensation. A heartbeat where there shouldn't be one. "How do you feel?"

"Like I killed my maker and almost died from magical silver poisoning." I manage a weak smile. "So, about average."

He doesn't smile back. His hand comes up to cup my face, and I feel the weight of what he's feeling.

"I'm okay," I say softly. "I'm here."

"I know. I can feel you." His eyes search mine. "It's strange. Having you in my head."

"I'm not in your head. I'm in your..." I press my hand to his chest, feeling the heartbeat beneath my palm. Feeling the warmth of the mark beneath his shirt. "Here. And you're in mine."

We stay like that for a moment, just feeling each other. The bond hums between us, a constant connection that makes the silence feel full instead of empty.

"I need a shower," I say finally. "I'm covered in..." I look down at myself. Dried blood, dirt, the remnants of battle crusted on my skin. "Everything."

"You need rest."

"I need to not smell like a corpse." I swing my legs over the side of the bed, and he's there immediately, hands steadying me. "I'm fine. I can walk."

"You were dying twelve hours ago."

"And now I'm not." I meet his eyes. "The bond worked. I can feel myself healing. Whatever was coming apart, it's stable now." I touch his chest again, feeling that heartbeat, the warmth of the mark beneath the fabric. "Because of you."

He's quiet for a moment, emotions flickering through the bond too fast to name. Then he nods.

"My quarters," he says. "Not here. You can shower there."

I don't argue.

He helps me stand, his arm around my waist as we make our way through the compound. It's quiet, the halls empty. I catch glimpses of faces in doorways, curious eyes following us, but no one approaches.

They can all hear it, I realize. Our heartbeats. Every vampire in this building can hear the rhythm coming from both of us.

Maximus's quarters feel different tonight. The same elegant space, the same king-sized bed where we've spent every night since we first came together, but something has shifted. Maybe it's the bond. Maybe it's almost dying. Everything feels more vivid, more precious. He leads me into the bathroom, and I don't protest when he follows. We're both covered in blood. We both need this. The bathroom is almost as large as my old apartment.

Marble floors. A shower that could fit six people. A massive tub that looks more like a small pool. Everything in shades of gray and black, understated luxury that somehow fits him perfectly.

"I'll get you clean clothes," he says, turning to leave.

I catch his wrist. "Stay."

He goes still. His reaction hits me instantly, a spike of want, quickly suppressed. He's trying to be noble. Trying to give me space to recover.

I don't want space.

"Stay," I repeat. "You're covered in blood too."

"Celeste..."

"I almost died." I step closer, still holding his wrist. "And right now, the only thing I want is to feel alive." I press my palm flat against his chest, feeling our shared heartbeat, feeling the mark warm beneath my touch. "With you."

His control wavers. I feel it like a tremor running between us. The desire he's been holding back, the desperate need to touch me, to confirm I'm real and whole and here. Centuries of restraint, cracking under the weight of almost losing me.

"You're injured," he says, but his voice is hoarse.

"I'm healing." I reach for the hem of my ruined shirt, what's left of it, and pull it over my head. The movement tugs at my wound, but the pain is distant, manageable. "And I don't want to be careful tonight. I don't want to be gentle." I drop the shirt on the marble floor. "I want to feel you."

His eyes travel down my body. The blood, the bandages, the bruises already fading. And the mark, the crimson bond mark over my heart, glowing faintly in the bathroom light. His want floods into me, hot and immediate, no longer suppressed.

"You're sure?" he asks.

"I just killed my maker, survived a magical assassination attempt, and bonded myself to you for eternity." I reach for the fastening of my pants. "I've never been more sure of anything."

Something snaps in him.

One moment he's standing there, fighting for control. The next, his hands are on me, pulling me against him, his mouth claiming mine with a desperation that steals my breath.

And I feel it. Not just the kiss, not just his hands on my skin. I feel what he feels. The relief of having me alive. The hunger he's been suppressing for hours. The overwhelming love that saturates everything else.

It's almost too much. Almost.

I pull at his shirt, needing it off, needing to feel his skin against mine. He breaks the kiss long enough to tear it over his head, and then we're pressed together, chest to chest, our heartbeats pounding in unison. Our marks pressed together, both glowing brighter at the contact.

"Shower," I manage against his mouth.

He reaches past me and turns on the water. Hot, steaming, perfect. Then his hands are at my waist, stripping away what's left of my clothing while I do the same to him. Boots, pants, everything, tossed aside until we're both bare, both exposed, both feeling everything the other feels.

He lifts me easily, carrying me into the shower. The hot water hits my skin like a benediction, washing away the blood and dirt and remnants of battle. I wrap my legs around his waist, my back against the cool marble wall, and pull his mouth back to mine.

The bond makes everything more intense.

I feel his hands on my body, and I feel his sensation of touching me. The softness of my skin, the curve of my waist, the weight of me in his arms. A feedback loop of pleasure that builds with every touch.

"I can feel what you feel," I gasp against his throat.

"I know." His voice is wrecked. "I feel you too."

He presses me harder against the wall, the water cascading over both of us, and I feel his need like it's my own.

"Don't hold back," I tell him. "Not tonight. I want all of you."

He groans, a sound that vibrates through both of us, and shifts my weight, positioning himself at my entrance. I feel his anticipation, his desperation, his overwhelming love, all of it amplified through the bond until I can't tell where his emotions end and mine begin.

He pushes into me.

The sensation is indescribable. Not just the physical feeling of him filling me. I feel that from both sides. His pleasure at being inside me. My pleasure at taking him. The bond weaving it all together until we're gasping, both of us, overwhelmed by the intensity.

"Celeste." My name on his lips is a prayer.

He starts to move, slow at first, controlled. But the bond won't let him hide. I feel his restraint fraying, feel how much he wants to let go.

"More," I demand. "Harder."

He obeys.

The wall is cold against my back, the water hot against my skin, and he's everywhere. His body against mine, his emotions flooding through me, his pleasure building in tandem with my own. Every thrust sends waves through the bond, echoing between us, multiplying.

I rake my nails down his back, and I feel the sting of it through his senses. He bites down on my shoulder, not hard enough to draw blood, not yet.

It's too much. It's not enough. It's everything.

"I need..." I can't finish the sentence. I don't have to.

He knows. He feels what I feel.

His hand slides between us, finding the place where I need him most, and the dual sensation, his fingers on me, my pleasure flooding through him, tips us both toward the edge.

He growls against my throat.

The orgasm hits like a wave, crashing through both of us simultaneously. I feel him shatter as I shatter, his release and mine tangled together through the bond until there's no separation, no distinction, just us. One pleasure, one heartbeat, two bodies sharing every sensation.

I catch a glimpse of our reflections in the bathroom mirror. Two bodies pressed together, water cascading over us. And on both our chests, glowing softly through the steam, the bond marks pulse with crimson light. Brighter now than before. Responding to our passion, our connection, the pleasure flooding through the bond.

Beautiful. We're beautiful together. Marked. Matched. Mated.

I'm still shaking when he carries me out of the shower, both of us dripping, neither of us caring. He makes it as far as the bedroom before I pull his mouth down to mine.

"Again," I say against his lips.

"You need to rest."

"I need you." I pull him closer, feeling his want surge through the bond despite his protests. "We have eternity to rest."

He kisses me. Deep, consuming, nothing held back. Then my back is against the wall, and he's lifting me, and I wrap myself around him.

When he slides back inside me, we both moan at the sensation. The bond has settled into something steady now, a constant current of shared feeling that makes every touch electric.

"I can feel how much you want me," I murmur against his ear.

"I've wanted you since the moment you walked into my life." He thrusts deeper, and I gasp. "Every night. Every hour. Every moment."

"Then show me."

He does.

He takes me against the wall with a ferocity that leaves me breathless. Hard, fast, desperate. I feel his need through the bond, raw and consuming.

"More," I demand, and he gives me more.

The orgasm builds fast, fed by the feedback loop. His pleasure fueling mine, mine fueling his, spiraling higher with every thrust. When it crashes over us, I cry out against his shoulder, feeling him shudder inside me as we break apart together.

But it's not enough. Not nearly enough.

I'm still shaking when he carries me to the bed, both of us trembling, neither of us finished.

On the bed, he's different.

"Now," he says, settling over me, "we do this properly."

The desperation has faded into something else. Still hungry, still wanting, but controlled now. Deliberate. He settles over me, bracing himself on his forearms, and just looks at me.

"What?" I ask, suddenly self-conscious under the intensity of his gaze.

"I'm memorizing you." His fingers trace the line of my jaw, my throat, the curve of my shoulder. "Every time I almost lost you, I kept thinking, I don't have enough memories. I need more."

"You have eternity now."

"I know." He lowers his mouth to my collarbone, pressing a kiss there. "And I intend to spend every moment of it learning you."

He starts at my throat, mapping my skin with his lips. Slow, reverent kisses that trail across my shoulders, down the valley between my breasts, over the curve of my ribs. I feel his focus like a laser, the way he catalogs every shiver, every hitch in my breath, every spot that makes me gasp.

"Here," he murmurs against the inside of my elbow, pressing a kiss to the sensitive skin. "You like this."

"I like everything you do."

"I know. I can feel it." He smiles against my skin. "But some things you like more than others."

He continues his exploration, finding places I didn't know were sensitive. The inside of my wrist. The curve of my hip. The soft skin behind my knee. Each discovery sends ripples through the bond, my pleasure feeding his satisfaction, his attention making me feel like the most precious thing in the world.

By the time he settles between my thighs again, I'm trembling with need.

"Please," I whisper. "I need you inside me."

"Not yet." He presses a kiss to my inner thigh. "I'm not done learning."

"Maximus..."

"Patience." His breath is warm against my core. "We have eternity, remember?"

His mouth finds me again, but this time it's different. Slower. More thorough. He explores every fold, every nerve ending, learning what makes me gasp and what makes me moan and what makes me cry out his name like a prayer.

I lose track of time. Lose track of everything except his mouth, his hands, the constant pulse of the bond between us. He brings me to the edge over and over, backing off each time, drawing out the pleasure until I'm begging.

"Please, I need, Maximus, please..."

Finally, finally, he rises over me. I feel his arousal against my thigh, hard and ready, and I reach for him, guiding him to where I need him most.

He pushes in slowly. Inch by inch, letting me feel every bit of him, watching my face as he fills me completely.

"Look at me," he says.

I meet his gaze.

"I love you," I whisper.

"I know." He starts to move, slow and deep. "I feel it."

We move together like we've been doing this for centuries instead of days. His thrusts are measured, deliberate, hitting places inside me that make stars explode behind my eyes. I wrap my legs around his waist, pulling him deeper, and he groans against my throat.

"I want to taste you," I say. "While you're inside me."

His rhythm falters. His desire surges at the request. I feel it slam into me, primal, undeniably vampire.

"Are you sure?"

"I want everything."

He tilts his neck, offering, and the scent of his blood, rich, ancient, powerful, makes my fangs ache. I strike without hesitation, sinking into his vein, and the taste of him floods my senses.

Pleasure floods through me, so intense it borders on pain. Him buried deep inside me, his blood on my tongue, the bond singing between us. I feel his satisfaction at the connection, feel us strengthening with every pull.

"My turn," he groans.

I release his throat and bare my neck to him. He doesn't hesitate. His mouth finds the curve of my neck, tongue tracing the vein that pulses beneath my skin. And then...

The bite.

His fangs in my throat while he's still inside me. I feel my blood flowing into him, feel his satisfaction at the taste, the connection between us deepening with every pull.

Everything intensifies.

We're drinking from each other while moving together, no barriers left between us. His pleasure is mine. My pleasure is his. Our heartbeats pound in perfect unison, racing toward something that feels like it might shatter us both.

I glance down at our chests, pressed together. The bond marks are glowing again. That soft crimson luminescence. His crescent against mine, the two halves forming one perfect glowing moon.

He thrusts deeper, harder, and I feel his control slipping. His desperation bleeds into me, the need to claim, to possess, to mark me as his in every way possible.

"Yours," I gasp against his throat, releasing my bite. "I'm yours."

"Mine," he growls. "And I'm yours. Forever."

He seals his bite and captures my mouth, kissing me deep, letting me taste my own blood on his tongue. His thrusts turn frantic, punishing, and I meet him stroke for stroke, both of us chasing the peak that's building between us.

The bond is a living thing now. Pulsing, growing, connecting us so completely that I can't tell where I end and he begins. A loop that spirals higher and higher until...

We break.

Together.

One orgasm shared between two bodies, so intense I lose myself in it. I feel him spilling inside me, feel his ecstasy crashing through the bond, feel our heartbeats stutter and then synchronize as we fall apart in each other's arms.

For a long moment, neither of us moves. Neither of us can.

He's still inside me, his weight a comfort rather than a burden. Our shared heartbeat pounds between us, gradually slowing from its frantic rhythm.

"I think you killed me," he murmurs against my hair.

"You're already dead."

"More dead, then." He rolls to the side, pulling me with him, keeping us connected. "Twice dead. Extra dead."

I laugh weakly. "That's not a thing."

"It is now." He pulls me closer, tucking me against his chest. "You've invented a whole new category of death."

I press my palm flat against his chest, feeling the heartbeat beneath my hand. Feeling the warmth of the bond mark.

"We have a heartbeat," I say softly.

"We do."

"Why us?"

"I don't know." He's quiet for a moment. He presses a kiss to my forehead. "I've stopped trying to understand it. I'm just grateful for it."

I snuggle closer, letting my eyes drift closed. The bond hums contentedly between us, warm and steady. His emotions settle over me like a blanket. Satisfaction, love, peace.

"We should probably talk," I murmur. "About Konstantin. About the trigger. About what comes next."

"Tomorrow."

"There's a war. And I'm apparently a weapon he can activate whenever he wants."

"The bond provides some protection. And tomorrow, we start figuring out how to remove it entirely." He tightens his arms around me. "Tonight, we rest. We've earned that much."

He's right. We have.

I let myself sink into his embrace, into the bond, into the heartbeat that connects us. Tomorrow there will be plans to make, enemies to face, and a kill switch buried in my blood that we need to find and destroy.

But tonight, I'm exactly where I need to be.

With him. Bonded. Whole.

Alive.

Sleep doesn't come immediately.

We lie tangled together, too sated to move but too wired to rest. The bond pulses between us, soft and steady, a constant reminder that we're connected now in ways that go beyond the physical.

"I can feel you thinking," Maximus says against my hair.

"Sorry. I'll think quieter."

"I don't think that's how it works." His chest rumbles with quiet laughter. "What's on your mind?"

Everything. Nothing. The weight of the last twenty-four hours pressing down on me like a physical thing.

"Valentina's dead," I say finally. "I killed my maker."

"You did."

"I thought I'd feel more." I trace idle patterns on his chest, around the edges of the bond mark. "She ruined my life. Stole everything from me. Told me I was nothing but a weapon waiting to be used. And when I finally killed her, I just felt empty."

"That's normal." His hand strokes down my spine, soothing. "Revenge rarely feels the way we expect it to. The anticipation is always bigger than the act itself."

"Speaking from experience?"

"Luciano." The name comes out flat. "I spent a hundred and fifty years dreaming of killing him. Planning it. Savoring every detail of how I'd make him suffer. And when I finally did it, when I finally ripped his head from his shoulders, I felt nothing. Just silence."

"Did the silence ever fill up again?"

"Eventually. With other things." His hand finds my jaw, turning my face to his. "With purpose. With the network." His thumb brushes my lower lip. "With you."

I kiss his thumb. "That's very smooth for someone who claims I broke his brain."

"I'm recovering."

We're quiet for a moment. His contentment seeps into me, a deep, settled peace that I suspect is rare for him. I want to wrap myself in it, let it drown out the lingering darkness of the night.

"Everyone heard it," I say, changing the subject. "The heartbeat. When you carried me through the compound."

"They did."

"They're going to have questions."

"They already do. Marcellus looked at me like I'd grown a second head." He pulls me closer. "Let them wonder. I don't have answers yet." He shifts, rolling us so he's propped above me, looking down at my face. "Does it bother you? Being visible?"

"No." The answer comes immediately, surprising me with its certainty. "I spent eight months hiding. Pretending to be something I wasn't. Trying to survive without being noticed." I reach up, touching his face. "I'm done hiding."

"Good." He kisses my forehead. "So am I."

"Nadia's going to have opinions about all of it. The heartbeat. The bond. The fact that I'm apparently a sleeper weapon."

"Nadia always has opinions. She's had opinions about me for years. I've learned to ignore them."

"What about the others? Julian? Isabelle? When they find out what Konstantin built into me..."

"They'll help us figure out how to remove it." His voice is firm. "You're part of this network now. Part of my inner circle. That means you're protected. And it means we face threats together."

"Even when I'm the threat?"

"You're not the threat. Konstantin is. You're just the weapon he's trying to use." He cups my face in his hands. "And we don't let enemies use our people against us. We find the vulnerability, and we eliminate it."

I absorb that for a moment. The certainty in his voice.

"And Marcellus?" I ask.

"Marcellus smiled at me." Maximus's expression shifts, something soft and wondering.

"Really?"

"He's not usually expressive. It's not his way. But when I told him I was staying with you instead of debriefing the inner circle, he actually smiled." He shakes his head slowly. "I think he approves."

"Of me?"

"Of us. Of what you've done to me." His hand cups my face. "I didn't realize how worried my people were. About me. About my isolation. Apparently, having a bonded mate makes me less terrifying."

"You're not terrifying."

"I am extremely terrifying. I've cultivated it deliberately for centuries."

"You're a marshmallow."

He stares at me. "I am a six-hundred-year-old vampire who has killed more people than you can count."

"Marshmallow." I poke his chest, right next to the bond mark. "Soft. Squishy. Sweet on the inside."

"I will end you."

"No, you won't." I grin up at him. "I can feel your emotions, remember? Right now, you're feeling amused. Fond. Slightly exasperated. And underneath all of that, ridiculously, overwhelmingly in love."

His expression softens. "That's cheating."

"It's not cheating. It's using the tools available to me." I pull him down for a kiss. "Besides, you can feel mine too. So we're even."

"And what are you feeling?"

"Right now?" I let the bond open fully, letting him feel everything. The contentment. The safety. The bone-deep certainty that I'm exactly where I belong. And yes, the fear too. The knowledge that there's something inside me that could destroy everything. "Happy. Really, truly happy. For the first time in maybe ever. Even with everything else."

He's quiet for a moment, absorbing what I'm sharing. Then he lowers himself beside me, pulling me close.

"I never thought I'd have this," he says quietly. "Any of this. I'd convinced myself I didn't want it. That I was better alone. Safer."

"And now?"

"Now I can't imagine going back." His arms tighten around me. "You've ruined me for solitude, Celeste. I hope you're prepared to deal with the consequences."

"What consequences?"

"I'm going to be insufferably attached. Possessive. Protective to the point of absurdity." He nuzzles against my hair. "You're going to get sick of me."

"I don't think that's possible."

"Give it a century or two."

"I'll let you know in a century or two." I yawn, exhaustion finally catching up with me. "For now, I'm just going to enjoy the fact that I'm alive, you're alive, and we have a heartbeat." I close my eyes, letting the sound lull me toward sleep. "It makes me feel alive. Human, almost."

"You're not human anymore."

"I know. But I'm not just a vampire either. Not anymore." I snuggle closer. "I'm something new. We both are."

"Something new," he repeats. "I like that."

Silence settles over us, comfortable, warm. The bond hums quietly, two presences slowly merging into one as sleep pulls at the edges of my consciousness.

"Maximus?"

"Hmm?"

"Thank you. For saving me. For the bond. For choosing me, even knowing what I might become."

"You saved yourself." His voice is drowsy now, too. "You killed

Valentina. You survived the silver. All I did was give you an anchor."

"Still. Thank you."

He presses a kiss to the top of my head. "You're welcome. Now sleep. You've earned it."

"So have you."

"I'll sleep when you sleep."

"I'm sleeping now."

"Then so am I."

I smile against his chest. I feel him drifting off, his thoughts growing fuzzy, his emotions softening into the peace of approaching sleep. I let myself follow, let the exhaustion finally claim me.

The last thing I see before sleep takes me is the faint glow of our bond marks in the darkness. Two crimson crescents pulsing in perfect unison. His on his chest. Mine on mine. Two halves of one moon, waiting to be whole. Proof that whatever we are, whatever we're becoming, we belong to each other now.

THIRTY-FOUR

Three days.

Three days of peace. Three days of waking up with Celeste in my arms, our heartbeat pulsing between us like a promise. Three days of learning the bond, the way her emotions bleed into mine.

Three days of pretending the war is over.

It's not, of course. Konstantin is still out there, regrouping, planning. The contamination crisis continues. The trigger buried in Celeste's blood remains a threat we haven't solved. A kill switch that could turn her against me at any moment.

But for three days, I let myself have this. Let myself be selfish. Let myself pretend that love is enough to keep the darkness at bay.

Tonight, reality intrudes.

"You're brooding."

Celeste's voice pulls me from my thoughts. She's standing in the doorway of the bathroom, toweling her hair dry, wearing one of my shirts and nothing else. Through the bond, I feel her amusement at catching me lost in thought.

"I don't brood."

"You absolutely brood. You have a whole brooding corner." She gestures toward the chair by the window where I've been sitting, staring at nothing. "You sit there and stare out at the grounds with your jaw clenched and your brow furrowed. It's very dramatic."

"I was thinking."

"Dramatically." She crosses the room and settles onto my lap, her legs draped over the arm of the chair. The scent of her, clean skin, my soap. "What were you thinking about?"

"The meeting tonight."

Her amusement fades, replaced by something more serious. I feel it, the flicker of anxiety she's trying to hide. "The inner circle."

"They need to know what happened. All of it."

"Including the part where I'm a weapon he can activate whenever he wants?"

"Including that." I tuck a strand of damp hair behind her ear. "They're my advisors. My allies. They can't protect the network if they don't understand the threat."

"And if they decide I am the threat?"

The question hangs between us. It's something we haven't discussed directly, the political implications of what she is. What Konstantin made her to be.

"Then they'll have to go through me." I pull her closer, pressing a kiss to her temple. "You're not just a weapon, Celeste. You're not a tool. Whatever Konstantin intended, you chose differently. You chose us."

"I know." She leans into me, and I feel her resolve settling. "I just want them to see me. Not what I was designed to be."

"They will. And if they don't..." I shrug. "I've replaced inner circle members before."

"That's not comforting."

"It's not meant to be comforting. It's meant to be true." I tip her chin up, making her meet my eyes. "You are mine. Bonded. Permanent. Anyone who threatens that threatens me. And I did not survive six hundred years by tolerating threats."

Her response washes into me unbidden. Love, gratitude, and underneath it all, a fierce determination that matches my own.

"Okay," she says softly. "Let's go tell them everything."

THE INNER CIRCLE assembles in the conference room at sunset.

The full council. Something that hasn't happened in months. Marcellus stands at his usual position by the door, face unreadable. Nadia sits at the head of the table, her expression sharp and assessing. Julian occupies the seat to her left. Elena is there too.

But tonight there are others.

Ethan sits near the window. His nervous energy is more pronounced than usual, fingers tapping against his tablet. Isabelle has come in from the secure off-site location where she manages the network's finances. Celeste hasn't met her before, I realize. The petite French vampire watches everything with cool assessment. Caleb, who runs the containment facilities, occupies a chair in the corner, dark eyes cataloging every detail. And Dr. Elias Sullivan, whose work in the human medical community keeps him away from the compound most nights, sits stiffly at the far end of the table, silver hair immaculate, bearing formal.

Everyone called in. Everyone present.

Whatever doubts anyone had about the severity of this situation, the full assembly eliminates them.

And then there's Celeste, standing beside me at the far end of the room. Not sitting. Not subordinate. Standing as my equal, my partner, my bonded mate.

Every vampire in the room can hear it. Our heartbeat, pulsing in perfect synchronization. I see Nadia's eyes flicker to my chest, then to Celeste's. See Ethan freeze mid-tap on his tablet. See Caleb's eyebrows rise almost imperceptibly. The questions forming behind their careful masks.

"Thank you all for coming," I begin. "I know some of you have traveled significant distances on short notice. What I'm about to share does not leave this room."

Nods around the table. Even Nadia, though her jaw is tight.

"Three nights ago, we walked into a trap. The meeting with Konstantin was a diversion. While we were occupied at the warehouse, his forces were moving on the compound. They were minutes from breaching the walls."

Marcellus goes very still. Nadia's mask cracks, revealing genuine shock. Ethan mutters something under his breath, pulling up data on his tablet.

"My contacts reported troop movements," Ethan says, "but nothing suggested a full assault. How did we miss this?"

"I don't know." I won't lie to my people. "Whether he fed us false intelligence, used routes we weren't monitoring, or simply moved faster than we anticipated, we missed it. That's something we need to address going forward."

I let the weight of that settle before continuing.

"During the meeting, Konstantin revealed his hand. He told us his forces were already in position, minutes from breaching the compound walls. Everyone inside, staff, donors, guards, would be slaughtered." I pause, letting them absorb the image. "Then he offered a trade. Call off the attack in exchange for one thing: Celeste."

I feel Celeste tense beside me, but she stays silent.

"Celeste agreed. She walked out with Konstantin and Valentina willingly, believing it was the only way to save everyone here."

"She surrendered?" Nadia's voice is sharp. "To Konstantin?"

"She saved every person in this compound." I let the weight of that settle. "Including everyone at this table."

Isabelle leans forward, her French accent soft but precise. "And yet she is standing here. How did she escape?"

"The exchange didn't go as Konstantin planned. Celeste killed Valentina, her maker, and I engaged Konstantin directly. He escaped, but not before we learned certain information."

"Valentina is dead?" Caleb's quiet voice carries from his corner. "You're certain?"

"I watched her die," Celeste says. Her voice is steady, controlled. "I killed her myself."

A ripple of reaction moves through the room. Isabelle's eyes widen slightly. Dr. Sullivan shifts in his seat. Even Nadia looks momentarily impressed before her expression hardens again.

"That explains the power shift I've been tracking," Ethan says, scrolling through his tablet. "Konstantin's communications went dark for almost six hours after that night. He was regrouping."

"There's more." I look at Celeste. I feel her steel herself, squaring her shoulders against what's coming. "Konstantin has been planning this for years. What Celeste learned changes everything we thought we knew."

Celeste steps forward, and I feel her reach for me, not physically, but through our connection, drawing strength from my presence.

"The fight where Valentina turned me, it wasn't random," she says. "Konstantin watched me for months before that night. Had people at my underground matches, recording me, analyzing me."

"Why?" Julian asks, genuinely curious.

"Because I was useful." Celeste's hands clench at her sides. "Konstantin has been building an army of enhanced vampires. Stronger, faster, more resilient. He finds promising humans, has them turned, modifies them, and releases them into the world. Sleeper soldiers he can activate later."

Silence. I feel the weight of attention shifting, reassessing.

"Activate how?" Dr. Sullivan leans forward, medical interest cutting through his formal demeanor. "What exactly did he do?"

"The turning happened in Atlanta," Celeste continues. "But while I was transforming, dead for the three days it takes to change, they transported me to Rome. I woke up there, not that I remember it. Three weeks of modifications. Experiments. And then they blocked my memories, flew me back to Atlanta, and let me wake up thinking only three days had passed."

"Three weeks of modifications." Dr. Sullivan's voice is clinical now, fascinated despite himself. "Do you know what kind? Chemical? Biological? Something else entirely?"

"We don't know the full extent." I step closer to Celeste, a deliberate show of solidarity. "We know she healed from contaminated blood faster than should have been possible. We know she's adapted more quickly than any fledgling I've seen. And we know Konstantin mentioned abilities that haven't manifested yet."

"You said activate," Nadia says, her voice sharp. "What does that mean? Activate how?"

Celeste takes a breath. I feel her brace herself. "There's a trigger buried in the modifications. A kill switch. When Konstantin sends the signal, I stop being me. I become a weapon with no will of my own."

The room goes very still.

"A sleeper agent," Julian breathes. "He built a sleeper agent."

"Pointed directly at you." Nadia stands, her chair scraping against the floor. "She was designed to get close to you, make you care, make you vulnerable. And then, when the moment is right, he activates her and she destroys you from the inside."

"That was his plan, yes." I keep my voice steady. "It won't work."

"How can you be so sure? She just told us there's a trigger in her blood that could turn her into a mindless killer at any moment."

"The bond provides protection." I press my hand to my chest, over the mark. "When we formed the bond, I felt the trigger. The bond wrapped around it, around the core of who she is. Whatever signal Konstantin sends will have to fight through our connection to reach her."

"Will have to fight through," Nadia repeats. "So you don't know if it will work."

"We know it's protection we didn't have before. And we know we need to find a way to remove the trigger entirely."

"Before he activates her." Nadia's voice is flat. "Before she kills you."

"She won't kill me."

"You can't know that."

"I know her." I meet Nadia's eyes. "And I trust her. That's enough."

Nadia makes a sound of disgust. "Trust. You've bound yourself to a weapon aimed at your heart because you trust her."

"My feelings are my own." Celeste's voice cuts through Nadia's tirade. "Yes, Konstantin built a trigger into me. Yes, he designed me to be a weapon. But I chose to stay. I chose to fight Valentina. I chose to kill my maker instead of letting her use me."

"How do we know that wasn't part of the design?" Nadia presses.

"Because Konstantin wanted to take me." Celeste steps forward, meeting Nadia's glare without flinching. "He wanted me as leverage. As a hostage. As a tool to break Maximus with. Instead, I killed his most valuable asset and escaped." She lifts the hem of her shirt, revealing the still-healing scar where the silver blade had driven between her ribs. "I almost died doing it. Does that seem like part of his plan?"

"The logic is sound," Isabelle says quietly. "Valentina was valuable. Losing her weakens Konstantin significantly."

"Or it was a calculated sacrifice," Caleb offers from his corner. "Remove an asset that had outlived its usefulness while deepening the deception."

"That's paranoid even for you, Caleb," Julian says.

"Paranoid keeps my facilities secure."

"There's more," I say, cutting through the debate. "The bond we formed. It was necessary to save her life. The silver Valentina used was designed to unravel the modifications. Celeste was dying. The bond stabilized her."

"And the heartbeat?" Marcellus speaks for the first time, his voice quiet. "We all hear it. That's not normal. That's not possible."

"We don't know why it happened." I press my hand to my chest, feeling the steady rhythm. "Blood bonds don't create heartbeats. Nothing does. We're dead. Our hearts don't beat."

"Except yours do," Julian says slowly. "Both of you. In perfect synchronization."

"Yes."

The room falls silent again. I can feel them processing, centuries of vampire knowledge struggling to accommodate something that shouldn't exist.

"There may be a connection to the modifications," Elena offers carefully. "Whatever Konstantin did to Celeste's physiology, it's clearly beyond normal vampire parameters. The bond might have activated something. Or combined with something already present."

"I'd like to run some tests," Dr. Sullivan says. "With your permission, of course. Blood work, tissue samples. If we could understand the mechanism..."

"Later," I say. "Right now, we focus on the threat."

"The threat is standing right there," Nadia says, pointing at Celeste. "A sleeper agent with unknown abilities and a kill switch that could go off at any moment."

"The threat is Konstantin," I correct. "Celeste is the weapon he's trying to use. We don't destroy the weapon. We disarm it and turn it against him."

"And if you can't disarm it? If he activates her before you find a way to remove the trigger?"

"Then I'll fight for her." I feel Celeste's surprise through the bond, her gratitude. "Inside her own mind if I have to. The bond goes both ways. If he tries to take control, he'll have to go through me."

Nadia stares at me for a long moment. Then she shakes her head. "You've lost your mind."

"Perhaps. But my mind is my own to lose." I look around the room. "Anyone else have concerns they'd like to voice?"

Silence.

"Good. Then let's move on to..."

"I have concerns." Celeste's voice is tight, controlled. "About what Nadia keeps calling me. A weapon. A tool. An it."

Nadia's eyes narrow. "If the description fits..."

"It doesn't." Celeste's hands curl into fists at her sides. "I am not a thing. I am not a creature. I am a person who had terrible things done to her without her consent. And I'm standing here, fighting against those things, choosing my own path despite everything Konstantin built into me."

"Pretty words," Nadia says. "But words don't change what you are."

"What I am is someone who killed her own maker to protect the people in this compound. What I am is someone who walked into enemy hands to save lives. What I am is someone who almost died rather than let Konstantin use her against the man she loves."

Her voice is rising now. Something builds inside her. I sense it gathering like a storm, something unfamiliar.

The mark on my chest flares hot. A warning. I press my hand against it instinctively and see Celeste do the same, her palm flat against her own mark. Both are burning now, responding to the chaos building inside her.

The water in Julian's glass trembles.

"Celeste," I say carefully, sensing the danger.

"She keeps talking about me like I'm not here." Her hands are shaking. "Like I'm not a person. Like everything I've done doesn't matter, like I'm just a thing waiting to be used!"

The water ripples harder. Papers on the table flutter despite the still air.

Ethan looks up from his tablet, alarmed. "What's happening?"

"Celeste." I take a step toward her.

"I gave up everything." Her voice cracks. "My old life. My sister. Any chance of being normal. I killed my own maker. I almost died. And it's still not enough? I'm still just a weapon to you people?"

The glass explodes.

Not falls. Not tips. Explodes, shattering outward in a spray of glass and liquid that peppers the wall behind Julian. He lurches back, eyes wide, as the shards rain down on the table.

But it doesn't stop there.

The chairs around the table begin to shake. The chandelier overhead sways violently. Papers lift from the table, swirling in a wind that doesn't exist.

Our bond marks are blazing now. Visible even through our clothes, crimson light pulsing erratically through the fabric in time with the chaos around us.

"What the hell is that?" Ethan points at our chests, backing further away. "They're glowing. Both of them. They're glowing!"

"Are those bond marks?" Julian's voice pitches high with disbelief, fascination breaking through his fear even as he ducks a flying sheaf of papers. "I've never seen bond marks do that. They're not supposed to... bond marks are black. Faint. They don't glow."

"And they don't pulsate," Isabelle adds, her cool composure cracking as she stares. "Bonded pairs have marks, yes, but not like that."

"The color," Dr. Sullivan breathes, medical curiosity momentarily overriding his terror. "That's not pigmentation. That's light. The marks are producing actual bioluminescence."

Nadia's eyes fix on the crimson light pulsing from both our chests, synchronized perfectly despite the chaos. For once, she has nothing to say.

Isabelle is on her feet, backing toward the wall. Caleb has risen from his corner, hand reaching for a weapon. Dr. Sullivan grips the table, knuckles white. Ethan's tablet clatters to the floor as he scrambles backward.

Nadia stumbles back, fear breaking through her composure for the first time. "What the..."

"Celeste!" I grab her shoulders, turning her to face me. Her eyes are unfocused, pupils blown wide. I feel her chaos pouring into me. Terror layered over anger, and underneath it all, power. Raw, uncontrolled power surging through her without direction.

"I don't..." Her voice is barely a whisper. "I can't... I don't know how to stop it!"

"Look at me." I cup her face in my hands. "Focus on me. Only me."

The room continues to shake. A chair tips over. The chandelier swings dangerously. Elena has ducked under the table, her human instincts for survival kicking in.

"I can feel you," I tell her, pouring calm into our connection. "I can feel everything you're feeling. The fear. The anger. Let me help you carry it."

"I don't know what's happening!"

"It doesn't matter. Focus on the heartbeat. Our heartbeat. Can you feel it?"

Her hand flies to her chest, pressing hard against the glowing mark. I cover it with mine.

"That's us," I say. "That's real. That's the only thing that matters right now. Just breathe with me. Match the rhythm."

I feel her trying, struggling against the power that wants to surge outward. I send her everything I have. Steadiness, calm, love. An anchor in the storm.

Slowly, agonizingly slowly, the shaking subsides.

The papers flutter to the ground. The chandelier stills. The pressure in the air releases.

Celeste sags against me, trembling. I catch her, holding her upright, feeling her exhaustion flood into me.

I glance down at our chests. The glow is fading now, the crimson light dimming to something barely visible through the fabric. But everyone saw it. Everyone knows.

Silence.

The inner circle stares. Seven vampires and one human, all frozen in various states of shock.

"In three hundred years, I've seen several bonded pairs," Nadia says quietly, her voice stripped of its earlier hostility. "None of them had marks like that. None of them had marks that glowed."

"The color alone is unprecedented," Julian adds, still staring. "Bond marks are always black or gray. Subtle. Easy to miss unless you're looking. But those..." He shakes his head. "Those are impossible to ignore."

"They pulse together," Elena whispers from where she's

emerged from under the table. "Did you see? The same rhythm. Like..."

"Like their heartbeat," Marcellus finishes. His eyes meet mine, and I see the weight of understanding there. "Add it to the list of impossible things."

Then Nadia's voice, shaken but recovering its edge: "So she's not just a sleeper agent. She's an evolving weapon. One that apparently goes off when she's emotional."

"Nadia," Marcellus growls. "Perhaps now is not the time."

"Now is exactly the time. She just destroyed half the room without even trying. What happens when she's truly angry? When she's threatened? When Konstantin activates her while she has these abilities?"

"Telekinesis." Julian is staring at the shattered glass on the wall, an expression of wonder breaking through his fear. "She moved objects with her mind. That's not a vampire ability. That's not any vampire ability I've ever documented."

"The modifications," Elena says, crawling out from under the table. "This must be what Konstantin meant. The abilities that haven't manifested yet."

"Fascinating," Dr. Sullivan breathes, fear giving way to scientific curiosity. "Absolutely fascinating. The neurological implications alone..."

"I didn't mean to." Celeste's voice is small, muffled against my chest. "I didn't even know I could."

"I know." I hold her tighter. "It's not your fault."

"How do we know it won't happen again?" Caleb asks from his corner, voice carefully neutral. "How do we contain something like this?"

"We don't contain her," I say firmly. "We help her learn to control it."

"Control it?" Nadia laughs bitterly. "She's a bomb waiting to go off, and you want to..."

A knock at the door cuts her off.

Marcellus opens it to reveal a young vampire, one of the perimeter guards. His face is pale, his hands shaking.

"Sir. A message just arrived. From Konstantin."

The room goes still.

"Bring it," I say.

The guard enters, holding a sealed envelope like it might bite him. The seal is the same old wax as before, pressed with a symbol I recognize all too well. Konstantin's personal mark.

I take the envelope and break the seal.

Inside is a single sheet of paper. In Konstantin's elegant handwriting. Celeste moves to my side to view the letter. I don't stop her. She has a right to see this.

My dear Maximus,

Congratulations on the bond. Word travels fast when you have friends in the right places.

She's finally waking up. The modifications are activating, one by one, just as I planned. You've accelerated the timeline, actually. The bond strengthened everything I put in her blood. I should thank you for that.

Did you think binding yourself to her would save her? All you've done is ensure you'll be there when I flip the switch. You'll feel everything when she turns on you. Every moment of her trying to stop herself and failing. Every second of her hands around your throat. The bond won't protect you. It will just make sure you experience the full horror of what I've built.

She's my masterpiece, Maximus. My greatest weapon.

And now she's pointed directly at your heart, closer than I ever could have positioned her myself. This is the most fun I've had in centuries, Maximus. You have truly brought life to my dull existence. Don't worry. I fully intend to take my time and savor these moments.

Give my regards to your inner circle. One of them, at least, already has mine.

—Konstantin

P.S. I have your sister, Celeste. She has your eyes. I can see why you fought so hard for her. Now let's see how hard you'll fight to get her back.

The paper crumples in my fist.

Celeste's reaction hits me before she speaks. Horror. Pure, absolute horror, flooding through our connection like ice water.

"Simone." Her voice is barely a whisper. "He has Simone."

I turn to her, and her face has the expression of someone whose worst nightmare just became real.

"He can't..." She shakes her head violently. "She wasn't part of this. She doesn't know anything. She's human, she's innocent, she..."

Her voice breaks. And I feel it. The guilt crashing into me. The terrible, crushing weight of it. Her sister is in Konstantin's hands because of her. An innocent human who knows nothing about vampires, nothing about this war, dragged into it because Konstantin needed leverage.

The mark on my chest aches. A deep, throbbing pain that mirrors what she's feeling. Her grief, made physical in the crimson lines etched into my skin.

"We'll get her back." I cup her face in my hands, forcing her to meet my eyes. "Do you hear me? We will get her back."

"How? We don't even know where he is. We don't know what he wants."

"We know exactly what he wants." My voice is hard. Cold. "He wants you. And now he has leverage."

"So I'll go. I'll trade myself."

"No." The word comes from multiple voices. Mine, Marcellus's, Nadia's, even Ethan's. We all speak at once, a rare moment of unity.

Nadia steps forward, and for the first time, her expression holds something other than suspicion. "Walking into Konstantin's hands is exactly what he wants. We'd be giving him everything."

"She's right," Isabelle adds quietly. "A trade would only strengthen his position. We need leverage of our own."

"Then what do we do?" Celeste's voice cracks. "He has my sister. My baby sister. The only family I have left."

I pull her against my chest, holding her as she shakes. Her terror, her grief, her desperate love for the sister she's protected since childhood. All of it pours into me until I can barely separate her pain from my own.

And I feel something else, too. Something growing beneath the fear.

Rage.

"We find him," I say over her head, meeting the eyes of my inner circle one by one. "We find where he's keeping her. We identify the traitor who told him about the bond. We find a way to remove the trigger from Celeste's blood. And then we burn his entire operation to the ground."

"The message mentioned friends in the right places," Julian says slowly. "And he told us to give his regards to the inner circle. He's saying one of us is feeding him information."

The room goes tense. I watch them, all of them. Marcellus, steady and unreadable. Nadia, bristling at the implication. Julian, frowning thoughtfully. Ethan, fingers frozen over his tablet. Isabelle, face carefully blank. Caleb, dark eyes revealing nothing. Dr. Sullivan, looking genuinely disturbed. Elena, the only human, pale and frightened.

One of them. Or someone close to one of them.

"I know." I let my gaze sweep the room. "But we're going to find out who."

"I've been in the field," Ethan says, an edge of defensiveness in his voice. "My loyalty isn't in question."

"Everyone's loyalty is in question," Caleb counters from his corner. "That's how moles work."

"Pointing fingers at each other accomplishes nothing," Isabelle cuts in. "We need to focus on finding the girl. And finding a way to neutralize the trigger before Konstantin can use it."

"And the abilities?" Nadia asks. "The telekinesis? Whatever else is coming?"

"We learn to control them." Celeste's voice is muffled against my chest, but steady now. Hardening. "If Konstantin made me a weapon, then I'll be a weapon. Just not his."

She pulls back, and I see the change in her face. The fear is still there, but it's being consumed by something stronger. Determination. Fury.

"He took my sister." Her voice is quiet, but I feel the steel beneath it. Sharp and unyielding. "He experimented on me. He put a trigger in my blood that could turn me into a mindless killer. And now he thinks he's won?"

She looks around the room.

"Konstantin has been planning this for years," Celeste says. "But he made one mistake. He designed me to be strong. To survive. To adapt." Her hand finds mine, fingers intertwining. "He just didn't plan on me using those gifts against him."

Her resolve crystallizes. I feel it hardening into something diamond-bright and unbreakable. The terror for her sister transforming into something more useful. More dangerous.

My bonded mate. My partner. My weapon, pointed exactly where I need her.

"We have work to do," I say. "Marcellus, double the perimeter guard. Someone in this compound is feeding Konstantin information, and I want to know who."

"Done," he says.

"Julian, dig into everything we have on Konstantin's operations. Properties, allies, anywhere he might be holding a human hostage. And research any precedents for removing implanted triggers or commands from vampire blood."

"I'll start immediately."

"Ethan, reach back out to your contacts. I don't care what it costs. Someone knows where Konstantin is operating from."

Ethan nods, already tapping at his tablet. "I have a few sources who owe me. I'll call in the debts."

"Isabelle, follow the money. Konstantin has to be funding this operation somehow. Shell companies, property purchases, anything in the last six months."

"I'll have a preliminary report by dawn," she says.

"Caleb, review the containment facility security. If there's a leak, it might have come from outside the main compound."

"Understood."

"Dr. Sullivan, I need you back in the human medical community. Listen for anything unusual. Missing persons reports, unexplained injuries, anything that might indicate where he's keeping hostages. And research any medical approaches to removing neurological triggers or implanted commands."

"I'll make inquiries," Sullivan says. "Discreetly. And I'll review the literature on deprogramming techniques."

"Nadia..."

I meet her eyes. She holds my gaze for a long moment, and I see her making a choice.

"I'll coordinate with Dmitri's people," she says finally. "If anyone has intelligence on Konstantin's movements, it's them. And I'll reach out to contacts who specialize in blood magic. If there's a way to remove what he put in her, they'll know."

A peace offering. Or at least a truce.

"Thank you."

"Elena," I say, "coordinate with Dr. Sullivan. If Konstantin is holding a human hostage, she'll need medical attention eventually. Monitor any unusual activity in local hospitals and clinics."

Elena nods, her face pale but determined. "I still have contacts from before I joined the network. I'll reach out."

Celeste turns to me, her voice strained. "Simone lives in Savannah. I need to go there. See her apartment, find out when he took her, how he found her..."

"Not alone," I say firmly. "And not tonight. Konstantin could be expecting exactly that." I turn to Ethan. "Send people to Savannah. Celeste will give you her sister's address and workplace. I want to know everything. When she was last seen, who she talked to, any security footage in the area."

"Savannah." Ethan frowns. "That's outside our usual territory. I'll need to call in some favors."

"Then call them in. Whatever it takes."

Ethan nods, fingers already moving on his tablet. "I'll have people there by dawn."

The inner circle begins to move, filtering out of the room, each focused on their assigned task. But I see the glances they exchange. The suspicion. The doubt.

One of them is a traitor. They all know it now. And until we find out who, no one in this room fully trusts anyone else.

Only Marcellus lingers at the door.

"Sir." His voice is quiet. "For what it's worth, I don't believe the trigger will work. Not with the bond in place."

"I hope you're right."

"And the sister?" He pauses. "We'll find her. Whatever it takes."

"I know."

He nods and closes the door behind him, leaving us alone.

Celeste is still standing where I left her, staring at the crumpled letter in my hand. The storm inside her batters against me. Fear and rage and guilt and love, all tangled together.

"This is my fault," she whispers. "I stayed away from her. Eight months, and I never once tried to contact her. I thought if I kept my distance, she'd be safe."

"Konstantin has been watching you since before you were turned," I say, crossing to her and taking her hands in mine. "He knew about Simone long before you ever walked into my life. This was never about your choices, Celeste. It was always about him. His obsession. His plan. We're just the pieces on his board."

"I don't want to be a piece."

"Then don't be." I tip her chin up, making her meet my eyes. "Be the player. Take the board from him. Make him regret ever setting this game in motion."

"How?"

"Together." I press my forehead to hers. "Whatever you're becoming, whatever gifts are waking up inside you, whatever trigger he buried in your blood, we face it together. We find your sister together. We end Konstantin together."

I feel her steadying. The chaos settling into something harder. More focused.

"Together," she echoes.

Our heartbeat pulses between us, strong, steady, synchronized. A miracle. A bond that shouldn't exist.

A weapon Konstantin didn't account for.

"I love you," I tell her. "Whatever comes next, I love you."

"I know." She manages a small smile. "I can feel it, remember?"

"Then feel this too." I let the bond open fully, letting her sense everything I'm feeling. The fury at Konstantin. The protective rage over her sister. The absolute, unshakeable certainty that we will win this war. The determination to rip the trigger from her blood before he can ever use it.

And underneath it all, the love. Vast and terrifying and unbreakable.

"He thinks the bond is a weakness," I say. "He thinks the trigger makes you his. He's wrong on both counts. The bond is the strongest thing either of us has ever had. And you are not his weapon. You're mine. Ours."

Celeste's hand presses against my chest, over the mark. I cover it with my own, feeling the warmth of the crimson lines pulsing beneath our touch. Proof of what we've become. What no one can take from us.

"Then let's teach him," she says.

She looks up at me, and I feel her fear transforming into something fiercer. Something unbreakable.

"He has no idea what he's started," she says.

"No." I pull her close. "He doesn't."

Konstantin wanted to create my downfall. Instead, he created my reason to fight.

Our hearts beat as one. Impossible, miraculous, ours.

Let him come. We'll be ready.

THANK you so much for reading! If you enjoyed Blood & Dominion, it would really help me out if you would leave a review. Reviews help other readers find my work and encourage me to write more books.

Before you dive into Book 2...

Did you know Marcellus has a secret?

While Celeste and Maximus were falling for each other, something else was happening in the shadows. Something I didn't show you.

Want to find out what?

Sign up for my newsletter and get his story free:

ABOUT THE AUTHOR

Taloria Pryce writes dark romantasy with morally gray heroes, fierce heroines, and the kind of tension that keeps you up way past your bedtime.

She's a sucker for enemies-to-lovers, slow burns that actually pay off, and love interests who would absolutely burn the world down for the right person. Her stories live in the space where danger meets desire, where power is seductive, and love is a mess. Expect ancient grudges, impossible choices, and heroes who are very bad at being good.

Her debut vampire romantasy series, Crimson Crescent, starts with Blood & Dominion. Fangs, thrones, political scheming, and a romance built on the worst possible foundation. Just the way she likes it.

When she's not writing, she's probably deep in a romantasy rabbit hole, annotating paperbacks with way too many tabs, or arguing with herself about whether her characters deserve redemption. (They usually don't. She gives it to them anyway.)

Also by Taloria Pryce